DENIAL
AND
EXCLUSION

K. M. Matthews

Copyright © 2024 K. M. Matthews

All rights reserved, including the right to reproduce this book, or portions thereof in any form. No part of this text may be reproduced, transmitted, downloaded, decompiled, reverse engineered, or stored, in any form or introduced into any information storage and retrieval system, in any form or by any means, whether electronic or mechanical without the express written permission of the author.

This is a work of fiction, based on the author's lived experience. Names and characters are the product of the author's imagination and any resemblance to actual persons, living or dead, is entirely coincidental.

The views expressed in this work are solely those of the author and do not necessarily reflect the views of the publisher, and the publisher hereby disclaims any responsibility for them.

Cover artwork by K. E. Matthews

ISBN: 9798337597980

PublishNation
www.publishnation.co.uk

Dedicated to my loving family.

Your unwavering love, support and shared experiences have been integral to the creation of this book. From our time together in Berlin, witnessing the fall of The Wall, to the countless discussions and moments of encouragement, your presence has enriched every page with depth and meaning. This book is not just a reflection of my journey, but a testament to our collective memories and shared history. Thank you for being my pillars of strength and inspiration.

With love and gratitude, x

PROLOGUE

Tobolmennaya Institute – Soviet Psychiatric Research Establishment – Soviet Union - November 1985

Locked within four walls, deprived of light and human kindness, all that was left for her to do was to keep her mind occupied. She recited poetry, lengthy passages from the Bible and the works of Shakespeare. She sang songs in as many languages as she was able to recall and made-up stories to read to her children in the future - the future she longed to have. Clinging on tightly to every vestige of sanity, she never once considered death to be the solution which would end her misery. She planned her future, knowing in her heart it would be hers to enjoy.

"England, my England," she began, but the words abandoned her and so she tried something different.

"I'd a dream tonight as I fell asleep,
Oh! The touching sight makes me still to weep:
Of my little lad, gone to leave me sad,
Aye, the child I had, but was not to keep."

She looked around her in the darkness but couldn't see what it was she was looking for. She cried as she remembered and then she pulled up her legs and wrapped her arms around them, her head resting on her knees as she cried some more, but not for long; she never cried for long.

Poetry evoked mixed memories. She strained to recall the words of everything that had once been so familiar and again her memory cheated her and gave her only snatches of what she'd known before this hell. She saw the face of the man she adored, and watched within her mind as he moved around their home. Suddenly the last verse of an old favourite became crystal clear as if etched upon her eyelids.

"So all my thoughts are pieces but of you,
Which put together makes a glass so true
As I therein no other's face but yours can view."

She drifted into sleep, a faint smile gracing her lips as they pressed against the cold stone slabs beneath her. As the memories faded, she stirred from sleep, the icy chill of the stone floor biting into her bare feet as she paced back and forth, and then she stopped, raised her face to look up into the blackness shrouding her and with arms thrown out wide she called out dramatically, as if playing to a vast audience in a large auditorium: "What have I sacrificed for you, England, my beloved? Is there anything I wouldn't endure for you, England, my own?"

Her voice echoed in her head and then the silence filled her mind and she cried as she whispered, "Why have you forsaken me? I've been faithful to you, England, my England."

For several minutes, she remained silent as she listened carefully for a response, and then she called out once again into the emptiness of the dark prison. "Dan! Where are you? You're my beacon in this darkness, my last hope. Please, my darling, find me before it's too late!"

With a little whimper, and as if to herself, she whispered, "Forgive me for what I've done. I love you above all else, you're my life and my reason to live. Please forgive me. I will never stop loving you."

PART ONE

Chapter One

British European Airways Flight BEA413 from London Heathrow to Tegel West Berlin - Monday 3 April 1967

For the cabin crew, there was nothing in the least bit unusual, exciting, or exacting about the flight, as the aircraft grew ever closer to West Berlin; it was routine for them, with passengers packed into the cabin with barely enough room to move. For Amy Harper, travelling under the assumed name of Amy Packard, this was the most exciting flight of her life, in fact, it was the single most exciting thing she'd ever done.

The tingle of anticipation travelled the length of her body. She felt more vital and alive than she had throughout her short but interesting life. Apart from years of hard work and then the basic training, parts of which proved challenging for her; this was the beginning of it all - the start. This was where she'd put her knowledge to the test. She could almost reach out and touch the excitement she was feeling; it was so tangible now.

The in-flight midday meal had taken up a little of her waiting time. She'd enjoyed three small cups of strong coffee and flicked through the magazine she'd bought at the airport, and then she found herself with nothing more to do than sit back and relax until the captain announced it was possible to see East Germany on the port side of the aircraft as they began their descent to 10,000 feet.

Amy knew the descent was necessary to comply with the legal flight path ceiling for travelling along the air corridor into West Berlin. All access routes into the walled city, both by land and air, were carefully charted and strictly adhered to. The Soviets would feel no compunction in apprehending any driver who was foolish enough to stray off the land corridor, nor in shooting down any aircraft which accidentally, or otherwise, happened to stray off their given flight path along the air corridor.

Amy was beginning to fidget and she despised herself when she became fidgety. Looking down on the land gave her something to concentrate on again, something positive.

Below them the shadow of the aircraft silently tracked their flight path like a ghost from the past or a shadow from the future. Amy shivered and fixed her vision on the unending fields, broken only by the occasional tree. She saw uncultivated land; barren of crops with a sprinkling of farms and isolated outbuildings. From the air she thought the land looked poor and unkempt, cold and unloved - frozen in time by politics and madness, it was a fair assessment of how it was down below for those who endured the control of the Communist Party

Her heart missed several vital beats as she contemplated the prospect of forced retention in such a dreadful place. She shrugged off the feeling of impending doom, and willed herself to relax for what remained of the journey. There was little point worrying about something which would hopefully never happen, especially something she was going to do her level best to prevent.

The big metal bird touched down safely, although a little inelegantly, on the airport runway and Amy gathered her few possessions and waited patiently in her seat for all of the anxious passengers to leave her sitting there. Amy had only been on three flights in her short lifetime, and certainly would never consider herself to be a seasoned traveller, yet even she could see little point in rushing to leave a paid for seat only to go and sit on another one inside the terminal building while waiting for her luggage to arrive. She used the time to calm her eagerness to rush into this adventure.

Having dealt with the strict passport control, she passed through the baggage collection area and with her suitcase in her hand she travelled in a large black Mercedes taxi to the house on Kuregenstrasse, Spandau, where she stood on the pavement alongside her suitcase, staring up at the magnificence of the architecture, feeling dwarfed and insignificant, and not for the first time since arriving in the city.

The building was a vast masterpiece with three floors, solid stone walls, shuttered windows and wide stone steps leading up to the front door which was massive and ornate. She was staring up at it when it suddenly opened and a stunningly handsome young man beamed down on her, his cornflower blue eyes dancing with the burning flame of youth.

"Well, Fräulein, are you going to stare all day, or are you coming inside?" The fire she saw there in his eyes was playing on his lips now as he spoke to her. He watched as she recovered her breath, satisfied she was suitably impressed with his ancestral home.

When at last she managed to speak to him, he hadn't been prepared for her to be so precise; so perfect. She looked deceivingly vulnerable, lost and confused; yet the woman who knew exactly what she wanted from life spoke to him in impeccable German.

"You must be Herr Hoffmann. I am Amy Packard. I am delighted to meet you." Her hand was outstretched to him as she moved forward up the stone steps.

They met halfway and shook hands. "And I too am delighted to meet you, Amy Packard." As if to prove a point, he reverted to near perfect Oxford English. "You are correct, I am Herr Hoffmann, you must call me Peter. Welcome to our humble family home."

He swept his arm in a wide arc and then he laughed heartily; the place was anything but humble. "Come inside and meet Papa. Mama is in church with my sister Lore, but they will return quite soon. Come, meet my father." He relieved her of her suitcase and led the way inside.

Amy followed the beautiful young man with the crystal-clear blue eyes and flaxen hair, into the sweetly scented building. She looked at the solid carved architecture and the ornately embossed walls and there ahead of her stood the rotund robust figure of Rudi Hoffmann.

He extended a plump right hand and pulled Amy forward to study her more closely through the small round lenses in their flimsy gold wire frame. He was just an inch taller than Amy, who was only five-foot-five, yet his eyes were almost level with hers. He looked deeply into her amber orbs as his spectacles began sliding slowly down his slightly crooked Roman nose.

"You are quite beautiful, Miss Packard. A rare English rose."

"Thank you, Herr Hoffmann," she replied, strangely unmoved by the compliment. It caused her neither embarrassment nor discomfort yet had his son said the same thing she would definitely have blushed bright crimson. "You have a beautiful home and I am delighted to be here."

"Why thank you, Amy. How was your journey?"

"Comfortable," she said, smiling happily.

"Good. Please sit and Peter will bring us tea."

Sitting straight backed on the edge of the elegant plush blue sofa with the firm cushioned seat, she waited in perfect peaceful silence for the return of Peter, bearing a decorated enamel tea tray laden with cups and saucers and an ornate silver teapot.

"We prefer Indian tea," Herr Hoffmann began; he too had been contented to sit silently waiting. There are some who find it impossible to sit in silence; who make constant small talk to fill what they feel is an awkward space, often proving annoying to Amy. "We do have China tea if you would prefer it," he added.

"Indian tea is fine, thank you. No milk or sugar."

The tea was poured and a cup and saucer placed in her hands before Herr Hoffmann spoke again. "My wife and daughter will return soon, and we will have a guest for our evening meal. A gentleman who is anxious to meet with you."

It was then Amy gave her full attention to the peculiar timbre of his voice; there was an oddly strained and synthetic quality about it. "Who is the guest?" she asked.

"You shall see," he replied with an air of mystery. "Peter will show you to your room, no doubt you would like to rest before we eat."

"Thank you, Herr Hoffmann, I think that's an excellent idea," she replied politely, feeling anything but tired yet still curious about his voice. She had barely had the opportunity to taste the piping hot tea. "I look forward to meeting your wife and daughter, and the mystery guest."

Her bedroom was as Germanic in design and as strikingly ornate as had been the downstairs rooms. A large oak four-poster bed, carved and regal, stood dead centre in the bedroom. A similar dark oak had been carved and fashioned into a dresser with an oval mirror. A magnificent panelled cupboard swallowed up the far end wall. A thick feather quilt was folded in half across the bed. The linen was snow white and Amy could smell the freshness of it from across the room.

Peter opened the window wide and pushed the shutters to one side to allow the bright sunlight to stream into the room and light up the richness of the wooden panelling. Amy's senses took a battering as a dozen pleasant fragrances reached into her head and confused her mind.

"Your Deutsche is Prima, Amy," Peter said as he turned to face her. "You will survive admirably, but if you do not mind, I shall continue to practise my English."

"I have no objections," she said, watching him sit down on the low windowsill, the sunlight shrouding him, highlighting his perfect Germanic profile every time he turned his head.

"Tell me, Peter, how long was your father in the concentration camp during the war?"

He looked completely shocked by her question and she hastily apologised. "Forgive me. I had no right to ask such a thing."

"No!" he exclaimed. "There is no need to apologise, but your question took me by surprise. How do you know? It is not normally discussed."

She smiled at him and replied quietly, "I suppose it was an educated guess. Do you mind talking about it?"

"Not at all, my father is not ashamed of his life, nor of his ancestry. He is Jewish and he was punished for being who he is. He was in Dachau, but unlike six million other Jews, he survived. He is proud of his ancestors. He is a good man, an honest man."

"Did they perform surgery on him?" Amy asked quietly.

Again, he looked shocked by her question but this time she made no apology and he answered her in a forthright manner. "Yes, upon his larynx. Experimental surgery they called it. I am pleased the men who did these terrible things are dead, they have paid the price for meddling with good people; besides, many would be happy to see them die a slow and agonising death over and again."

He looked around the lovely room and then his eyes rested on the young woman who'd moved to sit on the edge of the bed facing him. "Only with such wonderful care from the medical profession was my father able to survive the horrors of what they did to him. Until recently, he was unable to speak his thoughts properly, and now, with the wonders of modern science, and many skilled people, he can hold a normal conversation.

"Those men, those evil men of the Schutzstaffel; the Protection Squadron, the SS, as you know them, they and the Nazis, led by Herr Hitler, were mostly brilliant men." He huffed and shrugged his shoulders. "Had they worked for the good of mankind we would all be more comfortably situated today."

Then, as if the horrors of his father's past had become his own memories, Peter shivered violently. "They were inhumane and evil. They operated without anaesthetics. They took out appendix and other more vital organs, without first putting the person to sleep. They made no attempt to anaesthetise the area where they would be working. Open brain surgery was second nature to them."

He shivered again as he wrapped his arms around himself. Suddenly the heat had gone out of the sun for him. "My father survived Dachau. That is something he is most proud of. My grandparents were slaughtered because they were Jews. They were also proud people. They were taken to Sachsenhausen, which is not very far from here, just 40 kilometres north of the city."

Amy frowned and said, "I understood they only held political prisoners at Sachsenhausen."

"Ja, but my grandparents were active in destroying Nazi propaganda. They were not popular people, Amy. They were punished for their beliefs. We now know surgery was also performed at Sachsenhausen, the evidence is there and the Soviets have not covered it up. One day, when the wall is down, everyone will go and see for themselves and the world will be horrified by what has been hidden away."

He shook his head as if to clear the conversation from his memory. "But enough of this, tell me, is there a special man in your life, Amy Packard?"

"No." She smiled with her warm amber eyes and the tenderness of her voice. "I have no special man in my life. I am far too busy with work." She paused and then she asked, "What time is dinner served?"

"At seven," he replied. "You have an hour or two in which to rest or to explore. I suggest you rest. I believe there will not be time for such luxuries when you begin work."

It was evident Peter was aware of the purpose of her visit. "Yes, I think I will. Thank you, Peter, I will see you later."

On Monday 10th April, the soldier watched the beautiful stranger cross the parade square at Brooke Barracks, Spandau. It was a lovely morning and the stranger was like a breath of fresh air, and as glorious as any spring day he'd ever seen, especially in West Berlin.

Berlin had come alive again after a long cold winter. The Berliners were frantically buying up bedding plants to put a little instant life into their gardens and window boxes. They loved the myriad of vibrant colours spread out on display at the florist shops.

West Berliners appreciated being alive and free within the wall - free despite the wall. There was a certain discipline and orderliness about living behind the structure which divided families and cost good people their lives. While the barriers kept them confined, it also kept out those who would undoubtedly turn their beautiful city to ruin.

Faces brightened as the dullness of long dark and bitterly cold winter days faded into an already distant memory. Those who could afford to do so, exchanged winter clothes for bright new garments and the poor would be warm for another season.

The lovely young woman walked towards him with a spring in her step as the sun warmed her face. Her joy of life was obvious as she crossed Brooke Barracks, temporary home of Daniel Jones and the Welch Regiment.

"Yer!" the ginger-haired youth by the big man's side shouted loudly enough to be heard by everyone, including the stranger. "She's a bit of alright. Bet I could..."

"Shut your bloody mouth!" Dan growled a low warning.

"Sorry, sarge. I didn't mean no harm mind, just..."

"Shut it!" Dan growled again. "And keep it shut, Morris, or you'll find yourself cleaning the..." But the young woman was close enough for the fragrance of her perfume to reach into his head and cause him a momentary lapse of concentration. "Bugger off!" he said through the side of his mouth to young Morris who scurried away from him before the big man remembered exactly what it was he'd have him cleaning.

"Are you lost, Miss?" Dan asked politely.

"No," she said, smiling up at him as she continued to walk on by. "Not yet, but thank you all the same."

"My pleasure," he said as he touched his beret in a gentlemanly salute and watched her continue on into regimental headquarters. He hoped the major would be gentle with her. She looked so fragile and very young.

For two weeks Amy had lived in the magnificent home of Rudi and Eva Hoffmann. She'd shared their meals and experienced the warmth of their hospitality since being sent to the city following the successful completion of her training. She answered directly to Commander Bernard Cooper and it was with his words ringing in her ears she now faced an angry Major Philips.

"You'll be under the safe wing of a fine man," Cooper had assured her. *"I've known Doug Philips for a long time now, and he's proven himself to be most trustworthy. He'll take good care of you out there. You'll be in capable hands and you'll do fine. Good starting ground. Surrounded by your own people and a beautiful city to enjoy while you're*

at it. Go in, do the job and get yourself back here." He'd sounded as if he were reassuring himself rather than Amy.

"Yes, sir," she'd replied, wanting only to get on with it now he'd stirred her interest. *"Thank you, sir."*

"Any questions before you go?" he'd asked, sensing there was something on her mind.

"Just the one," she replied, *"What grade did I make?"*

She needed to know how she'd been categorised - how highly she was being trusted. It was a form of playful rivalry between the trainees. Who made the highest grade was vitally important to morale.

"H-four," he replied, knowing exactly how she'd react. He had not been disappointed. Her face beamed with delight. Amy, dear little Amy, fresh out of university, innocent and raw. Nine men and one female and she, of all of them, had passed with flying colours.

"The others made H-three," he told her, adding to her pleasure, knowing she had held the upper hand throughout the training period. Her mental strength and tenacity had by far outweighed the physical might of her male counterparts.

"You've done exceptionally well, Amy. Don't go letting me down."

"Never! I would never do that, sir." Her grin spread from ear to ear. She was smug and thoroughly contented, and rightly so. At twenty-two years of age, she was just a couple of steps from the highly acclaimed, and much sought after, top rung of the ladder in her career. Her smugness and contentment were well deserved; she'd earned her award.

Amy felt no fear of the unknown. It was the sheer exhilaration of the adrenalin coursing through her veins at the mere prospect of what lay ahead of her that made her shiver in anticipation.

"You'll be alone out there," Cooper reminded her unnecessarily. *"Despite all of the British personnel surrounding you at times, you will be alone, and if it became necessary, they would deny all knowledge of you.*

You will be excluded from the files here in Victoria House. Amy Harper would simply cease to exist."

"I fully understand the implications of falling into enemy hands, Commander." She paused for a second or two before asking, *"What are my orders, sir?"*

"You are to assume the name Packard. You will be accommodated with a local family." He handed her a single sheet of A4 paper containing all of the essential personal details of the family in question.

"Family name Hoffmann. Head of the family, Rudi. His wife of twenty-five years is Eva. They have two children, Peter and Lore." He correctly sounded the final vowel turning the German name into the English equivalent of Laura.

"You are to be companion to Lore," he went on. *"To all intents and purpose you are going there to help her improve her English language, and to brush up on your German. You will be contacted within hours of your arrival and you will be handed a document, which will be for your eyes only. The document will brief you more fully as to the exact nature of your mission."*

He stood and Amy knew the interview was at an end. *"Enjoy the flight, but remember, you are not on holiday. Lives are at stake, yours and those of innocent civilians. Do the job you are being sent out there to do and get yourself back here in one piece. Understood?"*

"Yes, sir." She lifted herself slowly and gracefully out of the comfortable chair and held out her hand to him. *"Thank you for everything you've done for me, Commander. Thank you also for trusting in me."*

His hand folded on hers and he felt the warmth that was Amy. *"Do the job, Amy. Prove me right to have placed my complete trust in you."* He nodded and smiling added, *"Good luck."*

As their hands touched, Amy knew the man; she knew all there was to know about him. He was a good and honest man, a trustworthy man whom she admired and respected.

The mystery guest on the first night in Berlin turned out to be Major Douglas Philips, friend of the commander. He was an extremely tall, uniformed army officer who shook her hand when introduced to her by Rudi Hoffmann and who then went on to ignore her completely throughout the entire meal, refusing to even make eye contact.

Before Amy had the opportunity to dwell upon the state of her waistline Herr Hoffmann excused himself and his family; it appeared the major had asked permission to discuss business with their young guest.

Herr Hoffmann was about to exit the room when he looked back over his shoulder and said, "Join us in the lounge when you have finished your talk. I have a magnificent old German brandy for you to taste."

"Thank you, Rudi," the major responded politely. "I look forward to it." His eyes were locked on Amy's face now, despite addressing the older man. He was wondering how a child could have become mixed up in such a crazy business; for a child was exactly how Douglas Philips saw Amy Harper, and Berlin was most definitely a crazy business, in his opinion.

The man spoke crisply and curtly to her the instant the double doors closed on the entire Hoffmann family. "How old are you?"

"Twenty-two, sir."

His eyes darkened as a frown creased his face and his brow furrowed menacingly. "Are you certain?"

Amy frowned too. "Yes, I am certain. I was born in 1945. I know exactly how old I am. Do you require proof, sir?" She had succeeded in asking the question without a hint of insolence.

"Of course not." He seemed slightly flustered by her response. "It's just you look so damned young, too young." His crisp tone and aloof manner did nothing to endear him to her. "Too young," he repeated.

She countered the comment with a pretty smile and another question. "Too young for what exactly, sir?"

"This, all of this." He opened his long arms in a sweeping gesture, encompassing Berlin in its entirety. "The cold war - the commies – death - all of it."

He shook his head as if to clear her image from his mind and then it was straight down to business; no more time to be wasted on trivialities. If the girl said she was twenty-two then he would have to accept her word for it, but he seriously doubted Commander Cooper's state of mind when he had made his final selection for this mission.

"As from today," he went on. "You must begin setting up your credibility. You are here as a companion to Lore and to improve your German; perfect your dialect."

It was not quite how Amy remembered it. The commander talked about her helping Lore with her English. Experts had spent many hours perfecting her German dialect long before she boarded the plane for Berlin. She wisely remained silent.

"Take in the sights," the tall man went on. "See everything there is to see. Miss nothing. Forget nothing. Checkpoints. Guards. Systems. Routines. You have two weeks in which to learn everything there is to know about Berlin and then you go into the Eastern Sector."

"Yes, sir. When will I be briefed?" The question ostensibly caused him some concern. It was written in his eyes and Amy felt it in her gut.

"I am briefing you right now, if you cared to listen, and any additional information will be passed on in due course," he growled, and even that sounded arrogant.

"Sir, I was informed I would be given an 'Eyes Only' document within hours of my arrival."

15

She saw him bite back the acid comment he was about to issue forth. He appeared to count to ten and then he said, "For now, the least you know the better. However, I will issue you with one warning, do nothing to endanger the lives of the Hoffmann family."

"That goes without saying," she spoke quietly to him. "But am I permitted to ask you a question?"

He almost smiled – almost - instead he inclined his head slightly and snapped, "Go ahead."

Quietly she asked, "How tall are you?"

With that, he threw back his head and laughed until tears formed in his big green eyes. "Oh, Amy! You are funny," he spluttered, succeeding in sounding almost human for the first time since they met.

"Am I, sir?" she asked, perfectly straight faced and serious. She had no memory of having actually seen a man crying with laughter.

"Yes, you are. I was ready to answer a serious question and you ask me how tall I am. Why do you need to know?"

"Curiosity, sir. I can't remember having met a man as tall as you." It was something else she couldn't remember. "You are exceedingly long."

He was still laughing when he replied, "I am precisely half an inch off seven feet long - or so I'm told."

"God!" she gasped and he began another bout of raucous laughter.

"Hardly! More like mere mortal I'd say. I can't ever remember being adored, more the exact opposite actually. My men think I don't know what they call me."

She edged forward and asked conspiratorially, "And what is it, sir?"

"Ah, now, that really would be telling." He wiped his eyes with a snow-white handkerchief bearing an ornately embroidered blue initial D in one of the corners before he added, "Suffice to say the most overused word begins with B and ends with D, and generally implies I have no father.

However, I daresay the names they give me are really terms of endearment, wouldn't you agree?"

She smiled and asked, "Are you a bastard, sir?"

Unflinching he replied, "I do have a father, but yes, sometimes I have to be. Although I try to be a fair bastard." His eyes took in her looks, her private beauty. He missed nothing. He fell in love with the child who claimed to be a woman.

Now, a full week later, Amy faced the man across the expanse of the office carpet, the man so warmly spoken of by the commander. Amy stared at him as his hand thumped down on the desk for the second time in as many minutes and pens and paper clips danced a merry little jig before settling down again.

"I said..." he resumed bawling at her, "What in God's name are you wearing? Kindly answer me."

"I thought that's what you said, sir," she replied calmly and seemingly unmoved by either his outburst or his comment on her attire for the day. "Actually, I'm wearing the latest fashion."

She spun on her heels and the circular pale blue skirt fanned out around her lovely legs, offering him a glimpse of seamed stockings tops, several inches of bare flesh and a layer of cream lace. The fluffy pink sweater clung to her firm breasts and as she stood before him bubbling with the zest and energy epitomising the sixties - he was furious.

"Please do not adopt that attitude with me, young woman!" he yelled and thumped again as the decibel levels rose to beyond decency. "I will not tolerate insolence."

"Ahem!" she coughed prettily into her hand. "Forgive me, sir, but I am not aware of having been insolent to you; either dumb or otherwise, or to any other person, now or at any time in my life. I was told to play the tourist and this is how respectable English girls dress nowadays."

"Huh!" he huffed, knowing he was wrong, hating being wrong. "Get changed into combat gear. I want to see you in action. Go! Move! What are you standing there for?"

Amy bowed her head and looked down on her patent leather shoes. She took a long deep breath, counted silently to ten and lifted her head to speak again. "You can ship me back to England, Major. You can put me against a wall and shoot me, but please do not think you can bully me. I work for British Intelligence. I am not one of your 'Chaps'. I was assured by the commander you would look after me, and I am prepared to follow your directives, obeying you to the letter, just don't bully me, sir."

The major's adjutant looked up at her as she walked proudly from the office, her head held high and a look of quiet satisfaction on her face. He winked at her, hardly having failed to hear what she'd said with his ear pressed up against the door.

"Good for you, Miss," he whispered.

It hadn't been Amy's intention for anyone to ever know what had taken place in the major's office that morning. The last thing she wanted was rumours spreading against the good name of the commanding officer. She touched the side of her nose and quietly said, "Not a word to anyone, please."

He saluted her informally held his right hand to his heart as he said," Not a word, promise."

Even so, the news travelled like wild fire throughout the barracks. Amy was a strong force; an independent woman, but it crossed her mind she may possibly have made an enemy of an ally. It was too late to do anything about it and by the time she'd changed into musty borrowed combat trousers and tunic which were too long and too baggy, the major was the last thing crossing her mind.

Amy had an inbuilt fear and loathing of military exercises and army assault courses. It was all too physical and masculine for her; she was not the athletic robust type. She admitted to being physically lazy. She preferred to exercise her mind to working up a physical sweat. She'd dodged almost every gym class at school, with some extremely imaginative excuses. She loathed netball, rounders and sports days. All the running around was too much like hard work for her.

Nothing had changed; trailing through mud and hauling her tired aching body over and under obstacles was hard work, and definitely not her idea of a fun day out. It was the downside of her chosen occupation - enduring times like this. It had been an integral part of her basic training and it would always be part of her life. Staying fit and knowing how to get out of a sticky situation was essential for survival - it was not an option. She might be able to get away with it throughout her school days but there would be no excuses with the military.

Eager grasping hands reached down and yanked her into the three-ton truck as she fended off a foray of playful comments, teasing and good-natured pats on the bottom from the men she was to spend the day with.

The men of 'A' Company marvelled at her stamina that day, but not just her stamina, her dogged determination never to admit defeat. Above everything they admired her constant cheerful nature. They praised her marksmanship on both the pistol and rifle ranges; they coaxed her over the obstacles she dreaded and detested on the assault course, and pledged their undying devotion to the auburn-haired beauty without a second thought for wives and sweethearts.

She proved herself to be a trier and never once used her gender or slight build as an excuse not to attempt the nearly impossible. Not once did she complain about breaking a fingernail or getting mud on her face. Amy was accepted as an equal into a regiment of tough fighting men.

There would never be a time in her career when she was without friendship or assistance. She earned respect and gained friendship by being herself.

By early evening, Amy Harper-Packard was in no mood for a further confrontation with Major Philips, but confrontation was exactly what he had planned for her. "I hear you held your own," he patronisingly commented with just a hint of disappointment sounding in his voice.

"I gave it my best effort; at least I like to think I did my best, sir."

"Good. Well, sit down and I'll brief you on your mission. It won't take long."

He watched with apparent satisfaction as she gingerly lowered her aching muscles onto the straight-backed wooden chair. He saw a fleeting grimace quickly hidden from his eyes as the bones in her buttocks touched the hard seat.

"Tea?" he asked.

"Please. Black no sugar."

"No sugar?" he queried. "Sugar makes energy."

"Sir, I'll drink it any way you like, out of a filthy combat boot if I must, but I would appreciate a hot drink."

He grunted rudely and ordered his adjutant to bring them two mugs of tea and they sat in silence until they arrived, neither had anything to say. Once the drinks were delivered, he broached the subject of her briefing.

"You are to board the U-Bahn at Spandau tomorrow morning. Head for the Eastern Sector of the city. You'll be a tourist, as you have been for the past two weeks. Go to the Museum für Deutsche Geschichte, that's the..."

"I know exactly what Museum für Deutsche Geschichte means. With respect, sir, I can speak the language." Her patience was being tested by this man.

"Yes, well." Obstinately he succeeded in translating despite her reminder. "Go to the German History Museum on Unter den Linden and on the first floor you'll be approached by one of the guards on duty there. He'll be expecting you to arrive at precisely 09:00." He raised his eyebrows and Amy repeated his words.

"Precisely 09:00." It was impossible for her to hide her annoyance. He was continuously treating her like a child and it aggravated her. Her father had never treated her this way.

"He will speak to you in German," he went on. "You will reply likewise. He will say, 'There is a more interesting exhibit in the annexe, 'and you will respond with, 'I do not speak German '- in German, naturally."

"Naturally," Amy whispered.

"He will then escort you to the annexe." The major flicked open the buff folder on the desktop and referred to the notes before going on. "It's vital you respond in German and not in English, even if it doesn't make sense. Is that clear?"

"Yes," she said, wishing he would stop treating her like a five-year-old. "Is that it, sir?"

"What do you want, a spy's guide to East Berlin?" came his facetious reply.

"No, sir." Amy was tired of him and of his immature attitude. "But I did expect to be fully briefed on my mission. I was told I would be given a document containing everything I need to know. I assumed you would give me the document. Evidently, I assumed incorrectly."

"Evidently!" He pulled himself up to his full height and glowered at her across the width of the desk. "You will receive everything you need in due course. For now, you know as much as I do."

Yes, she thought, and that's precisely what rankles you. You would dearly love to know more than me. She was not impressed with him. In fact, she felt she was wasting her time talking to him, but she made the effort. "In that case I'll say good night, Major. I really am tired."

"Report to me when you return to barracks," he snarled - his eyes on the contents of the buff folder and not a hint of warmth in his voice as he added, "Good night, and good luck for tomorrow."

Chapter Two

The pasty-faced East German border guard stamped Amy's passport and moved on to the next visitor. It was all very much routine for him and the young English woman could not believe how easy it had been.

Safe back home in England, she'd run through how it was going to be. She'd formed a picture in her mind of a massive wall defended with flesh, blood and ammunition, and in the two weeks since she arrived in Berlin, she'd seen the border defences; the barbed-wire fence, the few slabs of concrete and the armed guards. It had the makings of a mighty wall which would bring either death or freedom to many, but right then it was not hugely impressive in its design.

There was a cloying greyness on the other side of the border reflected in the faces of the people living there, as well as in the dullness of the buildings. The place was devoid of joy and life, flat and faceless, impersonal and unimpressive; apart from the magnificent architecture everywhere she looked.

There had been no apparent renovations or improvements throughout the city since the Royal Air Force blitzed the place during the Second World War. It reeked of poverty and appalling neglect. Any change was infinitesimal. Progress in the eastern sector; dictated by fear and caution was exceedingly slow. The Soviet government had spent very little money in rebuilding the magnificence of the city. Buildings still bore tell-tale signs of bullet holes and shrapnel damage.

Piles of rubble were remnants of bomb blasted homes. Monumental works of art were crumbling with neglect. The roads were unkempt, potholed and dangerous yet the splendour of Unter Den Linden took her breath away. Not even the wanton neglect could prevent the absolute beauty of the place from shining through the greyness.

The air hung heavy with smoke from the brown coal burned in East German homes. The air was foul with the pollution of ignorance. Stepping into East Berlin was like crossing time to go back decades.

From the Brandenburg Gate to the museum where she was to make her first contact in the East, Amy passed by people who refused to raise their heads to look at her. She saw only a few battered cars although Soviet army wagons were there in plenty. Soldiers bearing the insignia of both East Germany and the Soviet Union stood guard on every corner.

Unter den Linden was wide, rutted and flanked by massive works of pure genius and a population which seemed doomed to extinction. It confused her. She'd been spoiled for choice since birth. Here was a city with far greater beauty than London had ever known and yet it was almost devoid of obvious life. People were too afraid to leave their homes and places of business, too hungry and too used to the greyness that had become normality. Only the brave, the foolish and the tourists strolled idly in the spring sunshine.

As she walked towards the museum, it dawned on her these people had nothing to inspire them to leave their homes. The shops had windows crammed with displays of luxurious products yet inside there was hardly anything on sale. It was all for show. The scarcity of consumer goods behind the Iron Curtain during the Cold War era meant shops were barely stocked, besides, there was such a small amount of money to spend on what was available, the residents of the city were safely out of sight behind locked doors.

There hadn't been sufficient time to recover from the dividing of the city. From the time the first barbed wire was strung and roadblocks established along the inner boundary of the eight districts of the Soviet Sector on the 13 August 1961, the citizens remained in a state of deep shock. The barrier went up overnight dividing and devastating entire families. Those who worked in the West remained in the West and the same for the East.

It had been the decision of one man, Walter Ulbricht, leader of the communist party. He had the full approval and absolute backing of the might of the Soviet Union. It was a desperate bid to stop the exodus of his people. Over 2,000 people a day chose to leave until the borders closed and they became isolated from the rest of the world.

The irony of it was, in June 1961 that same man, Ulbricht, gave assurances at an international news conference in East Berlin that nobody intended building a wall. It wasn't possible for the people to trust the word of a man who made promises only to do the exact opposite less than two months later.

Six years on and Amy felt the fear and the pain which was East Berlin. Deep inside her head, conflicting emotions ran riot. Her footsteps became laboured, as her legs grew heavy under the burden of all the misery reaching out to her for help and understanding. She had never experienced anything like this before. Her highly compassionate senses were being bombarded, battered and bruised. It was all too much for her. How could she ever survive in a place like this? It would drain her core and leave her empty to wither and die.

Feeling weak, dizzy and sick deep inside, she stopped walking and raised her face to the blue sky, and as the sun shone down hot on her skin, she offered up a silent prayer for help. She thought about her parents and the fact that she'd had a full belly since birth. She'd never known anything but the joy of freedom of passage and speech.

Slowly the shock and the pain within her gradually diminished and she was able to move on again, as if guided towards her destiny.

The Museum für Deutsche Geschichte, the largest and most impressive Baroque building in the whole of Berlin, was awesome in size, and Amy felt instantly dwarfed, intimidated and humbled for the first time in her life as she entered through the main doors.

Slowly and steadily, she made her way through the first floor, passing exhibitions of the history of the GDR from 1945 to the present. As her eyes fell upon an interesting document pinned to a table inside a glass case, a uniformed guard approached her and spoke to her quietly in a gentle way.

He spoke slowly, unhurried. His speech was clear and articulate. He was clearly an educated man. "You cannot stay here. There is a much more interesting exhibit in the annexe."

Amy drew a long deep breath and responded exactly as she'd been instructed to do, "I do not speak German." No sooner than the words were out than she felt herself being propelled by the elbow into a cool dark annexe at the side of the building. Once inside, the stranger pressed a square of flimsy paper into her hand and pointed to a door behind her.

It was all so fast and surreal that when she stood outside once again, she couldn't even recall the exact words she'd used to thank him, but she felt certain she had thanked him. And now, bathed in bright sunlight and a thin film of perspiration, she unfolded the paper and saw an address scribbled on it: *Richtenburg Platz 106/9.*

It was rice paper, the ink a vegetable dye. She checked the address again before popping the message into her mouth in true spy fashion. Had the circumstances been different she might have burst out laughing, but lives were at stake now - her life was at stake, and there really was nothing funny.

She checked she wasn't being followed and found herself a quiet corner to study the tourist street plan she'd tucked into her handbag. Richtenburg Platz was close to the museum, two left turns and one right. It would take five minutes to walk the distance, no problem.

It was dark when a thoroughly weary Amy knocked on the major's office door and entered at his gruff summons.

"Where the hell have you been?" he yelled and she almost turned and walked back out again, however, the words which followed and the gentle tone of voice, told of his genuine concern for her well-being. "I was getting worried. I was about to send a man out to search for you. How did it go?"

"Fine," she replied wearily.

"Well?" he waited. "Do I get to know what happened out there?"

"No, sir. You do not."

His eyes widened and instantly darkened menacingly, warning of danger. His hackles began to rise and he snarled malevolently like a ferocious guard dog. "May I remind you, Miss, that you..."

"No, sir, you may not," she said, interrupting him just as he was about to launch himself into a full verbal assault.

"Let me remind you once again - I work for British Intelligence, sir, and not for you. The least said the better but when this is over, I will report to you. For now, it's my intention to stay alive. Suffice to say I have to go back again tomorrow."

He was dumbfounded, rendered speechless by her blunt refusal to discuss her day. "Well, ahem! Yes. Well, is there anything I can do to help?"

"As a matter of fact, there is something," she said now his tone was somewhat subdued. "I need a car, something rather old and ordinary - inconspicuous."

"And?" he asked, sensing there was more.

Amy smiled prettily; she needed this man as her ally. "A driver. Someone who is thoroughly trustworthy and totally dependable. I need safe documents for the two of us to go back and forth into the Eastern Sector without let or hindrance."

"British tourists," he said as if to himself.

"No, sir. I really don't think it would be a smart move. As tourists we wouldn't be popping back and forth. We'd do the tour then leave to look at the West." Her well-bred English accent and authoritative tone of voice left no room for doubt in his head that she knew what she was doing, and Amy herself believed she knew what she was doing, things seemed straightforward to the tired young woman.

He nodded understanding. "What time and where?" He was learning her ways at last.

"O-six hundred hours - the corner of Pichelsdorfer Strasse and Klosterstrasse. Directly opposite the café."

"Very well. Anything else?" He noted the weary, almost imperceptible shake of her head. "Go and get some shut-eye. My man will be there. He'll bring the documents you require."

He turned his back on her; the conversation had been rudely concluded. And once again he'd proven himself unfriendly and ignorant when all he really wanted to prove was that he was a caring and concerned man.

Douglas Philips had never had any significant problems with dealing with the opposite sex, nor indeed had he experienced problems with attracting women in the first place. On the contrary, getting rid of them when they got too attached was generally his real problem. However, this young woman, who turned his senses inside out and spun him around had succeeded in scaring him, tall and grown though he was.

At 05:55 on Tuesday 18th April, a mud-coloured rusting and seriously dented old Volkswagen Beetle drove up onto the pavement directly opposite the scruffy café where Amy was sitting with a cup of bitter-tasting coffee in front of her. The driver looked about him.

"Bless you, Major," Amy whispered, recognising her driver as one of the men from 'A' Company. She was thankful that finally Douglas Philips had done something to exonerate himself in part, if not in full. She moved away from the table and thanked the sleepy café owner on her way to the door. "Dankeschön."

"Bitteschön," he replied without looking up from the newspaper spread across the counter top.

Amy crossed the road and walked straight towards the vehicle. The soldier in civilian clothing jumped, instinctively ready for action, and then he smiled recognition as he leaned over to open the passenger door for her to get in. He'd spoken to her on her first day at Brooke Barracks and was one of the thirty soldiers she'd trained with a few days earlier. His strong hands had hoisted her over the obstacles she loved to hate. He was clearly a well-built man, muscular and strong, a man with a kind face, kind and expressive. There was a chestnut-red moustache on his top lip yet his fine hair was fair and sparse. His eyes were grey in the early morning light. Yes, she thought, all in all a likeable face. A man she knew instinctively she could trust.

"Dan Jones," he said, introducing himself briefly. "What do I call you, Miss?"

"Amy," she said as she succeeded in shutting the car door the third time she slammed it. "Please drive to Checkpoint Charlie." As the car bumbled noisily down the road she asked, "What documents have you for me?"

He reached into the inside pocket in his jacket and extricated a length of string, a small piece of chalk, two matchsticks, a paper clip and two tattered ID papers, the latter he handed to her. "Sorry," he said as he packed all the junk back into his pocket while he concentrated on his driving.

The papers were civilian and German, but only temporary permits. "I don't speak much German," he announced, dropping a bombshell which exploded in her expression of horror. "Although I am good at playing big and dumb," he swiftly and wisely added. "And I can understand more than I can speak."

Amy was determined nothing was going to prevent her from carrying out a successful first mission, not the major, and certainly not this big Welshman. She checked the names on the documents - Fräulein Angelika Stronberg and her brother Herr Willhelm Stronberg.

"Do these people exist?" she asked.

"No," he replied, "But according to the major, there are Stronberg's over there who will welcome us should we get into trouble. They've been advised of our existence. The major has connections."

"I doubt it," she responded without thinking first. It was different in action, different from all of the training classes, the talks and the lectures. Worlds apart from everything she'd experienced in basic training. And now, sitting in the little car that smelt of burned oil and stale cigarette smoke, she knew she was alone and she had to make things work for her. She felt young, vulnerable and a little insecure all of a sudden, yet she would never let anyone know.

"Okay," she said at last. "This seems sound enough. I'll do all the talking. You can neither speak nor hear. Is that clear? You are a dumb mute."

Her voice was quietly confident and soothing. Dan Jones shrugged his shoulders and with a gentle smile he shrugged again and pulled a face which made her smile. The warmth of her amber eyes reached in to touch his heart.

"Can I ask why we're going in, Amy?" he asked, finding his voice again.

"All I know is I have to bring two men out, maybe not today. It could take days or weeks. I want to set this up and do it properly first time."

"I see."

She turned and took a long hard look at him, admiring him while struggling to understand exactly what it was about this man that made her give up information so readily. Why did she trust him? "Don't you dare breathe a word of what I've told you to the major, nor to anyone, understood?"

"Yes, Miss." He smiled smugly to himself. "Does this mean I get to stay with you on this one?"

"If you're good, yes. If not, well, I'll have you replaced. Are you good?"

"Of course," he said with a cheeky grin. "Survival is my speciality."

He now had her full attention. "How do you mean?" She turned her body to study his expressive face - feeling comfortable in his presence.

"I'm a survival instructor," he explained briefly. "Specialist like. It's the only thing I do best."

The major had chosen well. Amy raised her eyebrows. "That makes me feel nicely secure."

"You'll be safe with me, Miss," he promised. "I won't ever let you down." She believed him.

Amy could not have been in safer hands than those of the man whose sometimes maverick, and often well beyond unconventional behaviour, landed him in more bother with the Regimental Sergeant Major than any other member of the regiment. Daniel Jones was born in a terraced house in dockland Cardiff in June 1940. Growing up there was hard, and every day a battle to survive. The fittest, toughest and the bravest of the children who played out on the street after school every day, they were the ones who succeeded in life.

There was nobody there to do them a favour or give them a friendly hand up. Dan wore cast-off clothes, ran errands to earn pennies and he found a job delivering newspapers before school five days a week and again on the weekend. The money he earned went into the jar in the kitchen to help his mother feed the family.

He left school at fifteen and headed for the hills and the Welsh forests where he worked alongside some of the roughest and toughest lumbermen Welsh mothers had ever produced. The men became his brothers, uncles and cousins, and one man in particular adopted him as a son. From old Tom came sayings and expressions, habits and eccentricities. Tom Pugh made a good honest man of a gangly boy. He helped transform soft flesh into hard muscle and in building the muscle he forged a steel-like character.

A forest accident drove Dan back to civilisation and into the army. His friend and mentor Tom Pugh lay crushed beneath an ancient pine and his last words were for Dan and for him alone. "Go see the world, Son. See it and love it like I have."

The Welch Regiment took him in and gave him a home. They tried to knock the rough edges off. They attempted to make round what was so obviously square, and vice versa, yet while Daniel Jones was the worst soldier on the parade square, he was the best man in action. They sent him on specialist training courses where he was taught everything about army survival. They forged him into a lethal weapon with the ability to outsmart any enemy.

At twenty years of age, he had sufficient pay every week to send half of it home to his tiny but tough mother, Katherine, and still have enough left for cigarettes and karate lessons. The lessons were a secret, none of his mates knew about them, and when his secret was out, they ribbed and riled him until he learned to ignore them.

Dan was devastated when the SAS turned him down, claiming a lack of agility on his part. He was too slow off the ground and too sluggish in action, or so they said. However, the truth was, he'd upset one of the assessors by showing off his skills and outdoing the man. It had not gone down at all well and Dan was destined for an ordinary life from that point on; or so it seemed at the time.

The Middle East gave him a taste of action. He learned enough Libyan Arabic to converse with the natives, which made his tour of duty even more interesting. And then the regiment arrived in Berlin for its first two-year tour of duty, to witness the inception of 'The Wall'. Solid slabs of reinforced concrete slowly but surely replaced the flimsy wire fence. Bit by bit the lovely city became divided and depressed.

The Welch Regiment and Daniel Jones left Berlin for a two-year tour of duty in Belfast, returning in 1967 at the turn of the year.

The border wall did nothing to prevent him from seeking excitement and adventure, in fact, the oppressive wall provided the perfect excuse. He trained in canoes on the lakes, rivers and canals of the city, taking an active lead in a crazy and foolhardy stunt with a young, fresh-faced lieutenant which almost cost them their careers and could so easily have cost them their lives. They'd ventured into East Berlin by travelling along a canal in the depth of night - risking everything for the sheer thrill of it.

Another time, Dan Jones led an expedition of battalion misfits down the River Weser, knocking the men into shape with each passing hour. They set off with neither food nor water, stealing and begging as they travelled towards Bremerhaven.

Somehow, although the senior officers never discovered how, the men managed to prevent him from crossing the North Sea to Britain, which had been something he wanted to do, in his words: *'For the hell of it."*

He and his team of bearded; half-naked drowned rats were rushed straight to Berlin Brigade HQ and to the brigadier's office where the man congratulated them. While there, Dan persuaded the brigadier to give him a hardback book he'd spotted on the shelf - 'The Gathering Storm 'by Sir Winston Churchill. He even got the man to inscribe and date it before he left his office. The book was always one of his most treasured possessions.

It was Brigadier Kingston Miles who steered Major Douglas Philips in the direction of Corporal Daniel Jones, and he who suggested the specialist team be set up within the regiment and Daniel Jones be promoted to sergeant to enable him to head the team.

While Dan excelled in the world of survival, he remained uniquely eccentric. As the years went by, he became more set in his ways, becoming more the bachelor than he had ever intended to be. He lived by a strict routine, or regime for want of a better description; within severe self-imposed lines, and while he turned up on the parade square with white socks on his feet and his shirt unbuttoned to his navel, to be disciplined by the RSM, his bed pack was neatly folded, his locker immaculate and his personal hygiene unfailingly without fault.

Dan took giant strides everywhere he went. He never walked slowly or leisurely. His chest was always puffed out to display his massive bulging muscles to their best advantage, and his head was never held any way but proudly erect.

He slammed doors without any thought of anger, banged cutlery and crockery down onto table tops, not even aware of his own strength, and he grunted his way through each and every morsel of every meal, oblivious to all but the eating, and the pleasure it brought him. He was a man who remained completely loyal to his superiors and totally dedicated to every task set for him. He was a man who had known infinite kindness in the arms of his mother, who could crack a walnut with finger and thumb, yet hold a newly born infant with loving gentle hands. Amy Harper was safe. Dan would not let anything happen to her, not while he had life in his body.

Amy felt no sense of strangeness to know exactly how safe she was with this man. She dared to touch his hand when he handed her the documents, and she knew all there was to know. However, Dan was not the problem, the border patrol was, and an immediate problem at that.

The car was thoroughly searched. It was turned inside out. They were 'invited' inside the makeshift building where there was a pervading odour they failed to recognise. Dan suspected it was fear he could smell.

A succession of rapid-fire questions was hurled at them. Amy explained patiently that her brother was both deaf and dumb and they'd been given permission to visit their aunt who was asking for them from her deathbed.

As she talked, she knew she'd been deluded into believing she could do it all so easily. She felt angry with herself for her negligence. She should have insisted on having the false documents earlier so she could set up a plausible cover story for herself and her driver. Lying wasn't something which came naturally to her and she felt certain they were finished if details of the relatives in the eastern sector of the city were required.

Her inability to assess the situation beforehand and to form a strong plan of action could cost them their lives. She knew exactly where she'd gone wrong and in the time it took the guards to search the car and interrogate the couple she made a personal promise never to take such foolish risks again.

Perspiration flooded over her as Dan steered the vehicle away from the border on the opposite side to freedom. "You're good," he commented, glancing quickly in her direction before returning his full attention to the uneven surface of the road ahead.

"I'm not good!" she argued with surprising aggression. "I'm too bloody careless by far. We could have shot back there because of my arrogance. If we get out of this in one piece, I'll make damned certain I have all of the facts long before the next trip."

He refused to argue. He was impressed with what he'd seen and heard. "You a soldier, Amy?" he asked.

"Good God, no!" she exclaimed. "I'd never survive. I hate all the crawling around the place in soldier suits, carrying ridiculously heavy junk in a backpack and a weapon designed to take life and break the arms of the person bearing it. I'm a civil servant. A pen pusher." She was grinning.

"Some pen pusher!" he said, laughing at her, but lightly, and then he asked, "Where to?"

"Aim for Unter Den Linden. I can direct you more fully from there."

Chapter Three

Sgt Jones, the twenty-seven-year-old bachelor, followed obediently. He watched, listened and learned, and by the time he was nuzzling the rounded nose of the Volkswagen Beetle into an empty parking place on Brooke Barracks, West Berlin, he knew he, like his commanding officer before him, had fallen in love with Amy, the pen-pushing civil servant.

"Can I ask you out for a drink some time?" he dared ask as she was about to leave him.

"You can. When?" There seemed nothing timorous or inhibited about her. She was bold yet succeeded in remaining powerfully feminine.

"Are you too tired this evening?" he asked. It was gone seven. They'd been together for thirteen hours.

"No, although I must sort out the grumpy major before I do anything else." She laughed as she admitted; "He's been a regular pig since my first day here."

This fact had not gone unnoticed. "Go and see him and we'll talk about it later," Dan said, a nervous smile playing on his face. He could hardly believe his luck, a whole day with Amy and now the opportunity to share her evening too. "I'll meet you back here in an hour. I can take you to your place if you want to get cleaned up and put different kit on."

He was a thoughtful man. She liked the way he took charge and made decisions. "Fine. An hour it is."

Washed, polished and smartly attired in his best, and only, suit, Dan waited impatiently outside the building. Amy was late, fifteen minutes late. He began shifting about from one foot to the other and then with a grunt he paced back and forth several times before grunting again, convinced she'd changed her mind and gone home.

He kicked a stone and instantly regretted it when he noticed the scrape in the thick layer of polish on the toe of his best black shoes. He bent over and examined it closely and when he straightened, his eyes rested on Amy, looking pale and drained before him.

"Hell, what's been going on in there?" he asked as he reached for her arm to offer support and changed his mind.

"He beat me into submission," she joked but when he rose to his full five feet eleven and three-quarter inches, looking about ready to kill for her, she hastily added, "Calm down, I'm okay. I need to unwind. I'm keyed up."

She soothed him with a reassuring smile. "That man would never dare lay a finger on me." Tucking her arm in his, she tugged him towards her. "Come on, let's go."

They walked down into Spandau and to the house on Kuregenstrasse and while Amy showered and changed into a pretty blue frock, Lore and Peter Hoffmann entertained the British soldier.

Lore, the eighteen-year-old daughter of Rudi and Eva Hoffmann showed positive signs of interest in the big man with the fascinating accent, and her elder brother asked simple questions about Wales and why the regiment was known as Welch and not Welsh. He learned that it was the archaic spelling and perfectly correct, and when Amy entered the room and Dan stood and stared in open-mouthed admiration both young Hoffmann knew he was in love.

"I'll get a taxi," Dan announced as they stepped outside together.

"No, don't!" she exclaimed, reaching for his arm to prevent him from darting off. "Let's just go into Spandau Centre and find a bar. Somewhere quiet. It's warm enough to sit outside this evening. I couldn't face the city centre, not tonight."

He agreed, feeling proud to have her on his arm. Hoping above hope that everyone in the regiment would see them out together.

They sat in the open air and talked about themselves, or at least, Dan talked about himself and Amy listened. He learned next to nothing about her and the less he knew the more he became captivated and curious.

"You intrigue me," he admitted at last.

"Why?" she asked, never having been attracted to any man before this day, nor had she felt so powerfully and utterly feminine. Her equilibrium was under threat because her heart was doing a song and dance. "I'm only a normal elderly teenager," she said, flirting outrageously with him.

"Normal! Never! You are extraordinarily unique, Miss...what is your name anyway?"

"Amy Packard, for now." She raised her eyebrows and chuckled mischievously.

"Okay," he agreed. "But one day I want to know everything about you, Amy Packard. Everything!"

They laughed and teased. Flirted and moved closer together and Amy let him hold her hand on the walk home. "Amy, I..."

"Shush!" she silenced him, ever practical. "Don't say a word. Go and sleep. I've requisitioned your services for tomorrow. This time we have to use the public transport system for cover. We don't need to leave quite as early. Seven sharp, don't be late." Then she stood on tiptoe and placed a gentle kiss on his cheek. "Good night, Dan."

He watched her trip gracefully up the steps and into the Hoffmann residence without as much as a backward glance.

She was such a confident young woman he wondered if he really stood a chance with her.

As Amy slept a peaceful sound sleep Dan stalked the barracks for hours, unable to rest. Sleep was the last thing on his mind. He sang to himself. He stalked, walked, and would have kept going all night had the RSM not bawled out a warning for him to get inside and get his head down - or else!

The bogus documents helped them gain access to East Berlin once again next morning. They crossed through the border on foot at Bornholmer Strasse, which meant they had a fairly long trek ahead of them. Amy was dressed in borrowed shabby clothing and Dan in a scruffy bundle of rags, which he assured her, was what the local working men were currently wearing.

Amy carried all the information she needed to fend off a barrage of questions. The information was stored within her head and nothing could cause her to deviate from the contrived story she had planned. Her memory was exceptionally keen.

They were grudgingly permitted to cross into the Eastern Sector. They were safe for the time being. Quietly and unassumingly, she led Dan to the dilapidated building on Richtenburg Platz, to where he'd sat outside in the car the previous day, wondering what she was doing and why he'd been ordered to wait outside for her.

They went directly to apartment number 9, where she introduced him to a skeleton of a character of indeterminate age, a man pathetically and inhumanely emaciated and malnourished, who lacked almost every known essential vitamin yet remained surprisingly bright and articulate.

"I am pleased to meet with you, Dan," Herr Schaffner said as the men shook hands. "Please to sit there." He pointed in the direction of a rickety stool in the corner of the sparsely furnished room. Dan shook his head in a polite refusal, preferring to stand by the door where he could watch Amy's every move - ready to spring into action and carry her away to safety should the need arise.

The conversation between the old man and the young woman was carried out in rapid local dialect, which meant Dan understood only one in every ten or fifteen words and he soon lost interest in what was being said. It went on for the best part of thirty minutes with Amy stopping the old man from time to time, making him repeat himself more slowly. Dan shifted his weight from one foot to the other but he never once relaxed his vigil as he watched over them.

At last Amy stood, shook the bony hand offered to her and signalled for Dan to leave the building ahead of her.

They crossed the city centre in silence; there seemed no real need to converse. Dan was at peace walking alongside Amy. Her zest for life oozed from her core. Amy felt the same peace, together with a sense of security in her companion's care. Her thoughts were centred on the task in hand. There was an urgency in her to make things work, in her own inimitable way.

The dingy apartment building two kilometres from the old man in the drab little room on Richtenburg Platz was unwelcoming and hostile. Amy went inside and knocked twice on the second slate grey door they arrived at on the ground floor. She paused and knocked again. The door opened and she stepped inside, Dan close on her heels.

"Herr Klein," she said her voice thin and strained for the first time.

"Fräulein Stronberg." She nodded to the man, who was anything but small in circumference.

As soon as the door closed on the world Amy said, "Können Sie mir helfen?"

He glowered at Dan, snapped out a curt comment to Amy and ushered them both to seats snapping, "Sitzen." Dan refused to sit. Instead, he took up position by the door where he then proceeded to take in the abject poverty of the room. This was another place Amy had visited the previous day while he hung around outside, but he would never have found it again without her guidance or a map, or both, he'd been far too intent on watching over her to keep track of where she'd led him. He chastised himself, knowing he needed to pay better attention, especially as he was the survival expert.

From the moment Amy sat down things were much the same as they had been in the home of Herr Schaffner. Amy talked and listened intently. This time, however, they were not in the building for more than ten minutes, during which time the grossly overweight German spoke only when questioned. Then they were hurrying through the city again. Dan admired her positive strength, her determination and her sheer guts.

It was as if she knew exactly where to go, as if she'd been there before. Her actions were wholly positive and she had no need of a street map.

She led him to a low wooden hut, long since abandoned to the damp and the rats in order to cut down on Communist Party funds. It was a prefabricated building on waste ground, originally set up in 1947 as a temporary abode for homeless families, for refugees. A hovel of a place that reeked of stale urine, both from animals and humans. Rats scurried ahead of them as they entered.

Amy was instantly overwhelmed by the feelings of sadness and misery which pervaded her mind. An evil blackness descended upon her, swallowing up the light, sucking out her energy - she fought against it, praying all the while for strength and guidance, glancing back to make certain Dan remained close on her heels. He smiled fleetingly, unsure of the way she was looking at him, as he had no way of knowing the fear filling her tender soul.

The mist which closed in on her mind lifted as suddenly as it came and she saw the bundle of rags stacked against the far wall. Beneath the bundle lay what remained of the man she'd come searching for. She went to him and placed her hand on his brow. He was ice cold and a blue tinge had set around his eyes, nose and mouth. There were no days and weeks left for this man, merely a matter of hours, possibly minutes. He'd given up fighting.

"Christ!" Dan exclaimed, seeing him at last. "Is he alive?"

"Barely," she replied as she shifted her attention to the open door of the hut. "There's someone out there, watching this place."

He'd heard nothing. He moved towards the window and took a good long look. He saw three similar huts - a vast expanse of waste ground, rubble and rubbish. There was nobody in sight and nothing to be seen or heard. She must have imagined it. This was nerves - nothing more.

"No-one," he called quietly to her, satisfied in his own mind that they were safe, but as he moved back towards her across the hut, she hissed out a warning command.

"Stand guard!" Alarm bells were ringing inside her head. Calmly she returned her full attention to the dying man. "Mr Jacobs, you're safe. We've come to take you home. Please hold on. Don't give up." Already the tremors of death were beginning to set in. Urgent action was called for. There was no more time to waste.

She removed her thin jacket, wrapped it around the man, and went to stand next to Dan. "We need transport. Can you find a car?"

"Steal one?" he questioned and saw her almost imperceptible nod. "Will you be okay here?" She nodded again just the once as his hand reached for the door handle.

Dan Jones had never had cause to steal an actual vehicle, although he knew exactly how to go about it. It was one of the first things he taught on survival courses. In theory, it was all quite simple. In reality, it proved to be a completely different matter. It took him thirty-five precious minutes to find the beaten-up Soviet-built vehicle, parked at the front of a large dilapidated apartment building, it was unlocked and seemingly abandoned with the keys in place.

Amy waited in silence, willing the man to hold on. Praying her efforts were not in vain.

Dan parked the car two blocks away from Richtenburg Platz, lifted the unconscious man from the rear seat and slung him carefully over his shoulder so that he could hurry to safety, Amy close behind him.

They crashed into the room without first asking permission and deposited the dying man on Herr Schaffner's bed. The Englishman was comatose. His lungs filled with pneumonia; his emaciated body unable to continue the fight for life.

"I am sorry, Herr Schaffner," Amy began. "I had no other option. This man is seriously ill."

"I understand," he replied. "How can I help?"

"You are helping," she said, smiling her gratitude. "I had no idea he would be in this dreadful state." She shook her head. "We can't wait for nightfall to move on. What the hell am I going to do? This man should have been..." she left the sentence unfinished, she felt ashamed she had not done her job properly - again.

Dan had no answers. This was a new situation for him. "Tell me what you want," he said. "I'll get it or do it. Just say the word." He was prepared to move mountains for her.

"No! You can't speak, or have you forgotten? I have to go alone. Guard him, Dan." She stood and pulled on the thin jacket. "Don't let anything happen."

"Amy!" he called as she made for the door. He was about to advise her to be careful. Better still, not to go at all but he thought better of it. She was a woman who he strongly believed, knew what she was doing and she'd made her decision.

"I'll be careful," she assured him as she moved silently and swiftly out of the building and down the stone steps onto the street. As she moved, she called on her reserves of energy for what she knew lay ahead of her, wishing and praying there was another way; regretting not keeping her body in better physical shape.

She returned three hours later. A bag of medical supplies slung around her neck. She was physically exhausted and near to collapse as she fell into Dan's arms puffing out instructions, "Drugs...antibiotics...hypodermic. Quickly!"

He found the syringe and the phial of sulphonamide but he had never administered a drug this way. He fumbled clumsily in a futile attempt to fill the syringe until Amy snatched it impatiently out of his hands and pushed him, not too gently, away from her.

She yanked down the shoddy trousers and swabbed the man's scrawny left buttock with surgical spirits before plunging the needle deep into his emaciated body. She then asked for cold water and proceeded to strip his prostrate body of clothing.

It became a half-hourly routine for the next twelve hours. Amy sponged the man from head to toe, turned him and proceeded to do the same to his back, rolling him over and wrapping him in filthy coarse blankets.

With a little ingenuity and improvisation, she set up a glucose intravenous drip, Dan fastened to a nail which had once supported a large crucifix. There was a feint outline of the cross on the wall. A memory of his Catholic upbringing flashed through his mind when he saw it on the damp wall, and then it was gone and he returned his attention to the task in hand.

Amy had been able to carry dextrose powder and the means by which to administer it; the knowledge came from her thorough field training. Great care was taken despite their unclean surroundings; the hypodermic syringe was placed in a dented saucepan, which she filled with water and kept boiling on the hob.

Every four hours she refilled the syringe and injected sulphonamide into the thin buttock, which had quickly become black and blue.

Herr Schaffner fed them watery vegetable soup and dry bread and made countless cups of strong black coffee. There was no milk or sugar, they coped, and they were grateful to their host for sharing what little he had with them.

The sun had left the sky for over an hour before Amy knew the time had come to make a move. Only Herr Schaffer got any sleep the previous night and both she and Dan had long since forgotten their need for it.

Simon Jacobs recovered consciousness, his fever broke and he spoke to Amy for the first time as she and Dan prepared to leave. He coughed and pushed back the blanket to free his hand.

"Lie still," Amy whispered tenderly." You're in safe hands."

"Who...are you?" He coughed again.

She offered him a sip of boiled water before replying. "My name is Amy. This is Dan. We're going to take you home."

"Thank God!" he sobbed and his eyes filled with tears. "I...had given...up. My wife...is she...?"

"Your wife is well and looking forward to seeing you again. You must lie still, don't upset yourself. You'll have all the answers you require when we get you home. Dan and I have to go back to the British Sector. Herr Schaffner will take care of you until we return."

Dan was choked when the frail man began crying, and big as he was, he wanted to join him. Amy had done this, she'd brought the man back from the brink of death, and all he'd done was stand back and wait for her to issue commands. It was her show. She was in charge, and she was doing a bloody marvellous job from where he was standing.

"We have to go and get the car," Amy said to him at last. "He'll be safe here."

Dan nodded and reached for his jacket, following her out of the building. There was a long walk ahead of them but neither of them felt tired. The questions rolling around in his head would have to wait. Why not take the Beetle in the first place? She knew they were looking for Jacobs.

They returned at midnight to find Simon Jacobs fully conscious and perfectly lucid. His eyes were alive again and his face beginning to look less like a corpse and more like a living being.

"You look better," Amy said quietly as she knelt and smiled down on him. "How do you feel?"

"Stronger," he assured her. "How can I thank you?"

"Time enough for thanks when you're out of the East. Just a little while longer, we're almost there. Now, do you think you can lie still for quite a long time?"

He smiled. "I have no prior arrangements to the contrary, my dear."

"Good. I'll give you another injection of antibiotics before we leave. I don't know how long it's going to take us."

Dan watched her fill the syringe from two vials this time. He would later learn she'd administered a relatively strong sedative.

"Okay, Dan," she said when Jacobs closed his eyes and slept peacefully. "Let's get this over with." With barely a nod of thanks to the man whose home had been invaded, she led the way out of the building and opened the bonnet of the old car.

During the hours of their absence, some subtle modifications had been carried out. In the eyes of the world, it was exactly the same vehicle, however, now it would carry the body of a frail and sick Englishman, hidden away from prying eyes and hopefully without anyone being any the wiser.

The engineers removed part of the interior of the car, fixed a false panel inside and an inner compartment under the luggage compartment at the front end. With the vehicle having a rear-mounted engine, there was already limited storage space. Under normal circumstances, it would have been near impossible to store a suitcase let alone a grown man, thin though he was.

All Amy needed to do now was to insert a small screwdriver in a tiny slot and remove the panel. It took only seconds and with Dan's help, they lowered the drugged body into the concealed compartment. He fitted snugly; his legs wrapped around the steering column. As long as he remained unconscious, he would be safe from prying eyes.

The border guards had stepped up their vigilance in their absence and were making thorough searches of all vehicles crossing back into the West. Too many times they'd been fooled into believing what they could see with their eyes. Many fine inventions had passed before them with bodies cunningly concealed from view. Dozens had escaped in this way, and so the border control guards were issued with calibrated rods as a means of measuring the inside dimensions of all types of vehicles. Mirrors were clipped on the rods so the underside of every vehicle could be checked and strictly controlled. It was up to the inventors to stay one step ahead of them. They were desperate people doing everything they could to outsmart the authorities.

The conversion work on the car opened up many new avenues of inventiveness, and Amy felt confident it would be of use over and again. However, despite her confidence, they had no way of knowing if they'd be discovered. All they could do was drive and pray.

That was exactly what they did. Neither spoke a word. Neither voiced their own personal concerns and fears. Neither had time to acknowledge the deep sense of belonging they felt in each other's company. It would have to wait. There was nothing to be said, nothing for now.

Dan now knew exactly why they'd left the car behind on this mission. There was no longer any need to ask questions.

At the border crossing, they were invited to step inside the hut where Amy instantly burst into a flood of tears during a heart-rending tale of how their elderly aunt died late that night.

"Go!" the guard snarled, shoving her away from him, seemingly incapable of admitting to any feeling of compassion. "Get out of my sight and take that imbecile with you before you bring my commander down here to see what all the noise is about!"

"Please, God!" Amy prayed aloud as Dan turned the key and the starter motor refused to work. "Please let it start." The engine fired, spluttered and then they were moving away. "Let him be alive. Please, God, let him be alive." She moved smoothly and quietly from one set of prayers to the next.

They crossed into the West and turned into the quiet parking area well away from prying eyes so that Simon Jacobs could be carefully removed from his hiding place. Tender, careful hands lifted him into the waiting military ambulance. With infinite care he was tucked beneath soft blankets and strapped down on a trolley.

Amy stood next to Dan as the vehicle drove away. It was over. He was safe. She turned her head and looked at her companion, seeing all the tension and tiredness etched in his ruggedly handsome face. "One down and one to go. You did well. Thank you."

He was choking. Words wouldn't form. He looked at her and then tore his eyes away to look up at the night sky and the stars shining down on them. He shook his head, took a deep breath and looked at her again.

"You are something else, Miss Packard." He rested his hand lightly on her shoulder. "Come on, little lady. You need to sleep."

Chapter Four

"You okay, little one?" Dan asked as she slumped wearily in the chair next to him in the British Military Hospital outpatient department. She'd refused to return to the Hoffmann residence to sleep until she knew how Simon Jacobs was doing.

The department was packed - wives with screaming infants - soldiers on crutches - one with a heavily bandaged knee. Others had bandaged ankles and arms, and many of them looked extremely healthy.

Amy nodded slowly and eventually asked, "Are you?"

"Bugger me," he said quietly. "I've done sod all," and then he apologised. "Sorry."

"No need to be. I feel like a jolly good cuss myself; however, I'll wait until the good major arrives before I let off steam."

She laughed lightly and the effort sapped her of her remaining energy, although she was happy and even contented. At last, she was doing something truly worthwhile with her life and she had strong support in Sergeant Daniel Jones. They were a good team.

No sooner than she'd mentioned the major than he arrived in a flurry of khaki and brass, seeming to fill the corridor with his presence. He was so tall it was difficult to judge if he had any muscle on his frame. He appeared to be slim and willowy. He reached for Amy's arm and whisked her rudely out of the building to where it was beginning to rain.

"How is he?" he demanded bluntly as he released his grip, leaving behind several deep imprints in the delicate flesh of her upper arm.

"I don't know. I'm waiting to hear," she replied as she massaged her arm. "His fever broke before we brought him out. The car was perfect."

"Um, good." He hadn't even bothered to look at her. "How did Jones perform in action?"

"Um, good," she echoed his non-committal tone and expression.

"Good," he responded. It was wasted on him. He was proving himself to be an insensitive oaf, giving neither praise nor thanks, let alone congratulations - not that Amy expected anything from him, or from anyone for that matter. This was strictly business, she trained to do exactly what she'd done, recover ailing British agents.

"Let's go and find out what the hell's happening in there," he said, and with that, he strutted majestically ahead of her, back into the casualty department, straight passed his sergeant who leapt automatically to his feet, completely ignored. He carried on into the surgery at the rear of the building.

"You want me to knock his..." Dan stopped short just in the nick of time.

"No," she said, smiling at what he'd almost said combined with the expression on his face, it amused her. "Not yet. I get the first chance to bop him." She sighed, suddenly exhausted. "Forget him. He's only the boss. We get to have all the fun."

Dan reached for her hand and squeezed it. "Amy, that's not the way to have fun. What we've just gone through is dangerous, bloody dangerous, and you are far too young and precious to waste this way."

She took a deep breath and looked right into his eyes, touching his soul with her gentle amber caress. "Thank you, Dan. You really are sweet." Then she freed her hand and changed abruptly, hardening before him. "I'm okay. I can survive."

"Christ!" he exclaimed. "I hope so." He took a deep breath." Promise me something, please?" He waited until she was looking right at him again before going on. "Promise me you'll take care of yourself - over and above everyone else. Promise me, Amy."

"I'll try," she half-promised and then she nudged him as she stuffed her hands into her pockets and scuffed her shoes on the tiled floor. "Watch it! Here comes Puff Adder."

The major was red-faced and appeared even taller and more dangerous with his colour rising by the minute, looking very much the venomous snake Amy had named him after – the puff adder.

"Outside!" he growled at the tired couple. Dan jumped to his feet again, standing to attention, but not Amy, she rose slowly and purposefully to follow the men out of the building at her own pace, in her own time.

It was as if he took a delight in seeing her standing pale, tired and bedraggled, with wet hair and rain trickling down her neck to seep into her underwear.

He spoke to Dan, "Follow me back to barracks, Sergeant." Amy turned at the same time as Dan, prepared to travel with him. "Not you, Miss, you can get into my car."

"No, sir, I think not," she began defying him again. "If you don't mind, I would prefer to travel to barracks with Sergeant Jones." Her expression was filled with the innocence and beauty of youth. She was impertinent but polite and irresistible.

With the first grunt of a series of grunts, the major watched as she pressed her little hand into Dan's large one and skipped alongside him as he took giant strides towards the car, muttering oaths under his breath with each step he took.

Steering the car out onto the main road directly behind the staff car the big Welshman asked, "Did he tell you how that poor sod in there's doing?"

"No," she whispered. "Not a word. Actually, it sounds as if I'm for the high jump. He went in to speak to the quack in a reasonably good mood and came out all hot and bothered. Yes, I'm definitely for the high jump." Nevertheless, the prospect hardly seemed to perturb her.

"Bastard!" Dan cussed. "Why is he so..." He shook his head, swallowed the words and went on. "Just listen to me! I never, ever swear in front of a lady, but why is he so bloody stroppy with you? Christ! I thought he was bad enough with the men but he really persecutes you, little one."

Amy was basking in his terms of endearment; lapping up the attention he was giving her. "Perhaps he feels threatened," she suggested. "Perhaps he's jealous. Don't let him worry you. I couldn't care less. If he crosses me, I'll take him out."

He flinched beside her. The steel cutting edge of those words sliced into his soul. One glance into her amber eyes told him she would indeed kill the man if need demanded. It was the first and last time he would see such hardness in her.

"Amy," he said quietly.

"Yes, Dan?"

"Meet me later, when you've slept."

"Yes, of course. Shall I ring you?"

"Three-seven-one," he said by way of an answer.

She repeated the number and then, "Later. Sleep first, for both of us."

Major Douglas Philips DSO was pacing the office floor when Amy eventually arrived; she hadn't hurried. "Close the door," he snapped before she had time to enter properly. "Why the hell did you risk moving the man?"

There was no offer of a seat and no sign of anything but anger and resentment. Amy stared questioningly up at him and then she spoke to him in much the same tone of voice.

"Why the hell do you think, sir?"

"How dare you!" he began spluttering as he rounded on her, his face as red as the shock of hair on his head. This time, however, she was ready for him and for anything he could dream up to hurl at her.

"I dare because I can't for the life of me understand your present attitude, sir. I came to Berlin to locate two British agents, ex-serving officers of Her Majesty's Armed Forces - two old and ailing, loyal and trusted men. One is safe in hospital here in the West, safe after years of ill-treatment and the other is in a living hell until I find him and bring him out. I'm doing my best and you have just been privy to information I should not have divulged. What exactly is your problem, sir?"

It was as if she hadn't uttered a sound. He drew himself up to his full height, puffed out his bony chest and spat words into her face like venom. "You were instructed to gain information and to report back to me. You moved without my command. You took it upon yourself to extricate the man, risking not only your life but you had the audacity to endanger one of my most valuable men in the process. Who the hell do you think you are, Miss, some superbeing, some angel of mercy who is invulnerable to danger?"

His voice was beginning to resound in her ears as it bounced off the office walls. The experience brought her pain. She wanted to cover her ears or silence his voice; whichever proved the swiftest and easiest. Instead, her eyes narrowed to thin orange slits and she hissed at him like a large marmalade cat.

"Get off my back, Major. Leave me to do my job as I think fit."

"I intend reporting you to Commander Cooper," he counter-attacked with as much arrogance as he could muster from everything he'd ever learned in his thirty-seven years.

"Your feet won't touch the ground when you get marched off this barracks and dumped on a plane, Miss Harper!"

She smiled, but there was no warmth, no glimmer of humour. "Do whatever makes you happy, Major Philips, but do it silently. Your voice is beginning to grate on my nerves."

Before he could open his mouth again, she added, "I have always believed one earns respect, sir, and to this point you have done nothing to earn mine, therefore, please don't expect it as a God-given gift. Now, if you'll excuse me, I am desperately in need of sleep, and you have a report to file with the commander." She turned away from him.

"I need to debrief you, young woman!" he called after her.

Turning back to face him, her eyes blazing angrily, she said, "For your information, Major - you have not, as yet, briefed me. When I've slept sufficiently, you can debrief me until your private parts fall off...sir!"

As the door closed, Douglas Philips slowly and purposely unlocked and opened the top drawer in his desk, took out a red folder and placed it most precisely between his hands. He poured himself a small brandy and sipped it. A full minute later he opened the folder and read the hand-written note attached to the top of the three-page typewritten document by a black paper clip, written by his old friend Bernard Cooper.

Amy Harper was no ordinary twenty-two-year-old female. She was special, and Bernard wanted him to know that, sceptic though he was, there was no way he could deny the facts on the documentation in the file pertaining to

Amy. For the third time in less than an hour, he read the message addressed to him.

'Douglas, I know you will be as sceptical about this young lady as I have been for a long time, but there's no getting away from the fact she has some extraordinary abilities. You must judge her on her own merit, and with your usual wisdom, but never underestimate her - never! Above all - keep an open mind.

Amy has been described as a "Sensitive" and a possible "Psychic". You know me, I have no room in my life for such ridiculous nonsense, yet facts are facts and I have witnessed many strange events since the first day Amy came to Victoria House.

She has been described as a young woman with an exceptionally high IQ who has received special handling since childhood. Possessed with the power to perceive thoughts with an uncanny precision. Known to have foreseen obstacles in times of trouble. Gifted with vision and extrasensory perception. There's a lot more. Yes, you can scoff, as I did before you, but I have witnessed her in action.

I was invited to sit through the long, tiring and often tedious sessions with the Zener cards. Should you be ignorant as to what they are, I will briefly explain - they are twenty-five cards divided into five sets of five. Each set bearing a different symbol - star, circle and cross, wavy line and a rectangle.

Amy was sealed in a soundproof cabinet, her eyes taped down and blindfolded. It was a scientific study; because most people wanted to prove her a charlatan. The soundproof cabinet was sealed in a vault with lead-lined walls, several feet thick. To the annoyance of many, and the amazement of everyone, she correctly matched the cards selected at random by the scientists with 100% accuracy. She could not have been guessing, they kept on testing her well past the point of endurance and she kept on getting them right.

In field training only Amy was able to spot the sniper, we all needed binoculars to pick out. We blindfolded her, muffled her hearing and took her by cargo plane to the desert where we dumped her unceremoniously with a Jeep, in the middle of nowhere, without a compass, food or water, on a dark and stormy day. We planted a tracking device on the vehicle to enable us to keep surveillance, just in case things backfired on us, but we need not have worried, she steered the vehicle back to base camp within four hours.

There was no bigger disbeliever than me, and I can't recall a single member of the United Forces Committee who didn't want to see her fall flat on her face out there. She dropped the Jeep keys in my lap and asked what time dinner was being served! The irony of it wasn't wasted on me, she had no driving licence, and what's more she'd never been behind the wheel of any vehicle in her life, she'd never had time to learn.

What I have not witnessed first-hand, I have heard or read about. I know just about everything there is to know about her and I can say with certainty that she has always respected the privacy of my thoughts, and the privacy of others. She's kind and considerate with an enormous heart and the wisdom of an old woman. By nature, she has a caring and sympathetic personality. Amy is friendly, spontaneous and excellent company, not to mention a terrific sport and a generally happy person. Granted, there's a certain spark of fire when her temper gets aroused; generally her emotions are extremely well controlled. It has always taken a great deal of provocation to ignite the spark, and it has never been unjustified.

Good luck.
Bernard.'

Douglas Philips laughed to himself as he returned the folder to the desk drawer and turned the key. He knew exactly what the spark of fire in her felt like. He'd been at the receiving end of it several times since the day she walked into the dining room at Rudi's house. Despite everything he'd read about her, there remained a terrible fear within him for her safety, it drove all logic out of his head, turning him into a man he'd hoped he would never become. He sounded more like his pompous brigadier of a father than the old man himself did, and it frightened him. He knew he was going to have to sort himself out sooner rather than later, or he alone would be responsible for the destruction of Amy Harper.

Knowing the telephone could ring at any moment recalling her to the London, Amy wrote a full report on the events of the previous three days. It was direct, unabridged and powerfully written. The handwriting was small, neat and precise. As soon as the last page was finished, she dropped the pen in her lap and lay back in the easy chair to rest her eyes.

She woke in the middle of the afternoon stiff and sore, and walked back to the barracks to place the report on the major's desk. By then she knew she wasn't going to be recalled. They would allow her to complete her mission. She had no regrets and no place in her life for them. Apart from assigning Sergeant Dan Jones to assist her, the major had failed to offer her his support and had done everything within his power to alienate her.

"Reporting for my debriefing, sir." Amy's eyes were locked on his trouser front, inches below his belt as he stood before her studying her face. A provocative smile played upon her lips and in her eyes. Her voice was heavy with unspoken innuendoes. She needed no additional words to convey her message. Then she lifted her eyes in time to witness the tail end of a frustrated flush, and she knew exactly what the problem with the major was - he liked her, or more importantly, he was jealous of Daniel Jones.

He was resolving his problems, or put more succinctly, his frustration and his lust, by being unspeakably unkind to her in the only way he knew possible. However, Amy knew the truth and he knew that she knew. It wouldn't work. He'd lost. Any hope of winning her was now dashed for all time and he was licking his wounds; bitterly regretting all of his impetuous heated words.

"Sit down," he said, more gently, much less militant.

"Sir," she began before she'd agree to sit. "How is Mr Jacobs?" Above all else she needed this information.

"Remarkably well all things considered," he said, swallowing hard as he sat down in the chair behind the desk so to attempt an apology and an explanation. "Please sit. I was regrettably very much out of order." It was a beginning. "I've had a great deal on my mind lately. I do hope you understand."

"I'm trying, but forgive me if I sound somewhat obtuse, Major, was that by any chance an apology?"

He smiled as he settled back in the chair with an enormous sigh of relief. "Yes, that was a pathetic attempt at an apology. I really am most terribly sorry, Amy. Can you forgive me?"

"I daresay I can, sir, but please, don't ever speak to me that way again. Never threaten or abuse me, verbally or otherwise, I might not be able to resist the urge to throttle you," she laughed lightly as she pictured herself attempting to do just that. "If I could reach."

"Can we start again?" he asked, desperately seeking a second precious golden opportunity.

"No, sir," she replied, noting his brief look of disappointment. "Let's move on from here. I don't want to retrace my steps in life, besides, there isn't enough time to live with regrets and bitterness."

With the briefest of nods he said, "Very well, we move on." He coughed into his hand, clearing his throat together with his disappointment and studied the hand-written report in front of him. "This looks fine. When do you intend going back across?"

"Tomorrow," she said, "However, I need to study the guard rota much more closely. They do three-day stints and we might hit lucky with a familiar guard." She paused briefly and went on, "There is one other thing, Major, I need time with both men, to help them with rehabilitation."

"I am aware of that." He smiled at her and his entire demeanour exuded warmth. "Actually, I thought that was what you'd come out here for, not the search and rescue bit. I was expecting a shrink and not a soldier!"

She nodded, "I guessed as much, but my work is always going to be far more complex than simply sitting talking to a patient. It would be a waste not to use me more fully than in psychological healing. I know you've read the report locked in your desk drawer, the one clearly stating I'm not normal."

Her eyes were wide as she spoke the last two words slowly and precisely, and then she laughed. "It's okay, I am aware of what they say and think of me, and I'm not in the least bothered by it. They can think what they like, providing I'm able to help fellow human beings in whatever way is best for..." she stopped suddenly, shrugged her shoulders and added, "Who cares if I am abnormal? This is my first taste of work, and to be honest, I have a lot to learn. You are far more knowledgeable than I am, I need you on my side, sir."

"Douglas," he said quietly. "And I am on your side. I'm sorry it didn't appear that way from the onset." He sighed, relieved he'd been able to apologise properly at last. "I've taken Sergeant Jones off prison guard duty. He's assigned to work with you for as long as you remain our guest here at the barracks."

"Thank you." It was wonderful news; her heart thumped with excitement at the prospect of seeing Dan. "I like him."
"I know you do, and I'm no mind reader." He waved his hand. "Now buzz off and enjoy what's left of the day. Good luck for tomorrow."

She was about to leave his office when she turned back and holding on to the edge of the door she said, "Incidentally, I'm not a shrink, nor am I a trick cyclist or any other name you can think of for a psychiatrist. I'm a psychologist, a clinical psychologist. I work on the mind, and the soul if you like, the theory of mental laws and phenomena, not how the brain works. And I can't read minds either, not the way you mean."

He touched his eyebrow in a salute and said, "I stand corrected, forgive my ignorance."

"You're forgiven. No doubt I'll spend the remainder of my career repeating the same thing, thank you for giving me the practice." She issued him with a cheeky smile and swung out of sight, closing the door quietly behind her.

Amy rang the Sergeants' Mess the instant she stepped out of the major's office. She asked to speak to Sergeant Dan Jones. "Who can I say's speaking?" a stranger asked.

"Amy Packard." The name still sounded strange to her ears.

"Oh, 'ello, Miss. Thought it was yewer voice. John Jones 'yer, one of a dozen of us Joneses. We was on exercise together - well, us an a bunch of 'ooligans was. 'Ow yew doin'?"

"Fine, thank you. Dan has been taking good care of me."

"Bet he 'as, lucky bugger," he said, laughing at the same time. "Sorry, Miss, no offence meant."

"None taken," she assured him.

"It's just we envy 'im like."

Amy was happy, boosted by the sincerity of the compliment. "You wouldn't envy him if you had to put up with my constant nagging," she said, covering her mild embarrassment, "I don't stop. Poor Sergeant Jones has a lot to put up with."

"Gerron, I don't believe you. 'Sides, it's not what Danny boy says. Ee's got stars in 'is eyes...ere, 'ang on, love. I can see 'im. Take care, Miss."

"I will, thank you." She heard him yelling. "Danny, boyo! Phone. She's got a sexy voice. It's Miss Packard. Want me to speak to 'er?"

"Sod off, you smelly little flamer!" Dan growled as he snatched up the receiver. "Amy," he breathed her name and his voice was tender and caring in an instant.

"Hello, Dan. Did you manage to sleep?"

"A bit. You?"

"I fell asleep in the chair, but it did me good. Do you still want to meet up?"

"Of course. Where are you?"

"Staff Sergeant Morris kindly let me use the office phone." She was sitting on the edge of the adjutant's desk. Her face was alight as she pictured Dan.

"Don't move!" he commanded. "I'm on my way."

No sooner than she'd replaced the receiver than he skidded to a halt in front of her. "You look more lovely every time I see you. What do you take, some sort of rejuvenating elixir?"

"No." She smiled into his eyes. "I enjoy life. How about you?"

"When I'm with you I do." Suddenly he found it hard to speak. "Where to?"

"Off barracks?" she suggested questioningly. "Does down by the lake sound okay to you?"

"Great!" He straightened his jacket collar, smoothed his already smooth hair and asked, "Bus or taxi?"

"Neither," she said. "Car." She dangled the Volkswagen Beetle keys in front of him. "I filched them off Puff Adder's desk. Let's go before the staff sergeant gets back and reports me."

That night, before they parted, she let him kiss her. It was wonderful. He knew exactly how to make it perfect. He neither pressured her nor forced himself upon her. He simply placed his lips against hers and enfolded her in his arms and she melted against him. He could have done anything and everything; she was completely powerless in his arms, but no, what he did was simple and beautiful. He kissed her. He told her she was the most beautiful woman in the world and then he released her.

"Dan, I feel I should..." Amy looked flustered and confused for the first time since meeting him.

"My little one, just go inside and get some sleep." He stroked her cheek with the backs of his fingers. "I'll be back, first thing."

"Six," she said with a bashful little smile. "I wish...oh, hell! Go away, you're bad for me."

"Am I?" he asked quietly confident.

"No, but I think I could well be bad for you." She stood on the second step, leaned towards him one last time and kissed his lips tenderly. "Good night, Dan Jones one of a dozen Joneses."

He frowned and then he laughed as she walked away from him. "We're a common bunch," he called to her. "But we're friendly enough, so I'm told. Sleep well, my little one."

When she turned out the bedroom light, she knew she would probably never sleep again. All she could think of was Dan and how he made her feel deep down inside. How her stomach fluttered nervously and her heart pumped almost too painfully to bear. She licked her lips and tasted the sweetness of him. The subtle fragrance of his spicy after-shave lotion lingered in her nostrils.

In just a handful of days, she felt she'd grown up. She wanted the man more than she'd ever wanted anything. Her body physically ached for him. She laughed and rolled over onto her stomach, burying her face in the snowy-white pillows. How she ached for him.

Chapter Five

"Amy! It is forty-five minutes after five, and you are going to be late if you do not wake up," Lore said as she gently prodded her through the thick quilt.

Amy opened her eyes and stared blankly at the girl. She had no recollection of even falling asleep. "Amy! Wake up. Your alarm clock has been ringing and you did not hear it."

"I'm awake! I'm awake!" she said as she leapt naked from the warmth of the bed to run into the bathroom leaving Lore staring in silent admiration.

"I really am sorry," Amy called to her. "I must have woken everyone."

"No, only I can hear your alarm clock from my room. Can I make you breakfast? There are freshly baked rolls in the kitchen."

"Thank you but no time." Amy said as she hurried back into the room, dragging a brush through the mass of auburn hair.

"Tut! Tut!" Dan chided playfully when she tumbled into the car six minutes later. "Who's a sleepy-head this morning then?"

"Shut up and drive!" she snapped, although not unpleasantly and then she hastily added, "Anyway, I'm not late, you were early."

"I was on time," he countered. "Spot on. You were late. Have I told you how much I hate being kept waiting?"

"Not yet," she said stealing a look at his smiling eyes. "But I'm sure you're about to. Go ahead. Don't let me stand between you and the soap box."

"Little lady," he began. "You can keep me waiting whenever you like." His voice was low, calm and gentle and he saw her squirm in her seat and found it impossible to contain his amusement.

"You are beautiful, you know," he said. "And that's another thing, have I told you exactly how beautiful you are?"

"Shut up!" She thumped his arm; embarrassed by his words and by the way he was looking at her. "Drive! Stay focused, we need to concentrate - I need to concentrate."

The closer they got to the border the more fidgety she became. Dan noticed everything but said nothing, knowing she would speak when she had something to say.

"I want this finished today," she said at last, almost tripping over the words tumbling from her mouth. "Do you think our luck can run that smoothly?"

"I hope so, but does it mean you'll go back to London?" He turned his face in time to see the small sad nod of her head.

"Then I don't want to get it over with today," came his admission "Sorry, it's selfish I know, but I don't want to lose you - not yet. Hell, I've only just found you."

Her eyes met his for the briefest of moments and her heart melted as she turned to liquid inside again. "Drive slowly," she advised, her mind instantly back on the business in hand. "Look sad. Cry if you can. We've lost a loved one."

"That won't be hard," he mumbled. "Not if I'm going to lose you."

"Dan! Shut up," she chastised gently. "Let's go through."

But how could she possibly be angry with him when she was feeling exactly the same way? The thought of leaving this man was already causing a constricting pain around her heart, which she knew was not indigestion. Everything, her strange emotions, the way she felt in his presence, it would all have to wait.

The guard stared into the car, passed fleetingly over Dan to check Amy and her slim brown legs. It was the same guard, the one who had previously witnessed the flood of tears, but would they win his sympathy a second time?

"Guten Tag," Amy greeted him solemnly.

The pale-faced man nodded by way of a reply, glanced briefly at the forged paperwork and waved them through.

"Christ!" came Amy's irreverent exclamation. "So easy! Pinch me. Am I asleep?"

"No, you're awake, but tell me, which way today?"

"The second house. Fat old Herr Klein's place."

"I remember, the grey door. Moody old bugger."

"One and the same. Actually, he's a damned handy person, but suspicious of everything and everyone and not altogether a nice man."

"What's he getting out of this?" Dan asked.

"Money, lots of lovely money. Thousands of Deutsche Marks for each person safely received into the West. Ten thousand West Marks to be precise, per live body."

"And the men themselves...who are they?"

"Agents," she said quietly, looking out of the side window with seeming disinterest.

"British?"

"Yes, men who've been locked away in prison for so many years they're almost dead and no longer of any bargaining value. The British government, with the greatest of respect, has no option but to deny all knowledge of these people. Just as they would me if things go pear-shaped."

She noted the look in his eyes and told him, "They can't afford to be blackmailed into doing deals. We know who their men are just as they know ours. It's a stupid childish game of hide and seek, with everyone knowing all the hiding places. Stupid!"

She sighed and it was the most profound of all sounds as she stared out of the window. "Klein pays backhanders to the Soviet guards. He buys and sells. He offers them to our government who usually accept and then he does his best to put the goods in a reasonably safe place for collection. People like us risk life and limb to rescue them. If he can't get them out, he makes certain their end is relatively swift."

"Jesus! Is this for real?" His eyes were wide, his colour drained away.

"Oh, it's definitely real. Personally, I would much prefer you to finish me than Klein. His way is cruel, inhumane, and painful."

Dan shook his head and then he slammed both big fists into the steering wheel. "Don't say that! Don't ever say that!"

She stared at him. "But it's true, Dan. I know you would make my end swift and painless."

He was grinding his teeth now. She could see the muscles tightening in his jaw. "I could never harm a hair on your head," he spoke quietly but firmly. "Don't ever mention it again."

"Dan, I..."

"Forget it," he advised, concentrating on avoiding a collision with a tram; his hands clutching the steering wheel and his eyes fixed with laser-like concentration on the road ahead.

The remainder of the journey was undertaken in thoughtful silence until they reached the street in which Herr Klein occupied one of the many dozens of apartments in the overcrowded blocks of dirt-encrusted buildings which closely resembled prison outbuildings. Paint was peeling off walls and wooden window frames - chunks of plaster was crumbling and falling from external walls.

There was no sign of life and no sound of laughter or of children at play. It was early morning, but not too early. Saturday morning in the West was filled with the sounds of children ringing throughout the closely-knit communities, through the blocks of apartments where everyone became involved in their neighbour's business.

Here, in East Berlin, it was as if the shadow of death had descended upon them, wiping out all traces of sunshine and the distant memory of past happiness. The younger children knew of nothing but this impoverished hell that removed smiles from faces and the sound of laughter from voices. The people were destitute. Their homes were nothing more than bare necessities with four walls and no comfort.

While the small children knew of nothing else, those who were old enough to remember, knew there was more out there beyond the wall - the wire and the guns. Colours bright and cheerful. Music and outrageously happy sounds and sensations. Fruit and vegetables unseen in the Eastern Bloc countries. It was all there, beyond their grasp and beyond their hopes and dreams.

Parents had long since stopped talking about how it had once been. They remembered in silence now. To speak of how it had been brought pain. This was how it was, how it was to be. There was nothing to be gained by dwelling on what they could no longer reach out and touch, and nothing to be gained by torturing themselves with the taste for freedom.

There remained, however, those who could not block such memories from their dreams and their hopes. Those who lived for the day when the walls would eventually fall, and those who lived each day to bring about the breaking down of the political barriers.

"This place stinks," Dan informed her as he parked the car.

"Yes," was all she said. "Come along. Let's go up." It was dirty and it did smell, but she could do nothing about it.

She knocked twice on the door and then twice again and it opened a fraction. She spoke to Klein through the crack and then the door opened sufficient only for them to squeeze inside.

They were not offered seats and were obviously unwelcome. Amy and Klein spoke in whispers, their heads close together, and within minutes, the conversation ended.

"There's a hitch," she informed her companion as she slammed the car shut on the stench. "Our man is being watched. Klein says he's safe but he believes him to be a trap and he wants nothing more to do with this one. He has generously waved his fee." With a contemptuous sniff she added, "It seems he no longer welcomes us here."

"So, what happens now, do we give up?" Dan asked.

She looked directly into his eyes to say quietly, "I never give up, especially not on a living being."

"Okay, you're the expedition leader." He studied her face, watching her grow thoughtful.

Then she said, "We'll go and take a look for ourselves. See if we can assess the situation. I'll get a better feel of things if I'm actually there. I do, however, have a large knot in my gut and it scares the hell out of me." Dan was to learn that when Amy felt the familiar knot tighten in her gut, it was time to take cover.

Together they found the place where his captors had unceremoniously dumped the long-missing man. He was huddling in the corner of a filthy cellar of a building not in the least dissimilar to a war blitzed ruin.

The shell of a man began whimpering as he cringed even further into the corner with each step they took towards him. He had been brutally beaten, burned, tortured and starved. Not even a glimmer of mercy had been shown to the broken old man. He was destroyed. Robbed of both sanity and pride. He reeked of excrement and stale urine.

When his usefulness ended one of the forward thinking, money-grabbing party members worked out a deal and sold him to Klein before dumping him like rubbish to be gnawed and nibbled at by rats.

Amy went to him and spoke to him quietly and gently, soothing his fears, persuading him to move towards the light so that she could assess his state of health.

"Tell me if you see any sign of life out there," she whispered to Dan who nodded briefly and moved towards the narrow open grid, high up in the end wall. It gave him a perfect view of the street, now at eye level.

There were horrific flesh wounds on the man's body, and with trembling hands, Amy smoothed salve from the first aid kit onto the most obvious wounds, which were mostly open and pus-filled. She injected him with a large dose of broad-spectrum antibiotics and wondered where to go from there. His pathetic emaciated body lay prostrate and vulnerable for her to examine for tell-tale signs of pneumonia, there was nothing.

She offered him water and he drank greedily from the flask, refusing to release his surprisingly firm grip when she attempted to slow him down. His eyes were dull and coated with a thin white film, but she knew he was studying her from within. When at last she succeeded in prising the flask from his bony clutch, he reached out and touched her hand, as if to thank her.

"You will be home soon, Joseph," she assured him; talking to him while she tended his wounds. "Back in England with your family."

"Amy!" An unspoken voice cried out inside her head. It was Dan, warning her. She hurriedly packed away the medical supplies, it was time to leave, and they were in grave danger.

"Amy!" Dan cried out, but this time it was reality and not a warning echoed from the future. He was hurrying towards her. "They're out there - two of them. Uniforms. Armed. They're watching this place. Christ! I should never have left the car out there!"

She was prepared for what lay ahead of them. "It's okay," she calmed him. "Everything will work out. Trust me, and please don't argue with me, no matter what I ask of you."

"What's the plan?" he asked; his eyes steady on the grid in the wall.

"I've given him something to knock him out for a while. Go and open the car bonnet, and come back for him."

"But isn't it a bit obvious?" he asked.

"Yes, and that's exactly why it will work if you do as I say. Please, Dan. You have to trust me."

He looked right into her eyes and with the briefest hint of a smile he said, "I do trust you, it's those mad bastards I don't trust."

She watched as he walked stiffly to the Beetle. His back was ramrod straight and his chest puffed out in a show of strength. He wanted them to know he was fit and healthy, he would do battle for his leader, and to the death if necessary. He reached in through the passenger's window and pulled the bonnet release lever, then he went to the front of the car and opened it.

From where Amy was standing, the old car looked like a brown animal with gaping jaws. In her heart, she knew things would work out, but she saw and felt pain ahead of her. She shrugged off the warning sensations and returned to the sleeping man as Dan hurried down the last concrete step.

He took one especially long look at Amy, grabbed a filthy piece of something resembling tarpaulin from the corner of the room and spread it over and around the prostrate body. He lifted the man onto his shoulder as Amy smiled at him, encouraging him to go on. "Right, little lady, let's get this show on the road," he said, "Follow me."

It appeared that Dan was stuffing something into the boot, it looked like an old carpet or a roll of blankets. He prayed hard. His lips moving as he repeated over and over his own prayer for guidance and strength, forgetting everything he'd ever learned from the nuns at the strict Catholic school in Cardiff, where he spent his formative years. *"Just give me the strength to pull this one off and I'll never ask for anything else."* He promised as his stomach churned.

With Amy's help, he closed the car bonnet. "Get in!" he said urgently but she shook her head and moved away from the car.

"Get in!" he repeated. "Amy! For God's sake get in the car!"

"Go!" she pushed him away from her. "I'll follow. Trust me. Go!"

As she ran back into the building, two men came out into the open. Dan saw her face, heard her call out something but he couldn't hear the words for the roaring inside his head as blood rushed like a tsunami through his skull.

He got into the car, turned the key and slammed the lever into first gear. The gears ground noisily, the engine grumbled in protest and Dan steered them away from the building, driving like a novice. He could no longer think clearly, he'd abandoned Amy.

"Oh my god! What have I done? God help me. God help Amy."

Chapter Six

Major Douglas Philips DSO had calmed considerably and was now steaming only slightly as his colour began to fade to a pale pink shade. He'd used just about every foul four-letter word in the book, and written a few of his own. He'd spluttered, splattered and blasphemed. He'd ranted and raved and then he began visibly calming.

"I'm going back, sir. I have to go back for her." Dan had to apply every ounce of patience he possessed not to first strangle the major and then charge off into the night after Amy. He'd already lost the best part of a day in which he could have been searching for her.

"She said she'd follow. You wait. We all wait."

"But, sir..."

"We wait!" he snarled menacingly.

They waited and sixteen hours later there was still no sign of Amy and Dan was desperate with worry. The forged five-day passes, which had given them access to the East had long since expired, there was no way Amy could now walk out, even if she were capable of doing so.

Dan had gone beyond the point where he'd decided he could no longer obey a direct order and go it alone. He was cramming emergency supplies into a backpack when the major summoned him.

"Go and get her," he snapped. "You have a twelve hour visitors permit. You can't take any longer, understood?"

They were the words he'd waited for. "Yes, sir," he snapped to attention to crisply salute the man before him.

"Don't come back without her, Sergeant."

"I won't, sir. Permission to go armed?"

"No..." he began but then he considered the request and changed his mind. "Yes, but for the love of all things holy, be discreet for once in your bloody career. No madcap, foolhardy, hair-brained bloody schemes and escapades. Go in and bring her out discreetly." He sighed and then he spoke again, "You do know the meaning of the word 'discreet', don't you Jones?

"Yes, sir. I do, sir." Dan offered him a hurried half smile. "Thank you, sir." He saluted smartly once again and was about to leave when he asked, "What about Amy, sir? Her pass has expired too. I can take one for her."

"No can do, Sergeant. You know they book everyone in and out. Their methods are primitive but they are efficient when it comes to head counts. You'll have to improvise."

"I'll take the car. I can bring her through in that." It all seemed cut and dry to Dan.

"No! How the hell would you have the VW, which is down on record as being owned by Angelika Stronberg, you being a British tourist, not even remotely related to the woman? Think about it man. Use your blasted loaf for once."

Dan nodded and left before he had time to think of anything else which could go wrong.

Daniel Jones strolled through Checkpoint Charlie with an air of confidence belying the fear clutching at his heart. The guards on duty sniffed when they saw his permit stating clearly he was a British tourist. They sniffed at his tweed jacket, cord trousers and the heavy brogues on his feet. He handed over a fifty West Mark note and received the current exchange rate equivalent in East Marks, which was customary and a way of boosting the East German economy by fleecing innocent tourists, they never sniffed at the money.

They practically threw the dog-eared notes at him and had they known about the pistol concealed in the small backpack, and the angry fire burning in the Welshman's belly as he pushed himself on relentless in his search for Amy, they might well have had cause to reconsider their actions.

His legs pumped like well-oiled pistons as he moved through the city to the building where he'd last seen her. His mind and body were as one in this quest. Adrenalin surged throughout him.

"Be alive, my little one," he whispered as he entered the building and cautiously descended the cellar steps into gloom, to where the last of the day's light was filtering thinly through the metal grid.

As his eyes adjusted to the poor light, Dan searched the area finding the first aid kit scattered and smashed in the far corner and a small brown shoe, flat heeled and Amy's. He clutched it to his chest as if to gain vital information from it. Where was she? What had happened to her after he left her there? The answers were not forthcoming and he was wasting precious time staring into space and wishing he'd done things differently.

Klein opened the door but made it apparent the big Welshman was not welcome. He grunted something incomprehensible and attempted to close the door on the heavy brogue.

"Where is she?" Dan demanded as he reached in and clutched the thick flabby throat in his big fist. Suddenly the hand that had gently smoothed the warmth of Amy's cheek turned into a cruel vice.

"Ich verstehe nicht!" Klein spluttered and Dan drew him up off the ground until their faces were almost touching.

"Yes, you do! You bloody well understand me just fine. Where is Amy? You have precisely five seconds to tell me.

Verstehen Sie? Wo ist Amy? Wo?" He was shouting at him, spitting angrily into his face, causing him to flinch with fear.

"Sie ist nicht hier!"

"I gathered that," Dan snarled impatiently. "Where the hell is she?" He shook him until his teeth began a familiar symphony.

"She came..." he gasped in English as if by a miracle. "She went."

"Where? Wo?" Dan was shaking him again. "Come on, you fat sausage eating bastard! Where did Amy go! Tell me or I'll kill you with my bare hands. I'll tear your..."

"No! No!" If this man had never before known true fear, he tasted its bitterness now. A sharp pain, hot and searing, penetrated his gut as his bladder threatened to explode.

"She go to Schaffner. Richtenburg Platz. Nicht hier. Go! Go!"

Dan thrust him away in disgust, feeling nothing but utter contempt for the despicable character who was growing fat and rich on the strength of the poor incapable human beings who depended upon the likes of him.

Klein lay shivering and weak on the floor - a dark stain beginning to spread across his trouser front. It had been that certain something within Dan's eyes which put the fear of all things holy into him. The big hands clutching at his windpipe were never a threat; he'd been held this way many times in the past. No, it was the look in the eyes of the stranger which froze his blood and chilled his soul.

"Believe me," Dan threatened before leaving, "If I don't find Amy I will be back, and you can kiss goodbye to your nice comfortable little life."

The door slammed shut on him and Dan began running. He ran until his calf muscles ached as never before. He ran until he reached Herr Schaffner's apartment. He wanted to cry out his regret for having abandoned Amy. Guilt was the burden he'd lugged around the city. He'd promised to look after her and failed to do so. He felt wholly responsible and unworthy of her trust.

"Amy! Where is she?" he gasped as the door opened and he saw the frail old man.

Schaffner reached for his arm and urged him inside where he smiled, exhibiting his stained plastic dentures. "She is well. She sleeps." He pointed to the bedroom door. "Go. See."

Dan found her curled foetal-like on the old man's bed. "Thank you, God," he said aloud, his voice breaking with emotion as he reached out to touch her. He kissed her forehead and she stirred and opened her eyes to look at him.

"Dan!" She seemed surprised he was there.

"Yes, little one." He knelt by the bed, resisting the urge to hug her to him; to crush her and possess her; to never release her again. "Did you forget to follow?" he asked.

"No," she whispered and then she flung her arms around his neck and clung to him with all her might.

"Here! What's this?" he said as he brushed hair off her face and kissed her cheek and then her lips. "Are you okay?"

"Sprained ankle," she gasped as she attempted to move her leg. "Couldn't walk. Damned nuisance."

"I was worried sick about you, little one. You shouldn't have gone and done that."

"I had to, Dan. You would never have been able to get away if I hadn't distracted them. I had to be certain you got Rook out." She looked deeply into his eyes and asked, "How is he?"

"Physically he's doing well, but mentally he's a mess."

On a tired sigh she said, "I want to see him again. Speak to him. I might be able to help him." She began pulling herself up on the bed. "We've got to get out of here."

"First things first," he spoke gently as he attempted to assess the damaged ankle. "I need to take a look at this, see what's going on."

"It's nothing," she said pushing his hands away, not wanting a fuss made. "I can walk now I've rested it." A spark had fired the obstinate streak in her. "It's nothing. Don't look at me that way."

"If it's nothing, let me take a look at it," he insisted.

She was struggling to her feet now, proud, obstinate and in more pain than she was prepared to admit to. "It's nothing more than a simple sprain," she managed to gasp between spasms of searing white-hot pain.

He caught her as her legs gave way. "Come on, Amy, let me help for God's sake," he pleaded with her; tortured by the pain he could see in her face. "I can put a bandage on it."

At last she agreed and his sensitive fingers explored the grossly swollen ankle and lower left leg. It was, as he suspected, no simple sprain. The jagged ends of broken bone were not far beneath the surface. "It's broken," he declared.

"Huh!" she sniffed haughtily. "Since when did you become an orthopaedic specialist?"

"I don't need to be a damned specialist," he argued gently. "Anyone with half a brain can see it's busted." He smiled at her. "I am over qualified in that sense, I've only got half a brain."

Despite her pride and her pain, she laughed with him, but she would never acquiesce, not for Dan Jones or for anyone. "It's sprained. Bandage it for me, please, Dan."

His eyes were full of concern and love when she made her first attempt to put weight on the broken limb and her eyes filled with tears of frustration. "Can you walk?" he asked, knowing in his heart it was a ridiculous question - of course she couldn't walk. He would carry her if he had to, but it would look better going through the checkpoint if she could at least hobble.

"I'll manage," she grunted through clamped teeth. "Let's get this over with."

The silent journey through the dark back streets of East Berlin to the quiet border crossing was infinitely slower than either would have liked, but each step Amy took was a step closer to the threshold of consciousness and to the barrier of freedom. She hobbled alongside him for almost twenty minutes and then he lifted her into his strong arms and carried her as if she were a small child.

Now, with the dilapidated East Berlin suburbs far behind them, Dan drove himself on in a state of automatism, his body and mind separate entities, yet as one in their task. His solid, muscle-packed legs pumped hard, driving him on as he pushed them further towards safety, and all the time his mind kept flashing back over the hours he'd spent scrutinising the maps of the area. He recalled clearly the route he planned to get Amy out once he found her again. He knew that by following the remote country lane he would eventually arrive at a quiet border crossing used mainly by agricultural vehicles. He also knew that precious time would be needed once there in order to observe the guards and form a safe and effective plan of action.

Amy was beginning to grow heavy as he headed down over the low hill a kilometre from the checkpoint and freedom. He turned off the deeply rutted road and found a suitable hiding place where he carefully lowered her to the ground. She moaned and he apologised, "I'm so sorry, little one," he breathed the words into her ear. "Ideally, I'd get you straight across and to hospital, but I need to study form, so everything works out right. Our lives depend on it."

She smiled through her pain and nodded. "I'm fine, it's only a sprain. No problem."

He checked his watch, seeming not to have heard her. "Fifteen hundred hours, we'll make our move." He spoke aloud now, so she knew exactly what he was planning. "I've seen enough to be able to handle things. I'm not waiting for dark because they might get a bit trigger-happy;

besides, I need full light to see exactly what I'm doing. If I've got to take action, I want to know I can make every shot deadly accurate. There are two guards outside the hut and one inside. I don't think there are more than, not on a quiet crossing like this."

"They're Soviet guards," Amy informed him through clenched teeth.

"No problem," he assured her.

"Dan, you should...oh, hell...this damned ankle. You have to take care."

"Don't you worry about me, little one, I'm used to getting myself out of tight corners. They'll be well trained and totally uncompromising, but I can deal with them. I just have to make sure my action is instant and incisive. There's a single-story guard room, looks like two or three rooms on either side."

He thought carefully and came to a decision and then he spoke directly to her. "I'm going to act the simpleton again, no speech, just lots of grunting. There's an outside chance they'll let us through if they think I'm a bit of a mental...well, you know what I mean...no threat to anyone."

"Don't kill anyone, Dan, not if there's an alternative. I'm here to save life, not take it. Not because of me. Please, promise me."

He smiled down on her and with the gentlest of tones he said, "I promise, little one, not unless there's no other option. I'll always take the easy way if I can."

"How can I help?" she asked, grimacing with pain.

"I'll hold on to you, but you're going to have to get along as best you can. I'll try and get them to see you're hurt and I'm not running on a full tank, if you know what I mean. If things don't work that way, I'll squeeze your hand a couple of times and I want you to stumble into the nearest guard. He should drop his weapon and as you go down on the ground, he'll stoop to see what's wrong with you. If all goes to plan, I can deck him quite easily and do the same with the other, without firing a shot. If it's a silent job, we'll get past the one in the building, he'll be making tea by the time we get there I expect." He attempted to lighten the gravity of the situation.

Amy smiled through her pain. "Tell him I don't want sugar in mine," she whispered and then she began attempting to stand. "Help me up and let's get this over with, but be careful, please. I don't want you to get hurt."

They made their way back to the heavily rutted road and on towards the checkpoint. The guards spotted them the instant they came into view, and one called out to the other, pointing to the stranger's heading in their direction. They'd reached the point of no return; the only way now was forward.

To his absolute horror, Dan suddenly caught sight of a two-storey building, previously hidden by trees when he made his plan. "Bloody hell," he complained under his breath. "Looks like a billet for more guards. I should have remembered. Christ, what a bloody idiot I am!"

His mind was racing ahead as he looked far beyond the checkpoint, across the vast expanse of no-man's land to the British sector crossing where he knew that 'A' Company from his own regiment were currently on border duty. He mentally chastised himself again for not remembering the building, where he believed they billeted the reserve squad of Soviet guards - the men sitting around waiting for an emergency just like the one Dan knew was about to erupt around them.

The control point, where his eyes now rested in the distance, was what the boys called 'Ice Kellar '- notorious for the bitter cold Siberian east wind that whipped down the wide open road, cruelly cutting through their thick layers of clothing to leave them miserable. Dan squinted so that he could just about make out the parka-clad figures. It could have been imagination but he was sure that they had him under observation. There was no way they could offer help if the Soviet guards took him and Amy. They were under strict instructions not to cross the barren waste of 'no-man's land', and under no circumstances could they fire a shot across the border. Absolutely no circumstances!

He felt a brief moment of comfort as the image of his comrades flashed within his mind. 'A' Company had more than the average concentration of hard cases than probably anywhere in the entire British Army. Big Smudge – six feet three inches, with shoulders nearly a yard wide. Mad Mick O'Malley – as Welsh as they come despite his Irish name. Punchy Will – Brigade Middleweight Champion and unofficial champion of all the public bars and the streets of Spandau – his face like a rocky crag.

But they were only three of many such hard men, all of whom were out there under the leadership of Guard Commander Lieutenant Hoare, the dashing but reckless young officer who was always as brave as a lion and whom the men affectionately referred to as, 'The Boss'. He would do what he had to do and he wouldn't give a damn about starting up a Third World war.

Dan knew if he was up against it, he would need only to shout out, 'Cymru Am Byth ' - 'Wales Forever', or the more familiar regimental slogan of 'Stick it the Welch', and they would all come running and to hell with international protocol! But no, he must not, under any circumstances, involve his friends and comrades; he would have to handle this one by himself. There was no way blood would be spilled on an international scale on his account.

Suddenly there was no more time for daydreaming or speculation on what might or might not happen, two guards were moving slowly towards them.

Bent over almost double, Dan held on to Amy's right wrist, her arm draped around his neck. His hand was inches away from the Browning 9 mm automatic pistol resting in a canvas harness under his left armpit. He supported her weight with his left arm and despite his ungainly stance; he was ready for whatever lay ahead.

The two guards stood firm now, legs spread, submachine guns trained on them, but Dan and Amy continued the slow and painful shuffle forwards. Dan prayed that they would be sympathetic and offer help but by the expression on their young faces, he knew they were not going to be that obliging. One of them shouted aloud that they would not let drunks pass and the other laughed as he began walking straight at them, his weapon levelled on Dan, his eyes locked on Amy.

The other shouted again but Dan had no idea what he'd said, it was all incomprehensible gibberish to his ears right then, yet he knew that the sounds were a warning and unless they stopped and complied there was sure to be trouble. Ice-cold fear wrapped itself around his heart but it wasn't for his own safety, merely for the safety of the woman in his care, the woman he loved beyond reason. He would do whatever it took to take her home again.

He was about to signify to her that he needed her to collapse when he realised she was already out cold and he'd been hauling her weight without even knowing it and so he scooped her up easily, and did his best with grunts and pleading looks to signify that he needed help, still banking on them dropping their defences, lowering their weapons, thus affording him the opportunity to make it through.

Both men stood menacingly right in front of them now, both were shouting aggressively while poking and prodding Dan in an effort to get him to turn around.

The big Welshman knew that there was no way he was going to get through these zealous young men and so he made a decision and moved into action.

Seeming to trip, he bundled Amy into the arms of the short stocky guard who happened to be closest, leaving the man with no option other than to let go of his grip on his weapon so that he could catch the unconscious woman. The Soviet guard lowered her to the floor and the instant he let the sub hang on its sling, Dan straightened in an almost explosive movement, whipped out the Browning, rammed it into the mouth of the guard standing to his right and pumped a 9 mm round of lead through teeth, brain and skull.

Without waiting to see him fall, and in a single split second, Dan plugged a round horizontally through the head of the guard hovering over Amy, ensuring that the bullet would exit his skull at an angle wide of Amy's prostrate figure.

As the soldier fell heavily onto Amy, Dan bounded across the forecourt of the building and leapt into the doorway of the guardhouse, like a tiger going in for the kill, levelling his pistol in a two-handed stance along the corridor, just in time to fire a shot through the eye of a third guard whose misfortune it was to be on duty that day.

He began counting and after three seconds, he knew that he was now alone in the building. He holstered the pistol and dashed back to Amy to hack the dead guard off her with his boot, no time for sentimentality in war and for Dan this was as close to a battlefield situation as he ever wanted to get. He scooped up her limp body and, in a snatch-lift movement he rested her comfortably across his shoulders.

As he ran towards freedom he apologised to her, "Sorry kid, no time to be gentle." He could hear the sound of someone shouting as studded boots pounded on concrete behind him. A cold sweat broke out on his brow with the knowledge that when the Soviet support guards got out onto the road, they would shoot him down like a dog. The thought impelled him to drive his strong legs as they had never been driven before. A thousand imaginary cockroaches crawled on the flesh on his back as he waited for the inevitable shots to rip through him. He knew he would never feel them; he knew he would be dead before he hit the ground.

Ahead of him, his comrades were strung out in a line across the road in the gap in the trees but still he refused to shout out to them.

In the meantime, Lieutenant Hoare watched as the squad of Soviet support guards tumbled out into the road in disarray far behind the escaping fugitive.

"Spread out, chaps," he commanded his men. "Let the buggers see us. I want this fellow to get across. I've been watching him through my field glasses for some time. I don't know who the hang he is but he's just taken out a couple of guards back there and he has a woman on his back. They could be our people." The young officer knew full well that the Soviets would open fire before the fugitive could cross the border if they had a mind to. "You men keep coming forward behind me. Cock your weapons now and make a good show of it."

On hearing the sound of so many weapons being cocked Dan broke his silence. "Don't shoot! Don't shoot!" he bellowed. "It's me, Dan Jones. I'm nearly there just give me cover."

"Good God!" Hoare exclaimed. "It's that mad bugger Dan Jones. Come forward to the line you chaps, at the double. The bastards are not taking him. Hold your fire until I tell you otherwise." Then at the top of his voice he shouted, "Come on the Welch!"

Although his lungs were near bursting, Dan kept driving on towards freedom. The boys of the Welch Regiment were lined up along the border; weapons sighted and ready to release a volley. The Lieutenant had drawn his revolver and Big Smudge was alongside him waving the heavy Bren gun around as if it was a flag.

By the time the Soviets sorted themselves out and felt inclined to fire their weapons, the sight of the mad Welshmen - weapons trained in their direction like a vast firing squad, was enough to put them off. The fugitive had crossed the border and was swamped by a sea of parka-clad Celts. They turned away and reluctantly walked back to the building to report to their superiors that criminal elements had escaped to the West after murdering three border guards. There would be a fuss made to NATO about aggression, and the KGB would be ready primed to make a supreme effort to identify the man who had killed with such vicious precision.

"Take her off me, sir, but gently please, she's got a busted leg." Dan turned so that the officer could help Amy. "She's in a bad way. We need to get her to hospital fast." Willing gentle hands took her and laid her carefully on the parka Hoare took off his back and spread out on the ground.

The officer then fired a round of orders in the direction of his men, commanding them to get a medic and transport and then he added, "Grab some blankets from one of the tents too…on second thoughts take mine, it's too bloody cold for a chap to get a decent night's sleep here anyway."

Dan smiled; knowing why this man was so loved by his men, he always considered everyone before himself.

Amy Harper recovered consciousness six hours later on Sunday 23 April 1967. Her left leg was a singular solid mass of burning pain, despite all of the drugs in her system. She moaned as she attempted to focus her vision. A myriad dancing lights stung her red-rimmed eyes.

"You're okay, Amy. Just lie still."

She blinked twice and succeeded in focusing on the uniformed nurse who'd spoken to her. "Where am I?" she asked and inside her head she laughed - it was the one thing she'd vowed never to say. Her voice sounded hoarse, her throat was dry and her lips felt like sandpaper.

"You're in the BMH in Berlin."

"BMH? I don't...where?" Amy was struggling.

"The British Military Hospital," she explained. "You have a couple of fractures in your leg but they've been put right and you're going to be just fine."

"Dan? Where's Dan?"

"Sergeant Jones?" the nurse asked.

She attempted to nod but the action brought a whole new set of pains to the fore and she gave up.

"He's outside. I'll send him in, but do try and rest, you've had a rough time."

Amy wanted to laugh and failed. She closed her eyes and struggled to recall the events of the previous night; the days that led up to that night, the chase and then the pain. Dan, Dan and...and nothing, it was gone.

He closed the door and moved silently towards the bed abhorring the smell of antiseptic that hung heavily in the air within the confines of the building. He was out of place here and conspicuous. Nothing, other than Amy, or a bullet, could have dragged him into this building.

"Hello, my poor little Amy." He stood away from her, almost afraid to touch her. She looked fragile and pale, yet beautiful. "How are you doing?"

Her eyelids opened slowly; with some considerable effort, she focused her vision on the man standing before her, and then she croaked, "Thank God you're okay."

"I'm fine," he hastily assured her. "How about you?"

"Fine," she offered him her hand and he reached for it and felt her weakness. He kissed her fingers and then he leaned forward and placed his lips on hers.

"You scared the hell out of me, woman," he whispered, tasting anaesthetic on his palate. "Don't you ever do that again."

She smiled at him, seeing and sensing all the worry and all of the relief flooding over him. Loving him for who he was and not for the way he looked. She cared nothing for the big macho-man image he projected; she loved the tender soul and the little boy within him, yet she sensed that the strongman image was important to him. It was his protective shell.

"My hero," she said quietly. "I owe you."

"Yes, you do. I won't forget." He kissed her again, and there it was once more - anaesthetic.

"What happened?" Major Philips tossed the written report onto the desktop. "In your own words. Not that bullshit." He waved his hand at him. "Sit down, man."

Dan sat uncomfortably and began his verbal report. "She wasn't where I'd last seen her, sir, only I could see there'd been a scuffle of some sort. Her medical kit was smashed and kicked about and I found one of her shoes. I thought they had her. I really did."

"Yes, yes, go on." Philips was impatient to know everything.

"I went to Klein's place. He's the one who..." And then he remembered Amy's warning not to tell him anything about the mission. "Anyway, the man told me where to find her and I went after her. I was relieved to find her there. Well, relieved doesn't quite cover it. How in God's name she got there I have no idea."

He sighed and went on. "She told me she'd sprained her ankle and insisted she could walk out of there. I could feel at least one fracture but there was no arguing with her and all I wanted to do was get her home, so I wrapped her leg as tight as I could and she hobbled alongside me, all obstinate and independent like. I can't figure out how she stuck it as long as she did. Takes some guts to cope with the intensity of the pain she must have had.

"When we got close to the border I saw two guards ahead of us, standing there, legs spread, subs trained on us." It wasn't difficult to recollect exactly what had happened, but it sickened Dan to have to repeat it. All the same, repeat it he did.

Douglas Philips sat silent and still when at last he finished. "There was no other way," Dan began explaining in fierce defence of his actions. "I used three bullets. I kept it clean. The men didn't know what hit them." Now, and only now, was he beginning to attempt to excuse those actions.

"And Miss Packard?" Philips asked.

"I got her seen to and phoned you. Her ankle's busted good and proper and there's a hairline crack in the shinbone. The damage wouldn't have been quite so bad if she hadn't done a bloody route march. The MO isn't worried about her; she'll be fine. They knocked her out to pin the bones, and she's plastered and drugged to the eyebrows. They say she'll be healed in about six to eight weeks."

What he failed to tell the major was that he was privately rejoicing at the prospect of having Amy in his life for a while longer.

"When are they discharging her?"

"Tomorrow, sir. They want her to rest for a few days." He paused and then, "Sir, how long will she be here, in Berlin, I mean?"

To that point Douglas Philips had only had his suspicions. He'd seen this man light up when Amy walked into a room. He could no longer harbour jealous emotions regarding that young lady. He knew that he alone was responsible for destroying any hope he'd had of impressing the enigmatic little agent. His emotions had levelled off at last and he wished her only happiness. He would always be fond of Amy; he would always love her just a little.

"How long do you think we can keep her here?" he asked the eager sergeant.

Dan was grinning broadly. "About eighteen months." That would fit in nicely with the regiment's return to the UK.

That amused the long thin man and he laughed aloud. "That's highly optimistic; however, I will see what I can engineer. Go and get a meal inside you and some shut-eye."

"Thank you, Major. Err, just one last thing."

"What is it?"

"Any chance of you wangling some leave for me, sir? I've only had the three days in ten months. I'd like to be with Amy, while I can."

He nodded just the once and his smile returned. "I'll see what I can do. Leave it with me."

True to his word, he spoke to the regimental sergeant major who owed him too many favours to count. Reminded the man that Jones was on special detachment, guarding and assisting a member of British Intelligence. The RSM agreed - Jones 7498399 could take fourteen days' leave, but only fourteen days and not a moment longer.

Amy looked so fit and happy when next Dan saw her that he couldn't help enthusing. "Wonderful! You looked wonderful. Are they giving you pain killers, my poor little Amy?"

She wanted to remind him that she was neither poor nor little, but it was Dan, and Dan's term of endearment, and he meant well. His words were gentle and kind and his love for her shone from his face as his eyes devoured every visible inch of her.

"If they had their way, they'd be sticking needles in me every five minutes and bed pans under my bum every ten," she complained happily, offering him her hand as she did so. "Come and sit by me. I've missed you."

"You have!" he exclaimed with obvious surprise and delight. "Good!" And with that he sat on the chair by the side of the bed, carefully avoiding the white cast slung in traction. Facing her with her hands enfolded in his, he asked, "How's the leg?"

She grimaced.

"That bad?"

"I'll survive - if I can stop them filling me with junk. Anyway, never mind me - tell me how you are and what happened last night."

"I'm okay." He coughed to clear his throat and then he straightened his back as if he was uncomfortably. "Last night's best forgotten." Alarm lit up her face and he knew that he'd be forced to explain. "I had to call time on the guards, that's all. I didn't have any other option, I had to get you out."

How many?" she asked quietly.

"Three?" he replied.

"I am sorry," she said and quickly moved on. "Anything else to report?"

"No."

"Honestly?" she questioned, needing to know everything.

"Honestly. I got you through the border and back here. It didn't take as long as I thought it would."

Then they became swamped in a profound silence, but it was a contented singular silence, like nothing they'd known. Just being together brought about a beautiful calm that neither had experienced previously. It was as if the world stopped turning and only they remained. Problems and worries were suddenly non-existent. It was an illusion, the pain and death and the cruelties of life were there, waiting for them to find their feet again, to return to reality. For now, they were contented to be together.

Amy sighed. "They tell me I have to wear this damned cast for six weeks. That means I can't fly out, and they'll want to keep an eye on me here, naturally."

"Naturally," he echoed, unable to contain his joy. "I can't think of anything I want more than for you to stay here, Amy. But will you stay on at the Hoffmann place?"

"I don't know, I haven't given that any thought. I was going back once my work was completed, however long it took me. And now, now I have to change my plans. I suppose I'll be hearing from my chief at any time. No doubt the Puff Adder will take a delight in informing him of my misfortune." She was annoyed with herself, it sounded in her voice and reflected in her face.

"Does that worry you?" he asked, still struggling to get to the bottom of her.

"Yes, it irks me somewhat that this should happen on my first job." It was not a difficult admission. "How could I have been so damned careless?"

"Were you careless?" he asked, prising the information gently from her.

"Must have been," she said matter-of-factly. "You didn't break anything."

"But I wasn't being chased," he argued in her defence. "You're lucky you're still alive, let alone lying there with a couple of busted bones."

"And that's just about the feeblest excuse I have ever heard to cover clumsiness, Sergeant. I was clumsy and you know it."

"Call it what you like." He smiled down on her. "I'm glad. I get to keep you here."

At precisely 17:15 Major Douglas Philips arrived in the ward. Dan had gone for something to eat and he missed the expression of sheer delight on Amy's face as she read the priority signal the major handed her.

"Is this on the level, sir?" she asked.

"Absolutely! What exactly are you implying, young lady?"

"Nothing, sir. Thank you." Her eyes danced and skipped over the words printed on the paper in her hand as she read them over and again.

"Can I take it that you're pleased with the news, Amy?"

"Yes," she replied quietly. "I am pleased." She looked up at him and asked, "How about you? It means putting up with me and my outrageous clothing for a while longer than previously planned."

"I'll survive," he replied dourly. "The only problem I foresee is that you might get bored with the tedium of a desk job. I can't possibly risk sending you back across. You have to realise that. You'll work here on the rehabilitation side of things. Put your psychology degree to good use at long last, Miss Harper."

Amy raised her eyebrows. "Have you been spying on me again, Major?"

"Studying form more like. You have an impressive record."

"Please," she was beginning to blush. "You're embarrassing me, sir."

He laughed. "What, with the degree and the languages! Come now, Miss Harper, don't be modest. You've achieved a great deal in a short time. But tell me, which was the easiest to pick up?"

"The degree," she said in a serious tone. "I stepped up onto the platform and they put a piece of paper in my hand. But I enjoyed learning Russian although I do prefer German." She sighed and said, "Now, if you don't mind, I would like to discuss Jacobs and Rook."

Douglas Philips settled back in the chair. "Do you mean to tell me you haven't already made enquiries?"

She smiled. "They wouldn't tell me anything. Kept referring me to you."

"Ah, I see. I wondered why I was being consulted at last." Just a brief hint of sarcasm sounded in his voice. "Jacobs is well on the road to recovery. His body is healing swiftly and his mind is thankfully quite sound, but Rook, well, he's a different kettle-of-fish. I'm afraid his mind is too far gone."

"Has he been assessed yet?" she asked as she heaved herself up in the bed.

"Yes, but frankly it might have been kinder to put a bullet through his head."

Amy shuddered at that thought and shrank back down on the stack of pillows. "Can I see him, please?"

"He's being flown out tomorrow."

"Please," she begged. "Give me the opportunity to try. Keep him here a little while longer. Give me a month, six weeks. Hell, don't I deserve the opportunity to help him? I brought him out. He's a human being, for pity's sake, Major!"

Douglas Philips looked at her and half-smiled, knowing just how beautiful she was. "We don't have the facilities here, but I'll see what I can do - no promises, though, and, in the meantime, I'll get someone to take you to see him. Just remember that you are supposed to be resting. Commander Cooper holds me entirely responsible for you."

"I'll be fine. God! It's only a broken bone and a small crack. Nothing worth half this fuss."

She never failed to cuss or blaspheme in such a precise and proper manner that the major delighted in hearing her. She spoke beautifully. Rounding her vowels and forming her consonants with the uttermost care. She had a wonderful grace of expression, of personal style, and a unique and innocent way of stating the obvious. There were no airs or graces about Amy. No falseness in the way she used the English language. She spoke precisely and quite beautifully.

"Do me one small favour, Amy," He appeared more relaxed in her company now. "Start calling me by my given name, Douglas or Doug. It's high time we were friends."

"Major, I..."

"No strings," he hastily added, "Promise." His smile was genuine and warm. It reassured her instantly.

"Friends," she agreed as she held out her hand to him. "Douglas."

"Does this mean you stop calling me names, Miss?"

"Names?" she said looking like the picture of innocence. "I really don't know what you're talking about. You told me that your men have a term of endearment for you, but you can rest assured, I would never, ever call you that. I remain convinced that you were indeed fathered."

"Oh, so innocent." He released her hand reluctantly. "But don't think you have me fooled for one minute, young woman. I know exactly what you call me behind my back."

Dan stomped back into the ward minutes after the tall thin officer bade Amy a temporary farewell.

"What's new, my little one?" he asked as he bent over to kiss her lips before pulling the chair forward and placing his backside on it.

"All sorts of things," she said. "I'm staying here in Berlin with the Welch Regiment. Sort of mascot."

"Um," he mumbled, distracted by the loveliness that was Amy. His ears picking up only the soothing sound of her voice and not the words she was saying.

"Yes," she went on, aware that she was talking to herself, and not for the first time. "Eighteen months in Berlin, then who knows where. I suppose you'll be fed up to the eye teeth with seeing me day in and day out long before your leave ends, let alone after eighteen months."

"Um." He was still daydreaming with stars twinkling in his love-struck gaze.

"Dan."

"Yes, little love?"

"I'm leaving Berlin."

His eyes widened in horror. His smile fell away. She had his full and undivided attention at last. "God! No! When?" He clutched her hands in his.

"September, nineteen hundred and sixty-eight."

His mouth gaped and he searched her eyes for truths, his brain working hard to sort the date out. "On the level?" he asked at last.

"On the level," she replied, laughing at his expression. "Are you pleased?"

"Pleased! Pleased! I'm overjoyed." He was a boy again, a boy on Christmas morning. He needed pinching to believe he wasn't asleep. "But how do you feel about it?" he asked quietly, nervously.

"Happy." As she spoke the word, she realised that she wasn't just happy - she was ecstatic. The prospect of seeing Dan every day for eighteen months filled her with a rare joy. She dampened down that joy and brought things back into a more basic perspective to reason out her happiness for him.

"I will be working on rehabilitation - the clinical side of psychology. It's what I originally trained to do, working for and with the British Military. My services will also be offered to the allies. This is a rare opportunity, Dan." She caught the brief shadow of disappointment, which was barely fleeting in his eyes.

"And I get to see you, of course," she added. "If I play my cards right, you might even..."

"What?" he asked. "I might even what?"

"Nothing," she was growing shy and uncomfortable." I dare not ask a question if I know I can't cope with the reply. I'm just not certain, not yet."

"Fine." He squeezed her hands gently. "When you are, you just ask away. I'll be honest with you. Right now, you need to rest, because tomorrow I'm springing you from this prison."

Amy spent three hours of what remained of that day with Joseph Rook. She talked to him about herself. She soothed him, placated his fears and the anger that was growing massively within his soul. She coaxed him to look directly at her and then she held his stare and searched deep within his mind, his hands in hers.

He was indeed a mental wreck, but while she saw and felt turmoil, doubt and fear, she also saw a vestige of hope, a tiny spark of sanity to which he was clinging on fiercely, and which she clung onto with him.

"I'm coming to see you again tomorrow, Joseph. We can talk." She released his hands and he snatched them back into his body like two lost children returned to their mother. There was no more to be done that day; time would be this man's healer; time and Amy. She would do nothing to push him further down into the abyss of insanity.

Alone in the sterile room, Joseph Rook remembered the girl with the amber eyes. He giggled, crawled back into the corner behind the bed and wrapped his arms tightly around his body.

Whenever a nurse, no matter their gender, attended his needs, he yelled aloud. He yelled at doctors too, but he never once attempted to yell at Amy, the girl with the golden eyes. It was as if he understood that she had saved his life and that she cared about him as a vital human being; a living, breathing person. The compassion that this young woman was offering him was something nobody had ever shown him in his entire lifetime.

Chapter Seven

Herr Rudi Hoffmann held the door open wide so that Dan could carry Amy inside. "Put her here, on this sofa, it is much more comfortable than the others."

"Please, don't fuss," she implored; embarrassed by all of the attention she was getting.

"The veelchair! Do not forget the veelchair." Eva Hoffmann was flapping about like a delicate swan attempting to take off from a frozen lake.

"I won't forget it," Dan assured her calmly as he placed both Amy and the weighty white knee-high plaster cast on the cushioned sofa. He gave her hand a little squeeze and smiled down on her as he whispered, "I won't be long."

She followed him with her eyes as he went to the door and there they rested until he re-entered carrying the wheelchair and a bag of heavy textbooks.

"I couldn't have managed without you," she assured him.

He was frowning down on her. "Hey! No need for thanks. This is what friends do for each other, remember?"

She nodded shyly. "In that case I have another favour to ask of you. Would you mind taking me up to my room? I really am shattered." She needed privacy more than rest. It was like being a museum exhibit with the Hoffmann family standing around her.

Dan turned to the senior member of the family to ask, "Do you mind if I take Amy upstairs, sir? She's tired, and a bit heavy at the moment."

"Please, go on up. Our home is yours. Amy is like a daughter to us. Stay as long as you wish and visit whenever it suits you."

"Do you think he meant what I think he meant?" Dan asked as he pushed the bedroom door open with his foot.

"Who meant what?" she asked being purposely obtuse.

"About me staying as long as I like and all that."

She looked into his pale grey eyes; her arms were around his neck. She searched for words, but they wouldn't come. Her colour was rising and she began muttering.

"I...err...I...don't know. Don't ask."

"But I have asked," he said as he lowered her to the bed, his arms still around her, reluctant to release her. "Tell me, Amy, are you afraid of me?"

"No," she said quite positively with an enormous sigh. "I'm afraid of myself."

"But why?" He was getting into his probing private detective routine again. His softly-softly act was almost always guaranteed success in worming the information out of anyone. He removed his arms and sat facing her. "Speak to me, little love. Please speak to me."

She shook her head, refusing to discuss her innermost fears. Her trepidation was increasing by the minute. Dan had the knack of being able to worm his way into her consciousness, making her feel guilty for not being more open with him than she had been.

"This is my first job," she said at last. "You are the first man I've worked closely with, apart from the men with whom I underwent basic training."

"I understand," he said patiently.

"I want my career to move on, not to end here and now."

"And you think I'll ruin your career, is that it?"

"No, Dan. Not you - me."

He sighed, unable to comprehend a fraction of what she was saying, or struggling to say. "You'll ruin your career by associating with a rough bugger like me, is that it?" he said, attempting to lighten his own worries.

She smiled at him. He was funny and kind and he loved her, she knew that. "Dan, I don't understand what's going on inside me at present. I'm scared stiff of the way you make me feel." There, it was out at last.

He frowned until his eyebrows met in the middle and his brow furrowed deeply. He rubbed his chin, fingered his moustache and then he spoke to her. "Do you want me to leave?" However, he remained seated all the same.

"No!" she cried out, wanting to hit him and hug him at the same time. "That's the trouble, I want you to stay. Damn it, Dan! Don't be so...so stupid!"

"So! I'm stupid am I, little one?" his voice was sufficiently reproachful to cause her to open her mouth in an attempt to explain.

"No! Don't say a word...I agree with you. I don't have a degree and my skills are limited to survival and combat, and I agree that I can be a bit dense at times. I even admit to not understanding what's going on inside me too. Since you arrived in my life, I've had to concentrate quite hard on even the simplest of tasks. Can't even tie my bloody bootlaces without concentrating.

"No. I don't understand this feeling, but I do know that I like the way you make me feel. I know how proud I am to be seen with you, and when that bunch of mercenary sods tease me at barracks, I'm thrilled. In fact, I think it's only fair to lay my cards on the table right now - I'm in love with you, little one."

Amy stared at him, completely speechless and shaken - rendered temporarily dumb. Her heart was racing and a fine sheen of perspiration appeared on her brow.

"Well, what have you got to say for yourself?" he urged lovingly.

"Dan, I...oh, God! What can I say?"

He was so utterly disappointed and deflated it showed in his face. "I suppose I hoped you loved me too," was all he could say as he almost choked on the words.

"Give me time," she begged, her hands beginning to tremble. "Isn't it enough to cause me to go to pieces this way? Isn't my craving for you to hold me enough for now?"

He smiled and the warmth of the smile filled her being until she glowed through and through. "Yes," he said proudly. "You're right, of course, but it's not every day I admit to weakness of any kind. You make me weak from my knees to my gut. Jelly, that's what I am."

Suddenly his mood swung to serious again. "It fascinates me how someone small and dainty like you, my poor little Amy, can turn a big lump of solid gristle like me to jelly."

Less shyly she responded, "To begin with, I'm not little, not really. I'm five feet and five inches tall, and I am rather solidly put together. My chassis is not dissimilar to that of a small armoured vehicle. I have a pair of nut-cracking thighs and biceps large enough to put Tarzan to shame. You make me feel small and feminine, but I'm no such thing. In reality, I'm chunky, clumsy and built to last."

"Prejudice," he said. "I'm prejudiced in your favour, and happy to admit it. Beauty is in the eye of the beholder, little one, and as I'm the one doing the beholding, I'm telling you, I see a lovely little angel."

He touched his lips to her forehead. "Don't you go putting yourself down, you ooze femininity. It flows from your pores. You can't do a damned thing about it either. Men turn and stare and women are jealous of you. I love you, just as you are."

"Prejudice," she agreed. "Blind to the truth."

"Amy." He lifted her hand and touched her fingertips to his lips and then he said, "You wanted to ask me something, a question. I told you I'd be honest with you. Now I'm forcing your hand, what was that question?"

"I don't...I can't." His grip tightened on her hands. "Hell, I wish I'd kept my big mouth shut."

"But you didn't. What is it? Tell me."

She told him. She asked her question. "What do you want from me? I have to know." Then she waited without daring to breathe.

He took a deep breath, released it slowly and without further hesitation he replied, "Everything and nothing. Whatever you want to give me. I expect nothing more than it pleases you to give me." He raised his eyebrows and asked, "And you, Amy, what is it you want from me?"

"Respect and loyalty," she replied, knowing exactly what she wanted from this man. "Your friendship, complete honesty and trust. Stolen moments, understanding and..."

"And?" he pressed.

"And love," she whispered shyly.

"You have it, and everything else. I'd move mountains for you, little one."

"I know you would." Her eyes were misting over. "Thank you for caring about me, Dan."

She placed a kiss on his cheek and hugged him at the same time. "How can I repay you for making me feel this wonderful?"

"Let me spoil you. I'm on two weeks' leave. I can bring you nice things and when you can get out and about, I'll take you to restaurants and spoil you a bit more. What about it?"

It was not quite what she had in mind, but it would do for now. "It sounds lovely."

"Amy is in zer garten, Herr Jones."

Dan had long since given up asking Eva Hoffmann to call him by his given name.

"Vielen Dank, Frau Hoffmann," he said, touching his fingers to an imaginary beret.

He'd been visiting the house for a full week, every day and all day. Arriving loaded with flowers, chocolates and mysterious, beautifully wrapped packages for Amy. He'd taken Amy to the hospital on three occasions to visit Joseph Rook, whose family were insisting on his being returned to the United Kingdom at the earliest opportunity to be locked away in an institution for the remainder of his days.

His daughter, Alison Rook, arrived in Berlin four days after his return from captivity, and he became violent and refused to look at her. It was then she decided he was to be locked up in the country of his birth. There would be no family reunion, no celebration of his return to the fold; he was to be hidden away until his dying day. Amy intended fighting for him in any way she could. She would never give up on him.

Hobbling about on crutches at last, and complaining bitterly about getting fat and lazy, she was able to take herself into the garden and it was there Dan found her.

"How you doing?" he asked as he kissed her cheek.

She turned her sun-warmed face for him to kiss her again, but on the lips this time. "I suppose I'm fine, but I am itching to go outside into the real world again, and I don't mean to the BMH and back like some damned prisoner under escort. Honestly, I feel like Hess in Spandau prison with you walking around the walls guarding me like you do him when you're on duty there."

"Okay, well we can't have that now, can we? Your wish is my command, Miss," he said with a grin and a sweeping gesture, as if he was Prince Charming and his feathered hat was in his hand. "Your carriage awaits you, Princess Amy."

"Carriage!" she exclaimed.

"Well, not quite," he admitted. "A battered old German Ford, but it's mine and it goes, and who cares. I bought it for a couple of hundred marks and a crate of American beer."

Her eyes were dancing on his. She was standing now, hopping about on one foot. "When can we go? Where can we go?" The world was out there, well, West Berlin at least, and she wanted to taste freedom again.

"Now and wherever you like," he said, delighted by her obvious eagerness. "I've got a packed lunch and a bottle of wine I borrowed from the Mess. We'll find somewhere nice and quiet. Come on, little one, don't keep the chauffeur waiting."

The sun shone down on them on that beautiful day. They talked at length, held hands and stole the occasional kiss, but they never once let each other out of sight for a moment longer than was necessary.

By the end of his second week of leave, Dan felt he knew almost everything there was to know about Amy, with the exception of her true identity. She assured him her name was indeed Amy, and one day soon he would know the rest. He learned she was a joy to be with, a constant source of knowledge, fun and affection and a delight to behold. She was quite beautiful and at times a touch shy of him.

Amy never failed to boost his moral, making him feel glad to be alive. She was there with him, for him and behind him, in decision-making and spiritually. He felt at peace and complete in her presence.

In private they enjoyed each other and in public, they shared each other. Amy joined sweethearts and wives in girl talk at the Sergeants' Mess, fitting in easily wherever Dan took her, never letting him down, especially when it came to the regimental formalities customary within the confines of the Mess.

On the last night of their two weeks of freedom, Dan took her to a quiet Bulgarian restaurant just off the Heerstrasse. They sat close together in a corner of the dimly lit room, a single candle burning on the tabletop.

Dan referred to the waitress as: "The mad woman" after she'd hurled a menu at them - continuing to hurl everything from then on. Firstly, the card drinks mats, and then their meal. She spoke excellent English and smiled a broad, pretty smile.

Amy hinted that perhaps the pressure of work was beginning to get the better of the young Bulgarian. "Stress," she whispered to Dan as a glass of beer landed with a thump in front of him.

"She's mad!" he declared, more to himself than to Amy. "Definitely mad. But the food's always great here and there's plenty of it."

It was a blatant understatement. Amy had never seen meat piled as high on a plate before. The large oval platter was stacked with different types and cuts of meat: pork fillets, beef steaks, gammon, and at least half a dozen other cuts of various meats.

Beneath every layer she lifted, another challenge opened for her. She was already full and feeling slightly nauseous long before she reached halfway down the stack, but not Dan, he ate as if there was no tomorrow. He ate anything and everything. He cleared his own plate and finished off Amy's meal, despite having politely refused several times. He spared only enough time to gaze lovingly at his companion between each forkful of food and large gulps of ice-cold beer."

Amy sat in silent contentment, happy to be with him, treasuring each moment. She waited until he'd cleared a large bowl of ice cream before announcing, "I'm going to look for a place of my own."

"You are!" he was surprised. "Why?"

"Because I can't keep on sponging off the goodwill of the Hoffmann family. Besides, I want some privacy. I need to be able to come and go as I please."

"I see," he said as he ran his finger around the rim of the beer glass. "Can I do anything to help?"

"Would you?" her eyes lit up at the offer.

"Of course. Give me a ring tomorrow and let me know what you've got planned. You can't go hiking about the city with that cast on your leg, not on your own. I've got the car."

"Can you spare the time?" she asked.

"I'll make time. For you, everything else stops."

When she pushed him away from her in his car late that night, she knew she couldn't go on resisting the urge to be loved. "Be patient with me, please, Dan," she begged. "I'm not prepared to have sex in the back of your car."

"You make it sound dirty," he said, sounding too much like a hurt schoolboy.

"That's how I might feel if we did it in here. Please try to understand, it has to be right, it has to be perfect."

"I love you, Amy. I don't give a damn where we are. I...I need you, little one."

Oh, but she already knew that much. She'd felt his need, his urgency. She'd seen the signs. The one thing she was not, was blind. Besides, her need wasn't necessarily obvious but it was just as great.

"When I give myself to you, Daniel Jones, it will be done properly or not at all. Trust me, this is not the way for us."

"Dan! I've found a little house to rent." She'd tracked him down in the Mess. She was breathless and excited and could hardly sit still as she held on to the receiver.

"It's perfect, Dan. Peter took me to see it. I've paid a deposit and I have the key. Please meet me there when you've finished work. I'm just dying to show you around."

"When and where?" he asked curtly.

"Are you okay?" she sensed his black mood. "You sound strange."

"I'm okay. Tell me where to meet you."

"It's easy to find, Falkenseer Chausee. Fourth turn right. Wilhelmstrasse, number sixteen. Is seven too early for you?"

"I'll be there. Amy - are you okay?"

"I am, and I'm happy. Peter's helped me move my few bits and pieces. Be a love and bring a bottle of wine."

It was a detached property, small and white, picturesque and continental in design - a doll's house of a place, super feminine and very suited to Amy. It was one of those prefabricated, but solid places, the Germans managed to erect in days. One day there was nothing but foundations and the next, a house ready for habitation.

He knocked and waited for the sound of Amy hobbling along the narrow hallway, her crutches clicking on the tiled floor. The door opened and he saw her. She looked excited, flushed, and so lovely his heart palpitated hard and painfully in his chest. She reached forward and pulled him inside, closing the door on the world to kiss him.

"Welcome to my new home," her voice was effervescent and young.

"Very nice too," he said and then he spoke for the sake of speaking. "Bet this place cost a bomb."

"I can afford it," she replied, still undaunted by his mood. "Don't you like it, Dan?"

"I said it's nice. What more can I say? It's only a house."

Amy frowned and then she chose to ignore his gruff response. "You could ask me to go to bed with you, and I could say I'd love to."

He shifted uncomfortably in the cramped space. "Stop larking about, Amy."

"I am not 'larking about', as you put it. I've made my decision and I never do anything I feel is wrong for me. So, how about you, are you shocked? Do you really want to run away?" He was edging back towards the door.

"No," his voice was as low and sombre, as was his countenance.

"Then in that case, I suggest we take a look around my lovely home, pour a glass or two of wine and see how happy we can make each other feel. Come."

The kitchen was neatly laid out and white. The lounge was small but elegant with a warm honey colour on the walls. Amy abandoned the crutches and lead the way upstairs. The heavy white plaster cast proved to be cumbersome and of great nuisance value. Her leg ached constantly, as did the calf muscles on her right leg, the undamaged one.

After just two and a half weeks, she was tired of the weight and the pain, it was grinding her down, but she never once complained, and she contained all the misery she was feeling; deeply hidden from the prying eyes of the world, deeply hidden from Dan, the man she had no doubt she loved.

He hadn't expected the bedroom to be quite as large, but then there was only the one of them and it did cover almost the entire upper half of the house.

Strange, he thought, how so much emphasis was placed on one room, the bedroom. It looked as if it was the central point, the core of the entire building, as if more time was to be spent here than anywhere. There was a radio on a tightly packed bookcase at the far end, several vases of flowers; candles; more books and he saw the large continental twin-mattress bed was centrally situated, covered in a forget-me-not blue bedspread, possibly duvet covers, two of them. He was not overly observant when it came to things like that - material things - but he did notice there were several large square pillows on the bed and inside his head he was working out how long it would take to declutter the bed to get a night's sleep. Forget-me-nots, tiny, blue dots decorated the wallpaper on all four walls. The carpet was deeply piled and a soft ivory colour.

"Pour the wine," she said, and he saw a bottle of Liebfraumilch in a wine cooler beside two tall-stemmed glasses. "I knew you'd forget." She could see he was about to apologise. She kissed his chin. "Forget it. At least one of us remembered."

She left him for ten minutes, returning wrapped in a pink silk gown. Her mass of auburn curls was slightly damp, and he concluded she'd taken a quick shower.

Dan was ill at ease and edgy; it sounded in his voice when he asked, "How do you manage with that thing?" He was pointing to the heavy cast.

"I wrap it in a plastic bag and stick it out of the curtain, resting it on a stool." She chuckled. "Not an easy or elegant task I can tell you, especially when I keep dropping the soap."

"No," he agreed. "Sounds awkward." He stood up, stretched his legs and prowled like a lion before eventually saying, "Okay if I shower? Don't want to stink of sweat."

"Go ahead," she said. "You'll find a towel in the cupboard in the bathroom."

Somewhere in Amy's plans, she'd forgotten to consider the likelihood of his taking three quarters of an hour to shower. In her naivety, she'd expected him to hurry to her, anxious to hold her and love her. But not Dan, Dan was in hiding, buried in the bathroom like a hamster in a bundle of hay.

"I thought you'd gone down the plug hole," she teased when at last he returned to the bedroom with a small hand towel wrapped around his lower half. "Couldn't you find a bath towel?" she asked for something to say, trying desperately to pull him up out of the peculiar black hole he was digging himself into.

"No. Managed with this."

Amy was about to tell him there'd been no need to 'manage' - there were a dozen large white fluffy towels in the cupboard. Instead, she sat back against the headboard and watched him pour another glass of wine for himself. He swallowed it down in a single swig and refilled the glass, then, and only then did he lie next to her on the soft clean bed.

"Strange this," he said. "Having two mattresses and two quilts. Big bed too." He was thumping the pillow, moulding it to fit under his head and neck.

"Germanic," Amy said. "Typically so. They don't have double beds like us, nor ordinary size bedding. Anyway, there's more room for us to stretch out on."

She turned and looked at him lying there on his back, his hands folded around the glass of wine, which was resting on his chest. "Would you care to explain why you happen to be so damned angry with me, Dan?"

"I'm not angry," he denied, sounding just that. "Mind if I smoke?" He was reaching for a pack of cigarettes.

"Yes, as a matter of fact I do mind. When did you..."

"Started again this morning," he explained, anticipating the question. "Filthy habit. Don't know why I do it."

"Nor I," she said quietly. His mood was most peculiar; it perplexed her.

"Want me to pull the curtains shut?" he asked, so obviously stalling for time.

"No. I want you to make love to me." The silence between them was earth-shattering. He made no attempt to move towards her and she felt both frustrated and embarrassed. "Damn you, Dan Jones!" she cried, flouncing away from him, pulling the duvet higher over her naked body.

He reached out to her, touching the warmth of the silken skin on her shoulder and she turned into his arms, burying her face in his neck.

"Amy, my little love. I'm sorry. I'm really sorry."

"Just hold me." Her lips searched for his, hungrily kissing his face. She became lost in him, enfolded in strong arms, secure and loved.

"Why didn't you tell me?" he asked thirty minutes later. "I hurt you, little one." He pulled her back into his arms and she kissed his chin, knowing she was content with this man.

"Absolutely not! You would never hurt me, Dan."

"Why didn't you tell me?" he repeated as he rocked her gently like a small child with a grazed knee instead of a grown woman who had willingly given away her virginity in the name of love.

"I thought you realised. I told you all about me, everything. I never once mentioned boyfriends, or lovers for that matter. What did you expect anyway, a tattoo on my left buttock 'Amy Harper is a virgin', right next to the 'Government Property' stamp and the little arrow? Someone had to be first. Do you know how happy I am that that someone, was you? I love you, Dan. I really do."

His soft grey eyes filled with tears. The big gentle Welshman was so overwhelmed with happiness all he could do was hold her close to him and thank his maker for blessing him this way.

"Marry me," he said when he found his voice again. "Marry me, Amy."

She thumped his chest with her hard little fist. "Don't joke. That's not funny."

"I mean it, marry me." He held her away from him. "Say you will."

"No, I will not." She gave a nervous little laugh. "We've only known each other for a few weeks. I need time. We both need time. I've hardly grown up yet. There's no need to do something we might live to regret just because we've made love. Besides, I want to know what was wrong with you when you arrived this evening."

"I was jealous," he admitted at last. "And scared."

"Jealous of whom? Scared of what?"

He laughed, nervous again. "Jealous of Peter for finding this place for you, and scared of making love to you. Scared of blowing it all first time. I did too. I rushed you like a mad bull."

"You did not!" she exclaimed, watching him swing his legs over the edge of the bed, reaching for his watch. "I was hungry for you. I couldn't wait a second longer," she argued. "Please don't demean yourself this way."

The truth was she had nothing upon which to base her comparison, Dan was her first lover; everything had seemed to be perfectly in order to someone who knew little or nothing about making love.

He stood embarrassed by his nakedness, his back to her while he stepped into his underpants and then his trousers. "I've got to go. Duty calls," he grunted.

"Do you have to leave so soon?" Amy asked. "Please stay with me."

"Can't do it, lovely one."

Bravely she asked, "When will you come back?"

"Tomorrow. Can I phone?"

"Yes," she whispered miserably. "The phone is in the lounge. I can't remember the number. Take a look on your way out." Hurt and anger were growing yet she forced herself to conceal the way she felt.

Dan tucked his shirt into his trousers and fastened the fly buttons before turning to kiss her full on the mouth. She clung to him, pulling him back down onto the bed. Feeling him resisting her embrace, her needs.

"Amy, please. I've got to go. I'll see you tomorrow."

And so, she released him in silence. Watched him hurry from the bedroom. Heard him clatter down the staircase, almost breaking his neck in his haste to leave.

The front door slammed shut and Amy was furious. She was hurt and felt cheated. She even detested him for a few minutes. He'd run away from her. He couldn't escape quickly enough. She'd wanted everything to be beautiful, romantic and memorable. It was all-important to her. He was her first lover - her last, she hoped. Dan, the man she hardly knew yet felt she'd known all of her life. Dan who made her feel comfortable and warm. Dan, the man she trusted implicitly. Dan - the man who'd just succeeded in making her feel like a five-mark whore.

There was time in plenty to analyse every throughout the night. Time to dwell on the do's and do not or on the why's and wherefore's. She'd rushed him, she reasoned. She'd hurried him into a situation, which he so obviously felt uneasy about, but no, he'd been pleading with her to let him love her, there in his car, just nights earlier.

'*No,*' she'd said. '*It has to be done properly, in a bed or not at all. No back seat love affair for me.*' He'd agreed, reluctantly at the time, but he agreed. She found the house. She set everything up, made it all too easy for him. They had privacy in plenty. Everything was favourable for a romantic affair. But what he did was flee like a scalded tomcat!

Amy fell asleep in the early hours, after the anger and confusion finally wore off, waking in pain, excruciating pain, less than an hour later. She took two painkillers and crawled back to bed. The night was long and painful, and she was lonelier than before she took Dan into her bed.

The following day proved interminable as she waited with her thoughts, her fears and her regrets, willing the telephone to ring. It rang at seven that evening. She snatched the receiver up. "Dan? Is that you?"

"Yes, it's me," he said sounding sheepish. "How are you, Amy?"

His voice was balm on her strained nerves. She'd longed to speak to him, to apologise for something she wasn't even certain she'd done. "I'm fine, and you?"

"Can I come and see you?"

Her heart took a nosedive into her stomach. He hadn't answered her. Something was wrong. He was angry with her. He wanted her out of his life. She would never again feel his body next to hers. Never taste his sweet loving. He was coming to say goodbye. The special senses she possessed were worthless that evening, her spirits were so low she had no energy to search for the truth in the situation, no reason to question her own common sense.

"You know you can," she said sounding braver than she felt. "You don't need permission. I'm here, alone."

"I'm on my way," he said. "Don't move." The line clicked and went dead.

He arrived fifteen minutes later, a bunch of wilting red carnations in his hand. His free hand encompassed her waist, scooping her towards him. His lips pressed down on hers with an undeniable burning passion and she knew everything would be all right. "Am I forgiven for buggering off?" he asked.

"You had to go," she said, making excuses for him again, ignoring her finely honed and special intuition. "Duty and all that." She closed the door and tugged him into the lounge.

"No," he said as she shoved him down onto the sofa and sat next to him, holding on tightly to him. "I cleared off. Needed time to think things through."

She sat back, staring at him, her eyes widening in disbelief and then they glowed like amber warning lights. "You bastard!" Shock and even anger had caused the exclamation to explode from her. "Do you mean to tell me you could have stayed?"

"Yes, but...look, Amy - I was shocked by you being a virgin and all that. I had no idea."

"You bastard," she repeated but without any malice or anger this time. "How about me being shocked and mixed up? Did you give any thought to me - to how I'd given you my all - my damned chastity? I wanted to prove beyond a shadow of doubt I loved you and it was the only way I could do it."

He smiled handsomely, proudly. "It worked," he said. "I believe you." The smile faded. "You said, 'loved'. Is there any significance? You know, past tense and all."

"None whatsoever. I'm actually amazed you even noticed," she replied tartly.

He took a deep breath and looked right at her and then away, as if nervous in her presence again. "I have a confession," he said at last.

"Confess away," she said with a shrug. "They say it's good for the soul. See if I care. I might not even bother to listen." It sounded childish and petty, yet she did listen.

"You were my first too."

She frowned. "First two what?"

"First, silly. I gave you my chastity - my damned virginity."

Amy stared open-mouthed at him; her eyes almost as wide as her pretty pink lips. Her mouth closed slowly, a smile crept upon her face, and she felt sorry for him.

"But you're twenty-eight years of age, Dan. What have you been doing? Why so celibate a lifestyle?"

"Why not?" he countered indignantly, and then he smiled right into her eyes, relieved she was still speaking to him. "Who gave you sole rights on virginity? Anyway, I'm not any more, nor are you, so it no longer applies. All I'm concerned about is you, and how clumsy I was. I was rough and...well...I got it over with as quickly as I could. Like a big scared child. I'm sorry, Amy, really sorry. I let you down."

"Shut up! Please, Dan, stop apologising when there's nothing to apologise for, except for running out on me. I have nothing to compare what we did with. There are no high standards for you to meet. You are the only man I've wanted to share myself with in this way. I love you, Dan."

He moved closer and she went on. "This is fast, and perhaps, well, just perhaps we should have slowed things down a little, but in my line of work there's no guarantee on there being a tomorrow to look forward to. I stole time with you. I want to steal some more. Please."

As she was speaking to him, he was winding her hair around his fingers. His smile was caressing and soothing her. He was forgiven and he was ecstatically happy.

He lifted her with ease and carried her to the bedroom where he set about making amends for his previous hasty act of inexperience. He stripped her of clothing and kissed her breasts and her stomach and then he tore off his own clothes to lie naked next to her on the crumpled blue quilt. He whispered sweet words of tender loving. He smoothed her velvet-like skin and then he kissed her lips.

Their loving was so profoundly passionate they were both dewy-eyed and completely at a loss for words afterwards. They clung to each other, unwilling to let go. It was when Amy expected him to get dressed and return to barracks that he loved her again, more slowly, much more slowly.

They learned together. They grew together and they shared love as pure as any shared by any human couple. They were secure and happy in the cosy bedroom in the authentic German house. The Wall, the communists and the worries of the world might well have been a million miles away for all they cared that night.

Again, Amy was woken in the early hours. Her face beaded with perspiration and her mass of hair clinging to her skin. She screamed out before she woke and as the nightmare broke, she sat bolt upright shaking and relieved it was over at last.

"You're okay, little one." Dan soothed as he pulled her towards him. "It was only a dream."

"That was no dream," she told him, a tremor of fear sounding in her voice. "That was a foretaste of reality."

He was fully awake now. He reached for the light switch and then he studied her face, almost afraid to ask for an explanation. "Want to talk?"

"It won't help," she told him as she wiped her face with a wad of tissues. "I don't really understand myself."

"What don't you understand, little one?" He was so patient with her; he was struggling to help her.

"Myself," she said as she looked at him. "I don't understand me."

He felt a complete dimwit. She spoke to him strangely, and she was looking at him as if he was just that, an imbecile. It was as if she was looking straight through him. "Because of a dream you doubt yourself? You'll have to explain that one. I'm only a common foot soldier, ma'am."

The comment raised a smile and served to drive away some of her fear. "Soldier you may well be, but common - never. I am fussy with whom I associate. It has to be a person of special understanding. A gifted person." She sighed deeply. "That's the problem, I'm fussy."

Dan raked his hand through his fine hair and sighed. "What are you on about, woman?"

"I get visions. Pictures if you like, warnings of things about to happen. It's something I have no control over and something I've lived with for twenty-two and a half years."

She saw him straighten as if to make better sense of what she was saying, and she felt obligated to explain more fully now she'd disturbed his sleep. "I'm not mad; at least I have been assured I'm sane. The problem is, my mind is more finely tuned than most. Almost all of the time I'm me, Amy Harper." She laughed and added, "That's blown my cover. Some damned spy I'd make!"

"You blew it before today, my love, when you talked about getting the virgin thing tattooed on your bum. Anyway, you're a beautiful spy. Don't stop, tell me more, Miss Harper, I won't say a word."

"As I was saying, most of the time I'm just me - an ordinary person with an ordinary mind doing an ordinary job of sorting out thoughts and ideas and so on. Then there are times when it is as if I have another person inside my head, making suggestions, feeding me with masses of information - mostly seemingly useless details - whole encyclopaedia type data. I see mental photographs of people. I cross continents without moving a muscle, and I have nightmares which leave me like this; shaking, weak and terrified."

"And this has been medically researched?"

"Oh, yes! Medically and scientifically researched. I, my love, am a statistic in a record book or two. Just another freak, phenomena, that's me. Some information is useless, but mostly what I receive proves useful. The ideas and suggestions save time cut corners and have been known to save lives."

"Like when we were in the East and you knew there was someone watching the building, and you insisted on me coming back with Rook?" She had his full and undivided attention now.

"Yes."

"And the nightmares, do they serve any useful purpose?" he asked.

"Yes, Dan. They prepare me for what is most certainly to come."

"Tell me about tonight."

"No!" The fear had returned to both her voice and her eyes. "Don't even ask." Her eyes were filled with unshed tears.

"Tell me, please," he persisted, deeply moved by the pain he sensed within her. "If it involves you, I should know. Are you going to be hurt?"

"Indirectly. I'm going to lose you." She attempted a smile and failed dismally. "I can't think of anything worse right now." Snuggling into his arms again, she began to relax. "Hold me, and don't let's waste a single precious moment of being together."

While Dan Jones performed the perfunctory duties of a soldier, Amy switched her time between sitting with Joseph Rook at the hospital and sitting at home in her cosy house thinking of the man she loved.
She tingled from head to plastered toes at the thought of his body, naked and splendid, lying next to hers. She went over everything they said and did - remembering all of his beautiful words and each of his tender caresses. She could see and hear only Dan's face and words. Her heart palpated madly. Her body was moist with perspiration. She felt feverish and ill yet at the same time she felt wonderful.
Dan lay with her at night, hurried back to barracks early each morning and raced to her again in the evening. While they loved and played her leg healed and all too soon, the six weeks had gone and Amy was declared fit for duty. She ached as she limped about when the cast was removed but with gentle persuasion from a skilled physiotherapist, the ache wore away into a distant memory, as did the lameness.
Joseph Rook arrived in England eight weeks after being recovered and returned to safety, but he was not to be institutionalised as his daughter previously planned. His future was far less bleak, there was hope for him, Amy was responsible for that. She knew he would remain withdrawn and moody, and his capacity for switching off reality would be far greater than she would have liked, but they were insisting on his return and she hoped to see him again in England.
Amy set up a rehabilitation programme for refugees from the Eastern Bloc countries, which proved so successful the West German authorities quickly adopted her methods. She then turned her skills to helping servicemen and women with stress disorders to settle back into service life. She was called upon to aid in the search

for a missing child and various other tasks, which utilised her special gifts, despite the scepticism of many men and women around her.

She was constantly busy, constantly in demand, spending many weeks in the American Sector working alongside top psychologists flown out of the States to help American personnel. The British government employees in Berlin kept her busy six days a week.

She and Dan made love at every possible and practical opportunity. They had a comfortable and understanding relationship. Everything seemed settled and easy, yet Amy was growing increasingly, and more noticeably restless and unhappy as the weeks rolled into months.

Dan had habits, strange habits. He was not altogether an easy man to live with. While he remained tender and loving, he also occasionally drowned and wallowed in the depths of his conscious concentration and forgot all about her.

A good example of this strange quirk was the report he was obliged to complete shortly after they began sharing a house and a bed. It was all the details on the latest survival course he was leading. It related largely to the men in his care. Major Philips expected to read and to be wiser. It had to be perfect and polished and Dan wouldn't hurry it.

To do justice to the task he'd taken three days' leave of absence and retreated to the comfortable lounge in Amy's house. She thought they were going to have a wonderful time together. She even rearranged her schedule so her days off coincided with his and she could wait on him hand foot and finger. She cooked and cleaned and fussed over him yet he hardly knew she was there, and so she returned to work on the second day. He seemed not to notice her leaving and barely acknowledged her return.

Amy felt isolated and lonely and the feelings were far worse than any she had experienced while actually living alone. Seeing him sitting in a chair, deep in thought, notebook on his knee and a cigarette burning in the ashtray, lost to everything except the job in hand, and being ignored by him, it hurt her terribly.

When he eventually noticed she was quiet, pale and withdrawn he demanded to know what was wrong and they ended up having their first real argument. During the heat of the row, Amy poured out a list of reasons why she could never live with him, why it would never work. He was too noisy, too untidy. He was barbaric at times. Single-minded to the point of the ridiculous. Too this and too that. He reached out for her and shook her gently and then he kissed her.

"You love me. I love you. Love can conquer everything and anything," he said quietly but firmly. "I'm sorry I'm a pig. I'm sorry I ignored you. I'm sorry, Amy, truly sorry."

"Dan, I..."

"I love you, Amy. Me." He prodded his own chest. "I love you. Not anyone else, just me."

"I love you too, but..." It was no longer enough for her, and she feared her love for him was not unconditional, and nothing but that would sit well with her.

He kissed her again and they went to bed and made love and everything that was wrong became instantly right, although nothing had really improved for Amy. She began regretting having tied herself down to Dan and to what was almost entirely a desk job.

After just nine months in Berlin, she faced the truth head on - she was not ready to settle down. She was, however, ready for more action. She was too young and inexperienced for this type of long-term commitment. The burning desire of first love seemed to have faded for her and despite the deep and lasting love she felt for Dan, it simply wasn't enough.

"But why have you gone and done it, Amy? Why? I need you. You can't go."

She raised her face and looked right at him. He was unhappy; tearing apart inside and it saddened her. "I have to move on, Dan."

"You don't have to. Your boss was in favour of you staying put until September. You could stay if you really wanted to."

The truth was she didn't really want to. Her eyes filled with tears and her words stuck painfully in her gullet, as the lump grew larger and larger. "But I don't want to stay."

He turned over onto his side, his back to her, contemplating leaving, walking out on her again. But he couldn't leave; not now, no matter how much he wanted to teach her a lesson. Time was running out. Suddenly he felt he was going to lose her for good.

"I love you," he said and she placed her hand on his back and smoothed his skin and he knew she was crying. "Don't do this to us, Amy."

"I've already done it," she whispered.

He rolled over and stared at her, too afraid to ask.

"I leave for London on Monday," she whispered.

His heart took a massive hit. That left them just five days together. "So soon," was all he said. He reached out for her, pulling her into his arms and the warmth of his body. "I'm going to miss you, my little one."

Not once in those five precious days did he beg her to stay. He knew that once she'd made a decision nothing would change it. It would be pointless even trying. He also understood her far better than she would ever have believed possible. He knew how she felt, how she was driven to seek adventure and excitement. She was a wild bird and he had no right to even contemplate caging her.

"What am I going to do when you've gone tomorrow?" he asked late on their last special night.

"Forget me," she suggested, a familiar lump building in her throat. "Find yourself a good down-to-earth woman who'll give you babies, who'll stay at home content to do the housework. You know it will never be that way with us."

"It could be," he said, still clutching at straws in a last desperate bid to change her mind. "We could get married. I'd never crowd you. I swear. I'd never ask more than you're prepared to give."

"Dan, you're already doing just that. Listen to yourself. I cannot be what you want me to be. Just trust me, it won't work. This way we part friends. I'll keep in touch and when I return to Berlin we can have a reunion."

He sighed - he'd lost her. "Just promise me one last thing."

"What is it?" Her heart was breaking.

"Promise me you'll always take proper care of yourself and you'll call me when you need me. Wherever you are."

She nodded and smiled into his loving and handsome face. "I will, and remember this, Dan, I will always love you, always."

They were both to discover that the sorrow of parting is in no way sweet. It was most unpleasant. It was a form of grief; a horrible blackness, which descended upon their hearts, turning out the light of hope that had burned so brightly for them.

PART TWO

Chapter Eight

Amy celebrated her twenty-third birthday the day after she kissed her lover of eight months goodbye. She celebrated alone. The day came and went, as did every day before it. Her heart was heavy and her spirits just about as low as they could get. She was missing Dan so badly there was a tight band around her chest; however, she'd made her own decisions and she had only herself to blame for her present misery.

With a full week's leave in which to drown in her sorrows, she visited her parents. Despite letters from her mother during her absence she still naively expected everything to be exactly the same as the day she left, yet things were not the same, the old man who looked up from his newspaper had shrunken physically. Flesh hung loosely on his frail frame. His eyes were set in dark hollowed sockets in a gaunt yellow face.

Amy kissed her father and imagined he'd recognised her for an instant. "Hello, Dad. How are you?"

"Who the hell are you?" he growled. "Don't know you, do I?"

"It's me silly, Amy."

"Amy?" he repeated. "Don't know anyone called Amy. Knew Amy Johnson once."

Amy smiled patiently. "Yes, Dad. You named me after her."

"Amy!" At last he remembered, but had he? "My girl's called Amy. She's a good girl. Works hard." He coughed a bronchial rasping cough which tore at the lining of his lungs and brought Amy actual physical pain.

Her mother rested her hand lightly on her shoulder and coaxed her away from him. "Come and have something to eat, my darling. Dad will still be here when you've finished." David Harper would not be going far ever again.

Amy could no longer swallow food and her appetite had left her completely. She longed to seek refuge in Dan's big strong arms. "How long, Mamma?"

Ruth Harper shook her head. "I don't know. Nobody seems to know for certain. It could be at any time. The cancer is..." She paused, drew a long strong breath and went bravely on. "It's advanced, and it's massive. His lungs are almost finished. They could do no more for him at the hospital. They couldn't risk removing anything and the last lot of radiotherapy hardened the living lung tissue, it's much more difficult for him to breathe now."

"He looks so old." Amy was close to tears now. "Aw, Mamma! He's only fifty! It's not fair."

Ruth could do little more than hold her daughter and offer words of comfort and wisdom. "It's not a question of fair or unfair, darling - it's one of those things we have to bear in life. There are no rules when it comes to illness and dying. It happens. I get my comfort from the fact that Dad doesn't have much recollection of anything. He's not troubled or upset. He eats, drinks, reads his paper and sleeps. His life is simple, and he is greatly loved."

Amy sniffed and dried her eyes. "I'm sorry. You don't need me like this, but it was a shock seeing him this way."

"How long are you staying?" Ruth asked.

"Until Sunday. I have to get back up to London by Monday morning. I'm sorry it's not for longer."

"Never mind." She covered her daughter's hand with her own and squeezed gently, gathering strength for the days and weeks to come.

"It's lovely having you here. You look wonderful." Then she frowned, as if trying to fathom out a complicated puzzle. "You've changed. Who is he, Amy?"

Amy smiled secretly. "Just someone I fell in love with. He's a lovely man, kind and gentle. Someone who deserves better than me."

Ruth tutted, "Don't belittle yourself. You're a good girl. Anyway, are you going to bring the young man home to meet us?"

"I don't think so, Mamma. I won't be seeing him again. He's a soldier and he moves about quite a lot. He understood when I told him I was leaving Berlin."

Ruth tutted again, as was her way. "But did he understand? Knowing you, he wasn't offered much by way of a choice. Once you make your mind up, there's no moving you." She sighed deeply. "Don't you think you should be considering a more sensible life? I worry about you."

"Well, don't!" Amy hadn't meant to sound quite so hard and angry. It just came out that way.

"I'd be a strange sort of a mother if I didn't worry about my only child." Another of her gentle tuts, and then she remembered something important. "I have a small gift for you."

She went to the sideboard and took a package from the top drawer. It was wrapped in pink floral paper and tied with a delicate lace ribbon. She placed the package in front of Amy. "I'm sorry, love, but I didn't get the chance to post it to you in time for your birthday. Happy birthday from Dad and me, I hope you like it."

Amy's eyes misted as she unwrapped the small silver photo frame, it was folded and opened to reveal two photographs, one of her with her parents when she was eighteen, and the other of her father sitting in his armchair, taken a year earlier, before his illness. The frame was a modern classic, simple and elegant, and perfect for Amy to carry with her when she travelled.

Amy hugged her mother and kissed her on both cheeks. "It's beautiful. I love it, thank you, Mamma, thank you."

Before leaving on Sunday night, she made her mother promise to contact her, wherever she was, the moment the end was close for her father. Ruth made the promise, and Amy also promised to keep in touch more often.

London was as hectic as ever. Amy rushed everywhere she went snatching snacks along the way and developing an irritating cough which worsened as January rolled into February and the weather closed in. During the third week in February, a message was handed to her. Her father's condition had become critical and there was only a matter of hours left. She caught the first train out of the city and arrived an hour before he died.

Within two weeks of his funeral, Amy was hospitalised with bronchial pneumonia. Her mother sat with her night and day and listened as she cried out for Dan. Ruth had no idea how to go about finding the young man. She had no idea exactly who Amy worked for. She knew only it was a government office and that the work involved a large element of secrecy. Ruth did nothing except pray and wait for Amy to recover. Her daughter almost lost her life.

On the first day of April 1968, Amy was discharged from hospital as fit to return to duty. She was anything but fit, she was frail and in need of tender loving care. Ruth persuaded her to return to their Kent home for a period of recuperation but Amy grew restless and left after just four short days.

When Commander Cooper set eyes on her, he told her exactly what was on his mind. "You look dreadful, dreadful! Who in God's name discharged you from the hospital? Was it some blasted maniac?"

"A doctor, sir," she replied. "I really am fine. I lost a little weight, that's all."

"That's all!" he exclaimed, still horrified by her gaunt appearance. "You'll take sick leave as from today."

"No, sir. I really do not require more time off. I need to be working, to keep my mind fully occupied."

Cooper immediately concluded she was referring to her recent bereavement. He had no idea she was grieving for a certain sergeant in the Welch Regiment, a sergeant named Daniel Jones. Amy had done all of her grieving for her father while his cancerous body lived, but Dan was different, he was alive and well and she was still struggling to live with her decision to leave him.

"Very well." Cooper conceded. "But I'm going to send you somewhere different, somewhere where you can relax and get strong again."

The two months she spent in the quiet little office in Prague set her up both physically and mentally. She still pined for Dan but the pain lessened upon her return to England.

In August 1969, the twenty-four-year-old spent an exhilarating month in the heart of Moscow. Despite the necessity of a constant secure escort, she succeeded in enjoying every second of every day.

Having quenched her thirst on Moscow's atmosphere, she missed the place like an old friend when at last she returned to London. As soon as she got back she learned she was booked on a training course: New psychological methods and new thoughts on the subject of psychology in warfare.

The course ran through the autumn of '69 and into the New Year when Amy packed and boarded a flight for America where for eight months she travelled extensively throughout the United States. During the time she learned, taught and enjoyed her life, returning to England looking healthier than she had since long before the bout of bronchial pneumonia. Her five feet five-inch frame had filled out and with the extra pounds she looked wonderful. She positively glowed with health.

It seemed that no sooner than she was hanging her few bits of clothing in her own wardrobe in the small basement flat in London than she was packing again. This time she was off to Holland, to Rotterdam and Amsterdam, to wherever she was ordered to go, and for eleven months this time - another long and interesting tour of duty.

She acquired a pleasant, traditional Dutch apartment in a large house in Amsterdam, a ten-minute walk from the Stedelijk Museum, just one of her favourite haunts, and with delightful views from both her bedroom and living room windows. The outlook was soothing on the eye, the accommodation was clean, and exactly what she needed. Her working days were short and she found herself with time to spare for sightseeing, shopping and the luxury of lying on her bed with a good book or listening to classical music.

Amy was happy and contented. There were friends if she needed company, a good social life and work, which was not in the least bit taxing. Being alone suited her admirably. She felt no compulsion to be possessed by a man. No feminine urge to breed constantly. She was comfortably happy in her own company and contented with her life - or so she thought until she bumped into someone from her past.

Her mind was filled with a psychological entanglement - a recent problem, part of her daily routine. A man in need of rehabilitation, who'd been a prisoner of war in Germany from 1944 until he was freed in 1945 when the allies stormed the prison camp. He went on to serve in Korea with the US Army in 1951.

He'd been living in Amsterdam - a mental wreck. His problem was almost as old as was his body. His mind was all but destroyed and Amy was there to help him, him and many others like him - men and women scattered around the globe, conveniently forgotten by their own people.

She stopped at the little café with the blue and white striped awnings and the pavement tables with the fresh red gingham tablecloths and wicker-backed chairs, ordered coffee and in deep thought she sipped it slowly. No sounds or sights penetrated her mind. Nothing from the world around her succeeded in breaking through, nothing other than a deep, rich and haunting male voice.

She gasped, looked up and saw him - Daniel Jones.

"Good God!" he exclaimed. "It is you, Amy! I thought it was you."

Then she noticed the short stocky woman by his side - dark hair, dark complexion and beautiful dark eyes. There was also a darkness about her entire being which startled Amy.

"Hello, Dan," Amy said at last, rising shakily from the chair. "It's been a long time. How are you?" She longed to hold him but she refused to offer him her hand.

"Fine. I'm fine," he said, his hands stuffed into his pockets and a look of boyish embarrassment on his face, and then he remembered the woman by his side. "I'm sorry. Damned rude of me. This is Jane, my wife."

Amy felt faint. The striped awning suddenly seemed to spin around her head. She was aware of her colour draining as her ears buzzed loudly and then the colour flooded back to her cheeks and she felt she might explode at any moment.

"Hello, Jane. I'm delighted to meet you." She purposely avoided extending her hand. "How long have you two been married?"

"We're on our honeymoon." Jane replied her accent the singsong sound of the Welsh valleys, the H dropped and a forced attempt at sounding English by abusing the letter H.

"Got married last week we did. How long you two known each other then?" What she said sounded incongruous.

It was Dan who replied, Amy remained in a state of mild shock. "Years," he said. "We met when I was in the army in the sixties."

So - he was no longer a soldier, just a married man, but Amy had heard enough. She was beginning to feel nausea sweeping over her.

"Look, I'm afraid I really must dash. It's been lovely seeing you again, Dan, and meeting you, Jane. Do enjoy your holiday." Wild horses could not have dragged the word "Honeymoon" out of her, with or without the H!

"Amy!" Dan called as she rushed off. "We're at the Waterfront Hotel. Come for a drink."

"If I have time," she said, knowing full well she'd do no such thing. "Thank you."

Jane Jones watched the pretty petite female hurry away. She looked up at her husband and snapped out the first of many questions. "Who is she?"

"I told you, someone I met years ago, she's a nice girl. Very kind."

"I bet she was. Sounds like a bit of a snob to me. 'Must dash' Huh! 'Do enjoy your holiday' who'd she think she is?"

Dan sighed, and in his heart, he knew he'd made a grave mistake, and not for the first time.

Amy cried herself to sleep in the afternoon. She was so unhappy she even wished she could die. When she woke, she took time to analyse her situation. She'd chosen to give up the man she loved. It was her own choice, and her own free will, and now she had absolutely no right to be feeling pangs of jealousy. No right to hurt because another woman shared his bed. She'd rejected him along with all of her rights, but it still hurt.

When she returned to the café with the striped awnings it was in the hope that she might once again catch sight of her dearest friend, but he was not there. She drank two cups of coffee and returned forlornly to her apartment. An hour after she closed the door on the world someone knocked and she went to see who was there. It was Dan.

She stared at him, questions tumbling through her aching mind. "Dan! How?"

"I went to the café hoping you'd go back there. I waited, and then I followed you. I couldn't bring myself to speak to you, not then, and it's taken me this long to pluck up enough courage to come and knock on your door." He smiled. "Can I? Come in I mean?"

"Err...yes. Please do." She held the door open wide and closed it after him. "Have a seat. I'll make coffee."

She boiled the kettle and made two mugs of instant coffee, two sugars in Dans and as she carried them through to the living room, marvelling at the emotions running riot inside her. It was as if he'd never been out of her life, just as if they were back in Berlin, in her cosy little house.

"Thanks," he said as he relieved her of one of the mugs. He sipped. "You remembered how I like it."

"I have an excellent memory." Inside her head a voice was screaming at her. How could you forget? You love him. You have always loved him.

"How are you, Amy?"

"Fine, and yourself?"

"Oh, I'm okay. You look wonderful. Are you still in the same line of business?"

"Yes, although things are a little less exciting these days. I don't think they trust me not to break a leg or something equally as careless," she smiled at the memory and hurried on. "I did have a thrilling month in Moscow and a few small slices of action, but nothing to shout about. How about you?"

"I work for a haulage contractor," he told her. "Sort of foreman I suppose. It's a living. I had no real qualifications when I left the regiment. I was trained in survival and killing the enemy, not in providing a wage packet for a wife and family."

"You should have stayed in," she said quietly. "You were good."

"Thanks for that, but things weren't the same after..." He half-smiled. "Amy, I...hell...I've missed you, little one."

Her heart began pounding. "And I you, but I made my choice."

"Why did you do it?" His voice was low and gentle. It soothed her pain. "You knew I was crazy about you. I'd have moved mountains for you. I've never met anyone so alive, so exciting. You're unique and I've missed you, my little Amy."

"You have a wife now, Dan." What she wanted to say was: "You missed me so much you went and got married."

"Jane's pregnant, Amy."

"Oh, I see," she said, as if it made all the difference. I got her pregnant because I couldn't have you.

"Are you happy, Dan?"

"Sometimes, but mostly no, I'm not. Are you?"

"I was beginning to be. I had rather settled into a routine. A good book some music. My own space." Then she felt angry he'd caused her renewed pain.

"Why the hell did you happen back into my life? I was doing okay." She saw him flinch. Witnessed the pain in his eyes. "Go away, Dan! Go back to Jane. Enjoy your baby. Go!"

"No. I can't, not like this. We had something special you and me. We've still got something special. Don't banish me from your life again. Please don't. I need you, Amy. I've always loved you. I will always love you."

She shoved the chair back and moved away as he reached out for her hands. "Please go!"

He left and she broke her heart once again.

Exactly one week later he returned to the apartment. Amy opened the door knowing he was there. She'd thought carefully about what she'd say to him if he returned, but now, facing him, all she could think about was being in his arms again.

"Come inside," she said quietly, signifying that he was to sit with a simple movement of her wrist. "What do you want from me, Dan?"

"I told you once - everything and nothing. Only what you want to give me. Damn it, Amy, I love you. How can I simply turn it off? I've made a mistake - a terrible mistake."

"But you are a man of honour," she said without bitterness. "You'll be a good husband and a wonderful father."

Her voice caught as she thought of him holding his child in his arms. She tilted her head back and willed the tears not to form. "Please don't come here again, Dan. I cannot and I will not have an affair with a married man."

"I'm not asking you to," he said, but her words had failed to surprise him, the thought had crossed his mind too. "All I want is your friendship and company whenever possible. Please don't cut me off again, Amy, please."

"Where does she think you are when you come here to see me?"

He smiled at her. "She's visiting some friends who live here in Amsterdam. She isn't interested in where I am or what I'm doing."

"She would be if she knew you were with me." She paused and then, "Why did you marry her? A baby is no reason to persecute yourself."

"I felt sorry for her. She's a good woman."

Amy reached out and touched his hand and then she gasped and recoiled as if burned. "My God!" she exclaimed. "It's not even your baby!"

136

"How...who...how do you know that?" he asked, shocked by her announcement. "No-one knows except Jane and me." His eyes narrowed as he worked things out for himself, the cogs of his brain grinding and turning slowly but methodically.

"You once told me about this. You can read minds. That's what you did, you read mine, didn't you?"

"No," she denied the accusation quietly. "I can't read your mind. I sensed it," she whispered, appalled by what she discovered when she touched him. "What have you got yourself into, Dan? Moreover, why? Why in God's name?"

He sighed and buried his head in his hands; everything was so damned complicated. "It's a long story."

"I have time. Have you?" She watched him nod his head. "Tell me why."

"Hell, Amy, I didn't know what to do. I felt sorry for her. We've known each other since school. I never really thought much about her. She was always a pretty kid, but a bit...well, she's a bit unpredictable. When I left the regiment, I took to hanging around the local pub, bored out of my skull most of the time. Jane was working behind the bar and...well, she was kind to me; at least that's what I thought at the time. We started going out a bit, although I wasn't interested in her, not really. All I wanted was friendship, someone to talk to. I was lost without you, and then I didn't even have the regiment, I was out, my mates gone and my life over in many respects."

He heaved a mighty sigh as the events of the past months caught up with him. "I got blind drunk at a wedding a few months back and Jane and me ended up in bed, not that I remember anything about it. Once we'd...the next day, she told me she was already pregnant. She asked me to marry her and admitted she didn't think she'd ever love me, but she needed my name and my pay packet. After we'd been married a couple of days, she started screaming and yelling at me because I'd left the lid off the toothpaste and when I tried to calm her down, she told me the truth, that the..."

"The child belongs to her brother." Amy completed the sentence for him and he stared long and hard. Stunned. Amy knew everything there was to know from simply touching his hand. "She used you in order to cover up for her own brother and you had no idea?" Amy was aghast at what she knew was the truth.

"None," he admitted, ashamed of the mess he'd become entangled in. "I felt she was a bit over-protective towards him, but it never entered my head. He's a bit...well, putting it politely; he's a bit simple. He's got more than one of his screws missing. Like I said, it never entered my head they were sleeping together. Why would it? I've never known anyone...never been subjected to...Look, I know I'm naive and stupid at times."

"That's as maybe," she said. "But you are also completely honest, Dan. You would never lie or cheat. How do you feel about her now you know the truth?"

"I feel sorry for her," he said, "And strangely protective. I'll take care of her, and the baby. They'll never want for anything, not while I'm alive. I'm sorry, Amy."

She smiled and sighed at the same time. Her voice was gentle as she spoke to him again. "Don't be. I love you even more for being loyal to her. If there's anything I can do for you, at any time, please ask me."

He reached for her hand and squeezed it gently. "Just be my friend, always. You give me peace and strength and I need that. I need you more than anyone or anything in the entire universe. I'm alone without you, Amy, completely alone and lost."

"Oh, Dan," she said as she pulled him into her arms and rocked him as a mother would rock her child. They cried together and when at last they felt comforted Amy made a pot of tea and they sat in silence until Dan noticed the time.

"Jane will be back at the hotel soon. I'd better go." He stood and stretched his legs. "Thanks, little one, for your loyalty and your support."

"No need for thanks," she assured him. "When are you returning to England?"

"Wales," he corrected and laughed at her expression and her wrinkled nose. "In four days. Can I see you tomorrow, or is that asking too much of you?"

"Come tomorrow. I'll be here. We'll talk." She kissed his cheek and closed the door on him. That night she slept soundly. Dan was hers. Dan would always be hers and that knowledge wrapped itself around her, warming her.

They shared three more evenings, and despite the powerful longing within them, they never once made physical contact until the time for them to part arrived and they moved into each other's arms, and became lost in a vast expanse of timeless love. They hugged and then they kissed. One kiss. One special, lasting kiss to carry them through lonely days and endless nights. It was all that remained, a memory of a time gone by, renewed in the passion of that single embrace.

"My precious little Amy. I'll miss you."

"And I you," she whispered.

"Write to me, my love," he begged as he kissed her forehead and pulled her closer into his arms.

"How can I? Don't be ridiculous, Dan."

"At work. It's safe. Please, Amy. If I drop you a line with the address promise me you'll answer."

She nodded. "I'll do my best."

"Good," he sighed, satisfied at last. "When are you going home?"

"In November," she replied quietly as she willed time to stand still for them.

"That's only seven months away. We'll meet and talk."

"We'll see," she said, suddenly wishing he would stop arranging her life for her, and stop confusing her too.
"You'd better go. Good luck, Dan."
"You too, little one, you too. Thanks for everything."
"Forget it. Take care of yourself, please."

When Daniel Jones and his pregnant wife left Amsterdam, there was a large void that only Amy noticed and felt. She was empty inside, drained and exhausted. She had given Dan as much strength as she could muster. She boosted him, filled him with confidence. She gave him her peace and her blessing. In those few short hours, she learned of his troubles; his decisions, be they right or wrong, and of the pattern he'd set for his life.

Amy seriously doubted her own ability to be 'the other woman' - it was not a role she envisaged for herself. It was asking too much. No - Dan had made his bed and it was up to him to lie on it. She would consider writing to him, if - and only if she knew it would not cause pain or problems for either him or his new wife.

True to his word, Dan wrote a lengthy letter telling of his loneliness and gratitude for her friendship. He wrote of how she and she alone succeeded in lifting his spirits. He was obviously depressed and her heart went out to him and so she wrote straight back, boosting his moral, reminding him just how essential a human being he really was.

She packed her possessions in November and left Holland, exchanging the smart Dutch apartment for her dreary basement flat in central London. London was dreary. The weather was dreary and Amy felt positively drab. Faced with a long miserable winter there seemed little to be thankful for, and then, on one of her lowest, most depressed days in January 1972, she saw Daniel Jones climb from a taxi in Oxford Circus.

She followed at a discreet distance. He went into several shops. Bought himself a shirt and tie and went into a small restaurant in a back street in the West End. Amy waited until she knew that he wasn't meeting anybody, and then she walked boldly up to his table.

"Can I sit here, or is this seat taken?" she asked. He looked up from the menu, stared in disbelief and then he exclaimed, "My, God! Is it really you?" Standing, he opened his arms to her and she went to him to be hugged gently but confidently.

"It really is me. How are you, Dan?"

"As you can see, I'm okay. You look wonderful, wonderful!"

"Liar!" she argued happily. "I look ghastly. I've had a cold and it pulled me down."

They sat opposite each other and Dan stared and smiled. He could not believe he was actually sitting opposite Amy at the little square table with the frilly tablecloth and modern cutlery. "I think you look wonderful."

"Then perhaps you need your eyes tested," she argued.

"Perhaps, but I know beauty when I see it and your beauty comes from within, so don't argue with me, little lady. I know about these things."

As the waiter approached, Dan reluctantly returned part of his attention to the menu. "Hungry?" he asked her.

"Just thirsty. I'll have a pot of tea and watch you eat."

"Only if you insist," he said as he checked the menu again. "Spanish omelette and a large pot of tea for two."

The stranger scribbled on the pad in his hand and then he asked, "Chips or salad, sir?"

"Chips. Thanks."

All the while Amy had been studying him. He looked healthy and incredibly fit. She'd missed him badly. There were hundreds of questions needing asking and answering and even more words needing to be spoken. Instead, she sat in contented silence while he talked proudly and a little insensitively of his life.

As soon as the meal was on the table, he wolfed it down hungrily and then Amy asked, "Why are you here, in London?"

"I work here, for your lot."

"My lot?" Her eyes narrowed to amber slits. "Who exactly are 'my lot', Dan?"

"The government. Special detachment work. Hush, hush." He lifted the saltcellar and jokingly checked beneath it for a hidden microphone.

Amy was not in the slightest bit amused. In fact, she was angry with him for turning the important work she undertook into a joke.

"You cannot be serious?" she said, unable to fully comprehend what she was hearing.

"I am."

"And what of Jane?"

"Jane and I are separated. The marriage was doomed from day one. She miscarried the baby, which wasn't much of a surprise considering her lifestyle. She's quite fond of gin."

"I'm sorry, I know you were looking forward to being a father."

"In a way I was, but it wasn't why I agreed to marry her in the first place, it was for all the wrong reasons. I thought I was doing something good for her. I was wrong, about a lot of things."

"Are you divorcing her?" She needed to know. It was vital she knew exactly where she stood.

"I'll go on supporting her."

"You haven't answered my question." There was a quiet insistence about her, a determination born of living a lonely and sometimes isolated life; an attitude hardened like tempered steel over the years since last she shared her body and her life with this man.

"Divorce hasn't come into question. We're married."

"And separated for all time." Amy added.

"Yes."

She sighed as she felt all hope for them fly out of the restaurant window.

"Amy, this won't affect us. We can..."

"No!" she snapped. "We have no future. You're a married man and I do not intend aiding you in committing adultery. I might be old-fashioned, but I have standards to keep."

He looked at her then and smiled lovingly. "I love you, you know. I need to be with you. Don't make me beg."

"I won't," she assured him. "We can meet for tea; a drink, but no more than that."

"We'll see." He too seemed determined now. He too had spent a long time dwelling on the error of his ways. He should never have permitted her to leave him - which had been his first massive mistake. There was no way either of them could turn back the hands of time. The wrong decisions they'd made were gone, and it was all recorded in the annals of time. It was up to them never to repeat their errors.

Dan saw and sensed emptiness within her, an unfulfilled longing in a beautiful woman. He understood it even if she failed to recognise its existence. She was a woman, powerfully feminine. Born to love and to be loved. Born to raise children and to make a home - a nest for them.

He knew he'd failed her, he should have pursued her and persuaded her to become his wife. They were made for each other and they'd missed hearing the voice of sensibility echoing inside their own heads. The voice of wisdom told them they were right and good for each other, and they were either deaf or stupid, or both.

That same voice rang out now, loud and clear, but Amy was a determined woman with a strong sense of loyalty and high moral standards. Daniel Jones was a married man, and not her man. She belonged to her sovereign and to her sovereigns' government. All of her, one hundred percent belonged to Great Britain and not even her heart was free to be given away.

Amy looked at him, admiring his looks not for the first time - wanting desperately to hate him while aching to love him. "You said you loved me," she began. "That you wanted to be with me."

"It's true. I do," he confirmed with a sigh, sensing her mood, knowing she was about to hurt him in any way she could.

"Then why haven't you looked for me? How is it I found you?" By accident, but she failed to mention that fact.

"Amy, I..."

"You don't need me, Dan. You need Jane and you need a mistress, a lover. Someone to comfort you when your marriage becomes too tedious and trying. Someone to ignore when it suits you and to acknowledge when you feel in need of being mothered."

It was cruel and she knew it. She wanted to hurt him just as she was hurting inside, knowing he was not about to divorce his wife, for her or for anyone.

"That's not fair, nor is it true." Pain reflected in his grey eyes and he could do nothing to conceal it. "I've always loved you. When you left Berlin, I told myself I'd never have you. I gave up, but I never stopped loving you and I know I should never have let you walk out on me. I should have moved heaven and earth to win you back.

"I was wrong when I didn't pay you enough attention when I put more into my career than I did into loving you. I regret having the manners of a pig and a total lack of consideration. I know my mistakes. I've lived with them all these years. But I have no regrets about what we had. I never stopped loving you, never, not for a single moment of every day I've lived since you left me."

He longed to hold her, but all he could do was offer words for now. "You're my life, Amy. I've lived every second for today, for every day I might be given a chance to be with you again. Every moment we've ever shared I cherish. All I want is to be with you. I want to die in your arms, to take my last breath telling you how much I love you. You have to believe me."

She did, every word, but it was too late. He wore a gold band on his left hand. He also wore the shackles of an unhappy marriage. She could not, and would not cut free his chains of bondage; it was not her place to even try.

"I can't help you, Dan. You have a wife, and you have too many responsibilities."

"And you?" he asked, almost choking on his disappointment. "Is there anyone in your life?" She shook her head. "Why not?" he asked, but he was glad she was still free.

With a tired shrug, she admitted something that raised his flagging spirits. "There was only ever you. No-one else matched up." Then she dashed his hopes again. "Perhaps I'll find my Mr Right one of these days. Who knows."

"Perhaps," was all he could manage to say.

Amy refused his offer to walk her home, and she refused it rudely. "If you don't mind, I would prefer to see myself home. I know I can trust myself not to let me down." The comment cut through him like a knife, causing him further pain and it hurt her too, but she really did want to hurt him so much and so badly this time.

"Can I call you?"

"I don't think so. It's not a good idea under the circumstances; besides, I'm leaving town. Off abroad again."

"Where to this time?" He continuously feared for her safety.

"Anywhere and everywhere," she said with a weary shrug of her shoulders and a quick flick of thick auburn curls. Her hair had grown longer than he had ever seen it. She looked radiant. At almost twenty-seven, she was a beauty. Despite the indefinable sadness etched in her features, she had never looked more lovely.

Her heartstrings tugged painfully as she made once more to move out of his life. She stood and forced a resigned smile onto her lips.

"Take care of yourself, and give my best wishes to Jane when next you speak to her."

"Don't go, Amy, not like this."

"I must. Goodbye, Dan. Good luck with the new career." She left him there, his eyes filling with tears, his heart aching and a pain cutting deep into his gut. He reached into his jacket pocket and took out a flat pack of foil-wrapped tablets. He chewed on two of the chalk-based antacid tablets and paid for the meal.

That night it was Dan who cried himself to sleep having gone over and over the conversation with Amy. He'd lost her again, perhaps for good this time.

Chapter Nine

"Amy!" the elegant female, wrapped up snugly in a thick Astrakhan coat, called across the width of the busy street. "Amy Harper!"

Amy focused her eyes and smiling happily dodged between passing traffic to cross the road, her arms wide open ready to embrace her friend. "Roushaka!" she shrieked. "My god, you look marvellous!" They hugged, kissed, and danced about on the pavement in front of passers-by. Five years had gone by since last they met.

The Russian girl spoke near-perfect English. Amy spoke near-perfect Russian. They darted verbally from one language to the other - playing with words. Teasing, laughing, remembering.

Roushaka Pavalovsky - indirect descendant of the Tsar of Russia. Roushaka and Amy studied psychology together at university. They shared accommodation, food and friendship before life and circumstances took them in opposite directions.

The Russian beauty stood tall and proud, there was a positive air of regality about her being. She was an extremely bright and lively character whose personality succeeded in sparkling even on the darkest of days. Roushaka had always been fiercely proud of her royal blood. A year older than Amy and the eldest of six children, all of them female, born into the semi-luxury of hard work and good food. She was always a happy and spontaneous woman who brought out a hidden mischievous imp in Amy.

"I am so happy to see you, Amy. You look absolutely fabulous. But tell me, are you married? Are you?"

"Heavens, absolutely not!" Amy squealed. "Who would have me? Are you?"

"I was," she admitted happily. "For four whole weeks." Roushaka giggled as she confessed, "He was wonderful until I wore him out."

"Oh, you haven't changed at all. But, were you really only married for four weeks?"

"Yes," she said, her head held proudly. "Four weeks and two nights." Not four weeks and two days! "He is a splendid specimen. A Russian count."

She sighed with the fond memory of his perfect form. "Alexander came directly from my father's side. He has no money but a wonderful body." She hugged Amy again. "My dear friend, you should have seen him naked. He was a god!"

In a flurry of arms, giggles and expensive perfume, the two friends hurried towards Amy's flat in Kensington. It was snowing and with those first white flakes of the year came stories from the Russian beauty of days long ago in her homeland, days of snow and love - of great wealth and beauty. Once inside the basement rooms they shed their coats, made hot chocolate and filled in the missing pieces of their lives.

Amy heard of the godlike Count Alexander who had lost his appeal after just four short weeks and two long nights. Roushaka's eyes widened to large sparkling brown jewels as she listened to Amy speak of Daniel Jones, the man from South Wales - strong and muscular, ruggedly handsome, with a heart of pure gold. There was no way Amy could disguise the depth of her love for him, and no hiding the pain either.

"But, darling Amy, why did you leave him? You are still very much in love with him. I see it. I hear it. God, how I feel it!"

Amy nodded agreement. "It's true. I want to hate him, Rou. I really do, but I can't."

"You have not answered my question. Why did you leave him there in Berlin, are you a fool?"

"Because I felt trapped - because I wasn't ready to settle. He started getting on my nerves. Poor lamb, he could never do anything right. I know we could have worked things out if I'd been prepared to settle down. I was too young, far too young. Yes, perhaps I was a fool."

She shook her head and sighed. "I blamed him for everything, for the way I felt and for my restlessness, but it was simply because I was forced to give up what I'd longed to do, just because I'd fallen in love. I went out there to do a job, a specialised job, and I got one damned taste of action and was told I could stay, but only on the condition I accepted a desk job."

Roushaka smiled sweetly as she nonchalantly asked, "What specialist work was it? Psychology?"

"Yes." Amy brushed the question aside. "Just work. The point is I only wanted Dan at the time. I thought I could give up the excitement because of the way he made me feel, but it was simply not enough, and everything got blown up out of all proportion in my head."

"You are greedy, Amy Harper. You always were a greedy little pig." Roushaka smiled affectionately at her. "Why don't you take him back into your life? He has given up his wife. Just take him as he is. Enjoy him."

"He hasn't given her up." Amy argued. "He will always have her there. He is too loyal a man not to be bound with guilt. I have to forget him and start to live a life of my own. If only I could sleep nights without seeing him, without longing for him. It hurts me feeling this way. It's been too many years to be so damned love-struck and celibate."

"How many years of celibacy, my dear friend?" Roushaka was completely captivated.

"Five." Amy replied with a weary sigh.

"After we last met."

"Yes." Amy remembered their previous encounter. "When I was sent to Berlin. Tell me, what are you doing these days? Do you still work at the embassy here in London?"

"Yes, but I have been promoted. I have my own office, with an electronic pencil sharpener!" She raised her eyebrows and they giggled again. "I have much more work now, Amy. Although I suspect my life is not nearly as exciting as yours is. I cannot remember feeling psychology is in any way an exciting career."

After a second or two of silence she asked again, "What is it you do? I am dying to find out. You trained as I did, but my life is not action packed, not at the embassy. Everything is sleepy there."

Amy sighed again. She needed to talk, but she dared not take even her oldest friend into her confidence, particularly not her oldest and dearest Russian friend. She had her work cut out guarding her thoughts without opening her mouth and speaking the truth. Together they became two parts of a lethal weapon, an atom bomb primed and ready for detonation. They were adept at mentally ducking and diving, ever alert and conscious of the other's capabilities.

"It really is nothing. I am sure your work is much more rewarding and far less tough on your feet." A change of subject was called for. "Tell me more about your count. Why did you part? Come on, Rou, tell Amy everything."

Roushaka Pavalovsky stayed the night. They talked until four in the morning and fell asleep simultaneously, unable to chat a moment longer.

The doorbell woke them at nine next morning. Amy clambered over Roushaka who was still sleeping soundly, oblivious to all but her dreams. She reached for her robe and staggered drunkenly to the door, thanking her maker it was Sunday and she was free until Wednesday. Knowing it would take her that long to recover from sitting up nights talking with her friend.

She brushed knotted hair from her eyes in an attempt to wake herself fully and look somewhat more civilised than she felt as she opened the door to the extent of the safety chain to ask, "Who is it?"

"Amy, it's me." It was Dan.

Her heart stopped beating for too long. A hot flush spread over her and then an icy chill cooled her instantly. Her head was swimming. "How did you...what do you want?" she asked her voice was cold and hard.

"Can I come in? I need to talk to you, about yesterday, I shouldn't have let you go like that...I..."

"I have a visitor...a friend," she informed him curtly.

"I see," he said, jumping promptly to all the obvious but wrong conclusions. "Sorry. I'll see you again sometime."

As he moved away from the door, Roushaka called out to her friend and Dan was quick to pick up her dulcet tones. He turned and looked hopefully at Amy.

"Go back to sleep!" Amy shouted back over her shoulder, half wishing Dan had not heard her voice. "That is my visitor," she explained through the crack in the door. "I'm sorry, Dan. We talked all night and I'm extremely tired."

Suddenly she felt inexplicably sorry for him; he looked so damned sad standing there in the passage she pitied him. "Can you come back in a couple of hours? When I'm fully awake."

"Yes." He smiled his gratitude. "Two hours. Thanks for...for giving me a chance to talk. I'll be back. Thanks."

"Damn him to hell and back!" Amy shouted as she flounced back through the building to the bedroom. "Damn! Damn! Damn! Why do I keep falling for it? Why do I feel so bloody sorry for him?"

"I had no idea you knew as many swear words, my dear Amy." Roushaka commented flippantly. "Anyway, are you alluding to the handsome Welshman?" She was deep within the warmth of the quilt. Her big brown eyes taking in every move, every gesture made by her frustrated friend.

"Yes! Damn him! Daniel Jones! Why do I care?"

"You love him. It is as simple as that," and it really was that simple to her. "Why not care? Every one of us has the right to love and to be loved. Even Amy Harper and Daniel Jones, big and handsome though you say he is. Why are you so angry always? Why can you not accept this man for what he is and for what he has to offer? Just love him, Amy."

Amy spun to face her, glowering now with eyes dark and menacing. "Since when did you become an expert on romance?" she asked, spitting the words at her friend.

"Since I married a count, my dear friend, and since I lost him." She held the quilt open. "Come back to bed before you freeze. This place, argh, it reminds me of Siberia."

"Have you ever been to Siberia?" Amy asked, a smile beginning to replace the heavy frown.

"No."

"Then how the heck can you compare my home with that godforsaken hell hole? Anyway, I can't come back to bed. I have to get up and get dressed. You just lie there while I turn up the heating. I'll take a bath and cook something delicious and if you would like it, I'll introduce you to Daniel Jones when he returns in two hours and ten minutes."

"So precise." Roushaka commented lazily. "Why two hours and an extra ten minutes?"

"He's almost always ten minutes late," she checked the bedside clock. "He'll be here at ten minutes past eleven or I'm not Amy Harper, and you are a Russian spy."

Roushaka laughed at the suggestion and then she suddenly leapt from the bed shrieking, "My God! I am going to be shot at noon if I do not get myself back to the office. There is a big noise official paying a visit!"

"It's Sunday, Rou," Amy reminded her.

"I am aware of that; work is work." She began heaping clothes upon her beautiful naked form. "Please help me, Amy, I am desperate. This time I could end up in Siberia, and although it will not be a joke it will be better than being shot - I think!"

"Better!" Amy exclaimed. "What can I do? I know Siberia." They were laughing and hunting for a stray stocking, and then Roushaka's handbag. She found it and tossed it at Amy as she headed for the bathroom.

"Telephone the embassy. Tell them I am ill. Tell them I am dead. No, a sudden illness will suffice, I need my pay at the end of the month. Please cover for me. I can be there in thirty minutes if I run like the wind."

"The number, Rou?"

"In my bag. You have it in your hand, silly child."

Amy struggled to remember when she had last been referred to as a child, let alone a silly one. She had always been treated like an adult. Her father said she had an old head on young shoulders.

She opened the black bag and rummaged tentatively about. A woman's bag was a sacred place. A tiny torch key ring with attached assorted keys. A small round fawn-coloured leather purse. It was soft and containing what felt like loose coins and nothing else. A compact pistol, ladylike and deadly, and lastly the allusive address book, well thumbed.

"In the address book!" Roushaka called, returning from the bathroom with Amy's hairbrush in her hand. "Markarevich. Vasili Markarevich."

"Got it." Amy dialled and heard a gruff voice respond by repeating the number, firstly in Russian and then in English. Amy used her native tongue.

"Mr Markarevich?"

He grunted again.

"This is St Mary's hospital, Sister Nightingale speaking. We have a Miss Pav...Pavalovsky here." She purposely struggled with the pronunciation and Roushaka giggled quietly. "She has received minor emergency treatment."

"What has happened?" he asked sounding genuinely concerned.

"I'm afraid she had a slight fall while travelling to her office. She slipped on a step and was knocked unconscious for a short time. Miss Pavalovsky isn't seriously hurt, just a few strained muscles and a slight concussion. Nothing a day in bed won't put right. She was concerned you'd wonder at her absence from the office. Something about an important appointment."

"Where is she?" he asked, sounding like a giant of a man. His voice was massive and thunderous.

"She left the outpatient department two minutes ago. Doctor discharged her, although she'll need plenty of rest. She was badly shaken."

"Da, I will see to it. Thank you."

Amy replaced the receiver and curtseyed before Roushaka. "Am I, or am I not, a wonderful actress?"

"You are the best." Roushaka applauded her daintily. "But I really must leave." She hugged her and snatched up her bag, snapping the clasp tightly shut. "You might just have saved my life, my dear friend."

"My pleasure, Rou. When can we meet again? We must not part so quickly."

"Tomorrow. I will come. Take care, and please, be gentle with yourself, and with Dan too." She kissed both of Amy's cheeks, and hurried out.

"Gone!" Amy addressed the empty room. "Just like that, but that's Rou for you. Here one minute and gone the next."

As soon as Dan walked into the flat Amy knew she wasn't strong enough to resist the urge to be loved. He looked miserably at her and smiling said, "I had to see you. I'm sorry."

"Don't keep apologising, for God's sake, Dan!" there remained an edge of annoyance in her voice.

"Sorry," he apologised for apologising.

"What do you want?" she asked, sounding far harder than she was feeling. Inside her a volcano burned white hot. "There's nothing more to be said," but when she looked at him and saw the tears well up in his eyes her heart melted.

"Oh, Dan!" she wailed and then she was in his arms and they were both crying.

He covered her face with kisses, tasting their mingled tears on his lips. "I've missed you, little one. I love you; you have to believe me."

"I do. I do. Dan, I...I need you. Please love me."

He lifted her easily and carried her through to the bedroom where he undressed her and wrapped her in the warm quilt. His lips brushed lightly against hers and he asked, "Can I shower?"

"Quickly, please," she begged.

"I'll be quick. Don't move."

She lay still and warm, burning deep inside with a fire of anticipation, which only Dan could have ignited and only he could now extinguish. When he returned to her side minutes later, he was naked and damp from the shower. He slipped silently beneath the quilt and eased her gently towards him and she shivered as he touched her flesh, telling him without words that she was ready for him, more ready than she had ever been.

Her body was firm and her breasts fuller than when he last held her this way. She'd matured and he couldn't recall her being more beautiful. When he entered the warmth of her body, he felt a tremor of excitement course through her. She clung to him and he became lost in her, drowning in her sweetness and her love.

They loved with an unknown fiery passion and lay together satiated and more closely bonded than they had imagined possible. There was no more disputing or denying the strength of the emotions they were feeling. To deny them would have been pointless - a barefaced lie.

"Why do you keep running away from me, my little precious?" he asked.

"Because of my conscience. Because I love you too much and it scares me."

He turned to study her face. "I didn't think anything scared you, Amy."

She laughed lightly at the thought. "Well, I have news for you, this does. I don't want you in my life, Daniel Jones, because every time I accept you and your love, I risk losing you."

It was his turn to laugh. "That's a cock-eyed way of thinking. If you'd married me five years ago, we wouldn't have wasted all so much time, and there wouldn't have been the complications there are now. Hell, Amy! I've already admitted I was wrong to let you go. I was wrong to marry Jane. To feel sorry for her and to get suckered into her vile family with their tiny valley minds and their disgusting habits. The only thing I won't apologise for is wanting to take care of the child. Nor will I ever make any apologies for loving you. You are my life. I'm useless without you."

She snuggled closer to him and kissed his damp skin tasting the salt of mingled perspiration. Feeling only moderately ashamed to need him again so soon yet completely unashamed to love him so wantonly.

She cooked steak late that night and they opened a bottle or red wine and sat practically naked at the dining table for the feast. It had been a wonderful day and a glorious evening. They touched, talked, and loved, and Amy made one small concessionary promise - never to run away from him again. They knew they would be parted by occupation, but not by desire - never again by desire. They made no other promises, either to themselves or to each other. It was mutually agreed to live each day as it dawned and they would love until such time as it became impossible or unnecessary.

They were together although fully clothed when Roushaka Pavalovsky returned the following afternoon. She greeted Dan with the same amount of warmth she afforded everyone - two kisses, one on each cheek and a friendly hug which offered him no avenue of retreat. She did the same for Amy, whispering to her in Russian as she placed the first kiss upon her cheek.

"Congratulations. You took my advice." She then went on to tell them she was returning to Moscow for three weeks.

"My brother is to be married at long last," she said as she settled down next to Amy on the sofa. "He is forty-five years of age and we had almost given up on him finding a suitable bride."

As she spoke Amy frowned and looked questioningly into Dan's eyes, but he failed to interpret the look.

"When are you going?" Amy asked.

"Tomorrow. Come with me - no, you have Dan. Next time you must come with me to my home. I shall bring you a gift - a Russian doll for luck. I have not forgotten tomorrow is your birthday, Amy."

"I'm trying to," Amy said, forcing a smile. "One year older and no wiser."

"Silly! You are wise, you have Dan." Suddenly she turned her attention to the man sitting directly opposite her. "Tell me, how are you occupied, Dan?"

He frowned, thought about her words and understood. "I do as little as possible. I drive long distance lorries, or rather I aim them in the direction I wish them to go and sit back with my foot on the accelerator pedal."

They laughed and he added. "I'll be in Manchester by this time tomorrow. Back to the grindstone. Someone has to buy the bread."

Amy was glad he too had sensed untruths. Roushaka laughed loudly, seeming to see something extremely amusing in what he had said. "That is so funny. Someone has to buy the bread. You English have such a wonderful sense of humour." She saw a deep furrow form on his brow.

"Forgive me, Dan. You are not an Englishman, but you are a gentleman and you are extremely interesting and amusing."

"I'm glad you find me amusing, Miss Pavalovsky."

"Oh, darling, I'm Roushaka, please." She was looking at her wristwatch, a fancy gold timepiece, which must have cost a year's salary for even a wealthy party member. "I cannot stay. I must go and purchase a suitable wedding gift, and something divine to wear."

Before Amy could protest, Roushaka was on her feet and making for the door, her coat already on her back again. "I wish you could stay longer, Rou. When will I see you again?"

"Only God knows, my dear friend. But we will meet again, that is a promise." It all seemed ordinary, but when she refused to take hold of her outstretched hands Amy knew Roushaka was lying through her eyeteeth.

When the front door of the building closed with a slam, Amy began a frantic search of her flat.

Dan was confused at first by her thorough search and then he knew what was on her mind. "She wouldn't," he whispered directly into her ear. "She's your friend, she wouldn't bug this place."

Amy dragged him by the arm into the bathroom and after flushing the toilet and turning on the cold-water taps she spoke to him.

"Yes, she would. She's Russian and a communist through and through, irrespective of her ancestor the tsar. She answers directly to the KGB. Forget the embassy - it's just a cover. She was tense and there were too many outright lies."

"Could it be her way of showing her disapproval of me, little one?"

"No, not Roushaka, and it has nothing to do with approval or disapproval. She lied to me. She has no brother, only five sisters, all younger than she is. I do hope she'll be okay."

Dan stared long and hard at her and then he asked, "What next?"

"Search again and if we find nothing we can assume the place is bug free and let the commander know what's going on, but we must remain vigilant. No loose talk. Not until this place is swept properly."

Turning off the water, she took hold of his hand to pull him back into the living room.

They searched in vain and then Dan began pacing the floor, deep in thought. He turned the radio on and reached for the note pad which was next to the telephone.

"What does she do for a living?" he wrote hurriedly but neatly.

"Embassy." Amy wrote as she dialled a number and waited to hear the familiar voice of Commander Bernard Cooper before speaking.

"Hello, Uncle," she said, sounding far happier than she was feeling. "I've been trying to get hold of Uncle Jim. He hasn't replied to any of my calls. I was hoping he'd be able to decorate this place when I'm away next time."

"I'll be seeing him later today, Amy. He's had problems with his home phone but I'll pass on the message. Are you okay?" he replied, aware of her needs.

"Yes, perfectly healthy. I'm sorry to bother you, I know how busy you are these days."

"Think nothing of it. I always have plenty of time for my favourite niece. I'll tell Jim, he'll probably call around on his way back home."

"Great! Thanks." They exchanged polite farewells and Amy hung up. The room would be swept for electronic bugs within the hour. In the meantime, she needed to get Roushaka back into her life to find out what was going on.

Dan took her hand in his and eased her out of the chair to lead her back into the bathroom. With the taps running once again he said, "Good thinking. Now, didn't you say Rou...Roushaka is a trained psychologist?" Amy nodded. "Where does a psychologist fit in at an embassy, little one?"

"I wondered about that a long time ago," she sighed. Dan always listened to what Dan wanted to hear.

Amy sat on the edge of the bath while he took up occupation on the toilet seat, his hand reaching out to flush it before he sat down.

"I've already said I believe the embassy is a cover," she reminded him, her head close to his. "All I can come up with is that she and I have similar occupations. Although neither of us is forthcoming on the subject. There was a time, though, years ago, when she talked about her people studying the human mind in order to perfect psychological warfare. She was all against it. It scared her and she needed to talk about it, about what was happening over there."

"Did you report it?" Dan asked.

"Yes, of course, I reported what I'd learned to my superiors, and I was assured it would be looked into. That was the last I heard about it and Roushaka has kept her silence ever since."

Amy was frowning again, her brow deeply furrowed. "I keep picking up..." she just couldn't clearly define her feelings.

"Messages?" Dan suggested, opting to stand, his legs too restless to sit still for long. "Feelings? Vibrations?" he persisted in trying to help find the right word.

"Yes," she said. "Suggestions. Thoughts if you prefer. If only I could have held her hands. I need to make proper contact to find the truth."

"Would it help if she came back?"

"Yes." It was exactly what she wanted.

"Then I'll bring her back." With that, he stood, turned the taps off and went to get his coat off the hook on the back of the door leaving Amy sitting on the rim of the bath.

She wanted to laugh but couldn't. It was too silly to be funny - him chasing a Russian spy around London, and far too silly to be practical, but he was doing just that. He had no clue where to find her and if he did, what could he possibly say to persuade her to return? Amy suspected he'd go to the embassy and ask for her if he had to.

However, find her he did, and without too much effort on his part, without going anywhere near the embassy. He drew the correct conclusion, applied logic and arrived at the answer. Roushaka had no brother who was about to get married, no gift to buy, no shopping to do. What she had in mind was keeping a close watch over her friend, which meant she couldn't go too far from her.

He found her in the cosy tearoom. The one with the genuine log fire and genuine English afternoon tea and scones served off delicate crockery by genuine English-rose waitresses, dressed in a neat black dress with lace aprons and frilly doilies on their heads.

What Roushaka needed most was time to put her thoughts together. She'd assured her superiors that she could handle Amy Harper, but faced with the daunting task of gleaning precious information from her she'd lost her nerve; made up the feeble and seriously flawed lie and fled. Now she needed a solid plan before she could face her superior - Anatoli Semenychev, head of the KGB in London. He was a hard man to please.

"Roushaka!" Dan faked surprise as he pulled out a chair and sat down next to her, leaving her no avenue of escape. "What a coincidence. Fancy meeting you here. You don't mind if I join you, do you?"

"Of course not." The shock failed to show as she composed her perfectly made up, lovely face especially for him. "I was chilled through," she lied. "Besides, I rather fancied a nice cup of tea before I get on with my shopping."

He bowed his head, showing visible acceptance of her lie and then he nodded to attract the attention of the waitress who was moving gracefully in their direction anyway. "Tea please," he said, smiling politely at her. "And one of those scones, the sultana ones." He looked to Roushaka and asked, "Can I get you anything?"

"No, but thank you. I have tea."

"Just tea for one and the scone then, thank you."

"Won't be a tick, sir?" the waitress said giving a hint of a curtsey before manoeuvring her way back through the obstacle course of tables, returning within a minute with a cup of piping hot tea and a plate with a small scone, butter and a tiny pot of strawberry jam. "Is that all, sir?"

"Yes, thank you," he said stirring the tea despite failing to add sugar. He'd given it up years ago when Jane complained about him using an excess of it. To her mind, every spoonful he used was in excess of his requirement. Now, thanks to her, he rarely enjoyed a cup of tea or coffee.

He cut the scone in half and buttered it, and as Roushaka homed in on his worried expression he spread jam on the upper half and started eating.

"You look like a man with more than his fair share of worry." It was hard not to notice his furrowed brow. "Is your heart so terribly heavy, my friend?"

"Um," he said absent-mindedly as he swallowed a mouthful of scone. "It is. I had to get out of the flat for half an hour, just to clear my head and straighten out my thoughts. I'm worried sick about Amy. I don't think she's well."

Roushaka straightened in her chair. "What is wrong with her?"

"She's supposed to report back to the hospital for tests but she won't go," he lied as he lifted the bottom half of the scone. "She had some sort of a brainstorm - a type of madness. There was no reason for it but she flipped. Since then she's been absent-minded and seems to have lost something."

"Something?" she asked, sounding deeply concerned, if not a little confused.

He wiped his mouth on the serviette, having cleared the plate of scones. "Yes, something of the old astuteness. You know - the quickness to sense what someone's thinking almost before they think it themselves. It was as if she could read my mind at times. Really uncanny."

"And she no longer does this...this something?" Roushaka was swallowing the bait, along with the hook.

Dan began reeling her in. "Gone," he said dramatically, and with a sigh he added, "I've been seeing her for months but all of a sudden she made out she hadn't seen me for years. Just like that, out of the blue, like I'd never been in her life."

"She said it was five years since you met, apart from when she bumped into you while you were on your honeymoon in Holland." Roushaka proved her memory was excellent, and even when she seemed distant; she was alert and absorbing information like a human sponge.

"Honeymoon?" he questioned, looking completely perplexed. "I'm not married, Roushaka." He held up his left hand, there was no gold band; he'd given up wearing that a year earlier. "Never could marry anyone. Not when I was in love with her all this time. No, only Amy for me. You must have misheard her."

"No, I think not. She told me you have a wife. That she could not have an affair with a married man. She was angry because you came to the flat yesterday when I was there."

He laughed. "Hell, Rou, I've been living with her. Didn't you see my clothes in the wardrobe? My toothbrush in the bathroom?"

"No." That confused her even more, she hadn't really looked, and it was remiss of her, Anatoli would be furious if he ever found out. She asked herself why she failed to notice Amy's lapse of concentration, of power. Perhaps she too was losing her touch. Suddenly Anatoli became an enormous threat. Without her special abilities, she was worthless to the KGB; they would put her down like a rabid dog.

"God! She's bunged everything in the bin again!" Dan exclaimed. "I work away a lot, driving, and I'm often gone for days, up to a week at a time. I wondered where my slippers had gone, but she was so loving yesterday when I got back I really didn't need clothes. It was more like my old Amy again. More like she was before this thing went on inside her head, this brainstorm."

"Are you sure?" she asked.

"Positive. I'd give anything to get her to go to the hospital for a check-up like she's supposed to." As if by some flash of inspiration he asked, "Could you try and persuade her for me, Roushaka? Please. I love her so dearly I can't bear to think she's got a brain tumour or something just as terrible eating away inside her head and nobody's doing anything about it."

"I don't know...she would guess...I..."

He leaned forward and clutched her shoulders firmly in his big hands. "Please. I am a desperate man. I'll do anything. You could be the answer to my prayers. Please."

"I will try," she conceded. "But..."

"Oh, thank you," he said, kissing her hand, giving her no time to reassess the situation. "Just don't mention anything I've told you or she'll go funny again. I don't think I could stand to see her like it again. It scares the hell out of me. She screams and raves on, and she throws things too, anything she can get her hands on."

Roushaka nodded agreement, too confused by her own sloppiness to concentrate clearly, and far too frightened of what would happen to her if Anatoli Semenychev learned of her dereliction of duty. The possibility that she was fast becoming useless to him was beyond comprehension. She wasn't naive, she was aware her powers of perception were not nearly as pristine as they had been five years earlier. Nor were they as powerful as those of Amy Harper who could sense emotion from across a room, or at least, she could before this...this brainstorm.

"I will not mention our discussion. I have exactly one hour to spare," she said as she reached for her coat. "The shopping must wait. Amy is far more important."

He almost kissed her as she stood to leave. "Go ahead," he said. "Tell her you need some advice on what to buy or something. I'll follow on and act surprised to find you there." He intended making absolutely certain the woman went straight to Amy.

Roushaka Pavalovsky knocked on the door and waited for it to open.

"Rou!" Amy declared when she saw her standing there. Genuine surprise showed in her expression. "What brings you back so quickly? I thought you had shopping to do?"

"I have, but I could not think what I could buy as a gift for a brother who has everything. How can I select some trinket when I have no idea in my head? I thought you would know what is best to take for him."

"Come in," she said, holding out her hands to her friend. Roushaka stared at them and then she placed her hands in her friends and gave a great sigh of resignation. She could not fight this woman. She was stronger, and much cleverer, besides, if Dan were correct Amy could no longer search her mind.

Amy led her inside and closed the door on the world. "What is worrying you, Rou? Why are you frightened?"

"I am frightened of everything, my dear friend, everything. I am also frightened to go home tomorrow. My country has changed. Communism has not done it any favours. The people are as scared children; they are all suspicious of each other. All afraid of being watched and listened to."

She shivered violently. "I am cold inside my heart. I have no man to love me and hold me. You are most fortunate. Do not lose Daniel Jones. Do not be the fool I was when I gave up my Alexander so readily."

"Oh, Rou, are you really unhappy?"

"Yes." It was the truth. "I envy you, dear Amy. I envy you your homeland and your work. I wish...but wishes are for fools, and I have been fool enough already. I must leave. But first, tell me, are you well, truly well?"

Amy laughed. "Inordinately so. I have never been better," she laughed. "Do not believe everything you hear, Roushaka. Dan has a fertile imagination. He thinks every time I kick him out of my life I'm having some sort of a brainstorm."

Roushaka caught her breath and almost choked. "You...you are so strong." She knew the truth; two clever and skilled operatives had duped her.

"Nothing changes, Rou. Nothing and nobody." She needed to say no more, the Russian understood fully.

"I should leave, before Dan returns. Forgive me, but I sometimes feel I was born in the wrong place and at the wrong time. Perhaps one day things will change for me and I too will come home."

"Perhaps," Amy said. She kissed her cheek and led her to the door. "Go now, and take good care of yourself. It would grieve me if you should come to any harm." The warning was clearly understood and accepted. Roushaka left without a further word as Dan closed the outer door.

"You going so soon?" he asked quietly of her.

"Yes," she smiled directly into his eyes. "As you know, there is nothing wrong with your Amy. Love her. Keep her safe within your home and guard her with your life." She smiled fleetingly and swept passed him into the street leaving him with the subtle fragrance she was wearing and a memory of her sad yet beautiful face.

"What the hell was all that about?" he asked as he tossed his coat onto the back of the chair. "You scared the living daylights out of her."

"I think not, but tell me, what's this about me having some sort of brainstorm, Mister Jones?"

"She told you, the traitorous little baggage!"

"No," Amy said, grabbing him and clinging onto him, her arms wrapped tightly around his neck. "She said nothing. You were the one who mentioned my mental state. Anyway, what is a brainstorm, my love?"

"You...you...witch!" He kissed her passionately. "Is the place...you know?" he asked when their lips parted.

"It's clear," she told him. "Jim came and did a sweep. We're okay."

"Thank God. Did you have any luck with her, apart from scourging her mind?"

"Hardly scourging, my darling Dan. I sense things, remember?" She was teasing him again. "She was lying. She is working for them and in a similar capacity to my line of work. They sent her to find out what I'm up to. They want me, Dan."

He held her at arm's length and studied her face, as was his way. "Explain for a simpleton please."

"They've wanted me for years. I suspected it a long time ago, but I had no proof until...until today. I still have no hard evidence. I just know I'm one step ahead of them.

Roushaka Pavalovsky is not as strong as they would like her to be and I think I'm going mad."

Dan left her and went into the kitchen to make two mugs of coffee, returning with them to sit silently next to her again.

"Thanks," she whispered as she took the mug off him. "What in God's name am I going to do?" she asked.

He sighed, a deep, deep sigh. "I don't know what to say because I'm not certain I understand any of this." Before she could speak, he hurried on. "I know I love you, little one. I also know that you are, without doubt, a special person. I think I see the real you, where others only see your beauty and your strength. I see a lovely being, a special, gifted person who gets lonely from time to time, who needs to be loved and protected but never caged. A free spirit."

Amy looked at him with large moist amber eyes and smiled lovingly at the only man she knew she could trust with her life. "You're too kind to me."

"Rubbish!" He returned the smile. "Don't ever argue with me on the subject of my Amy."

"When do you have to leave?" she asked suddenly, quietly, afraid of what she already knew he was going to say.

"Day after tomorrow."

"Then let's not waste a moment of our time together."

Dan stayed there with her, in the warm basement flat in the heart of the city. They celebrated her twenty-seventh birthday in style with a hamper of food from Harrods and a bottle of champagne, a gift from the commander.

They loved and they talked, but neither of them mentioned Roushaka Pavalovsky. A full report was filed with Commander Cooper and again a promise to 'Look into it' was made.

Dan came and went, in and out of Amy's life. The big Welshman with the enormous heart who worshipped the ground she walked upon. When Amy worked, he worried. When she was there in his arms, he prayed they could remain together always.

Chapter Ten

Exactly one year after Dan returned to her, Amy was forced into making necessary changes to her lifestyle. The telephone rang in the middle of the night on January 23, 1973. It was St Bartholomew's Hospital; her mother was seriously ill and asking for her. Amy dropped everything and left immediately.

Dan drove her to the hospital; kissed her passionately and told her quite firmly to ring him the instant she needed him. She had no idea what to expect and no way of knowing how she would react one month later when faced with another huge decision.

When given the choice of career or caring for a loved one, it was an easy decision for Amy, she chose to put her career on temporary hold and went home to look after her mother who was now a very frail old lady. None of the doctors or specialists told Amy the truth, but in the middle of May she knew that her mother was dying, she also knew without doubt she was carrying Dan's child.

Two long months had gone by since last she saw him. He was working in Germany again; somewhere in the south was all she could extract from the boss. All the comfort she received was one hastily written note and an even more hastily despatched telephone call.

"Amy, it's me. I love you, little one. Had to hear your voice. Can't stop. Take care, little darling."

As she replaced the receiver, she felt an overwhelming need to break something. He'd wanted to hear her voice yet all she'd managed to utter was his name and a brief goodbye. Damn it! She needed him, now, by her side. The mornings were waking nightmares with dizzy spells and nausea. Her knees were constantly weak and she felt helpless. Days were hell.

Her mother, who was a constant source of worry, was unable to rest, eat or do anything more than lie staring up at the ceiling. However, she remained cheerful although concerned about her daughter. The old lady was full of fight. That was what got to Amy the most - her fight. Her mother was relentless in her bid to survive.

"Commander Cooper, it's me, Amy."

"Good morning, Amy. How is your mother today?" The gruffness of tone, which he generally adopted for his operatives, was instantly dropped as paternal tenderness echoed along the line to her.

"A little weaker, sir. Every day I see a big difference in her."

"I'm very sad to hear that," he said, although she knew he really only wanted her back in harness. She'd been on indefinite leave for over six months, it was a long time to be off work. She was totally committed to caring for her dying mother. Everything else came second to that commitment.

"I'm actually ringing to let you know that I need to extend my leave yet again, sir. I am most terribly sorry."

"No problem," he said sounding cheerful. "Do what you have to do, there's no point living with regrets. Is there anything I can do for you, or for your mother?"

"No thank you, Commander." She paused and then she said, "There is one small thing actually, sir. Have you any idea where Dan Jones is at present?"

The commander was aware of their relationship. There was nothing he wasn't aware of, with the exception that an infant was growing within the confines of her womb -

growing larger and stronger every day. He knew nothing of that new life. Only Amy knew.

"Yes," he said. "As a matter of fact I do. He's back home Wales. His wife was ill; she needed a hysterectomy, or a mastectomy or something. He went home a month ago." Cooper paused. "I'm sorry, Amy. Don't you think it's time you stopped wasting yourself?" She remained silent and so he added, "It's none of my business, I know, but I think you're wasting yourself."

"I have to go, sir. My mother just woke up. Thank you." She hung up before he could utter another sound. Her hands were trembling uncontrollably as she fought tears and building nausea.

"You look ill," Ruth Harper observed later that same day. "What's wrong with you, Amy?" She missed nothing. Her eyesight was excellent and she'd watched her daughter changing, seen her body alter, her flat stomach growing and rounding, an infinitesimal change, but those sharp eyes had witnessed it happen. "Are you pregnant, my darling?"

Amy nodded forlornly. She'd hoped to spare her this, but now, as her mother opened her arms to her she was glad she knew. Relieved to have someone to share the burden, she clung to Ruth's frail body, sobbing bitterly and hating Dan - hating his wife - hating life and hating death more. Yet strangely without hatred, just the intensity of the emotion, just anger, frustration and confusion. She was suffering with her mother; feeling her pain, sensitive to her troubles and her massive swings of mood.

"Mamma, I'm so sorry. I didn't want you to know," she sobbed, a child again.

"Well, I do know. How far on are you?"

"Five months," yet she didn't look it; more like three. She was very small and very slim. Only a loving eye could have detected the swollen dome of her swelling womb.

"Five months!" she repeated. "Are you certain?"

"Yes. I forgot to take my pill. I know exactly when I conceived."

Ruth needed much more information. Amy had successfully kept her private life very private. "Who is the father? Will he marry you?"

Amy shook her head and began crying again. When her tears abated, she spoke to her mother, and for the first time she told her everything. "His name is Dan. He already has a wife."

Fresh tears began to spring to life again but she dashed them away, took a deep breath and went on. "We were in love...years ago, when I came home from Berlin. I left him for my career. We met up again, but there was nothing between us, just a loving friendship, no...no sex. Then he left her, Mamma, separated from her. I just would not...I could never have...not with a married man."

"No, I know, but what concerns me most is how poorly you look right now. I want you to tell Doctor Crawford when he calls to see me tomorrow."

"No, Mamma. I'm fine, really, I am," yet she was anything but fine, she'd been ill for months and it wasn't getting any better. Now, to crown it all, she was suffering recurring nightmares. Things were not right but she placated her mother, convinced her she'd talk to the doctor although she was perfectly well.

She permitted the family doctor to examine her during the following week. She underwent routine blood tests and a scan and learned that apart from being over-tired she was in fact perfectly healthy. The foetus was twenty-week gestation and healthy – a small but healthy baby, kicking and moving exactly as was expected at five months.

The news delighted Ruth who declared herself to be, 'On the mend.' It put roses back into her pale cheeks when she talked of the pleasure a grandchild would bring her. She and Amy talked about the baby and despite the pain deep within her; Amy looked forward to holding Dan's child.

She knew that her life would alter. That she would be housebound and responsible for a new life, but the sacrifice was worth it. The child was Dan's and she loved it already. If only the terrible fear, which was also growing exponentially, would cease. If only Dan could come back to her. If only - there were too many if only's.

There were always too many of those in her life. If only she hadn't gone to Berlin and met Dan in the first place. If only she'd married him and stayed in his life. If only they hadn't become lovers again. If only. Those two words had to be the saddest Amy knew.

Ruth Harper lived for three more weeks. During that time Amy and Ruth grew closer than they had since she was a child. They reminisced and went through all the family photographs, laughing and even crying with fond and sad memories. Then one morning in late July, Amy went to help her wash, her mother looked at her, smiled and slipped quietly away. There was no pain for her - she simply stopped living. Despite all of her preparations, Amy was devastated by her death. She felt as if she was completely alone in the world, alone apart from the little infant tucked safely inside her.

She laid her mother to rest alongside her father in the quiet graveyard in Bromley, Kent, and returned to work two weeks later, August 20, 1973.

Commander Cooper noted her pale complexion and far away looks. "Are you holding up okay?" he asked pulling out a chair for her to sit down. She'd changed during her many months of absence. He wasn't altogether certain he knew exactly what was different about her, and whatever it was, it disturbed him enormously.

"I'm okay," she assured him. "What I need more than anything is to return to work, to keep my mind occupied."

Amy was immaculately turned out, although Cooper had never seen her anything but immaculate. The suit, which had cost her a small fortune, was so beautifully cut it cleverly disguised her swollen body. With soft folds of fabric drawing all-seeing eyes away from her middle, there was no way anyone would have guessed she was so far into her pregnancy.

She knew that she'd have to face the truth one day very soon, but she really did need the occupational therapy, which, in her estimation, was the only thing to help her sleep nights right now. Just one last job and then Cooper would know everything. She would retire gracefully and become a devoted mother.

"You're on the service flight out of Innsworth, first thing tomorrow, heading for Brugen. They have someone they want you to work with, a bad case. Needs sorting out and fast. Lost his nerve. You'll get a detailed report before you leave here today."

"Fine. How long will I be there?"

Cooper frowned. Amy had never before asked such a trivial question. "As long as it takes." He replied suspiciously. "What's your hurry?"

"No hurry, sir, just curious."

The Royal Air Force flight to Brugen in West Germany was as crisp and efficient as was to be expected of a military flight. Had they been aware that Amy was six and a half months pregnant they would most certainly have questioned her need to fly and suggested she board the first available ferry across the English Channel. As it was, she said nothing and they welcomed her on board the VC10, made her comfortable and left her to enjoy the flight.

With her eyes closed, she focused her attention on relaxing her body and mind. She thought of Dan. She saw his face and heard his voice and she ached for him. Her life was empty without him. Until the death of her mother, she'd had someone to talk to. Once more she found herself lonely and afraid.

At RAF Brugen she was made welcome, and given officer status so that she could be accommodated in the Officers' Mess. The accommodation was superb, as was the food. The company was excellent whenever she sought it, and the work was very much routine for her - the evaluation and rehabilitation of a psychiatric patient in the British Military Hospital.

Her patient was thirty-year-old Squadron Leader Angus Neerson, who had experienced the terror of internment in an Eastern Bloc country. A simple holiday in Yugoslavia turned into a nightmare from which he would undoubtedly never fully recover. He'd inadvertently crossed a border into a Soviet training area and had been arrested as a spy.

The Soviets despatched Neerson to a 'special diagnostic department' for thorough investigation by white-coated doctors who employed drug therapy to induce the required answers to their questions. They bound him like a mummy in wet canvas and as the canvas dried, it contracted very slowly and Neerson suffered excruciating pressure on his body.

When the psychiatric examination ended, they led him back to a cold damp cell without food, water or light where he lay in the corner for two full days. They then turned a spotlight on him and blinded him for a further day and night. They got nothing from him, there was nothing for him to give, and so they handed him to the British Consul in Belgrade.

Neerson was thin and pale and yet he continuously insisted that he'd been properly treated and that the whole thing had been his own mistake. He said he'd fallen, hurt his head and broken his arm, and they took him to a hospital and treated his wounds. The doctors at the BMH could find no proof of his having been injured, other than superficially. There was no evidence of a fracture, old or newly healed, on his arm. He took two weeks' sick leave, convinced the medical officer that he was perfectly healthy and returned to work.

He seemed fit and happy until he began a gradual mental breakdown, in which he attempted to throttle his senior officer and rampaged throughout the station brandishing a precious ceremonial sword. He wasn't drunk on either occasion and afterwards had no recollection of having done anything untoward.

When Amy spoke to him, he answered very precisely and he was polite at all times - a true gentleman in fact. It was on her seventh visit that she reached across the table and placed her hand on his. "Tell me about it, Angus."

He laughed. "About what, Miss?"

"The Soviet hospital, the prison cell. How did they treat you?"

"There was no prison cell," he laughed several times. "What are you talking about?" As he spoke, he attempted to extricate his hand from beneath hers, but she held on to him.

"The Soviets," she said quietly and with infinite compassion. "At the institute and the prison. How did they treat you?"

"I...I really do not know what you are talking about, Miss." Each word bore heavy emphasis. He was beginning to perspire profusely yet the room was cool enough to be considered cold.

"In the Soviet sector, Angus. They held you at Rastich for three months. They locked you up and beat you. They took you to the institute where doctors gave you drugs. They bound you and tortured you. They starved you and deprived you of water and light and then they blinded you with light."

The man was beginning to panic. His eyes darted around the room searching for an escape route, but Amy held on to him and he listened to her, there was something compelling about her voice.

"There was an iron bed with a hard mattress in your cell," she went on. "You remained on the floor, in the corner. There were bugs and lice. They bothered you at first but you got used to them."

"No!" he exclaimed. "I got bitten when I had my accident. I fell and I lay on the ground for a week. Broken bone in my arm. My head was hurt, damaged. I couldn't move. I was scared half to death. Then someone came and helped me. Insects in the fields bit me. There were rats. I was..."

"You were in a cell, Angus," she interrupted. "You were drugged and starved and beaten. There was no fall or head injury, you had no broken bones. You urinated in a small tin can until it was full and spilled over onto the concrete floor. You had diarrhoea and they refused you the use of a toilet. They laughed at you and left you to lie in your own excrement."

Amy paused, as the horrors of what she was sensing became reality to her, she shivered violently. "They tortured you yet you told them nothing of any interest and they released you. You're telling me exactly what they programmed you to tell me. It is not the truth. You must face the truth and together we will help ease out all of that pain from inside you."

His eyes were wide and filled with terror; Amy had seen that look too many times before. He began screaming as he shoved the table into her and headed for the door. "Let me out!" he demanded and within seconds the door opened and a male nurse led him out of the room.

Winded and still shaken by what she'd sensed from Neerson, Amy sat with her eyes closed. When she opened them, Group Captain James Bishop was standing looking down on her. He raised his eyebrows and asked, "Are you going to explain what just went on, Miss Harper?"

When she shook her head, he reached across the table and pressed the rewind button on the cassette recorder.

When the tape was running and her voice seemed to fill the room, he picked the chair up off the floor, placed it back on four legs and sat on it.

"Is it true?" he asked as he turned the recorder off.

"Yes," she said quietly, still visibly pale and shaken.

"How do you know all of this?" he asked.

"It...it isn't possible to explain to you, Group Captain, but I know I can help him. I have done it many times before."

"How can you possibly know something, which is not documented, and that the patient has not spoken of? Are you privy to Soviet information, Miss? Because if you are...well, I cannot permit you to remain in my..."

Her eyes were locked on his. "Sir, I am most certainly not privy to Soviet information, nor am I working for the KGB. My credentials are genuine; I am a psychologist with many years of experience in this field. Given time, Squadron Leader Neerson will tell us everything that happened to him. At present, he is unwilling and unable to divulge the information because he's been brainwashed into believing that his family will be slaughtered should he speak of what happened to him. I need time with him."

"I don't think I can agree to that. He was doing well until this session, and now he's being sedated for his own good. I can't permit you to undo the good work we've already done, Miss Harper."

"Sir, I can help him. Please, just trust me."

He sighed deeply. "I will consider your request, together with the well-being of my patient, and you'll have my decision by the end of the day."

There was nothing more to say, she watched him walk out of the room. Amy would not give up without a fight.

Amy was sitting alone at the dining table in the middle of the day when an extremely handsome man approached her and asked if she minded sharing his company.

"I hate eating alone," he said. "Do you mind?"

She smiled and acquiesced with a slight inclination of her head and a brief smile. Her face was still very pale and a pain cut into her middle where Neerson had rammed the table into her. "Amy Harper," she said as she held out her hand to the stranger.

"Roger," he said. "Roger Longhurst. I'm pleased to meet you, Amy."

A petite young waitress approached the table and spoke to him, "Good evening, Flight Lieutenant. Would you like to see the menu?" He looked politely at Amy and the waitress hastily informed him, "Miss Harper has ordered, sir."

"Then in that case I don't need a menu, I'll have my usual please, Vicky."

Amy, in the meantime, was studying the stranger who had proven a minor distraction for her. He wasn't a tall man, about five feet eight inches and slim in build with the makings of a paunch, which seemed a contradiction in terms, yet it was how she saw him. He gave off the appearance of being skin and bones. Upon closer inspection, she could see he was merely of small frame with no visible excess body fat. Having had many experiences of living in various officers' accommodation Amy knew that the budding paunch was a result of rich food and most probably an excess of strong liquor.

She had no way of knowing that Roger enjoyed the niceties of life - a fast car, wine women and the very best cuisine. His entire life had consisted of home-cooked food in plenty and then the Royal Air Force mess halls in which he could indulge himself to the excess if he so wished. The Mess at RAF Brugen provided him the opportunity to be waited upon with extremely rich food and a plentiful supply of low-cost alcohol. His work involved sitting behind a desk. His social life offered him the only exercise he extended to his body, and that entailed lifting a glass at the bar.

Roger Longhurst was a linguist, fluent in Russian and Polish. His work largely involved the translation of documentation, usually information gleaned from monitored telephone calls, and occasionally he was called upon to act as interpreter.

He was a lazy man in general, one with no ambition other than to one day procure a wife. Marriage would prove a convenience to him, if he could fall in love at the same time, it would be most fortunate. Socially polite at all times and a wonderful companion when under the influence of any intoxicating substance; he preferred his overseas tour of duty to being UK bound. The tax-free tobacco and drink entitlements were largely responsible for that preference.

At 38 years-of-age the most he could look forward to, was retirement in twelve years' time and a big fat pension, with which he could settle back and do nothing for the remainder of his days. After a thirty-year career in the Royal Air Force, he would be well taken care of.

"Sorry?" she said, realising he was speaking to her.

"I wondered if you'd care for a drink while we wait."

"No, thank you. I'm sticking with water tonight. I have important work tomorrow and I need a clear head."

"On the base?" he asked.

"At the hospital," she replied.

"Ah, a doctor," he said, certain he was right.

"Actually..." she hesitated for a moment, "I'm a psychologist." What the hell, she thought. There is no secret in what I am.

"Ah," he said again. "A trick cyclist."

Amy smiled. It was a common misconception. "Not psychiatrist," she corrected him. "Psychologist. There is a subtle difference, or so I'm told."

"Sorry. Don't want to sound ignorant but I never had much to do with hospitals and all things medical, although

I did go out with a rather pretty little nurse a few years back. Black as the night she was, a real beauty." He poured water into a glass and sipped it before speaking again. "What exactly is the difference?"

"Psychology is a scientific study of behaviour. I specialised in clinical psychology. I work mainly in hospitals, playing a role in diagnosis and treatment, working closely with the medical team. My work involves research and teaching and it's very interesting."

"Sounds very like a trick cyclist to me." Roger said, laughing at her now.

"Hardly," Amy countered. "Psychiatry is the study and treatment of mental diseases, or disorders if you like. I work on the mind and the soul, mine is a theory of mental laws and phenomena."

"I see, and this important work you have to do tomorrow, it doesn't mean you're about to fly off and leave me all on my own again, does it?"

She looked around the dining room at the other military personnel eating or about to eat, at least two dozen in all. "You are hardly alone, Roger, but to answer your question, I don't know. I really have no idea how long I'm going to be here. I could well find myself on a flight out by tomorrow morning," she looked at her wristwatch. "I should know one way or the other before the sun goes down. Ask me next time you see me."

If anyone had asked Amy what it was she liked about Roger Longhurst, after she'd shared the afternoon with him, she would have no doubt replied: "He's good company." But then, all she was doing was drowning her sorrows in soda water and the company of a stranger. Any stranger, particularly a man, was better company than no company at all. She wanted Dan and she knew that she could never have him.

She was heading for her room when a Mess steward chased after her and informed her that Group Captain Bishop wanted to see her at the hospital at 17:00 prompt. She thanked him and went to tidy herself up before facing the music.

Jimmy Bishop invited her to sit down. He poured her a cup of tea and placed it on the low table between the two leather sofas in his vast office. When he sat facing her, he crossed his legs and folded his arms and then he seemed to come to a decision. "I'm going to let you speak to Squadron Leader Neerson just one more time, Miss Harper, and I will sit in on the session."

"Fine," she agreed, relieved that she had partly won the battle. "Thank you."

"I spoke to the commander," he informed her. There was no warmth for her in his voice. "He signalled me a few notes from your file and I want you to know that I don't go along with all this psychobabble. I believe in calling a spade a spade, so you can rest assured that I will not tolerate anything unconventional."

"Not even if it saves the sanity of one of your officers, sir?"

"Frankly, I don't believe there's much wrong with the man," he argued, unable to respond to her question. "Nothing a few months of hard work won't put right. I believe he's looking for his ticket out of the force - a medical discharge and a healthy pension."

"With respect, sir, you could not be more wrong. What he's been through I pray we will never know." A shudder travelled through her leaving her cold. "There's nothing mysterious about me, Group Captain. Take a look - I'm just an ordinary woman. The only difference is that I am fortunate to be blessed with some extra senses, or at least, the ability to use the senses we are all born with and generally waste. Despite what you may or may not have read about me, I think you should know here and now, I cannot read minds. It is not how it works. I sense emotion. I am very perceptive and receptive." Briefly, she wondered how many more times she was going to be saying the same thing.

He remained silent and she went on, "I have no way of explaining to you what goes on in my head, it's been scientifically studied at great length, not to mention great cost. I had two choices when I came to selecting a career, I could go with the circus freaks and put myself in a sideshow, or I could use my precious gifts to help others.

"There really wasn't any choice for me. I'm not interested in getting rich quick. My values and priorities lie elsewhere. I work for our government, just as you do. When I have the opportunity, I work very hard and I aim to achieve excellent results. I set high standards for myself. You don't have to believe in anything, sir, but I can assure you that your patient has been to hell and back and he is currently terrified for the safety of his wife and three daughters. You see, Group Captain, subconsciously he knows what the Soviets can do to destroy a human being, and there is no way he can permit that to happen to the women he holds more dearly than his own life.

"I'll speak with him at nine in the morning. You're welcome to sit in on the session and to speak your mind at any time during that session. I ask only that you trust me implicitly."

"I see no way I can make that sort of promise, Miss Harper; however, I will try to keep an open mind in the light of what you've told me." He heaved a sigh and made to move out of his seat. "At the end of the day, I really am only interested in the welfare of my patient, you know."

"Yes, sir, I am very aware of that, and I promise you I will do nothing to jeopardise his well-being. Thank you." As she stood beside him, she offered him her hand and he took it. In doing so he felt the warmth of her pass into his body, and it was as if he'd known and trusted her all of his life.

There was a wild look in the eyes of the Squadron Leader as he watched the young psychologist enter the room and sit down in front of him the next day. "Good morning," she said smiling at him. "How are you today?"

"There's nothing wrong with me," he assured her before she had the opportunity to say another word. "I don't know why everyone is making such a damned fuss. I just want to get home to Polly and the girls."

"I know, and that's why I've been asked to speak to you, so that I can help you get back to them, and back to work too, you must miss work."

"I suppose so," he agreed reluctantly.

"Do you recall our conversation of yesterday?" she began. He nodded that he did and she went on." Good. Then in that case you can tell me what happened to you when the Soviets took you prisoner."

He turned his eyes and looked slyly at the Group Captain sitting to his left at the far side of the room. "Nothing happened," he said.

Patiently, so very patiently, Amy coaxed him to speak to her, assuring him that anything he had to say would be in complete confidence, and when he did attempt to speak, he was close to tears and very angry with her for drawing the truth out into the open.

"I know this is hard," she whispered as she placed her hands over his. "I understand. Please talk to me, Angus. I can help you. You need help. Talk to me, there's no shame in what you did, you survived."

Suddenly everything burst out of him as if some giant floodgate opened. He cried, he laughed and he told her everything he could recall of what happened to him, everything he believed to be the truth.

He learned to trust her, and she began the slow process of clearing away his fears.

"Thank you," Group Captain Bishop said as he shook her hand at the end of what had seemed to be a very long but fruitful session.

"You are very welcome," she told him as she gathered up her notes. "With your permission I'll do all the groundwork and then I can leave him in your safe hands. I need two weeks at the very least."

"You have it," he assured her. "Take as long as you need. I'll inform the commander that you are to be our guest for as long as it takes."

Amy sensed there was something on his mind. "Thank you," she said again, waiting for him to spit it out.

"Can you spare me a couple of minutes in my office?" he asked.

"Yes, of course. When?"

"Right now, if that's okay with you."

He waited until she was sitting comfortably with a cup of tea in her hand before he said what was on his mind. "I owe you an enormous apology, Miss Harper."

"Amy, please, and you owe me nothing. I came here to do my work to the best of my ability. I don't expect anyone to understand how I work, or to approve of my methods, unconventional as they often are. I really am accustomed to being treated like a leper by those who prefer to stick to what they know and trust. It isn't a problem for me. I never was your run-of-the-mill little girl. It was often difficult at school, even after I went to a special school, where I was supposedly amongst my own."

"It must have been hard for you."

"Yes," she agreed. "But it's going to come in useful when the first aliens land on earth. They can send me out to do the meeting and greeting, I'll know exactly how they feel."

He laughed and for the first time since meeting her, he actually relaxed in her presence. "Is there anything you need?" he asked at last.

Yes, she thought, the man I love. "Nothing," she said. "I'm very comfortable at the Mess. The only problem I'll have during the next two weeks is keeping my weight down."

They chatted for another few minutes, he thanked her again and she took a leisurely stroll back for lunch.

By dinnertime she was feeling one hundred percent better. The pain was gone from her stomach and she had a deep sense of satisfaction from her work with Angus Neerson. She ate properly for the first time in days and decided to sit in the bar for a couple of hours - it was either that or her lonely room and thoughts of Dan and the child deep within her. She was still grieving for her mother and she had nobody to help her through it.

"Hello, stranger," Roger called to her from where he was propping up the bar. She hadn't seen him there until he spoke to her. The truth was, she didn't intentionally look for him. He pulled out a stool and she climbed up onto it. "What would you like?"

"Ginger ale, and a parachute please," she said as she adjusted the front of her blouse. "Just in case I fall off this perch."

He raised his left eyebrow, smiled and asked, "Are you staying?"

"For a while."

"Good." He ordered the drinks and invited her to sit further away from the bar and closer to the ground.

When they were comfortably seated, she asked, "What are you doing here, in Brugen I mean, not the mess bar?"

He smiled and tapped the side of his nose with the index finger on his right hand and she laughed. "What's so funny?" he asked, his face bright and smiling at her.

"Oh, it's nothing," she replied. "Just the secrecy. My life is dull in comparison."

"What exactly does a psychologist do at the BMH?" he asked, mildly curious about her, sensing there was more to her than was visible, but she too tapped the side of her nose, and they both laughed.

And that was how Flight Lieutenant Longhurst entered her life. Some rare quality about him appealed to her. There was also a certain weakness, which was a challenge to her. He was insecure and he drank far too much alcohol during the course of the day. Even so, she liked him and she was in desperate need of a friend.

After three full weeks, Amy wrote a report recommending that her patient be referred for evaluation and extensive treatment in the RAF Psychiatric Unit at the Princess Alexander Hospital, in the United Kingdom. The hospital was close to Swindon and Amy would have easy access to him to monitor his progress.

In the report, she also stated that in her opinion he should be given early retirement from the Royal Air Force. She doubted his ability to function as he once had. His mind was unbalanced after the three months of drug abuse and the primitive torture methods used by the KGB in all its many guises. Some patients were able to adjust, but in her opinion this man was permanently scarred, of that she had no doubt.

At some stage during her return flight to London, Amy experienced severe stomach cramps. She was almost eight months into her pregnancy by this time, yet she remained small and slim. Naked she could see the swelling that was her unborn child. Clothed, it hardly showed. She looked plump and content. The child squirmed, kicked and turned. Amy loved the feelings within her. They were feelings that brought Dan back into her life. She knew in her heart he would never be hers, but this little one would be. It was someone for her to hold on to and someone who needed her just as much. Amy loved the life growing inside her.

The cramps grew in intensity until she knew she needed to seek urgent professional help and the minute she'd reported to the commander she headed for her doctor.

"How long have you been like this?" he asked.

She looked into his all-seeing, all-knowing eyes and decided to be honest, for the sake of her child. "For the past six hours," she took a deep breath and said, "I'm losing my baby, am I not, Doctor?"

"Not if I can help it," he replied. "But it is a warning. You need to rest, young lady. Feet up. No work, or you will lose your baby."

"I've only just started back," she complained.

"Look, you've gone this far, why risk everything now, just for the sake of getting back into harness?"

She went home and confined herself to bed. Two days later, when she went through the living room to answer the hall telephone, she felt what she thought was her waters break, something seemed to pop and then a hot, sticky liquid trickled down her legs. To her horror, when she looked down, she saw she was bleeding profusely, with the shock came the first of many excruciating pains which threatened to sever her in two.

"Hello," she said through clenched teeth as she silenced the telephone.

"Amy, it's me, Dan."

Her heart stopped beating for two full beats. "Dan...I...I can't talk. I'm busy."

"Okay, when?"

She needed him, and now, not later. She knew she couldn't and wouldn't ask him to come to her.

"I don't know...I'll ring you." She replaced the receiver, knowing he hadn't given her his number, but the pain was so severe she doubled over in agony. Her cry reached out into the emptiness of her home and she fell, pulling the telephone receiver down with her.

After moments of unconsciousness, she recovered sufficiently to dial her doctor's number. A recorded message told her that the surgery was closed. There were numbers to ring for a variety of services, and advice to call 999 in an emergency. She blacked out again.

When she woke, she was lying in a massive dark pool of congealing blood. She cried out again. Her baby - she was losing her precious baby! She and gave her name and address to the operator and then she prayed help would arrive in time.

Fifteen minutes later, the unlocked side door burst open and strong hands lifted her. Kind voices sounded in her head, offering reassurance and comfort, but all she knew was she was losing Dan's child.

So intense was her misery that she retreated into her own silent private place while those caring hands helped deliver her baby.

Amy cut herself off from the searing pains and from what was now certain. Without Dan and his child, she had no reason to live.

Chapter Eleven

Her son lived for six hours. He was perfect. Amy held him and loved him and she watched him take his last precious breath. She named him David Daniel and the vicar arrived to baptise him. He stayed on with Amy, offering her words of comfort but he had no answers that made sense for her. He made all of the necessary arrangements for the burial of the tiny infant and left her alone with her grief.

Nobody could feel her pain or her terrible sorrow. Nobody could possibly know how very lonely she was. She was a private person who had grown up keeping her feelings locked within herself. She cried inside, in silence. She grieved privately and her grief was destructive and evil, as is always the case. It ate away at her sensibilities. She bled deep inside for the death of her precious son, and then she vowed never to tell Dan.

However, Amy had not reckoned on the commander telling him. There was nothing the man didn't know. He learned of her being hospitalised within hours of the birth. One telephone call to the hospital administrator and he knew exactly why she was there. He pulled rank, told lies, did whatever was necessary, but he did get to the truth.

Dan arrived in time to take her home. She looked tiny and delicate. Shaken firstly by the death of her mother and then shattered by the death of the little boy she'd learned to love as only a mother can. Amy was devastated by circumstances, by fate.

She stared at him when he stood in the open doorway of the single-bedded ward. She stared, wondering how he knew. She stared, wondering how he dared just turn up after so long. And then she returned to packing her few bits and pieces into a carrier bag. Three days after the birth of her son she was going home to bury him.

"Amy, I'm sorry. The commander thought perhaps you could use a friend."

"Is that what you are, Dan?" she asked quietly, looking at him now. "Are you my friend?"

"Yes. I am your friend." He longed to reach out and comfort her.

She sniffed at his words. He was her friend, so perhaps she should get it in writing this time. Proof of friendship for a rainy day, rainy and lonely - damned lonely.

"I have news for you," she said. "I don't need you." And with satisfaction she saw that her words had cut deeply into him. But the satisfaction was shallow and short-lived because she had never truly wanted to hurt him - she adored him.

He followed her into her flat an hour later. She'd agreed to accept his offer of a ride home. There was no conversation between them, no warmth at all. They were worse than strangers. As he closed the front door and turned to face her, he saw the massive dark stain on the hall carpet and Amy staring down on it. "Why didn't you tell me?" he asked.

"Tell you what, that I was pregnant? It was none of your damned business!" she shouted at him now, "That's why!" She began tugging at the edge of the carpet in an attempt to tear it up.

"Leave it," he said, "I can do that."

"I can do it myself!" she yelled, shrugging off his hand.

"Amy!" He reached for her arm and pulled her towards him but she fought him. "Amy, my little one. My poor baby." As those words left his mouth, she swung both of her fists at him - lashing out angrily, pounding his chest. He

192

stood holding her, taking the punishment, permitting her to vent her anger on him. He loathed himself anyway and he fully understood why she needed to hurt him.

Suddenly she fell limp against him, she could fight no more, it was futile, and her baby was dead. She wept then, for her parents and for her precious tiny son and she wept for herself and Dan. Then the sadness and regret took hold and she wept some more. At last, the tears ran dry and he lifted her, carrying her into the bedroom where she slept in his arms, waking to see him looking at her, studying her, his eyes full of love just as they had been when they were together in Berlin.

"I'm sorry," she whispered.

"No need. I understand." He wanted to know about the child, but he was afraid to ask. Amy sensed what was on his mind without him uttering a sound. She began moving away from him.

"You shouldn't have come here, Dan. You have a wife. This is not your place."

"Amy, I love you."

She turned away. "I know you do. But you're a married man with commitments and I won't come between you. You must go, and stay gone this time. There's no place for you here."

She spoke each word slowly and precisely, wanting him to understand that she meant exactly what she was saying, no more and no less. "Please go."

"I love you," he repeated.

"I know."

"I'm sorry, Amy."

"I know that too."

"Do you still love me?" He asked and she nodded sadly. "Was that my son, Amy?"

As she moved her head to look at him a hard shell formed around her, cutting him out of her life. He saw it in her eyes and felt it with his soul. She refused to reply and that refusal told him everything he needed to know.

"I'm always here for you," he said as he stood to leave. "Always. I've made mistakes but never in loving you. Take care of yourself, little one." He touched her cheek with the backs of his fingers, brushing the velvet-like skin.

"I wish you happiness," he said and as the door closed quietly behind him, she went back to sleep.

There remained a quiet anger within Amy following the death of her son. It was an anger that grew in magnitude and intensity, brewing, stirring, ever restless. Yet it was indeed a very quiet anger. To the world she was the same gentle, caring, understanding Amy. To those who'd known her as she'd once been, the change was obvious and frightening. There was a deep-rooted need burning inside her. It was an unspoken need to be loved, to be useful in a completely new way. She recognised that need; that desire for fulfilment, yet there was nothing she could do about it. She'd closed the door on her own fate and sealed it as tightly as was humanly possible. All she could do was exist from day to day, and exist was indeed all she did.

Commander Bernhard Cooper asked her how she was coping on the day of her return to work and left it at that. Inside him he wondered how she, of all people, had not trusted him enough to confide in him, to tell him about the pregnancy in the first place. However, he respected her privacy and continued to keep vigil from a distance. He would never doubt her ability to cope with life. He had no idea of the bitterness settling around her heart and soul.

Amy purposely sought out danger. Constantly looking for ways to challenge the new hardness, which was her heart. A parachute-jumping course gave her reason to fear for a short time. An expedition to the South Pole offered her all the danger the elements could rain down upon her. She survived it all, but then, she was a born survivor when all was said and done. Without putting in any effort, she survived.

Almost two years after closing the door on her lover, Amy returned to West Berlin, flying into RAF Gatow. It had been her one and only stipulation on acceptance of the mission, that the Royal Air Force accommodates her. She had no plans to return to Brooke Barracks, or to accidentally bump into Dan again.

Berlin was familiar territory but many things had changed in the city. The barrier, which sealed the East Germans into their country, had grown stronger, reinforced now and massive. It was much more colourful than she remembered it to be in the sixties too, with many wonderful works of art daubed along the length of the wall.

West Berliners were as fashion conscious as ever and their homes just as elegant. The city centre modernisation was under way; crowds of people were rushing around, everyone was in a hurry. It all seemed so familiar, just as it had back in the sixties. She'd long since learned that the best place to get lost in, was amongst the crowds in any city centre.

She knew that she would be amongst strangers on the RAF base, and for her it was like beginning again. Starting over for a while with a clean slate. There was, however, one person whom time had not changed in the slightest. It was uncanny because Roger Longhurst looked for the all the world as if he'd been translocated by some act of magic, from propping up the bar in the Mess at RAF Brugen, to a very similar bar here at RAF Gatow in West Berlin. Amy smiled to herself; some things never changed.

She saw that the symbols of rank on his uniform jacket were different, and noted he'd received a promotion, but he remained as handsome as she remembered him.

Roger was on his fifth whisky by the time he looked up and recognised the amber-eyed beauty. The whisky did nothing to affect either his eyesight or his manners.

"Well!" he declared as he stood, placed a kiss on her cheek and pulled a stool out for her to sit down on. "What a wonderful surprise. You've made this old man very happy. How are you, Amy?"

"I'm fine, as you can see. How are you?" He looked wonderful.

"Like I said, you've made me very happy. You're like a ray of sunshine in this damned prison of a place. When did you arrive? Nobody mentioned your name."

"Nobody knew," she told him quietly. "I landed two hours ago." She was suddenly glad she was there. The prospect of returning to Berlin without Dan had been somewhat daunting. Meeting Roger put a new complexion on the whole thing. "Congratulations are in order, I believe, Squadron Leader."

He glanced at his left epaulette. "Oh, that. A hard-earned promotion, my dear girl." Laughing he added, "The extra salary helps soothe the burden of responsibility. But enough of me, are you still a ginger ale drinker?" His memory was excellent; it was another thing that, miraculously, had not been impaired by the alcohol.

"Roger," she said, reaching for his arm. "I will drink anything you'd care to put in front of me right now."

He caressed her with his eyes, soothing her pain slightly. "You look tired, but apart from that you look simply wonderful. You've lost weight."

She took a deep breath. Yes, she had lost weight, six precious little pounds to be precise - six pounds of David Daniel, a child with no future

"I'm not tired," she assured him. "I've been busy lately, and yes, you are correct, I have lost a few pounds. Do you approve?"

He laughed at her, she was flirting with him, and this was not the sensible Amy he remembered so well. "Oh, yes. I approve. But tell me, is there a man in your life?"

"No," she replied positively. "And you, have you a woman in yours?"

"Hell no! But I could be tempted. Here, drink up." He placed a glass of wine in front of her and she had no recollection of him even ordering it. "Drink up and I'll get the next round in ready."

Amy Harper was well and truly drunk that night. She was so intoxicated that she woke the next day with no memory of reaching her room, nor of undressing, but she could recall every drink that passed between her lips and her headache served as a painful reminder of the foolishness of drowning one's sorrows.

She also remembered kissing Roger Longhurst good night, which had not been a wholly unpleasant experience, in fact, she'd enjoyed it.

A car drew alongside her as she made her way down the long straight road leading to Station Headquarters. She'd staggered into the dining room an hour earlier for a glass of orange juice and a slice of dry toast.

"Amy! Hop in, old girl." It was Roger in a bright blue Alpha Romeo Spider. "I'm going your way."

As she lowered herself into the bucket seat, he turned to kiss her cheek. "God! You look positively awful, old girl. Are you going down with something?"

Staring at him through dark glasses, she wondered if he was making fun of her. "Yes," she said. "Alcohol poisoning I wouldn't wonder. I was as drunk as a skunk last night thanks to you, Roger Longhurst."

He smiled and she thought again how handsome he looked despite her hangover. In his uniform he was an extremely good-looking man.

"The demon drink eh!" he said. "Of course, I hadn't thought of that, but then, I am immune to the bloody stuff. Has no effect on me whatsoever. Just seem to soak the bloody stuff up like a sponge." He squeezed her shoulder gently.

"You need the hair of the dog, my girl." She moaned at the suggestion. "Trust me, it's guaranteed to put you on your feet. Anyway, where are you going?"

"Your way," she reminded him, her hand on her temple. "Or SHQ, whichever you reach first."

"Work eh! That's not much fun. You meet me afterwards and I'll show you real fun."

Two impressively burly men waited in the small windowless office on the first floor of Station Headquarters. The room was sealed and secure. The walls were lined with copper. The Berlin Wall and communism, the KGB, listening devices and spy towers were all just a few hundred metres from that sealed office - across the airfield and over the main road. But the enemy would learn nothing of the meeting between the two big men and Amy Harper.

It could be taken for granted that the Soviets, the KGB and the East Germans in power, knew that Amy was back in West Berlin. It was common knowledge that Berlin was home to more government agents than any other country in the world. It could also be taken very much for granted that each and every person in Britain had met a communist, and possibly an operative in the employ of the KGB, at some stage during their lives. To the common people that theory would be disregarded as nonsense. To those in the know, it was a terrifying fact.

The men waited alone and silent, both in a pensive mood. Both were apprehensive - neither had met this woman but they'd heard a great deal about her. Amy knocked and entered and instantly felt dwarfed as both giants leapt to their feet. One was ebony-skinned with black hair and a goatee beard, but not the taller of the two, his skin was fair and clean-shaven. His hair was a light-golden colour, cut short, standing erect on his head.

The taller, fair-skinned man, made the introductions. "I'm Michael Devereux, Miss, and my colleague is Allen Bramford. Come in, and have a seat."

There were only three chairs and a table. Two chairs had been previously occupied; Amy took the third, and faced them. Diminutive though she was, she felt not the slightest bit intimidated by these men. There was no small talk. No preamble. No discussion on her having had a safe journey. Devereux went straight ahead and opened the discussion.

"We're glad you've come, Miss Harper, we need your help to bring a young woman out of East Berlin."

"Why me?" she asked when he paused.

"Because the young woman in question is almost your double, appearance-wise. That is the only reason you were brought out here."

"A straight switch?" That suited her, nothing too complicated, or so she thought.

Bramford took over and replied, "Yes. You'll go across on a fake German passport, meet the woman and switch clothes and documents." His voice was soft and his manner mild.

Back to Devereux, the more formidable of the two. "You'll need to get yourself down to Potsdam once the switch is made and come home through the back door."

"Why?" she asked, frowning.

"Because we know that the authorities are waiting for Miss Bremman to make an escape attempt. She's under constant surveillance. Makarevich has been seen near her home."

Her amber eyes narrowed to slits. "He was expelled from Britain...four years ago!"

"Yes." Devereux looked impressed by her knowledge of the KGB agent who'd been engaged in clandestine operations and expelled from Great Britain before any further damage could be done.

"Because we know they're watching her we feel certain the only way to bring her out is by using your ID. You will then be the one under scrutiny. Miss Bremman has relatives in Potsdam. They're prepared to shelter you until things quieten down and you can then cross back through. It's all very simple."

But was it? Amy looked suspiciously into his dark brown and eyes and knew there was more to it than he was letting on. "If I go in on a West German passport and I look exactly like this woman, don't you think someone somewhere will be just the slightest bit suspicious?"

"We feel it's a worthwhile calculated risk," Bramford informed her, sitting ramrod straight on the chair. "She has family in other areas, including the United States and Great Britain."

"Yes," Amy persisted, "but does she have a relative who looks almost exactly like her?"

The men exchanged glances. "Monique Bremman has many female cousins, Miss Harper. We haven't been able to obtain photographs of them all. We can only assume that there'd be a family likeness somewhere." Bramford again.

But that was not good enough for Amy and she told him so. "An assumption like that could cost me my life, Mr Bramford. Why were you unable to obtain photographs?" When he remained silent, she asked, "What has this woman got to offer us that's worth my putting myself at such risk?"

They exchanged questioning looks again and Devereux answered her. "Information, something worth the expense and the effort. We've still got a lot of good people over there, Miss. Some will never make it home. Some are dying while we speak."

"Yes," Amy agreed patiently. "I'm well aware of the communist situation, especially regarding the Soviet sector. I have actually tasted it from time to time. I'm not naive enough to think I'm out here on a picnic, Mr Devereux." She sighed, deeply troubled by the arrangements and extremely disturbed to be considered expendable in such a cavalier manner, as was being displayed by these burly government agents.

"When is this expense of my person going to take place?" There was no mistaking the acid in her tone. Her hangover was long gone and her wits were as well honed as ever.

"Tomorrow morning." Devereux told her. "You'll go through Checkpoint Charlie in a car bearing West Berlin plates. You'll drive to the address that we will provide, and you'll enter the building where Miss Bremman will be waiting for you. She then leaves the building at precisely 12:00, using your vehicle to cross into the West through Charlie.

"At 14:00 you exit via the rear of the building. It's entirely up to you which mode of transport you adopt but we suggest you use the public transport system."

"Clothes? Money?" she asked, her mind sifting through each and every possible combination of things, which could, and probably would, go wrong.

"Everything will be provided in Miss Bremman's home."

"How much time do I have to get back here?"

"As long as you need, Miss, but we suggest you get it over with as quickly as possible. We will expect you to have made contact with us by the day after tomorrow at the latest. If we haven't heard from you by then we begin a search. Saves a lot of wasted time if you can let us know you're okay," he said, attempting a touch of humour and failing miserably, and the look on Amy's face told him so. "Now, have you any questions for us?"

"Hundreds," she confessed with a wry smile. "Names of relatives? Addresses? Contacts?"

"All here." Bramford handed her a buff envelope. "And if there's anything else we can help you with, don't hesitate to get in touch. We're on three-zero nine treble two-one. Got it?"

"Yes." Her memory was exceptional.

"You can study the information in that envelope for the remainder of this morning, within the confines of this office. Do not take photocopies or remove any of the pages. Hand it back to us before you leave the building."

Amy sighed and nodded agreement. It was their silly game she was playing. She would abide by their silly rules, providing there were no fouls committed against her.

Devereux stood to leave. "If you need food or drink ring the bell on the wall and one of us will get it. My colleague and I will be in the room directly opposite."

He nodded a curt thank you to her and his partner lifted his body from his straight-backed position on the chair to stand up, without appearing to move any of his muscles in the process. They left her alone in the room.

"Dear God!" she whispered to herself as she removed the sheaf of papers and began the tiresome process of remembering everything she was about to read. "This woman had better be worth the risk, that's all I can say."

Roger was on his third double whisky when Amy approached him at 13:00 that day. Her mind was cluttered and untidy, and it wasn't the way she worked best. She knew that she would have to sort herself out or she risked failing in the forthcoming mission. That failure could cost lives and not only her own.

"The rest of the day's my own," she whispered into his ear. "Any suggestions?"

He turned very slowly and smiled directly into her eyes. He raised his right eyebrow and nodded slowly. She joined him for a drink, just the one, and then they went through to the dining room to see if there was anything left to eat. They had wine with the meal and wine after the meal.

By 15:00 Amy was light-headed and giggly, but she knew exactly what she was doing when she followed Roger into his room in the Mess.

He drew the curtains tightly together, plunging them into darkness. "No," he said when she was about to turn on the light. "It's much more intimate in the dark."

Amy cried when he undressed her, but she cried silently and he neither knew nor cared. She cried again later when she thought of Dan and the way he'd loved her with such infinite tenderness. She saw Dan's face and felt his hands upon her flesh and then she cried out as a massive orgasm coursed through her body exploding inside her head. It had been Dan who caused that explosion, but she felt a stranger in her arms and a stranger deep inside her body. A stranger whom she had permitted to touch her most intimate parts as only Dan had done before.

Burdened with guilt she crept back to her room like a thief in the night and locked the door. She showered for the best part of an hour in piping hot water in a futile attempt to wash away the act, which had made her feel like a novice prostitute and then she cried herself to sleep.

There was no sign of Roger next morning when she breakfasted alone in the big dining room and for that she was grateful. After breakfast she took possession of a silver Mazda saloon bearing Berlin registration plates. She drove out of the main gates, turned left onto the main road and headed towards the city centre.

The Mazda was immaculate and Amy could see and smell the newness of it. It had really low mileage. It was an easy drive; a comfortable vehicle and she chuckled as she wondered if the person who assigned this vehicle to her had been aware she'd only held a full driving licence for a year. However, she was a calm and confident driver and it was possibly the only thing that gave her pleasure nowadays. The rage and anger inside her calmed the instant she sat behind the wheel of a car.

Even now she wondered why she'd never had time or desire to learn to drive long before she did. But then, had she been a driver she wouldn't have met Daniel Jones. Of all of her regrets, Dan was not amongst them. She never regretted one moment spent with him. She only regretted that initial decision to leave him.

She was driving along Strasse des 17. Juni, (17th June Street), with Ernst Reuterplaz behind her, the Wall directly in front of her and the Brandenburg Tor standing nobly behind it.

The day was clear and warm and her eyes were focused on the road ahead, taking in everything, missing nothing, and then she saw Dan filling her vision! He was stooping over a workbench, examining a weapon; it looked like a sniper rifle.

Suddenly Amy felt her heart lurch, her grip tightened on the steering wheel and her knuckles turned white. He raised the weapon to his face and looked along the barrel, down through the telescopic sight. Amy could smell the warm familiar smell of him and then the pervading odour of gun oil touched her senses and she shivered. It was all there before her, alive in her mind's eye.

By the time she reached the border crossing at Checkpoint Charlie, the image of Dan had become transparent. She could see right through it while she drove. She was left shaken by the clarity of the vision and of what she'd learned, more certain now than ever before, that his life was in danger. It was as if eight years had rolled into ten minutes. She could still feel his presence in the car with her. The smell of his spicy cologne mingled with his manly musk. He was in the car with her.

Amy handed over her pass to the East German border guard and subjected herself to the ordeal of the silent interrogation of his glowering expression. There was no time for her to worry about him. She was concentrating on the image of Dan as he lowered the rifle to the bench.

He was telling himself that he'd just imagined seeing and feeling the presence of his precious Amy. "Amy?" he whispered. "Where the hell are you?" But he knew she wasn't there and he also knew that he was not losing his mind. He'd reached across land and sea to where she was. He knew without doubt that she was sitting behind the steering wheel of a silver car at Checkpoint Charlie, the border crossing in West Berlin.

"Christ!" he gasped as he leaned back on the edge of the bench, a cold sweat breaking out on his body. "What the hell is going on?"

"Who you talking to, sarge?" An elfin-like young soldier yelled across the expanse of the empty hangar.

"Myself!" he yelled back. "Mind your own sodding business and do some work, Mitchell!"

"Okay, sarge!" The boy knew better than to argue with Sergeant Jones, whose temper was inclined to run short occasionally. He found it hard to believe the rumours that the man was a cool-headed tough guy, an expert in survival, not when he could be seen close to tears most nights, a glass of unfinished beer on the table between his hands.

As a civilian instructor who carried the rank of respect by all of the soldiers, young and old he was Sergeant Dan Jones and he would always be 'sarge' to those in his care, even if he did cry into his beer.

"Fräulein! Fräulein Koryakusky," the guard repeated, having trouble with her name. He spoke to her in a rapid-fire gruff country dialect and she held up her hand to him, signalling that he should slow down.

In broken German she slowly spoke out the words she needed to pass through the border safely. "I am sorry. I do not speak good German. My father Russian and my mother Polish. My mother died when I was child. I speak only Russian and little German."

She smiled at him, giving him a really close look at her lovely amber eyes.

"As you can tell, that is not such good talk for me."

At thirty Amy was a stunner. She flirted with him, pulled her skirt higher so that he could take in her slim legs and ankles and then she held out her hand for her passport.

"You are very kind man. I will tell them when I reach to the house of my cousin. I will tell them how kind you have been to simple country girl."

He'd written the passport number down and studied each page, even the blank ones in the small book, made a note of the car number on his pad and a mental note of the auburn-haired beauty with the inviting eyes.

"Where are you going?" he asked, more slowly and much more friendly now. Then he checked that none of his comrades were in the vicinity. Fraternisation was strictly forbidden.

"To my cousin. She has house in Rummelsburg."

When he frowned Amy hastily added, "Oh, do not tell me I have taken wrong checkpoint." And then she broke into fluent Russian and jabbered on; bewildering him with words he could never hope to understand. He had no love of the Soviets, but this woman was different.

"No! No!" he exclaimed. "But it is a long way, and difficult if you are new here. I will make you a map if you wait over there."

He pointed to the area of land most commonly known to the British military as, 'The Sin Bin' - a patch of rough ground where anyone travelling through the border and failing to observe the strict rules and regulations, including showing impatience with the guards, was put to wait as punishment. Sometimes left there for up to three hours with no way of turning around and getting out of the situation. At the end of their punishment, their allotted visiting time would be close to over and so they'd have no option other than to turn around and go home.

Amy knew that she had no time for this, but she would have to be careful in dealing with this problem. "Thank you, kind guard, but I have map sent by cousin. Do you think you could take time...err...to show me city? One day next week I think is best, yes?"

His eyes lit up and he was about to respond when he caught sight of his superior officer approaching to see why there was a delay. The traffic was beginning to build behind the Mazda.

"That would be good. Come here on Wednesday at this time and I will be free." He saluted and with the broadest of grins on his face he spoke louder. "Thank you, Fräulein. Please have a good visit with your family, and drive carefully."

As she drove away from the crossing, her hands were trembling and her clothes were saturated in perspiration. Dan was no longer with her.

It took her over an hour to reach Rummelsburg. The East had changed so much so that she kept taking wrong turns, getting lost long before she got out of the city centre. The map her people had provided was all but useless. They hadn't bothered to make note of the one-way systems currently in operation, nor of the obvious problem spots where there was simply no access to anyone other than a true-blooded communist with a fully paid-up party card.

Several times she turned into a side road only to be confronted by stern faced East German or Soviet soldiers standing on duty, turning back anyone who was not qualified to pass that way. Politely they shook their heads and gestured for her to turn her vehicle and go, as quickly as possible. It was not a problem for Amy, the last thing she wanted was a confrontation leading to incarceration in some stinking Soviet prison.

When at last she parked the car and stepped up to the apartment block on Volkrad Strasse, she could see there were two parked vehicles parked on the opposite side of the street just down the road from where she was standing. There were two men in each car and all eyes were on her as she approached the building. KGB.

"Is it you?" the woman asked as she pulled the door open and stared at Amy, almost in a state of shock as if having seen a ghost.

"Yes. It is me," Amy told her in Russian. The apartment block was a decaying monstrosity. The passageway was dark and dank and the place a musty drab dwelling.

The woman, who appeared to be in her early sixties, welcomed Amy inside and still staring open-mouthed at her she spoke to her in broken Russian.

"I speak a little of your tongue, but not so good. My sister taught me before she died." She was proud of her dexterity, and of the opportunity to practise. "Please, come in. Welcome to our home. You have not been here since you were a small child."

"Thank you, Aunt." Amy chose here words carefully; knowing that the building was bugged and that every word they spoke would be monitored. The likelihood of there being hidden cameras was something she would have to risk.

"Is Monique at home?"

"Yes. She is in there. Go. Go. You have many things to catch up on."

Amy pushed the door open and stepped into the middle room, a small and equally dismal living area. Standing before her was a mirror image of herself. She was a slightly younger woman, with harsher features. Her eyes were cold in comparison to the warm glow of the amber-eyed English woman. Monique Bremman had mouse brown hair and dark brown eyes, but nevertheless, there was an uncanny familiarity about her, which sent shivers down Amy's spine.

"Monique!" Amy said, sounding as if she were greeting a long-lost relative. She'd reverted to poor German. "You look wonderful."

"I am pleased you came, Tanya. How are you?" she held out her hand to welcome the stranger, drawing her forwards to the hard two-seater sofa where she continued the friendly dialogue while writing hurriedly on a note pad. *"Have you brought the papers for me?"*

Amy unfastened her shoulder bag. "I have news of our cousin Alexander," she replied and Monique understood that everything was prepared for her to leave.

They sat close together and held two conversations, sometimes three. They spoke aloud for those who were eavesdropping, made notes on paper with questions and answers and occasionally whispered directly into the other's ear.

Amy quickly learned that Monique was a good person and she liked her almost instantly.

The grandfather clock in the hall struck twelve as Monique Bremman left the house to drive the silver Mazda back towards the border and the freedom of the West. Amber tinted contact lenses warmed and brightened her dull brown eyes. A shoulder length curly auburn wig turned the mousey female into Amy Harper, alias Tanya Koryakusky. The touch of make-up brought life into her face. The new clothes gave her confidence and a lift in her step as she left her home and her family behind her. Amy warned her about the young border guard and advised her as to how she should deal with him if he approached her.

Two hours later, Amy climbed aboard a bus bound for Potsdam. She too was disguised in wig and contact lenses.

The drab clothes of Monique Bremman hung on her lovely body. She looked thinner and ill with the pale make-up hiding her beautiful complexion. The shoes on her feet were thin-soled and uncomfortable, and not for the first time she wondered if Miss Bremman really was worth the risk and the trouble.

Staring out of the dirty side window at the grey of the outside world, she knew deep in her heart that Monique and all the Monique's of the world were worth the hardship.

In two short hours, she'd shared a lifetime with the younger woman. She learned more about the DDR, and of the hardships involved in living there than she ever learned back in the sixties.

All the misery and the suffering, the years of poverty, starvation and of political injustices and cruelty - yes, Monique and those locked behind the bars of inhumanity, placed there by the Communist State, they were all worth the small amount of pain and discomfort she was now experiencing.

Amy was tempted to close her eyes and rest as the bus trundled and clattered along rough rutted tracks and cobbled roadways, but she resisted the temptation and concentrated her thoughts upon her escape plan.

Within minutes of focusing her attention on the problem in hand, she'd drifted off daydreaming of Dan and then of Roger. She was shocked to the core that she'd slept with him, with a virtual stranger. The fact that she made the decision to be intimate with anyone other than Dan, without as much as a second thought for the consequences, left her stunned to the core. How could she ever face Roger again? He would undoubtedly avoid her now. But she needed love. It had been too long, far too long.

Roger appeared to like her and they were certainly attracted to each other. He was pleasant and good-looking. He'd been considerate with her the previous day. He'd also been silent and secretive. Once inside the room with the curtains drawn and the lights out, he was stone cold silent. She told herself that he would change; she would help him to change. If he were shy or in the least bit inhibited, she could bring him out. He was, indeed, quite a challenge.

By the time the bus bumped its way into Potsdam Amy was convinced she'd done the right thing in accepting this mission. She was no agent - definitely not a spy. She had never pretended to be one, although she did know a great deal about the Soviet system and with her special gifts, she was an asset to her country. It was her sole aim in life to assist in any way she could to bring about the emancipation of mankind. Working in this way was exactly what she'd been trained to do and it made her happy to be of service once again.

There had been times when she behaved naively regards entering an Eastern bloc country. Times when she led Dan into situations that she should have known instinctively were wrong. Blinded by an overwhelming need to help, she failed to apply common sense and logic to her actions. Only luck had saved her then, her and Dan. She'd done a great deal of growing up since then. She'd lost Dan and survived the ordeal, and now she intended living properly again.

Amy had never been deluded into thinking that crossing back into West Berlin was going to be easy. Hundreds had died doing exactly what she was about to do, and she had no intention of becoming another statistic, especially as the freedom of the West was hers by right of nationality.

Potsdam hit her with its decay, sadness and depression. It was a beautifully ornate city, sadly neglected. Prussian royal palaces including Frederick the Great's Sans Souci and the original Brandenburg Gate were there in Potsdam. It was a wonderful place steeped in history and tradition, rotting away for want of repair. More of the pale-faced people scurried about their business with hollow dull eyes trying not to see. Dozens of Soviet soldiers wandered freely throughout the city with their overlarge uniform caps on their tiny pale heads; their barracks close by.

Wondering what the place held for her, Amy stepped down from the bus, tripping and falling into the arms of a handsome, uniformed, Soviet soldier. He was a boy, no more than seventeen and he smiled down on her as she regained her poise, uttering thanks to him in German before moving on. His eyes bored into her back. Ahead of her there were three more soldiers in mud brown uniforms with the red star of the Soviet Union on their over-large caps.

They were complaining bitterly about the cruelty of their new captain but their complaints grew silent as the pretty girl passed by and they cast admiring glances down the length of her body. She ignored them and moved on.

A group of people was massing ahead of her, an illegal political uprising and a march against the state. She witnessed the dozen or so arrests as young men and women were dragged off by the hard-line police force; people who would broach no argument and who cracked down on skulls with heavy sticks in an effort to prevent a minor uprising becoming a major problem; knowing it would be reported back to party headquarters.

Amy ducked and dived, continuously avoiding the angry blows and the man who followed her out of East Berlin. Yes, she knew he was there. She saw him with her eyes and with her mind. She had his full measure and she knew he was dangerous. The Ministerium for Staatssicherheit, more commonly known as the Stasi, had its own undercover agents, spies, ordinary people snooping and reporting on friends and neighbours.

Amy knew all about the Ministry for State Security in the German Democratic Republic, she understood the power they possessed and the damage they were doing on a daily basis, and they had their headquarters in East Berlin. The reputation of the Stasi was described as effective, destructive and repressive; it was a powerful and very dangerous organisation to take a risk with. Amy would be careful and stay one step ahead of those watching her. Her heightened senses and perception could keep her alert and aware of everything around her.

She remained calm and appeared to be happily going about her daily business, travelling to visit a family member, nothing more, nothing less.

In the guise of Monique Bremman, she made her way to the home of her elderly uncle. She had not anticipated his unwelcoming greeting. The door opened a fraction and he spoke gruffly to her through the crack.

"Go away! You must not come here. We want no trouble from you and your friends. I have told you before today to stay away from me. You will get me arrested. I will report you to the authorities if I see you again. Go."

At first Amy thought he'd seen through the disguise and then she realised that he was addressing his niece, and it was Monique he wanted out of his life.

"But, Uncle," she pleaded with the old man. "I have come all this way to speak with you."

"Go away!" The door slammed on her and her only refuge in the East.

At a nearby café, she bought herself a small pot of coffee and brooded over it.

The stranger who'd followed her was conspicuous by his absence, yet she knew there were other strangers, and that they were watching her every move, and she was left with no choice, she needed to return to the Bremman apartment in the city and wait for nightfall.

The plan was simple apart from a single drawback - there was no public transport returning directly to Berlin until late afternoon. She decided to take herself on a short tour of Potsdam. It was only her second visit there and she was genuinely fascinated by the place. She quickly realised that all that was needed to restore the city to its former glory was for someone with a little foresight, and a great deal of hindsight, to realise they were looking at an original massive work of art. This was one city that had not been abused by progress. So many architectural masterpieces were torn down throughout the sixties and early seventies to make way for the modern abominations the world was growing used to and mostly detested.

Amy knew that society would one day realise their mistake and take down the modern eyesores in favour of the old-fashioned beauty once again, but Potsdam was rare, it was perfect despite the decay. It was as it had been so very long ago, and despite the gloom and depression of tyranny, there was a rare beauty in this wondrous place. I needed restoration, nothing more.

She went to the gardens of the Sans Souci Palace and sat in the warmth of the late June sunshine, watching a small group of tourists taking photographs as they strolled in the place where King Frederick II found refuge from the world during the 18th century.

It was while she took the time to dwell on the state of ruin of the beautiful city, she realised that while life had not always seemed to deal kindly with her, everything could be a great deal worse. Dan would always be her friend, and the memories of their love and the loss of their son would remain with her to her death. It was time to move on, and she knew it.

At ten minutes to six, Amy boarded the bus for the uncomfortable return trip to East Berlin. The only thing that had gone as planned was she'd exchanged places with Monique Bremman. She had no idea if the woman arrived safely in the West. For all she knew, there could well be a welcoming committee awaiting her own arrival at the border. Logic told her that she would already have been swept up off the streets of Potsdam if anyone had an inkling of what was going on.

Hilde Bremman, Monique's mother, was distressed to see her on her doorstep again that day. She stepped aside for her to enter and quickly closed the door on the eyes of the East. In the main room, she placed her finger to her lips and said aloud, "How was your visit, my dear?"

"Uncle was strange, Mother, but you must forgive me," she coughed and spluttered as she spoke. "I have a sore throat. My voice is not so good." She hoped the excuse would cover the many differences between her voice and that of the actual Monique.

Hilde nodded. "I will give you something for it. Now tell me, what news have you of my brother in Potsdam, why do you say he was strange?"

"He must be losing his mind," Amy told her. "He would not even permit me to enter his home. I returned as quickly as I could. There are not many buses now. Why do you think he has changed so much?"

"He was always a little different, my child. He was not a healthy boy. I will go and see him before winter arrives. Perhaps I can persuade him to come here for a while." She paused and reached for a note pad and as she spoke aloud, she wrote a message. "Do you want tea or coffee?"

"Tea. Thank you, Mother." Amy looked at the pad and read: *'What has happened? Why have you returned? Is my daughter safe?'*

Amy replied on paper: *'Your brother would not let me in. I had to return. I do not know if Monique is safe. I believe they would have come for you if she was not. Please, do not worry. I will leave as soon as darkness falls.'*

Both women rested for an hour. The old woman slept but Amy was very much awake and alert to each strange sound from outside that brought her instantly to her feet. Every voice echoing through the building caused her heart to lurch uncomfortably. Night was a long time arriving.

Chapter Twelve

At midnight the moonlight picked out the unmistakeable silhouette of the man standing on the corner of the apartment block. Another concealed figure lit up a cigarette three doors down on the opposite side of the wide road. A black car lurked menacingly north of where Amy waited. It would be this way morning, noon or night. Nothing would change. They were watching Monique Bremman, waiting for her to make her break. It was a good sign; it meant Monique was now free.

"I must go," Amy whispered to the old woman as she changed out of her East German clothing and put on the sweater, slacks and flat shoes she'd carried in her rucksack. Once again, she was Amy Harper. The passport tucked inside the lining of the bag said so.

"Please do not worry. You will have word of Monique soon, I promise," she whispered as she kissed the woman and left the apartment.

The rear door of the building creaked on rusty hinges and Amy waited a full ten minutes before she crouched low and performed a crablike shuffle away from the building into the shadow of an identical building immediately behind it.

Twenty minutes later she was standing on the platform of the overhead railway. She boarded the train as soon as it arrived and crossed through to the West at Lehrter Bahnhof. The fake visa declaring her to be a tourist, tucked into her British passport, brought her safely home.

It had all been an enormous risk. Had she been picked up at the onset of the mission they would most positively have found forged documents and three passports. One in the name of Monique Bremman, another for Tanya Koryakusky, and the third, which Amy now used, a British passport, and even that was part of her government cover, nothing was genuine, it was all a large expensive bluff.

She'd risked internment in an East German prison while awaiting deportation to one of the Soviet prison camps. Her clandestine operation would have daubed her a spy, despite all of her protestations to the contrary.

Once in the West she travelled by taxi, arriving at the main gates of sleepy RAF Gatow at five in the morning.

"Congratulations, Miss," Devereux said as he rubbed the sleep from his eyes. He and his colleague were notified the instant Amy walked through the main gates. "You made marvellous time."

"Any problems?" his colleague asked, as he was about to ensconce himself, straight-backed, on a chair in the small bug-proof room.

Amy studied both men closely, Bramford, with his black skin, bent and broken nose and a tiny glimmer of humanity shining in his deep brown eyes, and the other one, Devereux, the exact opposite. Fair of face with fierce green eyes, totally devoid of warmth and a voice so gentle it was soothing. When he smiled there was no hint of comfort. Such contrasts - such opposites.

"No problems," she said with a sigh. Her voice was quiet and she sounded tired, she was too tired to point out what they could have done better. "My report will be on your desk by midday tomorrow..." She paused before correcting herself, "Today."

"Fine," Devereux spoke again. "Thank you once again, Miss."

"Is that it?" she asked.

"That's it. Go and catch up on some shuteye and we'll see you later on."

"Miss Bremman," she said, knowing that if she failed to bring the woman into the conversation they clearly wouldn't. "Is she..."

"She's safe, Miss. Sleep well." Bramford stood as he spoke. It was apparent that there would be no further information divulged that day.

Amy was suddenly hurtling back in time to 1967, to Brooke Barracks and to the office of Major Douglas Philips, so stern yet such a marvellous leader. He was a man of fine qualities whom she greatly admired, despite the rough start to their association. How he loved keeping things to himself.

"Thank you," she said to the men as she left them to make their private call to London.

The sun was up and warm on her face as she walked back along the road, straight passed the married quarters where airmen and their families slept soundly, to the Officers' Mess. The freedom she felt at that time filled her with warmth. The freedom which countless hundreds of thousands took for granted and far too many knew nothing about.

As she walked, her thoughts turned once again to Dan, who was never very far from her at any time of the day or night. She reflected on how he'd looked when she pictured him there in that hangar, the rifle in his hands. God! How she missed him.

Her loneliness was so great it weighed her down and her feet became leaden. Her entire body was a mass of aches and pains. There were blisters on her heels from the ill-fitting shoes and she felt the need of a strong drink before sleeping.

She approached a steward in the lounge and asked if it was possible to have a large brandy and he assured her that it was no trouble and invited her to take a seat. Roger found her there minutes later. He was returning from a stint of duty at his place of work.

"Well, hello!" he said, touching her arm and causing her to jump. "Where have you been, young woman? I looked everywhere for you yesterday."

"This is yesterday for me," she told him sleepily. "I've been working." She noted the creased uniform trousers and asked, "You too?"

"Yup, work," he groaned. "It has the habit of coming between a man and his drinking time. Where have you been?"

"Here and there," she replied evasively. "Around and about. I'm waiting for a drink and then I'm off to bed for a couple of hours of well-earned sleep." The drink arrived and she emptied the glass in one easy swallow.

"Do you think someone could wake me at ten? I have a rather lengthy report to write and I need to be at SHQ by noon."

Keeping her eyes on his was difficult, he was looking right at her and beyond, as if he was making some monumental decision, which would alter his entire life.

"I'll wake you," he said sounding gentle and loving. He kissed her cheek and walked away from her. He would put a couple of strong drinks inside himself before he thought about sleeping.

He woke her, as promised, but with a bottle of champagne and two glasses.

"What's this in aid of?" she asked, struggling to cover her nudity. Strange, she thought. I slept with this man, yet I feel ashamed for him to look at me now.

"This, my dear, is to show you how much I care about you. You deserve champagne in bed every day for the rest of your life, and much more too - furs and jewels and everything money can buy." Dan never offered her anything like that, nothing in the least bit commercial or crass. He offered her stability and love, loyalty and devotion, his gifts had delighted her, and they were freely given.

"Really, Roger," she said eventually, "There's no need to go overboard."

He kissed her and it was a pleasant experience, which brought her to submission, giving herself in an effort to feel something for this man, something other than friendship and a longing to be loved. She wanted to love him, desperately, much more than he would ever know or understand. But it wasn't right. "Roger..."

"Shush!" he said as he went to lock the door. He undressed with his back to her and climbed into the single bed, taking her into his arms. He kissed her and fondled her breasts clumsily. He said nothing more while they had intercourse; it could never be classed as making love. When it was over, he slept.

Amy left him in her bed. She showered and dressed and walked out of the building. In the quiet of the room in Station Headquarters, she wrote her report for the two men from London who arrived at noon to thank her again for her help.

They advised her to take some leave. She could board the military flight out of RAF Gatow on Wednesday next. That gave her four days of freedom in the city she loved most in the entire world. London was her home and she was undeniably fond of the place while a small part of her lingered on in Moscow, but it was Berlin where she always left her heart.

Roger was sound asleep in her bed when she returned. She hoped he'd have woken and gone. She needed time to consider her actions. All too often of late she seemed to be acting in haste. The last thing she wanted to do was repent at her leisure.

"Ugh!" he groaned when she drew the curtains back and let the sunlight stream in, flinging the window open before turning to look down on him as he asked, "Where have you been? You keep vanishing."

"I had an appointment," she reminded him. "I like to be on time; besides, I had a report to write and I knew I'd never get it done if I stayed here with you. Haven't you got work to go to today?" She wanted to shout at him to leave. To order him out of her bed and well out of her life, yet her voice was gentle with him and he looked very handsome and young as he smiled up at her.

"Nope! Three days off. I hate these bloody split shifts."

Amy had no experience of shift work. "I fly out on Wednesday," she told him.

"You do?" He sat up in bed, propped a pillow behind his back and invited her to sit by his side by patting the bed with the flat of his hand. "Don't go."

"I have to. I have a career."

"Sod that, marry me."

Amy looked horror-struck at first and then embarrassed. "Why?" she asked.

"Because I asked you to. Because I...I...believe I love you."

"Do you?"

"Of course," he said, reaching for her hand. "I don't hop into bed with everyone I meet in the bar." In fact, he had never hopped into bed with anyone before Amy. He knew the rudiments of making love, he'd read the books and seen enough porn in his time, but he'd never actually had the opportunity to put the knowledge into practice, not that he would ever tell her that. There had never been any shortage of girlfriends, just an acute shortage of love.

She opted for complete honesty, before it was too late to speak out. "I don't love you, Roger. I like you very much and I care about you, but..."

"You will," he said confidently.

"This is ridiculous!" Amy declared. "I don't know you, or you me."

Adopting a serious expression he asked, "How old are you?"

"Thirty."

"And I'm thirty-five. What religion are you?"

"I don't really know. I was brought up Church of England, but..."

"Well! There you are!" he declared as if positive proof of their suitability had been supplied with those few words. "So am I. We have loads in common, and now we know everything there is to know about each other. So, will you marry me, Amy Harper?"

"You're mad!" she declared, meaning it.

"Mad, and a bit drunk. I finished the booze while you were out. But will you say you'll marry me, please, Amy?"

"Yes." She heard the sound coming from her mouth but she couldn't believe she'd agreed to his ludicrous proposal.

He grabbed her urgently and pressed his lips on hers. "Wonderful! I'll find out what the procedure is. Now, what about something to eat?"

She shrugged her shoulders, somewhat bewildered by the latest turn of events. "If you like."

"We're going to celebrate tonight. This building is about to see some action, my little love."

"Please," she said quietly to him. "Don't call me that. Anything, but not that."

"Fine, whatever you say, old girl. Now, if you'll clear off for ten minutes I'll get dressed and we'll grab us some food before we spread the good tidings."

"Roger!" she called as she reached the door. "Are you sure this is the right thing to do?"

"Never more so, old girl. You'll want for nothing."

They were married in London on the last Saturday in July. It was a simple registry office affair, with two of

Roger's colleagues acting as witnesses. Amy had no support, no family or friends, and she felt alone again, alone and very vulnerable. She knew as she went through with it, that it was a mistake, but she'd committed herself to this man and nothing would make her break that commitment.

Roger was thrilled with the arrangement. He was like a spoiled child at a birthday party, and Amy succeeded in convincing herself from time to time that she could change him. He was a charming and pleasurable person to be with while under the influence of alcohol, she had yet to see him sober.

Having been allocated one of the officers' married quarters close to the main gates on the air base; they moved their personal possessions in and attempted to turn the large semi-detached property into their home. The RAF provided everything, furniture, bedding, towels, and even a cruet set and dishcloths. It was filled with everything they could ever need and much more. They could live comfortably there, if not entirely happily.

They moved in after a brief honeymoon in Paris, a long weekend, which turned out to be a disaster from start to finish. Roger failed dismally in his attempts to make love and took to leaning against the hotel bar, clinging tightly onto a whisky bottle for three nights.

Amy cried her way through the entire time and through almost every night afterwards. Having endured several weeks of misery, she wondered if it was her destiny to spend the remainder of her days crying.

Commander Cooper kept her fully occupied from the London office. He despatched work for her on a regular basis and when she wasn't working, she attempted to make contact with the deprived locals in the hope that she would find someone to whom she could offer hope of bringing their relatives through from the East. She needed to be discreet because if the Stasi got wind of her attempts anything was a possibility.

The officers' wives united once a week, exchanging gossip and cookery recipes. Many voluntary tasks were put Amy's way upon request for something to keep her occupied. She helped out at the kindergarten, and even read stories to the little ones in infants' school. Her home life was not sufficient to keep her from getting bored and up to mischief. Her life was tedious and Roger was habitually drunk.

During the autumn of '77, she spoke to him about the prospect of raising a family. "No!" he replied firmly.

"But, why not? I do all the housework and it would be my responsibility entirely." Just like a family pet, hers to clean up after, hers to walk and hers to talk to. She felt inclined to add, "And I'll clean the bloody cage out once a week!"

"No! And don't talk to me about doing all the housework. You could have helped like the other wives, but no, not you, you have to prove something all the time. Why don't you just settle down and accept what you have, Amy? You want for nothing. You have money in the bank. A wardrobe so tightly packed with clothes you'll be old before you wear them all. You have a great social life and a husband who does his damnedest to please you. Why the hell do you want to spoil everything by having children?"

"I love children," she replied weakly.

"Well, I don't, so just forget it." He returned his attention to the television set, ignoring her completely. The subject was very firmly closed.

Yes, she had everything with the exception of love. Roger had not uttered a word of love to her in two years. They hardly talked at all. He went to work, came home and ate. He then walked to the Mess and filled himself with alcohol before returning home to sleep it off. They had sex once a month on the first Saturday, as if it was the thing to do. Everything was closeted and secret. There was no love.

Amy longed to have children of her own.

"Are you coming tonight, stranger?" the young woman called to her across the NAAFI car park. It was snowing, the first snow of the winter of 1980. "To the Mess ball. Are you coming?"

Amy crossed the road, slipping and sliding despite the thick-soled boots on her feet. "I don't know, Diana. Roger has a dreadful cold. He hasn't actually mentioned it. I think he's forgotten it somewhere in the misery of feeling ill."

The women laughed together and then Diana James asked, "Fancy a cup of tea with your neighbour?"

Amy checked her watch and reached out to relieve the heavily pregnant woman of the loaded shopping bag; chastising her as she did so. "You shouldn't be carrying this much, not in your condition, not with all this snow and ice." Diana was almost eight months pregnant, and seeing her brought everything flooding back to Amy. The pain and the suffering involved in the loss of her infant were fresh in her mind once again.

Diana unlocked the front door when they arrived at her home, closing it quickly on the icy blast. She struggled out of her boots while Amy did the same thing before going through to the kitchen with the shopping.

"Put the kettle on, there's a love," Diana called to her.

But when she walked into the kitchen a few minutes later, she found Amy with her head bowed over the sink. She laid her hand lightly on her shoulder and when Amy lifted her face, Diana saw that it was tear-stained and her eyes were swollen and red.

"I'm sorry," Amy apologised. "I don't know what came over me."

Diana knew. Every last one of the wives knew. Roger Longhurst was a drunkard and a belligerent pig. He did nothing to deserve a wife as good and caring as Amy. She was never anything but kind and helpful. She'd do anything for anyone. Roger needed a housekeeper and window dressing for when he was entertaining. The marriage had been convenient for him and destructive for poor Amy.

"Want to talk?" she asked.

Amy half nodded and made a feeble attempt to smile her way through her misery. It was the first time she'd given into tears in years, and the first time she was prepared to open up and share her sadness. The kettle boiled and Diana made two mugs of instant coffee. "Come on, let's go and put our feet up. This weather makes me tired all the time."

Sniffing and sobbing a big dry gulping sob, Amy wiped her eyes again and blew her nose. "I'm sorry, Diana. You don't need this."

"Stop apologising, for crying out loud, we're friends, this is what friends are for. Sit down and tell me what brought this on."

Amy rested her hand lightly on the mound of precious growing infant. Diana was much larger than she'd been. Her friend actually looked eight months pregnant.

"Is it my being pregnant, Amy? Are you jealous?" Diana asked cautiously.

"Oh, no!" Amy exclaimed at last. "No. How could I be jealous of you?" Her bottom lip quivered and she fought fresh tears. "It's just that...that I was pregnant a very long time ago."

"You were! When was that? I had no idea."

"I was twenty-eight and naive."

"Roger's baby?"

"Hell no! But I did meet Roger while I was pregnant. I came out to Germany for a week, I was working down south. We shared a few drinks, nothing more." And then she felt she owed it to her friend of five years to tell her everything, well, almost everything.

"I fell in love with a soldier when I was twenty-two years of age. He was here, in Berlin, at Brooke Barracks with the Welch Regiment. He and I were lovers and he asked me to marry him. I refused but agreed to stay on here with him. I'd known him only two weeks when we became lovers, but it was natural and right."

She sighed deeply. "I wanted to stay with him forever but eight months of sharing days and nights with him and I started getting restless. I had to leave. I felt caged and I wanted to go. He was the last person on earth who would have caged me.

"Dan was everything a young girl could hope to find in a man. He was ruggedly handsome, big and strong, kind and tender. He was a wonderful lover, understanding and generous to a fault, and what I did was run off and leave him. I used all manner of excuses to justify my actions.

"Years later I bumped into him in Holland. He was on his honeymoon. He said he'd made a mistake by marrying the girl because she was pregnant and he felt sorry for her. It wasn't his child but he was such a caring man he was prepared to give her a home, the child too. He asked me to be his friend, to keep in touch."

"Did you see much of him after he got married?" Diana asked.

"I could have," Amy admitted. "I could have been his mistress, but I refused to share my body and my bed with a married man; despite aching for him. The next time I saw him she'd lost the child and they'd separated. He said he couldn't take any more of it and he'd left her. We ended up in bed and we saw each other on and off for a long time. Things just sort of happened naturally, and then I chose to look after my dying mother. I was pregnant and Dan had returned to his wife. Mamma died and within weeks I lost the baby."

Amy looked up at the ceiling and there was nothing she could do to prevent her tears from falling. She cried as she spoke of David Daniel. "He was so beautiful...so perfect...another month and I'd have delivered him safely...three weeks even. He weighed six pounds and he looked so much like his father it made it even harder to bear...they said his little heart failed. He just went to sleep in my arms and never woke up again...I held him for six hours, just six hours...don't...don't risk losing your baby, Diana...please."

Diane cradled Amy against the squirming infant and Amy felt it move; marvelling at the miracle of life. They drank another cup of coffee and talked.

"Why did you go and marry, Roger?" Diana needed to know although she continued to feel that it was none of her business. "Don't tell me if you don't want to, it was rude of me to ask."

"It's okay. The answer is simple, because he asked me," came her pathetic reply. "Because I thought I could change him. Because I was so damned lonely. There was only me. I have no siblings and my parents were gone. Dan was...belonging to someone else. He'd returned to her in Wales. Roger asked me to marry him and I had no idea I could feel even lonelier trapped in a house with a man who pretends to care. I was better off alone. I'm so miserable and I want a baby."

"Don't do it," Diana warned. "Don't get pregnant for those reasons. Roger would only resent it, and resent you even more." It was then abundantly obvious that Diana knew that Roger had no paternal instincts.

"How do you know he'd resent it?" Amy asked.

"Come off it, Amy. I've seen the way he looks when you hold Michael." She was referring to her three-year-old, currently in nursery school. "He dislikes children as much as he does animals."

"Yes," Amy agreed. "He does. And you're correct. I can't get pregnant for the reasons I've given. Anyway, I can't because Roger..."

"What, Amy? Roger what?"

Amy bowed her head and balled her fists tightly in her lap. "I believe he got sterilised the last time he was in London."

"He what! Good God! He wouldn't!" But they both knew he would. "Oh, Amy, I am sorry." She had no idea what to say to comfort her distressed friend.

"That's okay. Please don't tell anyone. I should never have..."

Diana patted her hand. "It's our secret. But are you certain?"

"The MO sort of let the cat out of the bag when I went for another supply of the pill. He joked about not needing to bother in a few more weeks, when Roger's tests were back and there was a negative read." She shrugged her shoulders. "I pretended I knew what he was talking about. I should have known."

"Poor, Amy. Are you okay now?"

"Yes, and thanks for listening to my pathetic tale of woe."

"It was not pathetic. It's sad, and now you've told me I can understand things much better." She reached for Amy's hand and squeezed it gently. "You're a very brave lady, you know that, don't you? I could never have gone through what you've gone through."

"Yes, you could," she argued. "If you had to. Just promise me you'll take care of that child in there, and love him or her with all your heart, just as you do Michael. Promise me, Diana."

"I promise. This child will want for nothing."

PART THREE

Chapter Thirteen

One dull and exceedingly cold day, while Amy was walking through Spandau shopping centre, an elderly man shuffled up to her on painfully arthritic feet. He reached out a bony hand and gripped her arm urgently as she attempted to move away from him.

"What on earth are you doing?" she asked in fluent German, and then with a shock she recognised him and her eyes became alive again for the first time in years. "Herr Hoffmann! Rudi! How are you?"

"Older, my dear Amy." He croaked; his voice sounded very weak. "But how are you these days? I have not seen you for many years, four to be precise." Amy had visited the family home a year after marrying Roger. Lore and Peter were already married with families of their own by then and Rudi had lost his lovely wife Eva. And now Amy felt pangs of guilt for having neglected the old man while drowning in her own misery.

"Rudi, forgive me. I have been so wrapped up in my own life I have neglected to think about you. Where are you going?"

"To my house," he told her. "Will you come with me and share my humble meal? I am having knödel." His bright button eyes glistened mischievously when he saw her lick her lips in anticipation of the delicious German potato dumplings, which would be served with schnitzel and vegetables with a rich meaty sauce.

"Oh, you seducer of a woman's taste buds," she said as she tucked her arm in his. "Come. Let us get out of the cold." It was a week before Christmas, the 18th of December, 1980, and three days before Diana was due to produce her second child. Amy had been shopping for gifts for her Godson Michael and the new baby. The gifts would have to wait. Rudi Hoffmann was obviously in need of company.

Arm in arm they strolled back to the magnificent house on Kuregenstrasse. Nothing had changed in thirteen years, nothing, apart from the fact that the big old building was devoid now of the sound of laughter. Rudi Hoffmann lived alone with his memories, content with what he had, biding his time until he could join his precious wife.

"How is Lore? Peter too? Are they well?" Amy had broken into English now, excited to be in Rudi's company, just as lost in happy memories.

"Ja, they are well. Lore is about to give birth to my third grandchild. She said this one must be a girl. She wants to call her Amy."

"Are you serious?" Amy asked, her eyes widening in disbelief.

"Perfectly." His eyes narrowed as he asked. "It is your name, is it not?"

Amy laughed loudly and happily, filling the room with joy once again, lighting the darkest of corners and waking her sleeping soul. "Of course it is! Oh, Rudi, I really am very sorry I have not been to visit you."

Within an hour the old man knew everything there was to know which was not likely to contravene the Official Secrets Act. Amy told him everything without shedding a single tear. But the most difficult part was talking about Dan and the son he never saw.

Rudi Hoffman wisely let her talk until he knew there was no more and then he said, "You must stop living with regrets, my little one. Time now to put right your wrongs.

You must leave the man before he pulls you down to his level and buries you in misery."

Amy was visibly shocked by his advice. "I can't do that, Rudi. I have made a commitment and I cannot and will not walk away from it. I did it once, a long time ago, and just look at me now. No, I can't do it to him, nor to me."

"Then he will kill your soul, Amy. You will die lonely and sad. Is it worth the price?"

She shook her head. Tears were close to the surface now. "If only it were easy," she whispered. "If only I loved him, but I don't. I have never loved him. I told myself I did, but it was a lie. I tried very, very hard. I have longed to love him, to feel...to feel the way I do about Dan. Oh, Rudi, I have never once let him know how I feel inside. I keep it to myself. I could never hurt him - he doesn't deserve that. He can't help the way he is."

The old man sighed deeply, suddenly feeling his age. "I can see I am not getting through to you." Another deep sigh and he changed his approach slightly. "Are you still working for your government?" Amy nodded. "Does he know you are a spy?"

"But I am not a spy, Rudi!" she exclaimed, shocked he had thought that of her for so many years. "I have never traded secrets. I have never snooped or enquired. I have simply helped the oppressed reach the freedom we all take so much for granted, both mentally and physically. I am a psychologist; I am trained to help those in need."

"You are also oppressed and in need of help, my child," he replied and before Amy could respond he asked, "What does he think you do when you work?"

"He never asks. He...he is more interested in his own social circle. He never asks me about my life before we met, or what I desire from life. When he's had a drink, he's a very nice man, a considerate man. The man I met and became attracted to as a matter of fact. Sober...sober he's a moody and rude person. He abuses my friends to their faces and I make excuses for him. No, he has no interest in what I do, only what's in the bottom of his glass."

"Have you discussed this problem with anyone else?" he asked.

"Only my neighbour and best friend, Diana, although I believe everyone on the station knows what he's like. I cannot for the life of me understand why they keep him in the Royal Air Force. Either he's damned good at his job or they really don't know him at all."

"What is his work?" he asked.

Amy shook her head. "You know I can't discuss it with you, Rudi, besides, officially I don't know. All I can say is he works up the hill."

"Ah!" The old man understood everything now, and much more. "So! He works at Teufelsberg. Then I understand, my child." Rudi Hoffmann became lost in thoughts as he recalled taking his small son to the top of Teufelsberg to fly his kite.

Teufelsberg - Devil's Hill created by man with over twenty million cubic metres of rubble. Everything which had been West Berlin before the wartime blitz was piled up there for all to witness. The ruins of a beautiful city bulldozed into a lasting monument to the horror of war. A place where children play and men like Roger work.

Rudi sighed deeply. "I understand, although I cannot tell you what to do, I can only advise you to leave him while you have your sanity and your youth. Do not wait until you are old to make a new life for yourself. Best to do it now, while you can."

"I'm not strong enough to leave him, Rudi. I'm a coward. If anything happened to him, I could never live with myself."

"Nothing will happen," he assured her. "He will survive without you." But he could see he was wasting his breath in trying to convince her. "Whatever you decide to do, I want you to remember I am here for you. You can come to me at any time of the day or night. I consider myself to be your friend and I hope you will take advantage of my friendship. Never feel you are alone, because I am here. This is your home. Do you understand?"

She nodded as tears began flooding down her cheeks and an enormous lump stuck tight in her gullet. "Thank you, Rudi. Thank you."

"And now, before we eat, I have something to ask you, a favour. Please, dry your eyes. I have something to take your mind off your unhappiness."

"What is it?" she sniffed, taking the big white handkerchief out of his hand.

"Help me to bring a family out of East Berlin. Please, Amy, help me to do this thing. I have the money needed and I have all the details you will require. These are good people. Herr Doktor Koch is elderly and his wife is very sick. She needs to be treated in a civilised western hospital or she will die very soon. They have a grown son with a wife and young child. They are all trapped there, and I cannot speak of this to anyone. I have nobody to ask to help them. They need your help."

Her tears stopped suddenly, as if a well had been capped. Her eyes sparkled with anticipation and she sat forward in her seat, reaching for his hands as her pulses raced and adrenalin began surging through her once again. "Tell me more. Tell me everything."

Diana James gave birth to a daughter. The baby was born on Christmas Eve, 1980. Allen, Diana's husband, was ill in bed with a particularly bad bout of influenza when her waters broke and she went into labour. Despite all of his protestations, he had been banned from the delivery room.

Diana asked Amy to be present during the confinement, to hold her hand and mop her brow. Amy accepted with pleasure and immense pride, watching Megan make her noisy arrival in Berlin, red-faced and angry her arms and legs flailing wildly about her.

Megan objected to the disruption of what had been routine for her for nine months. She objected to the rudeness and the harshness of the world into which she'd emerged. She objected to the big strong hands and the brilliant blinding lights. Megan objected while Amy hugged her mother.

"She's beautiful, Diana. So big! Just look at her."

"Big and noisy," Diana agreed happily. "Just like I was when I was born. God help me if she gives me half the trouble I gave my poor mother. I yelled for the entire first year of my life."

While the father of the new infant rejoiced, Roger hadn't wanted to hear anything about Megan. He looked up and smiled at Amy as she burst into the room full of excitement and joy, and then he returned his entire attention to the film on the television set.

He was watching a German channel and a badly dubbed 'White Christmas' starring Bing Crosby. Amy knew he spoke only a handful of words in German. After almost twenty years of living in the country, he'd never made any attempt to learn the language. He was, however, fluent in Russian and Polish. She'd heard him talking in his sleep. He talked a great deal, about many sensitive subjects.

"Why are you sitting there watching that?" she asked.

"What?" he snapped rudely, as if she'd broken his concentration.

"I asked why you're watching something you can't understand."

"You watch what you want to watch and I'll watch what I want to watch. Okay?" He was drunk, and in an unusually obnoxious mood. The lethal fluid usually took him one of two ways, into a state of euphoria, when he sounded almost loving, or the exact opposite, when everything Amy said was a constant source of irritation for him.

"For God's sake, Roger," she began, still managing to sound pleasant and patient. "How many of those have you had?"

He rose from the chair and pulled himself up to his full height and walked menacingly towards her. Standing almost touching her, he leaned his face over until she could feel his breath on her flesh and then he spat words at her, "Clearly not enough to block your nagging. Mind your own damned business!"

He visited the bathroom before putting his overcoat on and slamming the front door shut behind him. He'd sit at the bar for the remainder of the night, possibly until morning. There were no hard and fast drinking times at the Mess.

Amy spent Christmas Eve alone, wrapped up in memories, a Polaroid picture of the new baby in her hand.

Roger stayed away all of Christmas Day. He booked himself into the Mess and slept there. Amy visited Diana and Megan and took gifts to Rudi Hoffmann.

It was Sunday, the fourth day of the new year, 1981, when Roger Longhurst walked back into their home. His face was red and bloated and his eyes bulged. He was angry again, only this time it was more than anger, he was blind with fury.

"What the f..." he began and Amy turned away from him, blocking her ears to his foul language. "Tell me!" he yelled as he took her by the shoulders and shook her. "What have you been doing? I got dragged out of my office and brought back here to be paraded in front of the CO like some bloody criminal to be informed that you've been bringing illegals through from the East! For Christ's sake! Tell me it's not true, tell me they made a mistake."

Amy stared at him, right into his angry eyes. She saw the person she'd grown to detest. There remained no visible trace of the funny, almost loveable Roger. This man looked at her with nothing but contempt in his eyes. He must have hated her from the onset of their relationship.

He raised his fist but Amy warned him with two little words, "Try it!" and he lowered his arm and walked away from her, his hands deep in his uniform trouser pockets. Amy asked, "Why do you care what I do?"

He spun on his heels. "You stupid little fool! You're ruining my career."

"I'm ruining your career!" she laughed. "Who are you kidding now, Roger? You have no career. You drank it out of the window years ago. You have no future with the Royal Air Force. They know what you are. There's nothing I can do which could possibly harm your fantasy career. You've done it to yourself, without my help!"

He slumped defeated and deflated in front of the television set, staring at the blank screen. "Why did you do it, you stupid, stupid fool?"

That morning Amy crossed the border into East Berlin, having filled out all of the appropriate forms to go on a harmless sightseeing trip with the blessing of the British military. She, and a wife of a senior ranking officer, signed out at Brigade HQ and it was all perfectly legitimate. As a dependent she was entitled to visit the eastern sector of the city on a special six-hour pass. She was to drive through to the checkpoint and with the windows tightly closed, display her identity card for the border guard to check the details and make notes on his clipboard. No speaking to the guards. No making contact with anyone in the East, other than during the process of eating, drinking, or shopping. Food was to be consumed while there. There was a long list of prohibited items and a strict ruling on assisting in the illegal emigration of any East German citizen.

They were two adults over the age of eighteen on a simple sightseeing tour. The shops were closed that day, as were the museums, but they said they wanted to go while it was quiet, to take photographs of the architecture.

It was exciting. Amy loved every minute of it. It reminded her of all the times she'd crossed the border with Dan. She parked her car in the middle of the road, in the designated parking area directly opposite the Staat Hotel in East Berlin. She then led her new friend into the hotel for a meal. That was also permitted. They had just over two hours left in which to relax and get back to Checkpoint Charlie. They'd walked miles that day, taking photographs and enjoying the architecture in the city.

While they were inside the hotel, a young man opened the boot of her car and closed it again from the inside.

An hour later the two women left the hotel and drove at a leisurely pace back through the city towards the East German side of Checkpoint Charlie. The guard signalled for Amy to move towards the barrier and she obeyed. The women held their ID cards to the windows and after a thorough inspection of the cards and the female occupants of the vehicle, he eventually signalled for her to drive away.

Amy looked back in the rear-view mirror and saw him standing in the middle of the road watching them. Something was not right this time, she felt it in her gut. The border guards were not permitted to undertake any search procedure. They simply reported their suspicions and left it to be dealt with by the Allied Forces. They missed very little.

Once parked in the military car park Amy invited her companion to go with her through the clearing procedure in the little cabin in the middle of the road. "Just in case you fancy coming through with someone else one day," she explained and the young woman was happy to follow her, curious as to what went on in there.

The military policeman on duty behind the counter accepted the package of documents Amy had been given to assist in any emergency while they were in the Eastern Sector. He then logged the return time on the official form and passed it across to her to sign the declaration stating she had not broken any of the stringent rules, which she had previously agreed to abide by at the start of her journey.

Amy signed the document and then a voice from behind her asked, "Have you any objections to my colleague and I searching your car, Mrs Longhurst?"

Slowly and calmly, she turned and faced the two senior ranking officers of the Royal Military Police. "None at all," she replied confidently, knowing her illegal passenger would be far away by now.

One of the men opened the boot of the car and saw it was completely empty. "The shops are closed," she said, laughing lightly. "Just as well, actually, I have a tendency to spot a bargain."

"We are more concerned with bodies than with shopping, ma'am," he told her politely. The man had been seen climbing from her car, and now Amy was about to face the music. She was invited to step back into the cabin at Checkpoint Charlie.

"My friend and I did some sightseeing and then we went for a meal in the Staat Hotel. I parked opposite there. When we'd eaten, we came straight back through. We were within our six-hour limit and we bought only the food and drink we consumed whilst in the hotel. There's nothing open over there! What could we have brought across if there's nowhere to buy anything?"

"Bodies, Madam." The MP said once again. "Illegal persons to be precise." But Amy argued, protesting her innocence. "If you wouldn't mind just following us back to Brigade Headquarters, Mrs Longhurst, your companion too."

There was no positive proof that Amy or her companion was aware of assisting in the escape of an East German resident, and they were eventually permitted to return to RAF Gatow, to where a large black cloud of suspicion loomed over them - or more correctly, over Amy. The gate guards glared at her upon her return and now Roger had returned spitting blood.

He had no way of knowing she'd brought an entire family out of the country since a week before Christmas, since the day Rudi Hoffmann asked for her help. The young man, on this quiet Sunday in the New Year, was the last of them. They were all safe now, and Amy could not have cared less what happened to her, or to Roger and his precious fictitious career.

"I have news for you, Roger," she began when he'd finished lecturing her again; rounding everything off with a tirade of foul language, just to make his point. "I don't like you. I'm lonely in your home, and I intend leaving you just as soon as I've tied up my business commitments this end."

He stared at her, his mouth sagging open in utter amazement. "You what? You can't be serious. You can't leave me, woman. I need you."

"Like a hole in the head," she informed him. "You don't need me. You need a skivvy - someone to clear up after you. You need to be mothered when you have a poorly head. You think more of your precious bottle of whisky than you ever have of me. I was a convenience. I fitted the bill, passed selection. You needed a little wife for your image. Well, you had one, but you no longer have her."

Heaving a sigh of relief, she went on. "I deserve more than this. I deserve better treatment. You don't love me. You have never loved me. You never touch me. You never need me. You make me feel dirty and cheap. I used to think there was something wrong with me and I was failing you in some way, but I know there's nothing wrong with me. I know it's you. You're always drunk. Too drunk and incapable to want to make love."

Amy laughed at the suggestion of making love. "Actually, that's very funny. You have never made love to me. You stab at me as if I'm eight and a half stone of meat on a butcher's slab. Stab! Stab! Stab! That's if you can rise to the occasion." It was a terrible and cruel attack but he really had invited it. "Everything is done in the dark," she went on; there was so much more needing to be said. "As if you're really ashamed of me and my body."

Before he had the opportunity to draw breath, let alone the living room curtains, Amy tore open her blouse and stepped out of her skirt. Within seconds she stood naked and very beautiful before him.

"This is me!" She said, turning for him to take a good close look from every vantage point. "This is what I look like without my clothes on. I'm not ashamed of my body, but you make me feel like a common whore. You inhibit me with your peculiar ways. You make me feel dirty. Look at me, Roger! For God's sake look at me!"

He raised his eyes and stared at her, seeing her naked for the first time in five years of marriage. He'd have needed to be blind, or completely insensitive, not to have known how beautiful she was. Her breasts were firm and her stomach flat. There was no surplus fat on her body. She kept herself fit. She was lovely.

"Amy I..." He turned from her and drew the curtains, worried a passer-by might see her. "I'm sorry. I had no idea you felt this way. Will you give me a chance to make things up to you?"

She knew it was a mistake, just as she knew she had to agree and with a sigh she said, "I can't promise you anything, but I am your wife and I have always done my level best to be a good wife. I'm not one to walk out on something I walked into with my eyes open." She picked up her clothes and went upstairs.

Roger tried hard to make amends. He was attentive and loving in a clumsy sort of way. He made love to her that night although he could not bring himself to leave the bedroom light on and he still completed the act in total clumsy silence. When he wanted her to turn or move, he prodded and poked. He could never express himself with words, although he knew he loved her and he certainly needed her in his life.

There was an enquiry into the alleged incident at Checkpoint Charlie and the judgement was reached that Mrs Roger Longhurst was to be banned from visiting the Soviet Sector for the remainder of her stay in Berlin. Her privileges were revoked and life threatened to become even more tedious than ever before for her.

Within days of promising to try, Roger slipped easily back into his old ways. Drinking through the day when off duty, and through the night when on duty. Lovemaking became a thing of the past; he had no need of her once again. Nothing was any better, and if anything, things were worse because he watched her every move now. He was still smarting from the severity of the reprimand he'd received.

The Station Commanding Officer had warned him to keep his wife in order or suffer the consequences. Roger was a frightened man. He knew only of life in an overseas 'duty-free' situation with cheap alcohol and cheap cigarettes. It was a good life for him and he dreaded the very thought of returning to England a moment before it became necessary. Sobriety was not a prospect he relished.

Amy could see no way out of the life she'd made for herself. She knew she would keep on forgiving him and he would continue to be a self-centred, conceited bastard.

Plans were in force for Amy to share her 34th birthday with the new baby. Megan was to be baptised during the afternoon of the 16th of January, and a massive double celebration was planned for later on. There would be two cakes, champagne and a great deal of delicious food. The party would begin at three, immediately after the church service at RAF Gatow, and would go on into the evening when the adults who'd been on duty could join in. All that was needed to do to finalise the preparations was for Amy to collect the cakes from the NAAFI shop at Theodore-Heuss Platz on the way into the city centre.

The cakes should have been delivered the previous day but there'd been a mix-up and Amy was none too pleased that everything was being left in the balance until the last minute.

"What's planned for today?" Roger asked, attempting to take an interest. He'd forgotten to buy either a card or a gift for his wife and he was feeling a modicum of guilt, which served him right and there was no way he'd derive sympathy from Amy, who was beginning to feel a bit stressed.

"I have to go and collect the cakes," she said. "Do you think you could organise more champagne? I don't think we have enough."

"Yes, okay," he happily agreed, this was more up his street. "Another dozen bottles?"

Amy smiled now, liking him when he spoke to her as if she were something more than subhuman. "Fine. But do you think they'll have that many bottles left at the Mess? I have bought up rather a lot lately."

"If they haven't, I'll find some," he assured her as he reached for his jacket. "Don't worry about it. It's all in hand."

There were only six bottles of the better-quality champagne left in the cellar at the Officers' Mess and Roger had promised to buy more, the last thing he could afford to do right now was upset his wife. She was a good housewife and easy to live with, and he knew exactly which side his bread was buttered.

He and his colleague Simon Newman hurried off to the NAAFI shop to be told they were out of stock and they had only a good quality sparkling wine in stock. It wasn't good enough for Roger. He needed to buy champagne, as promised. The men returned to the bar for a couple of quick drinks while they pondered over the problem in hand.

"Try the main shop," Newman suggested, slopping beer down his sweater. "If they haven't got any, we'll nip into town." In town they could pick up a few more drinks at the bars, which were never closed, and eventually they might even find someone selling champagne by the case.

The plan suited Roger. He contemplated another whisky before setting off, wisely changed his mind and after paying a visit to the toilet they set off in the direction of the city centre.

Roger spotted the blue Opel; the car he'd bought for his wife the year they were married. It was parked in a restricted zone right outside the main NAAFI shop, at Theodore-Heuss Platz. He shook his head; she just kept on breaking the rules. What was he going to do with her?

"Needs a firm hand, if you ask me," Newman voiced his shallow opinion.

"I didn't bloody well ask you," Roger informed him without any hint of malevolence sounding in his voice. "Go and park the bloody car and I'll move that thing before I get hauled over the coals again."

He carried a spare key for the Opel on his keychain; however, the door was unlocked and that made his blood boil even more. He opened it and climbed in, inserting the key in the ignition, still muttering about his wife's carelessness.

The explosion that followed his turning the key shattered every pane of glass within a radius of 200 metres. Thirty-four German civilians in a nearby bus were injured. Twenty more civilians in passing cars and in the bus stop close by were wounded, one with life-threatening injuries. Two members of the German Defence Unit, the security guards outside the NAAFI shop, were critically wounded.

British service personnel, their wives and children, were also injured in the blast. Over two hundred people checked into hospitals in Berlin that day, mostly with minor injuries caused by flying glass.

Roger Longhurst was killed outright. His legs torn off, and his stomach ripped open. He knew nothing about the blast. He died cursing his wife. His was thankfully the only fatality that day.

Amy was deep in the heart of the big shop, looking at the lace underwear, wondering if she should dare buy anything so blatantly feminine in an effort to win Roger's attention when the explosion tore through the building. As the floor beneath her feet shook, a tremor rippled from one end of the building to the other. Plaster and dust rained down on bewildered shoppers who became instantly panic-stricken. They ran blindly, uncertain where to go or why they should be going there.

Dropping everything where she stood, Amy made her way through confused people and broken glass. The sound of hysteria was beginning to ring out through the terrible silence that immediately followed the explosion. Amy remained calm and in full control. She intended helping in any way she could.

When she stepped out into the street and saw what had once been her little blue car lying on its side like a broken toy on the pavement some twenty metres or more from where she left it, she struggled to make sense of what she was seeing. Her car was in two pieces, with what remained of the wheels still spinning. There was no fire, just smoke, and the terrible stench of explosives, fuel and burned rubber. Debris was scattered everywhere.

Confused and shocked she went down on her knees as her legs buckled beneath her weight. She knew exactly what had happened - an explosive device had been attached to the underside of the vehicle and that something or someone had triggered it. What she didn't know was that her husband was now dead.

Simon Newman staggered drunkenly towards her. His face black apart from the streak of red down his right cheek from a small cut on his brow. "Holy Mother!" he cried out. "Sweet Jesus. Where's Roger?"

"Roger?" Amy called, grabbing at his leg to pull herself up. "Roger was here?" she screamed at him. "He was here, in my car?"

He looked confused and Amy realised he couldn't hear her properly. "Simon!" she yelled at him, shaking his arm. "Was Roger in my car!"

"Yes," he replied at last as the second shock wave hit him and he began trembling uncontrollably. "He was going to move it." His teeth started chattering and he wrapped his arms around his body, hugging himself in an attempt to get warm. "It was illegally parked. Christ! What happened, Amy?"

But Amy was feeling nauseous. Bile began rising from her gall bladder and she moved towards the gutter to vomit, coughing and spluttering. Alone again. Alone!

She telephoned Commander Cooper from Diana's house. Her hands shook as she held on tightly to the receiver. Her voice was unsteady when she spoke to him. She told him what had happened. The line was not secure but that fact mattered little to her now.

"Sit tight," he said. "Leave everything to me."

"They want me," she said quietly.

"Amy! Leave things to me. You're coming home."

"I have no home," she replied.

"Sit tight. Trust me."

She smiled as she lowered the receiver to the cradle. How many times had she uttered those same two words? 'Trust me.' They were easy words to use and comforting words to hear. The truth was that there remained only one man she trusted even now and God alone knew where he was.

A small, unmarked aircraft landed on the airfield at RAF Gatow exactly four weeks later on Friday 13 February 1981. It had been sent to lift Amy Longhurst away from danger. She carried only a small holdall and an enormous guilt complex. For all she'd yearned to be released from her marriage vows, she would never have wished for Roger to be killed, not for her, or for anyone.

She would never again see her good friend Diana, nor would she witness Michael and Megan growing up into beautiful people. Rudi Hoffmann would wonder about her, and then he would grow even older and die never knowing the truth.

Amy slept on the return flight. It was the first real sleep she'd had since Roger's death. For four weeks she'd remained isolated from the world, locked up in her home for her own safety, with only the men from the SIB, the Special Investigations Branch, to keep her company.

Police and military enquiries took place, an inquest into the death of Roger Longhurst was conducted and then at last, when it was all over, she was permitted to leave. Nobody laid claim to the murder of a member of Her Majesty's Armed Forces in Germany.

Amy took only a handful of photographs and enough clothes to get by with. She wanted nothing else, although it would all be packed and sent to London. She wanted to forget that the past five and a half years had ever happened. It was all a bad dream and a terrible, terrible mistake.

"How are you?" Cooper asked as she stood and faced him in his large intimidating London office.

With a sigh she said, "I'm alive. What more can I say? A month ago, someone killed my husband. They thought they were killing me. Tell me what you want to hear, Commander."

"Sit down," he said and she obeyed mechanically. "The situation is this, Amy, all of those personnel who knew you at the time your husband was killed, are sworn to secrecy as to your identity. You are, as far as anyone is concerned, lying in bed in a private West German hospital. Your life is hanging by a thread. Nobody will damage your cover. I want you to take a holiday. Go away. Lose yourself for a while."

"Do I have any option as to whether I take this suggested holiday or not, sir?"

"No. Do you have friends you could go to?"

Amy tipped her head back and stared up at the embossed ceiling and then she returned her gaze to the commander. "I had a friend or two out there in Berlin, my neighbour, Diana and Rudi Hoffmann - you must remember him." With a tired sigh, she went on.

"How is someone like me supposed to accumulate friends, sir? I'm forever moving on, forever wearing a different disguise, a new identity. They know what I look like." Her amber eyes blazed angrily now that she'd begun venting her guilt-ridden anger and frustration.

"They know what I look like and they want me. If they can't take me alive, they're prepared to kill me. You know how many times they've tried to snatch me. What am I supposed to do, have plastic surgery?"

"Do you want out, Amy?" It was the first time he'd offered her such an option.

"Yes. I want out! Right now, I wish it were me who was dead and not Roger Longhurst. I have nothing. I'm thirty-six years of age. A month ago I was celebrating my birthday. Huh! What a present someone left for me. I'm a widow. I have a widow's pension from the government and what...grey hairs by fifty?"

He sighed before he spoke to her. He was tired of this stupid game. "If you are really sincere that you wish to retire it can be arranged."

"Yes," she responded sarcastically, "Permanently." And then she sighed again. "No. I don't want to retire, but where do I go from here? Can you tell me that?"

"Take a holiday," he repeated. "Go away, a long way away. Wear contacts and a wig. I'll get you papers, a passport, and money. Don't go near your old flat. You can stay here. There are rooms upstairs. By Monday morning I'll have everything arranged. Is there anyone I can contact on your behalf?"

"Rudi Hoffmann," she said. "Tell him...tell him I wish him well. Tell him that I will never forget his kindness. Tell him it's over. He'll understand and he will have heard about Roger dying."

"No problem. Anyone else?" He was still wondering about Dan Jones and her. He had no idea when they last set eyes on each other. Dan had been in Berlin several times in the past eight years. They could easily have met again.

"There is no-one else." Amy rubbed her aching eyes and then she looked at the gold band on her left hand. She felt no pride as she removed it and tucked it into her bag.

"How about Dan Jones?" Cooper asked at last, unable to bear her pain.

Those amber eyes turned on him, flashing angrily, warning him to stay out of the private area of her life. "What about him?" she snapped.

"Do you want me to contact him?"

"No!"

"But, Amy. He's divorced and his wife has remarried. Within weeks of the divorce going through, she'd remarried."

"And you're telling me this because…?"

"Because he'd like to see you again. He often asks about you. I kept him..." but she interrupted angrily, leaping to her feet, her hands on the desktop and her face stretched forward to spit words at her senior officer.

"How dare you! How dare you discuss me with him! What gives you the right to meddle in my life?"

"Amy! Calm down." He saw the tears of frustration and shock beginning to form in her eyes. "I have never once divulged any personal details. I simply informed him that you were alive and healthy. He knows nothing about Roger Longhurst, or of your marriage. He only ever asked if you were safe. That was all. If you are interested, however, he still works for the department and he lives in a small house on the sea front at Southend. He's a good man."

"I'm not interested. I'm tired." She moved away from the desk. "If you don't mind, I would like to sleep."

She went to bed in the luxurious room two floors above the commander's office. She thought about Dan. About seeing him again. He was divorced. But no, it was too late for that. He'd gone running back to that woman. Then she felt guilty for that thought, she'd been ill. He was a man who took responsibility seriously. Naturally, he had to be with her.

And then her mood darkened towards her lover, he'd let her down when she needed him most. She would survive without him now. She had no option. She alone had shaped her destiny. She had brought the misery and the guilt upon herself. What good would it do bringing him back into her life? She would only get him killed alongside her.

Cooper sent for her on Monday morning and he couldn't help but notice the lack of spring in her step. Without that old confidence, he wondered how she could survive. She appeared broken and it saddened him deeply.

"You asked to see me, sir?"

He looked at her; checking her appearance, and he was satisfied with what he saw. There was barely a trace of the old Amy there, only the voice remained hers. The shoulder length black wig, made from human hair, and dark brown contact lenses, altered her appearance dramatically. The hairstyle was elegant and natural; a straight cut fringed bob. With her eyebrows darkened and a deeper shade of make-up, including carefully manicured and painted red finger and toenails, and matching lipstick, the disguise was perfect.

Her clothes were elegant. Paris models had once paraded in fashion shows in the outfit on her back. Her underwear was also Parisian, lace and silk. Her shoes were handmade Italian leather, designed and manufactured in Rome, as soft as peach bloom against her skin.

The chequebook in her small suede bag told her that her name was Ruth Miller. The balance, on paper, was well in excess of a million pounds. She carried a passport in the same name: Ruth Miller, a 34-year-old spinster - supposedly a writer - daughter of dead financier Herbert Compton-Miller - unsuccessful with her writing yet wealthy enough not to need worry about working for the remainder of her days. She liked to travel extensively. Her cover story was strong enough to hold up anywhere in any country. The commander was an influential man and circles had been opened around the world in which Amy could move freely and without fear of being recognised, other than by those who could help her.

"You look good." He approved of the new image. "Have a seat."

"Is this for life?" she asked. Terrified of the thought of spending a lifetime in a black wig, putting irritating contact lenses into her eyes and painting her nails an obscene shade of crimson.

"No, but it is for now, for your safety. Things will die down again."

"If not?" she asked.

"Things will die down," he repeated patiently. "In the meantime, you can relax and rest. Look upon this as a little bonus. You have enough real money in your own bank account to take things easy and enjoy life for a while. Have you decided where you'll be going?"

"Not really, probably abroad. I don't know. There are places I've always wanted to visit and never had the time. Now I have the time and the money and no inclination to leave."

"You'll decide," he told her. "You've always been a practical woman." Choosing to ignore her sniff of contradiction he asked, "Is there anything else I can do for you, Amy?"

She smiled at him, grateful for his help and his extended kindness. "No. I'll be fine. Thank you for...for putting up with me all these years."

"Go on," he said firmly. "Get out of here before I change my mind and make you earn your living."

It was strange how things happened suddenly and all at once. Within weeks she'd been widowed, moved away from her house and home of over five years, and now, dressed like a stranger, she walked into Harrods in Knightsbridge and stood so close to Monique Bremman she could almost feel her breath upon her skin.

Monique looked wonderful. Amy couldn't help but stare. The young woman had filled out, looking healthy and fit. She also looked extremely happy and contented. She was, however, currently experiencing some difficulty in getting the sales woman on the Elizabeth Arden counter to understand her broken English. Amy felt a brief moment of disappointment that the young woman hadn't taken the time to improve her spoken English.

"Can I be of assistance?" Amy asked politely. "I speak a little German."

"You do!" Monique exclaimed, delighted to find help. "That is wonderful. Only six months I have been here. My English is still not so good." And then lapsing into German she said, "Ich möchte bitte eine Reinigungscreme und Nachtcreme. Dann hätte ich bitte noch einen dunkleren Lippenstift, da mir meinen zu hell ist."

Amy smiled, understanding exactly what she wanted. She turned to the patient consultant and translated the request. "The young lady needs night cream, cleansing cream and a darker shade of lipstick than the one she is currently wearing. She is of the opinion that her present shade is far too light."

Removing her sunglasses Amy looked back at Monique who was staring at her now. "Vielen Dank. Entschuldigen Sie bitte." She said as she held Amy's arm. And then she spoke to her in English. "I am sorry, but I know you."

Amy shook her head. "I think not, my dear. I am sure I would have remembered such a beautiful face. Now, is there anything else I can do for you before I continue my shopping?"

"No. Thank you." Monique could not shake the feeling of déjà vu. "You have been most kind."

"Nicht der Rede wert." Amy had told her not to mention it. It was good to see her looking so wonderfully free and happy. She was wearing lovely clothes and she obviously had money to spend on cosmetics. She had truly been worth the effort. "Auf Wiedersehen."

Monique remained uncertain. "Auf Wiedersehen, and for your help I thank you once again."

From then on Amy began walking with a lighter step. Whenever she passed a mirror, or caught her reflection in a shop window, she stared, wondering who the stranger was and if she would ever grow used to her, but she was happier than she had been in many years, despite everything. It had not all been in vain.

She was passing Dixon's window when the news appeared on dozens of different television screens at the same time. She saw images of the remains of her blue Opel, and there was an old photograph of Roger looking handsome in his uniform. Her heart pounded painfully as she entered the shop, hurrying now, wanting to hear what was being said. One small set had the volume turned up and she rushed towards it.

"The IRA has today claimed responsibility for the horrific car bombing in West Berlin last month in which a Royal Air Force Officer lost his life when the booby trap placed beneath the car belonging to his civilian wife exploded. Government spokesman Hugh Gregory-Harper has condemned the attack as inhumane and..."

Amy moved away as a salesman approached her. "I was just looking, thank you," she said, heading for the exit and fresh air. She needed to telephone the commander immediately.

"Commander Cooper, this is Ruth Miller. I need to speak to you, urgently."

"I can meet you at the usual place in...shall we say half an hour?"

"Yes, thank you." She hung up.

Cooper was sitting on the park bench with a newspaper spread between his outstretched hands. Amy sat down on the opposite end of the bench. She looked around her; she was certain she had not been followed.

"I saw the news. They're saying that Roger was killed by the IRA."

"Yes. Seems we were mistaken. You had a right-hand drive car with British Forces Germany registration plates. Don't forget, those BFG plates stick out like sore thumbs. You were parked outside the NAAFI shop. They didn't much care who it was they got, man, woman or child, just as long as there was a connection with the British military. Roger was the perfect target. They're delighted with such a high-profile murder and you can breathe easy again."

"Can I return to normal?" The wig was beginning to itch and annoy her.

"No, not yet. Give the dust time to settle." He turned a page in the newspaper. "By the way, your belongings will be here tomorrow. I'll hold everything in storage until you decide what you want done with it."

"Dump it," she said without hesitation. "Give it to the poor."

"All of it?" He turned the page again, his eyes scanning the words before him without seeing them.

"Yes."

"I'll hold it for a few months. We'll discuss this again later. Go away. Take a holiday. Contact me every Friday as planned."

As Amy prepared to move, she said. "I spoke to Monique Bremman two hours ago."

His head snapped around and he stared at her, the colour rising in his cheeks. "You what!"

"You heard me, sir. I spoke to Monique. She looked wonderful. I'm glad I saw her. I now feel happier with myself."

"Did she..."

"No, sir. She didn't recognise me, but she felt she knew me from somewhere and I didn't hang about to give her any clues. Is she living in London?"

"Yes, newly arrived. She's working for the department. We held her in Germany for a while and decided it was time for her to come across. She's a good girl. Useful to have on our side of the fence."

"I'm pleased." Amy sighed. "And now I really must go. I have a train to catch."

"Somewhere exotic in mind?" he asked.

"Hardly," she said as she stood. "Southend-on-Sea."

Chapter Fourteen

Amy took possession of a comfortable suite at The Grand Hotel in Southend-on-Sea. The suite contained a lounge with telephone and colour television. The bedroom was luxurious by any standards and the king-sized bed hardly did anything to fill it. Despite the size of the suite, it was a homely place and Amy was grateful to kick off her shoes and lie on the bed. She was chilled through. The train had been nothing more than an icebox, with cold air blasting in where there should have been heat. She kept her long grey cashmere coat on, wrapping it around her legs, wishing she'd bought herself sensible boots and thermal underwear instead of the smart shoes and frills.

She fell asleep and woke with a start in the now dark room; someone had knocked on the door. "Come in," she called, without moving a muscle.

The door opened and she saw the silhouette of a man. "Miss Miller?" he questioned. It was the hotel manager. The light switch clicked and Amy blinked against the blinding light. "Are you cold, Miss Miller?" he asked, seeing her cocooned in her coat.

"I was," she said, smiling warmly at him. Praying that her wig remained securely in place and was not sitting at some obscure angle. "I was also very tired and I'm ashamed to say, this is exactly where I fell when I came into the room, and I have not moved a muscle since. I've been comfortably fast asleep. Was there something you wanted?"

Returning her smile, he sighed with relief that she wasn't complaining of inadequate heating, and that she wasn't ill. "As long as you're well, Miss. Actually, I came to tell you that dinner is being served. You did ask me to remind you when it was time, and you seem not to have heard the telephone."

"I turned the ringer off," she explained. "I needed to sleep. Thank you for calling me. I'll freshen up and come straight down."

He thanked her and was about to leave when she called him back. "Could you tell me where I can find the address of an old friend here in Southend? I seem to have mislaid it and all I know is that he lives on the sea front."

"Do you have his name, Miss Miller?"

Silly man, she thought. He'd hardly be a friend without my knowing his name! "His name is Daniel Jones."

"I'll make enquiries for you. It should be a simple enough task. Do enjoy your meal."

She thanked him again and he closed the door.

Heads turned as she glided gracefully into the crowded dining room. She ignored everyone by focusing her attention on the waiter who signalled to her that the table at the far side of the room was reserved for her. She thanked him with a simple nod of her head and a gracious smile and moved between the staring diners.

It was Monday evening, 16 February 1981. Four weeks and three days after the death of her husband and she was sitting in a packed dining room in an opulent hotel on the sea front at Southend-on-Sea. It really was quite unbelievable how much had happened in so short a space of time.

Her hands trembled as she lifted the knife and fork and began eating. She kept asking herself what she was doing there. It was madness to even contemplate looking for Dan. Yet she was free again, and so was he – so why not? Why not take the chance that he still wanted her in his life? She needed him. She was lonely without him. All those wasted years - so many wasted years and so many bitter regrets.

"Would you care for dessert, Miss Miller?"

She looked up at the waiter. "Just coffee please, and do give Chef my compliments. I cannot remember eating this well in a very long time."

It had been good food. English fare. Neither over-spiced nor over-fancy. Roast beef with an abundance of fresh vegetables. She was full and almost happy again. Not a soul knew who she was. She was an enigma in this place, the beautiful and mysterious lady with the lovely legs and expensively cut clothes.

"Thank you, Miss Miller," he said, delighted with her praise. "I'll pass on your kind words to Chef. Your coffee won't be a moment."

She was on her second cup when the manager arrived with news for her. "You were enquiring about a gentleman, Miss Miller." With that he placed a folded sheet of paper on the snow-white linen tablecloth. "I believe this will be of help. Is there anything else I can do for you this evening?"

"No, thank you, you have been most helpful."

It took her all of her strength of will to force herself to walk back to her room. She longed to run, to grab her coat and bag and fly out of the hotel and down the promenade into Dan's arms.

Alone in her room she calmed herself down again. The paper clasped in her trembling hand, still folded just as it was given to her. Roger was four weeks dead and she was trying to contact her lover, the father of her dead child. She should feel shame and remorse because she was behaving no better than a slut in lusting after a man. Longing to hold him, to be naked in his arms again, to feel his body against hers. To be loved for who and what she was. But it wasn't just that, not lust, not truly lust.

Her conscience wrung her out and squeezed her dry. It shook her and frightened her and then logic rang out loud and clear. She'd been faithful to Roger for the full term of their marriage. Never once had she wished him dead. Happiness is what she'd longed to share with him within the bounds of their marriage - happiness and companionship. And now that he was dead, well, it made her sad, for she had cared very deeply about him. She couldn't mourn him in his passing, just as she found it impossible to cry for him.

God forgive me, she thought, but I'm relieved that I no longer have to watch him drinking hour upon hour, day in and day out. I'm relieved that he's no longer my responsibility.

As Amy lifted the telephone receiver, she prayed that her maker would understand what was going on inside her head and her heart. She looked at the neat writing on the paper and dialled the number written there.

His voice reached down the line. He repeated the number she'd dialled seconds earlier and Amy felt panic overtaking her. "Who is this?" he asked but she found it impossible to speak. Her heart had stopped beating. Time itself had suddenly stood still for her. It was Dan, her Dan.

"Amy?" he asked, but how could he possibly have known. "Is that you? Speak to me. Please speak to me? Where are you, my little one?" How could he have known?

"Dan," her voice was trembling as much as her hands. Tears filled her eyes and choked her throat. Seven years of misery had passed since she heard his wonderful voice speak those words.

"Amy! Where are you?"

"That really doesn't matter," she whispered. "How are you, Dan?"

"I'm fine. God, woman! You sound bloody marvellous. I've got to see you."

"No!" she gasped in blind panic.

"Amy! Don't do this. You called me. You must need me. Let me come to you, wherever you are." His knees felt weak and he found himself sitting on the sofa whereas he'd been standing when he answered the call. The one thing he'd longed for in all the passing years was the opportunity to hear her voice again and to make amends for what he believed he'd done wrong by her. "Please, let me come to you," he repeated.

"No!" she repeated urgently.

"Are you in trouble?"

"No." She was calmer now.

"Are you ill?"

"No." His voice was so gentle that her eyes filled with fresh tears.

"Hell! Where are you?"

Amy lowered the receiver as she lost her nerve for the first time in her life.

Neither of them slept that night. Dan paced the living room floor all night long. He washed and shaved with the first of the morning light, made himself a plate of scrambled eggs and toast and ate as if there was going to be a famine, but this morning was different, Amy had made contact and he knew that she needed him. He was going into the city on the midday train to pressure the commander into telling him exactly where she was.

Amy lay on the big double bed staring at the ceiling until by morning she'd made a decision she knew she would never regret. She showered and dressed and went down to the dining room for a light breakfast.

After breakfast she returned to her room where she studied her image in the dressing table mirror, still not sure that she knew who she was any longer, but more comfortable with the stranger than she had been the previous day. She removed the contact lenses and dropped them into the special cleaning solution so that she could check her make-up and apply a touch more lipstick to her pretty lips. She then put the lenses back in place; covering the amber lights, and looked to see if her stocking seams were straight before putting on her coat.

At one minute past nine, Daniel Jones closed his front door and crossed the road to stroll along the promenade. He walked briskly for five minutes and then he stopped and leaned on the sea wall, staring out to sea. It was a lovely day, bitterly cold with a biting easterly wind, but fine and clear. He thought that perhaps it might snow that night, perhaps not. It was very cold though.

He was a troubled man. He'd heard Amy's wonderful voice on the telephone the previous night and he'd felt her hand on his brow, her perfume filled his senses in the confines of his home. Knowing he needed her and that he could not reach out and hold her made it all so difficult to bear. All that was left for him was to dream about her and live with his memories of days gone by. He felt old and tired. Without Amy there was little point in going on, but he lived on in the hope that one day she would return to him, and if that glorious day should ever dawn, he vowed he would never let her to leave him again.

With a tremendous feeling that something was changing in his life; that he was on the brink of the greatest adventure yet, he turned and took a deep gulp of sea air and watched the woman in the grey coat walking towards him. The coat was long, covering all but six inches of her legs. She looked classy, someone with a bit of money. She stopped walking and stood there staring at him, ten metres away.

He hadn't the slightest idea who she was and he was irritated that she was looking at him in that way, her with her fancy sunglasses. When she began walking towards him again, he saw nothing familiar about her. The walk was that of a stranger, as were the clothes and the hairstyle. Her heels were high and she swung her hips in a way completely unfamiliar to him, but she was sexy and there was no denying it, and that annoyed him even more than everything else about her.

He cried out Amy's name in his head. He longed for her to be right in front of him and not the stranger who was having a profound effect on his heart - which was now pounding painfully in his chest. He looked away from her, at the fast-turning tide. Why was she looking at him like that? Why was she still walking towards him? He rose to his full height and puffed out his chest, glad that he'd been exercising in the gym every day, proud of his full muscles. He was 41 years of age and still extremely fit.

The stranger stood alongside him now, looking out to sea. Her eyes were focused somewhere on the horizon but Dan was staring at her again. Her perfume reached his nostrils yet it was as alien to his senses as she was. She removed the dark glasses and looked at him. His heart flipped, but he still had no clue why he felt so confused and excited.

Was she an agent? A Soviet agent! Christ! *'What the hell am I going to do?'* He asked himself. *'Run?'* He'd never had any direct dealings with agents. He'd met that Russian woman, Roushaka; she could have been a spy, of course. And once, just once, he'd asked Amy outright if she was a spy and she'd laughed at him and denied it. He loved Amy, spy or no spy. This was different, if this woman was a spy and she was after him...what then? What was he to do? He was not used to running away. He'd run away from Amy, a long time ago, but never again, and certainly not from a woman, spy or no spy.

Her eyes were dark and mysterious like deep pools. Her complexion was also dark, and her red lips too inviting. What was she up to? He looked away again; frightened of her, of the way his heart kept lurching and pumping. And then a voice sounded in his head and he froze on the spot.

"Don't you know me, Dan?" It was Amy's voice. He stared at the stranger but she was looking at the turning tide. He spun on his heels and looked behind him yet there was nobody there - just the mysterious stranger by his side. "I'm here, Dan," she said again, yet the woman had not uttered a sound, nor had she moved more than her eyelids.

He stared long and hard at her. It was a trick, a bloody cruel trick! They were playing with his mind and then those luscious red lips parted and the tip of a pink tongue moistened them and she smiled, content that she was with him again. Glad that she'd contacted him. There were no regrets, not now.

"Hello, Dan," she whispered and her lips moved this time.

"Oh, my God!" His knees buckled and gave way and she reached out to support him. "Is it really you? Really, really you?" he asked, unconvinced that he was still sane.

"Yes," she breathed the word. "Can we go somewhere and talk?"

He took a deep breath, shook his head to clear it and said, "Well I'll be damned. I'd never have recognised you, never. And there was me bragging about knowing you anywhere." He shook his head again before taking her arm and propelling her across the road to his house where he whisked her through the front door and took her in his arms.

"You feel wonderful," he told her. "I've missed you." He kissed those red lips and clung to her, drinking up her presence. There was no doubt in his mind now; he was holding Amy again. "I've missed you."

"And I you," she confessed. "Can I sit down and breathe?"

He laughed. "Sorry. I'm forgetting my bloody manners. Sit, please. Tea?"

She nodded. "Love one. No sugar."

"Tea it is."

Dan remained in the kitchen during the time it took to boil the kettle and make the tea. There were many things to say and ask and he couldn't afford to lose this woman again, never again. He'd blown it too many times before. This time he was going to slow things down and take it steady, no more the crazy headstrong young soldier of long ago.

She was removing her coat, placing it on the back of the cottage-style two-seater settee, when he handed her a mug of steaming tea. She placed it on the low table upon which she saw a variety of magazines, including 'Soldier'. She waited for him to speak.

"Are you working?" he asked.

"No, I'm hiding."

"Who from?" he asked from his seat a good two metres away from her.

"Probably nobody," she admitted. "It's rather a lengthy story."

"I've got all the time in the world," he told her. "I'm at the start of fourteen days hard earned leave. I just got back from a month in Sweden."

"Sweden!" Amy was impressed. She had never been to Sweden.

"Okay, talk to me, Amy. Tell me what's been happening to you."

"Have you seen the news lately?"

"Yes, every day. Anything in particular?"

"Car bomb - Berlin - last month," she jogged his memory.

"Yes, or course! Right outside my old haunt, the NAAFI at TH Platz. Bad thing that. Never could understand the mentality of those mad bastards."

"Me neither," she said and then she shocked him to the core. "It was my car they blew up, Dan."

He was suitably stunned, she heard him gasp. "They said a 'blue job' copped it. An officer."

"Yes," she agreed quietly, unable to look at him. "That 'blue job' as you put it, was my husband." She had his full and undivided attention.

"No!" he exclaimed. "I'm sorry, Amy."

"Me too. I'd parked my car illegally and he arrived to do some shopping and decided to move it for me. He was a very neat person when it came to sticking to the rules. Anyway, seems it was a car bomb. I had no idea, none. I'd never have parked it there if I'd known. I was bloody careless about things like that, always in a hurry. Always cocking things up."

"You've had a bad shock," he said, excusing her of blame. He wanted to hold her again but she looked so much the stranger that he was almost shy of her now. Only the voice and the shape of her nose belonged to Amy. The rest was strange - different. This person moved, walked, behaved differently. Yet his heart told him who she was. It was Amy; he felt her presence there in the room.

"So," he began. "What's been happening to you?"

"Too much." She was reluctant to get into things, just happy to be there with him, looking at him, listening to him. Knowing he loved her in the same old way.

"When did you meet him?" he asked at last.

"About seven years ago. When I was in Brugen, just after my mother died, and then I returned to Berlin five...nearly six years ago and he'd been posted there. We shared a few glasses of something or other, I can't remember what, and I got drunk." She laughed but the sound was devoid of humour.

"I had a job to do out there. A simple mission, a straight exchange with an East German female. We swapped places. The afternoon before the mission I got plastered and ended up in bed with Squadron Leader Roger Longhurst." Amy still felt the exact same shame, as if it had been yesterday.

"I left early next morning and headed for the East. As I said, a straight switch and I was to make my own way back. It all went more or less to plan, although I was forced to use my initiative for once, and I didn't have a handsome strong soldier to watch my back." She laughed again, this time, however; there was warmth in the sound.

"When I got back to Gatow I had a few more drinks and ended up in bed with Roger again. It was pretty callous of me actually because I didn't love him, I used him."

"Why?" Dan asked feeling overwhelmingly sorry for her.

"Because I missed you, damn it!" She paused and then she added, "The trouble was, Roger was never a substitute. No man ever could have been a substitute for you, Dan Jones."

A big sigh escaped her. "After we…after we had sex, because it wasn't making love, it was never making love; afterwards he asked me to marry him and I foolishly agreed. There was no love; although he did tell me just the once that he loved me. I was straight with him from the onset of the relationship, I told him I was fond of him, that I didn't love him and I couldn't promise I ever would, but I tried, God knows, I tried."

"Christ!" Dan hated the dead man without ever having known him. "He must have been stupid. Not telling you he loved you."

"He was honest not to say it, I don't think he ever felt true love for me. No, I was the stupid one. I went through with something I knew to be very wrong for me. I thought he'd give me security and companionship. I was wrong."

"Was he cruel to you, Amy?"

"Not exactly cruel, not physically so anyway. He was a drinking man and he drank far too much. When he was under the influence, he was often kind to me, although he suffered greatly with 'brewers droop'. When he was sober, he was moody, miserable and poor company." She shivered violently.

"You stuck five years of that?"

"Yes," she whispered.

"Why didn't you leave him?"

"Because I knew he cared about me in his own way, and because I was a coward. Because I kept giving him one last chance. Because I'm me and I hate having to back out of a situation without giving it my best shot."

Dan shook his head. "Sometimes it's the right thing to do. Sometimes withdrawal is the only thing that'll save your life. You were wrong."

"I know that now," she agreed. "But I couldn't bring myself to hurt him. He'd never really done anything to hurt me, not purposely, not apart from..."

"From what?" he pushed.

Amy sighed. "He had a vasectomy without telling me. He knew I wanted a family."

"Did he tell you he'd done that?" Dan was aghast at the thought of any man doing such a thing.

"No. The medical officer hinted that I wouldn't need to keep taking the pill for much longer, not as Roger had had the snip. I hoped that one day I could come off it and conceive again, I longed for a child to love." She looked down at her hands, sighed and went on. "Roger detested children and animals and sometimes I believe he detested me."

Amy drank the tea slowly; there was nothing more to be said - she felt she'd said it all.

"Did you ever love him?" he asked.

"No. I cared about him and I tried very, very hard to love him, but his most endearing features were alcohol induced. I got to the stage where I had to have a drink myself in order to let him touch me - a sort of anaesthetic. I kept the bottle under the bed for Dutch courage. A good slug of vodka and he could do what he liked to me."

Another big sigh and then an apology for her lack of sensitivity, "I'm sorry. It really isn't anything to be proud of. Everything was unsuccessful and very sad."

"It's over," he reminded her and moved on.

"Is it?" she asked. "What about your wife? She's still alive."

"My ex-wife," he reminded her. "She's living in Wales with someone she met and married."

"You went back to her when she was ill," she reminded him.

"She was never ill. It was a lie. She just wanted me back under the same roof as her so she could pretend everything was okay between us."

"She lied about being ill?"

"Yes, made out she had cervical cancer and needed a hysterectomy. She even had me take her to the hospital a few times. I'd sit in the waiting room and she'd go off and come back half an hour later to tell me how desperately ill she was."

"Why would she do that to you?"

"For the same reason your old man got the chop without consulting you first, because she was selfish and needy, because she drank too much, just like him. She was an alcoholic who liked having sex with her brother. Then she liked reporting back to me. I caught them together one day when I got back earlier than planned, and without saying a word I packed while they lay in my bed, and then I left. The divorce was quick going through, she didn't dare contest it."

Amy sighed, he was right, it was over and then Dan asked her, "Where are you staying?"

"The Grand. Nice place. Clean. I arrived yesterday. How long have you been here?" She was glad to have changed the subject.

"Three years, since the divorce came through."

"At least you're free now to make a life for yourself."

He shook his head. "I only ever wanted you in my life and I made a pig's ear of everything I ever did regarding you. One big sodding mess after the other."

Amy smiled lovingly at him with those big brown eyes; eyes he failed to recognise. "Oh, I don't know about that," she said. "Not everything was a mess. We had wonderful times. Happy times."

He nodded. "I still love you, Amy. I still need you in my life."

She stood slowly, adjusted her slim-fitting skirt and lifted her bag. "Is it okay to use your bathroom?"

"Of course," he sounded relieved, he'd thought she was about to leave. "Top of the stairs, straight in front of you, you can't miss it."

When she returned to the room, she'd removed the black wig and the contact lenses, which disguised her unique amber eye colour he knew and loved. Her hair had been cut short but it was still a rich auburn colour that reminded him of the beauty of autumn. She'd washed off the thick make-up and removed as much of the red from her lips as would come off with soap and water, and she stood before him now, Amy. A few extra worry lines and a thread or two of silver in her hair, but Amy, mature and gloriously beautiful.

"My God!" he gasped. "I'd forgotten quite how beautiful you are. You take my breath away. Come here." He enfolded her in his strong arms and held her to his chest as joy filled up his soul. He had her in his life again, all of her, this was how it was meant to be.

He smiled down on her and kissed her lips and as he lifted her easily, she wrapped herself around him and snuggled into his face. He took her to his bedroom. It was a very neat room. Everything was in order and clean.

He laid her down carefully and knelt by the bed, looking at her, delighting in her very presence. "I've longed for this day," he admitted. "I've prayed for another chance with you, my little one. Can you ever forgive me?"

"There's nothing to forgive. We have both made mistakes."

"I deserted you," he argued. "When you needed me most I wasn't there for you."

"You had no way of knowing. Besides, I survived."

He kissed her lips and then her face and slowly he undressed her so that he could kiss her breasts and her stomach. She was as beautiful as he'd remembered, only more so. Mature and lovely with skin the colour of honey. It felt like silk beneath his touch. She smelt sweet and good and he moaned deep in his throat as a pain of ecstasy coursed slowly throughout his body. Each time this woman returned to him she was lovelier.

Amy let him take control. He stripped himself of his clothing and embraced her. He worshipped and adored her. He spoke gentle words of love to her, whispering them in her ear all the time he was loving her. Words, sweet and tender, words she'd missed with all of her heart and soul, and when he entered her body, he felt that he had come home at last. She was his home and his life, without her there was nothing worth living for. He existed for Amy. He drew every breath in her name.

They lay together, silent now that they'd loved. Amy touched him, his cheek, his lips and his hands. She marvelled at her memory of him. She knew every contour, every familiar line on his wonderful face. He too was her life and her breath, and she knew exactly how much she'd missed him. But once again she was snatching stolen moments; taking what he had to give, while she could. How long would they have this time? How long would they lie together, loving and giving in this way? How long?

She telephoned the hotel in the early evening and asked to speak to the manager so that she could explain that she wouldn't be returning for dinner, and that they were not to be concerned about her if she didn't show up for breakfast. He thanked her for her consideration and bade her a very good night.

Dan laughed loudly at her as she replaced the receiver. "You speak so beautifully I sometimes wonder why God caused our paths to cross. Me a rough old Welsh soldier and you a lady."

"Me!" she exclaimed, standing before him naked and lovely, her hands on her hips and a mischievous glint dancing about in her eyes. "I'm no lady. I'm Amy. Or I should say - Ruth."

"Ruth is a lovely name. Old-fashioned, like Amy."

"Yes," she agreed as she climbed back onto the bed and touched his arm. "It's ironic really, it was my mother's name. She was a lovely lady, very special. She wanted to meet you, my love."

Suddenly his expression grew serious and Amy sensed what he was about to ask. "Was he my son, Amy?"

"What difference does it make either way?" She took his hand in hers. "He's dead, Dan."

"I need to know. You see I believe he was my son. I believe there was only me in those days. I want you to be completely honest with me, please."

She lowered her eyes and an old pain wounded her once again. "There was only ever you. You were my first and only love. Roger was...a mistake." Still unable to look at him, to see his sadness and his grief she said, "Yes, David Daniel was your son."

When she looked at him, he was crying and something snapped in her heart and she cried with him, holding him close, her arms wrapped around him, soothing his pain, rocking him gently. These were tears they should have shed together, long ago.

"What went wrong?" he asked at last.

"I don't know, exactly. But I do know that our little boy was the most beautiful baby I have ever set eyes on. He was perfect. He looked at me once, just once. Oh, I know what they say, new-born infants can't see, can't focus, but he looked at me, Dan, as if he knew me, he was saying hello and goodbye. I thought I was going to die too. I'd lost you to your wife and your son to our maker. It was as if I was never meant to be happy - only in the briefest of snatches like this, the stolen moments. I wanted him to live, I longed for him to live." Her lip trembled as her voice broke.

"I would gladly have given up my own life to save him. He was you - from out of me. A product of our love and he died. He died, Dan!"

Dan reversed the roles now and comforted her as they cried together. After they cried, they made love and Amy prayed that she would conceive again. She wanted his baby as much as she wanted him in her life for the remainder of her days.

Two days later Amy was still in Dan's house. They'd loved and talked and shared everything, and now, when Dan turned on the television set Amy saw a photograph of her dead husband filling the screen.

"My God!" she cried out.

The remains of Roger Longhurst had been buried that day, flown back to England, to his parent's home in Lancashire - parents Amy knew nothing about. He never mentioned them to her. He said nothing about his life. She knew his age and his religion, his name, rank and serial number and nothing else.

The news reporter spoke about him with a familiar fondness as if she'd known him intimately. She told of his service to the Queen as a member of Her Majesty's Armed Forces in Germany and of his 22 years of loyalty and devotion to duty. And then she told the nation about his wife who was lying in hospital in Berlin; recovering slowly from the injuries she received in the blast. There were no children, she said, just a wife and his grieving parents.

Tears of remorse, anger and sheer frustration rolled down Amy's cheeks. She was inconsolable. Dan left her to cry. He sat back and waited for her to return to him. She cried for an hour, long past the natural span of crying. It just seemed to go on and on.

And then she looked at him with swollen red eyes and a red nose. Her mouth was miserable and turned down, trembling spasmodically as she sobbed in massive gulps. "If I hadn't left the car there...if I hadn't wasted time looking at underwear in the hope I could spark some interest in him. I hate myself for that day. I tried to love him. I tried."

"I know, baby," he soothed as he went to kneel by her on the floor, pulling her into his arms. "I know."

"He told me I was no good in bed," she sobbed as all of the anger and bitterness that had been locked away burst out.

"He told you what?" Dan asked as he held her away from him.

"We were bickering...I complained that he never wanted...to make love...he said I was...no good in bed...he said he felt nothing at all. He hurt me saying that, Dan. How could he say that?"

"Christ! I don't know, Amy. He was obviously an insensitive bastard. I can't think of anyone being more loving than you. Did he really say that?"

"Yes," she wailed again.

"The insensitive bastard!" he repeated.

"I feel so guilty. I knew nothing about him, nothing at all. I didn't try hard enough...I could have tried. I just thought about you all the damned time. I wanted to be with you, not him. Now he's dead and I can't tell him how much I wanted to love him."

"Forget him." Dan was doing his best to avoid hurting Amy further by saying something he might regret and ended up sounding uncharacteristically hard.

"Oh, Dan! Help me to forget him. Wipe out those terrible wasted years. Don't let me leave you again. Don't let me go. Tie me down. Chain me to the bed."

He laughed and brushed her hair away from her eyes so that he could kiss her face all over. "Can you imagine me doing that to you, my little wild bird? I said I'd never cage you and I meant it."

"Cage me," she begged as she clung to him. "Lock me up and throw away the key. Please, please, don't let me lose you again. It would destroy me if it happened again. I want to stay here with you, in this lovely little house. I want to have your babies. I want to make love to you every night, to cook your food and clean your house. I love you, Dan. I have always loved you. Please, please keep me here."

"You can stay, lovely one. You can stay." He paused briefly and then he said, "Marry me, Amy. Tell me you'll marry me. Say it!"

"Yes. Yes. I will marry you. I will." She laughed, why hadn't she thought of that? It was so simple!

He kissed her again, tasting the salt of a thousand teardrops on her lips. "When?"

"Now," she said. "Tomorrow. Next week. Today." She was crying again, but happy tears now, none of regret and remorse, just joy. He took her back to bed and loved her most thoroughly, as if to prove to her that she was special and that he loved her more than heaven and earth, more than life itself.

Chapter Fifteen

They travelled to London on the 4th of March. Commander Cooper was not in the least bit surprised to see them together. By Amy's own volition he'd known exactly where she was going when she left him sitting in Hyde Park, and besides that, he knew exactly what had been going on between them for the past two weeks. None of his people had any true privacy. The day they signed on the dotted line to work for his department was the day they gave up the privilege of a life of their own.

"What can I do for you both?" he asked a little gruffly as he settled back in his seat and they sat close together on the low-backed leather couch.

Dan spoke to him, having first glanced at Amy as if seeking her silent approval. "We've decided to get married, Commander. We've come to..." he hesitated, what had they come for exactly?

"For your blessing," Amy added happily.

The beady all-seeing eyes of Bernard Cooper looked directly at them. "You have it," he said, and then he smiled warmly. "I wondered when you'd see sense and get around to tying the knot. Does this mean you wish to terminate your employment with this office, Amy?"

"Not yet, sir. We've agreed that I should work for a while." Only until she was blessed with the miracle of a new life growing within her, that was the agreement between them, Dan wanted her to stop immediately, to remove herself from the danger of it all, and when she'd argued about that, he told her he would see to it that she got pregnant just as soon as was humanly possible.

"Fine," Cooper agreed. "Regarding the other business." That other business was one dead Royal Air Force Squadron Leader, namely Roger Longhurst.

"It was definitely an indiscriminate attack on a member of the British forces by the IRA. They have said as much. They have no regrets and accept full responsibility, which means you are no longer under direct threat and in, say a week, ten days you can stop wearing that ridiculous wig."

Amy smiled at Dan, knowing how much he hated seeing her in it. He'd made her promise to grow her hair again. To the same length it had been when he first met her; down over her shoulders in a glorious auburn mane. She promised only to grow it longer, declaring herself to be, *'Too old to go around looking like a Disney princess.'*

"Am I alive or dead, sir? Am I still Amy the grieving widow, or do I assume another identity looking like my old self?"

"It is my intention to declare you almost recovered. We'll issue a press release tomorrow. Tell them we've flown you back to the UK and that you should be up and about soon. The disguise is necessary until you're officially let out in the public eye again, then there'll be the media to face, and you'll have to make contact with your husband's parents."

"But why?" she asked, stunned by the suggestion. "He never mentioned having a family. I know nothing about them. As far as I'm concerned, Roger was a five-year mistake on my part. I've buried him and I'm prepared to go through the pretence of being the grieving widow; however, I draw the line at making friends with people I had no idea even existed."

Cooper sighed. "Very well. I'll leave it to you to be discreet when the time comes. Should they contact you, I expect you to say all the correct things. Don't ever forget that he was your husband, and not some complicated story we set up for cover. You chose that situation, not me."

"Thank you for reminding me, Commander I won't forget again," she responded sarcastically. Dan was staring down at his shoes, feeling embarrassed and awkward, and he looked up when Amy asked, "And when do you consider it proper for us to get married, sir?"

"Give things a few months to die down, six even. Be sensible about it. You have the rest of your lives ahead of you, why make things uncomfortable. I'd also like you to be discreet when you're out together in public until that day. The press is going to be watching you for a while, Amy. Until they find some other poor soul to sink their fangs into."

"Great!" she exclaimed. "Terrific! That puts me right into the public eye and refreshes the very long memory of my Soviet friends. Naturally, the KGB will need reminding that I'm still alive! Perhaps you should put a bullet through my head here and now. Kill me off on paper and give me a fresh start."

Dan stared at her and then he spoke his mind. "That means you spend the rest of your life walking about wearing contact lenses with your hair dyed black, or a bloody stupid wig stuck on your head, always checking to see if you look the part. Jesus! Amy, what sort of a life's that?"

"And what sort of a life do you imagine we'll have if I'm forever worrying about getting lifted by the KGB? It only takes my dear friend Roushaka Pavalovsky to walk back into my life and I'm eating dry bread in a Soviet cell for the remainder of my days. Do I have any choice? Really?"

He shook his head, she was right, of course. "No, but can't we compromise here somewhere?"

"With Amy's eye colour, Dan?" Cooper asked and Dan looked at Amy, but what he saw were large dark brown orbs. "Do you remember what they looked like without those contacts?"

He couldn't possibly forget; he'd been staring into them not two hours since. Great big warm amber lights, which caressed his soul and soothed his mind.

"How many women do you remember seeing with eyes that peculiar shade of brown?" Cooper persisted. "If brown is indeed what they are. They are unique; they are pure molten amber. They were always my one big concern when I enlisted her. How the hell was I going to keep her low profile with eyes like that?" He smiled at Amy. "Not an easy one to answer. You make the choice now, Amy. It's your life."

"I stay as I am. Bring me back, but keep it low profile. Why bother to tell the press anything? I'm only an ordinary housewife, widow of a Royal Air Force officer who was recently blown into oblivion by a terrorist bomb. Leave me to mourn my loss in private, please, sir."

"Very well. I shall do my best. Is there anything else?"

"Yes, sir." It was Dan this time. "Can you keep me here, UK-based, just for a while? I'd like to assume a more regular role and see Amy too, now that I've got her back."

Cooper nodded assent. "Leave it with me. There's plenty to be done on the home front. I'll keep you busy."

Amy received a telephone call from Mr and Mrs Longhurst three weeks after her supposed return from Berlin where she'd lain so desperately ill since the demise of her husband.

She and Dan were in the kitchen in her London flat, squabbling over the last slice of bread, laughing and punching each other playfully as the bread crumbled onto the floor.

"I was given your number by a chap in Whitehall, someone who knew you some time ago," the man explained. "I'm Roger's father, Malcolm Longhurst."

Amy took a deep breath. "Oh, yes. Please, you must forgive my seeming ignorance, but Roger never spoke about you. I had no idea he had family."

"I know," he said sounding both sad and disappointed. "He was like that. We were surprised to learn he'd gone and got married. My wife and I would like to meet you?"

"Mr Longhurst," she began. "I really don't think that would be advisable." Amy paused, knowing she had to stop it now, before it got out of hand and tentative family ties were formed.

"I have no wish to add to your pain at this dreadful time, but Roger and I were not exactly up for nomination as couple of the year. We shared a name and a home. We were never really close. It was a marriage of convenience for us both. He needed a wife and I needed the security of a husband. That was it. I believe he was fond of me, and I certainly cared about him, but we were not in love." She regretted having to talk about it to him, and more importantly, that she hadn't been able to love his only son.

"I'm sorry to hear that." Malcolm Longhurst said. "His mother and I thought..."

"Please, just forget me. You had no idea I even existed, forget me again, please, let me get on with my life."

But he was saddened by her choice and duty-bound he asked, "Are you okay?"

"I really am fine," she assured him. "I have to make a new life for myself now. Get things back to normal. Pick up the threads and start again, but are you both all right?"

"Yes. We're over the shock. We were never close to our son either. I understand the way you feel and despite everything, I'm sorry we never got to meet you, Amy. Thank you for your honesty. Forgive me for disturbing your day."

Amy wept as the line went dead. In his innocence he'd opened up the wounds of contrition.

"What is it, my little love?" Dan hurried to her and held on to her. "Who was that on the phone?"

"Roger's father." She was sobbing miserably. "Damn it! He sounded really nice and kind." And fresh emotion sprang instantly to life in her and she shoved Dan away.

"I hate Roger for this. He used people. He abused their friendship and their loyalty. All he did was pickle his bloody insides with booze and trample over everyone whoever tried to get close to him. He never even mentioned me to those people, not a bloody word. He was a callous, uncaring bastard and I hate him for being what he was."

"Hate, Amy? You don't hate him. Just forget him. We've got each other again. We'll be married soon. Think about that. Focus on what we have now, and not what he was. Forget him." Anger bubbled inside the big Welsh man. He longed to be able to stand face-to-face with Roger Longhurst, so that he could wrap his strong hands around the man's neck and choke him for everything he'd done to hurt Amy. He could taste hatred in his mouth as he held on tightly, comforting the distressed love of his life.

PART FOUR

Chapter Sixteen

Daniel Jones and Amy Longhurst, nee Harper, were joined together in holy matrimony on Saturday 12 September 1981. The service was held in a small Tudor church in South Wales and was attended by Dan's two older brothers and his younger sister. He'd told Amy all about his family many years earlier, having spoken of them with deep affection and of how he longed to show her off to them.

Now, as she walked towards him swathed in soft cream silks, her auburn hair touching her collar, falling in tiny ringlets around her lovely face, he was prouder of her than any number of words could ever express. His heart felt so full of love for her he was afraid it was going to burst before they managed to sign the register.

He looked to his family, to his brothers Peter who was his best man, and Jonathan, who had agreed to support Amy, and Dan was proud, the proudest man on earth.

"I love you," he whispered as he kissed her afterwards. "You do know how much I love you, don't you?"

"Yes. I do," she whispered back. "I'm so happy I can't think straight. I only dreamed of feeling like this. It will last, won't it? Promise me."

"It will last," he promised without the power of clairvoyance to know what was in store for them.

The press was kind to Amy. They used the story of the wedding as a happy ending to the tragic tale of a young woman robbed of her husband by terrorism and the bloody hands of the IRA. The front-page story showed a photograph of her kissing her new husband, Daniel Jones. It would have been virtually impossible for anyone to recognise either of them from the angle of the photograph. The press was happy and Amy was satisfied that it was over at last.

At the Soviet embassy Roushaka Pavalovsky studied the newspaper and the photograph of the happy couple. "So! My dear friend married her strong man from Wales!"

She sighed deeply and regretfully. "Oh, Amy, if only you had accepted the offer we made to you many years ago. If only you were with us and not with your own people. It is going to be so much harder for you now that you have married. Much harder." She had long since given up hope of convincing Amy to willingly change sides. "Enjoy him while you can, my dear friend. Enjoy him while you can."

Amy and Dan slipped into an easy, comfortable pattern of life. They worked office hours in the city. Both were content with what they had. They met up at lunchtime and shared a sandwich or a pizza, and sometimes they sneaked off home and made love. It felt naughty and exciting and they were blissfully happy together.

Amy had grown fond of her new family, Dan's three siblings; they were happy people. They exchanged visits. And after three years and seven months of married bliss Amy only had one real regret - she had not conceived again.

"I've invited Stephanie and Chris for a meal," she announced as she served dinner late on Thursday evening, 17 April 1985. Dan had been away for two days and she was both relieved and delighted to have him safely back home again.

"That's nice," he said, looking forward to seeing his baby sister and her husband. "When?"

"Tomorrow evening. I wanted you all to myself tonight."

He looked up at her and smiled and her heart did a backward somersault; just as it did whenever he looked at her with so much love burning in his smiling eyes.

Raising his eyebrows he asked, "What are you planning? Not...not sexy underwear?"

She nodded happily. "Can you stand it?"

He appeared to think deeply about the question, and obviously it was taking a great deal of effort. His face contorted and then he nodded slowly. "Um, I think so. What colour?"

"Black lace," she told him as she sat down opposite him, touching his leg with her bare foot.

"Good God!" he groaned. "How are you so incredibly sexy?" He reached for her foot. "How do you do it? You never fail to turn me on." Suddenly he warned. "I'll choke on this if you carry on." But he laughed and held onto her foot - preventing her from moving away. "I love you, Amy. My life's full now."

"Good!" she said matter-of-factly. "Eat, before it gets cold, and don't bolt it. The black lace can wait an hour." He groaned again, yet he continued to eat as instructed.

Amy and Dan had moved out of the small basement flat in Kensington within months of getting married and into an elegant two-story Victorian terraced property off Pimlico Road. They had three large bedrooms and everything they needed in a home, including a spacious study lined with books. Amy took leave of absence to decorate the place and enjoyed every minute of it. Both she and Dan derived great pleasure from being there together, in their own home.

They scoured the second-hand shops until they found all of the pieces of furniture for the house. Good pieces in general, but some were mostly just well-loved antiques.

"Did you bring it?" Amy asked as she hugged Stephanie.

"How could I forget; didn't you remind me no less than an hour ago?" Stephanie shrugged herself out of the duffle coat, shook her head so that the short straight fair hair became instantly tidy and checked her appearance in the hall mirror.

Amy laughed and Dan sighed with contentment as he watched them together. They were up to something, his sister and his lovely wife. "What are you two planning this time?" he asked but Stephanie ignored her brother so that she could pursue the subject with Amy.

"You did speak to me fifty-five minutes ago, didn't you, Amy Jones?"

"Maybe. Maybe not." Amy laughed again and Dan demanded to know what was going on, because less than an hour ago he and Amy had been rolling about on the bedroom floor. It had started as a game and ended up with them making love. Amy had definitely not telephoned his Steph.

"I think it's time you came clean," Christopher Williams announced to his sister-in-law as she led the way into the dining room. He and Stephanie had undergone a lengthy discussion on the subject of Amy, up to and including the entire journey that very day. There were questions to be asked and hopefully answered.

"Will someone please tell me what the hell is going on?" Dan was shouting now, but he was happy.

"Keep your shirt on, my love," Amy soothed. "Dinner's ready. Let's eat."

They ate and talked, discussing many varied and interesting subjects and before Amy could begin clearing away the dirty dishes her sister-in-law asked her again, "Did you send me some sort of a telepathic message or did you not? I really have got to know, Amy. If you don't tell me the truth, I'm off to see a shrink first thing on Monday. Because if it wasn't you, well, I'm going around the bend, and fast."

Amy sighed and settled back in her chair and Dan reached for her hand and squeezed it gently. It was tiny in his. She smiled at her husband and wrinkled her nose affectionately and he acknowledged the affection by winking his eye very slowly.

"Yes, I suppose I must have," she admitted at last. "I wanted you to remember the package."

"What package?" Dan asked, still openly curious.

"A surprise for you, for later," she told him. "Something you wanted and only Steph knew where to get it. You shall see, be patient. You know what they say, everything comes to he who waits, and waits, and waits."

They laughed together and Amy added. "Look what waiting got you - me. Aren't you the lucky one?"

"Yes, I am," he said with a warm sigh of utter contentment. "But what's this about messages to Steph? Have you had your broomstick out of the cupboard again?"

"Yes." Amy was full of fun tonight. She laughed until she cried.

"Seriously," Christopher tried again. "Will you tell us about yourself, Amy, please?"

"There really is nothing to tell. I'm weird, that's all." But they pressed her and when she kept insisting that there was nothing to tell, Dan stepped in. He had questions of his own and some of them had been on hold for several years.

He broached a subject he'd been meaning to bring up yet never got around to. "A long time ago, when I lost you the last time, I was working inside a disused hanger down on the south coast. I had a bunch of raw recruits I was supposed to be knocking into shape. Combat training. Self-defence, that sort of thing. One of the weapons we'd been training with jammed up and I took it into the hanger to dismantle it. You know me, little one; I'm not the most patient person when it comes to fiddling about with mechanical things.

"Anyway, to cut a long story short, I saw you, I touched you and I could smell your perfume. You were driving a silver car, down towards Checkpoint Charlie in Berlin. The car was new and shiny, not a big one. It looked like a Toyota or a Mazda. It was really weird at the time because I was convinced you were there, right in front of me. You seemed to be warning me about something but I didn't understand what it was. Then later that day the damned rifle jammed again and I almost copped it." He reached up and touched the silver scar on his left temple where the bullet grazed his flesh.

Amy nodded. "I remember that day. I was missing you like crazy. It was a Mazda with something like 200 kilometres on the clock. I remember it well, especially as I'd only had a licence for about a year and I knew the powers that be would never have trusted me with a new car if they'd known. They'd have gone out and requisitioned a rusty old banger, especially for me."

She paused, and then she said, "Funny that, everything was measured in metric, even the mileage on the car, but all the Brits talked about miles, yards, feet and inches."

Dan reached out for her hand and said, "You're right, it is odd. We travelled in kilometres over there, we just accepted it, like driving on the wrong side of the road. Anyway, you digress."

Both Stephanie and her husband sat enthralled as their two favourite people held hands across the table, caressing each other with their eyes as they reminisced.

"You did things with your mind a lot back then. Whenever we were apart. It was as if you'd come to me in the night and lay down next to me. Sometimes you'd talk to me, and other times you'd just fill me with your peace. The most moving experience was when you finally came back to me.

"All night long I was haunted by you. You were filling my mind with images and memories. Then you phoned me, we spoke briefly and you hung up and I saw you in my room, I even touched you. I couldn't sleep. I intended going to London the next morning, demanding to know where the hell you were. I went for my usual walk on the sea front and I saw an elegant woman who was a stranger to me. She had black hair and really dark eyes. She walked up to me and a voice spoke to me, inside my head, your voice, saying hello to me. The woman never opened her mouth."

"Who was it, Danny?" Stephanie asked, unable to remain silent a moment longer. "Was it Amy?"

"Yes," he said, smiling briefly at his sister before returning his undivided attention to his wife. "It was Amy. We've only been parted a few days at the most since then. Amy, my Amy had come back to me and I walked on air."

"Why the black hair?" Christopher asked.

"A wig," Amy told him. "I'd been married to an RAF officer who'd been innocently involved in a car bombing incident in Berlin. My car was booby-trapped and...and he was killed outright. The government bods were concerned for my safety and so I was forced to suffer the gross indignity of painting my lips and nails bright red. Ugh!" She shivered at the memory. "And contact lenses too, to change my eye colour. They irritated like the very devil. It was dreadful."

"You never said." Stephanie looked at her sister-in-law firstly and then her brother. "We had no idea."

"None of your damned business," Dan told her with a loving smile. "You're all too damned nosey for your own good."

"Cheek!" Stephanie reached out to thump him. "Go on, Amy, tell us more."

Some fond and some painful memories surfaced once again as Amy recalled her search for Dan. "I had no intention of looking for him at first. Not so soon after Roger's death - perhaps never, but I couldn't help it. When I looked with my mind and saw him, I knew I could never stay away. I had to touch him physically, to hold him and to love him, and never be parted from him again."

"Oh, my God!" Tears streamed down Stephanie's cheeks. She wiped them away and had a good blow in her handkerchief. "That's beautiful. You two are very lucky. But how do you do it, Amy? Won't you tell us? How do you look with your mind? Please tell us."

Amy smiled. "There's nothing to tell. I've been doing it since I was a child. Since before I could walk and talk. I don't know how or why. Without wanting to sound in the least conceited, I think I use more of my brain cells than the average person." She laughed and then her expression grew more serious as she went on with her explanation.

"Albert Einstein is reputed to have used four times more grey matter than the average person. What could we do if we utilised the whole damned lot at once? We'd move mountains." She shivered. "Actually, the whole thing frightens me somewhat."

"Why does it frighten you, little one?" Dan had never ventured to probe this subject before today.

Her reply came sad and quiet. "I've told you before, the Soviets have been working on psychological warfare for many, many years. They invited me to aid in their research - to perform tricks for them, like a circus animal. They offered me great inducements, money, fabulous treasures and works of art. Anything I wanted, a big house in Moscow where I would be treated like a royal subject with servants waiting on me. I told them to deposit their theory, together with the inducements, in a part of their anatomy which is best left to the imagination at the dinner table."

She smiled at her husband, who laughing said, "That's my Amy. Never one to mince words."

"What else can you do?" Christopher asked, much more interested in her special gifts than in the Soviets.

"I don't know, Chris."

"You don't know?"

"No, not everything. Some things just happen when I'm least expecting them and I'm more surprised than anyone. Generally, I need to concentrate very hard on getting where I want to go. It takes my energy, saps my strength." The mischievous imp in her surfaced once again and she said, "I can hypnotise people. Would you like me to have a go on you?"

"Yeah! Would you?"

"Certainly. Go and lie on the sofa." He missed the wink that passed between her and her husband.

Obediently he lay stretched out on the long sofa. Amy stood over him and whispered a few verses from Kipling's 'Mandalay' in rapid-fire Russian, and Christopher was convinced that she was uttering some mystic incantation or other.

She left him there, having pushed the others out of the room and back into the dining room, where he found them fifteen minutes later. He'd lain silent, waiting for the hypnosis to take effect, uncertain as to how he should be feeling. When he opened his eyes and saw that he was alone he felt a complete fool and knew that a practical joke had once again been played on him.

"Ha! Ha!" he said as he dug his hands deeply into his trouser pockets. "I suppose you think that's funny, Amy Jones?"

"You nodded off!" she exclaimed as she hugged him and placed a kiss on his cheek.

"I did not! You cleared off more like. You idiot! I'm going to get you for this, and for all the other times you've made a mug of me."

"My dear Christopher," she whispered into his ear. "I apologise from the very depths of my heart. You know I love you and I'd never do anything intentional to hurt you. It was just a bit of fun.

"Yeah, yeah, and I'm a gullible fool for falling for it every time."

"You are neither gullible nor a fool, so hush. Besides, how do you know you weren't hypnotised?"

"Because I'd know, because you just cleared off and left me...didn't you? Did you hypnotise me? Amy, did you or not?"

"I definitely did not, I don't know how to. But just think about this, how would you know if I had?"

As Dan climbed into bed that night, his leg brushed against a hard package. He looked at Amy who was propped up in bed reading a book.

"What's this?" he asked suspiciously, and then he joked, "A bomb?" The shadow that crossed her face made him kick himself mentally for being so insensitive.

"I'm sorry, little one, that was tactless."

"Forget it," she said, shrugging it off, leaning forward to place a kiss on his lips. "Open the box."

He did and then he stared in amazement at the leather-bound edition of Shakespeare's Sonnets. It was something he'd wanted for a long time. She'd bought him an old Bible the year before; he'd wanted that too. "Aw, for crying out loud!" he groaned. "I forgot again."

She nodded; he had forgotten. "Never mind, it's not a real anniversary."

It was the anniversary of their first working day in Berlin - 18th April. The day he'd driven her into the Soviet Sector of East Berlin in 1967 - eighteen years earlier.

She kissed him again. He was a wonderful man. He never forgot her birthday or their wedding anniversary. He was always thoughtful and considerate, the exact opposite of Roger. Dan never felt the need to attempt to buy her affection with expensive gifts, coats, rings or a car. He loved her and he gave her the simple things in life, such as a single red rose or a box of chocolates. Sometimes he saw a book or a soft toy he knew she'd love. She was inordinately happy with this man. He was a rare find, a true treasure, and she valued him for what he was, priceless.

"It's a real anniversary," he argued, and then he said, "The only good that came out of me living in Wales, before we got back together, was my getting back in with my brothers and Stephanie. It's wonderful having them in my life again."

"I'm glad," Amy whispered as she kissed his cheek. "They certainly are remarkable people."

Before they slept, she spoke to him again about the conversation they'd had with his sister and her husband. "I know they don't understand me, Dan, but, do you?"

"I think so, little love. I think so. I like to think I understand you better than anyone else does at least. Why? What's on your mind?"

"If anything should happen..." He was about to silence her. "No. Let me finish, please. If anything should happen and we're separated again, promise me you'll open your mind and let me in. Promise me you'll find me. Promise me, Dan."

"I promise you, little one, I won't let you go, but if it should happen, God forbid, I will move heaven and earth to find you again. Nothing will stand in my way. Nothing." He pulled her into his arms. "Now stop this daft talk, give me a kiss and get some sleep."

They eventually fell asleep at three in the morning. One kiss had led to another, and another.

By the beginning of July 1985, Amy knew that she was carrying Dan's child, but while her heart rejoiced with the life growing within her, she chose to withhold the information from her husband, intending to tell him when she was safely into the sixth week of the pregnancy.

Dan noticed the subtle changes in his wife. He knew that mornings were no longer a happy time for her; that she woke pale and touchy. He prayed that he was right, that he was going to be a father, that his precious Amy was carrying his child. But he could be an exceedingly patient man when it suited him and he knew that she would tell him in her own good time.

The weeks flew by, and Amy said nothing to him. She began eating breakfast again and was her normal happy self, waking with a smile and a whispered word of love for her husband who was naturally disappointed but he never mentioned it to Amy, not a word.

"Phone for you, little one," he called one morning. "It's the boss." He heard his wife groan from under the quilt. "Come on, lazybones, shake a leg."

She took the phone out of his hand and reached her face out to him for a kiss. "Good morning, Commander," she said sweetly. "What can I do for you this beautiful Sunday morning?" It was her way of reminding him that she worked Monday to Friday now that she and Dan were married.

"Sorry to disturb your weekend but something's come up. It is something that simply cannot wait. Can you spare me an hour?"

She sighed and said," Give me time to brush my hair." She was uncertain of what she was picking up from his tone of urgency.

"Amy - come alone."

As she handed the receiver to Dan, her left hand reached down to rest upon the life within her, his child. She shivered, said a silent prayer and began to rise from the warmth of the bed.

"Duty calls," she told him. "The boss wants to see me right away."

"I'll drive you in." Dan never argued with her. If he felt she was wrong he applied logic to what she said or did, and then he discussed it with her.

"No!" She said a little too urgently. "You start the dinner. I won't be long. By the time I get back, I'll expect to smell the essence of roast beef to be coming through the letterbox, and don't forget the Yorkshire pudding. I love the way you make it."

"Crafty!" he said, pulling her back towards him. "But why today?"

She shrugged her shoulders and kissed him, wanting to drown in his love, and not for the first time in the eighteen years she'd known him. "He didn't say. But I'd better get going. Don't worry."

"I always worry. I love you, Amy."

"I know you do, and I love you too, just stop worrying. I'm a big girl now. I have you and there's nothing more I need. Besides, if I didn't go anywhere without you, I wouldn't have you to come home to."

Dan laughed at her odd logic. "Okay then, go, because I want you back here safe and sound ASAP."

A smile lit her face as she drove towards Whitehall. Dan was going to be overjoyed when she told him about the baby. She knew he'd had his suspicions and that he'd given up hoping that she was indeed pregnant. This was the day she'd chosen to tell him. She was exactly six weeks pregnant and the doctor had happily confirmed her diagnosis two days earlier.

With her mind closed to everything except the love of the child and her overwhelming love for Dan, she failed to sense danger. Her mind was dancing about with giddy abandon. She found it increasingly more difficult to concentrate nowadays and she even cracked the offside parking light, as she pulled into a vacant space in the underground car park. She'd tell Dan about it after he knew she was pregnant, not that he was ever cross with her. She made her way to the lift and up to the fifteenth floor where Commander Bernard Cooper was sitting behind his desk awaiting her arrival.

"Good morning, sir." She swung into the room, crossing the vast expanse of vermilion carpet with a spring in her step.

"Good morning, Amy. I trust you are well?"

"Never better, sir." A smug smile lit her face. It was a smile that threatened to break into a silly grin at any moment. "What's happening, Commander?"

"Pavalovsky." His eyes remained fixed on hers, waiting for a reaction. There was none. "She has voiced her need to defect immediately."

Amy stared at him; the smile became a distant memory as he received the reaction he'd previously expected at the mere mention of the woman's name. "Never! Not her!"

"That's precisely what I said." Cooper had not been able to believe the coded messages he was receiving from Moscow. "That's why I'd like you to go out there and find out what the hell is going on."

"Out where?" she asked, her eyes narrowing with suspicion.

"Moscow," came his quiet, calm reply.

Amy leapt to her feet, her face growing hot and red. "Forgive me, sir, but are you completely insane? You intend putting me right into their hands!"

"You'll be safe in the embassy," he argued with marginally more confidence sounding in his voice than he was feeling. "They won't be able to touch you there."

"No!" Amy shook her head. "No, sir! I will not do it. Not for you, not for my queen or for my country. Not for Roushaka-bloody-Pavalovsky or anyone. Find someone else."

"There is no-one else." Cooper said quietly, signalling for her to retake her seat. "You're the only one with the capabilities needed to probe that woman's mind. We need a psychologist out there, and...and something more - insight."

Amy smiled at that as she lowered her bottom onto the chair again. "Good God, sir! I thought for one moment you were going to acknowledge my alleged abilities."

"Huh!" he grunted. "You know how I feel on that score, but I've never denied that you have something special. We need you there. Pavalovsky could be very, very valuable to us."

"She could also be lethal, sir. Forgive me, but you cannot possibly even contemplate bringing that woman in. She's a killer, a cold-blooded killer."

Amy shivered. "She alone was responsible for the death of both her father and one of her sisters. She turned them in to the authorities for subversive behaviour. She as good as executed them single-handed. She would never betray her country or her precious communism."

But Cooper was not to be swayed by what she was saying. "We want you to go out there and find out what's going on inside her head and why her comrades want her dead. Why she wants to defect. Only you can do it, Amy. We can't afford to bring her back unless we're one hundred percent certain we can trust her."

"Forgive me, Commander, but this...this stinks! I won't go. I'll resign if you order me to go."

"Amy! We need you there. We'll protect you."

She smiled at that and his blood turned to ice water. "Oh, please spare me this horse crap, sir! You have no way of protecting me, not you or the whole damned British Army. Nothing will stop them getting to me, nothing. You know how I feel about this, I have Dan now, he needs me. I am no longer a free agent; besides, I have to think about myself and..."

"And?"

"And I won't go," she replied defiantly.

"Very well, Amy. Go home to Dan. I shall find someone else to do the job, that, in my opinion, only you are capable of doing."

"You do that, Commander," she said as she headed for the door, slamming it shut behind her, driving home in a blind rage to face Dan who caught hold of her as she flounced passed him in the hall.

"Hey, little one! What's wrong?"

"I bumped the rear light," she said, and then. "Just leave me, please, Dan."

He left her. She went to the bathroom and lay in water that was hot enough to be safe for her baby for almost an hour, topping it up every time it got cool, and then he went to her and asked, "Better?"

"A bit. I'm sorry."

"Don't be. I know you. So, what happened beside the cracked light? What did the old man do to put you in such a foul mood?"

"I cracked the light before I saw him. He wanted me to do a job and I refused. That's the first time I've refused him anything in all these years. But I had to put..." She sighed again and then she looked up at her husband and into his concerned grey eyes. "I don't want to go working away from you." She smiled at him, hoping to reassure him. "I'm okay. Is dinner ready?"

"Ready and waiting. Dry yourself off, get dressed and come and eat. You'll feel better when you've got a full tum. We'll talk."

"No, Dan. There's nothing to discuss." She reached for his hand and kissed the palm. "I love you, that's all there is to it. Go and serve dinner."

There was no mention of the baby that day as planned, and no mention of it on her fourteenth week either, when the commander contacted her again. "Jackson is dead," he said as she stood before him in his office. "His body turned up at the Moscow embassy last night."

She sank into a chair and felt the turmoil mounting inside her. "I can't go, Commander. I have never refused you anything, but this is asking too much of me. You know they want me. They've wanted me for years. Roushaka Pavalovsky knows me. She knows what makes me tick. She's the only person in my life who has been anywhere close to my level of parapsychology."

Amy sighed a long and tired sigh. "She really is very good, you know, sir. She's a genius and a killer. Her people have her and they want me too. Together our minds could do the most destructive cataclysmic acts imaginable. We've gone through this a million times, why won't you listen to me?"

"I hear you, Amy, but I have a job to do too, and the powers that be want Pavalovsky. I have my orders, just as you do. They want her on our side. If she's not on the level, they want her dead."

Amy's heart sank. Not only were they asking her to risk her own life and that of her unborn child, but they expected her to kill an old and dear friend, because she knew there was no way Roushaka would ever turn her back on the country of her birth.

"Roushaka and I are like sisters, Commander. I don't trust her, and she doesn't trust me, but we love each other, and we hold each other in deep respect. I can't go out and kill her; not in cold blood nor any other way."

"But she'd kill you, and you know it." He opened the top drawer of his desk and reached in to remove something. "It wasn't my intention to resort to blackmail, Amy, it isn't my style, but this arrived two days ago. It came via the embassy. It seems it was handed to them by a peasant girl who delivers the vegetables to the kitchen." He handed her the single sheet of inferior coarse paper and watched as she read the words written on it.

It was addressed to her, in her maiden name - Amy Harper, and it read:

'You have lost one husband, Amy, and the death of another can be arranged by my people unless you help me fight them. I need your help. I am desperate. Only you can help me, my dear friend. My own people are attempting to kill me. I beg you, come to me. Please come to me. Help me, Amy. I would do this for you. You are my only true friend. Roushaka.'

Amy lowered her head. She wanted to cry out, to run and never to return to this terrible place. But she'd signed away her right to privacy and she was both loyal and conscientious in her dedication to her country and to her sovereign. She loved Dan more than life itself. She loved the child growing inside her body, but Dan was her priority, her first love, and she would not risk losing him again, and not to death which is so very final.

"When?" she asked quietly.

The old man gave her the consolation of a resigned sigh, which told of his distaste for his work. He had always admired her resilience and tenacity and now he was breaking her spirit by forcing her to obey his commands. He knew that he would lose her because of this. She would die in doing as he said or return and walk out of his life forever. Either way he would lose her respect. He loathed his profession. He yearned for the long overdue retirement they kept promising him. Now he knew that he was finished, that this was his last deed for them.

"Tonight," he told her. "You go tonight. What about Dan?"

She looked at him and saw that he was tearful, gone was the man of steel. "What about Dan?" she asked coldly. "He'll survive. I don't want him told anything. Let him think I'm safe. A short mission, somewhere secure. God willing I'll be back soon and I'll tell him everything."

He nodded. "As you wish. Go and pack. Transport leaves at midnight."

Before she walked through the office door she said, "Your decision to retire is very wise, Commander. I believe my husband is going to be seeking answers and revenge before too long. This world will not be big enough for you and your superiors." With a sigh she added, "I understand your position, and I forgive you."

Bernard Cooper would never forget those words; they would be the last ones on his mind as he drew his final breath. "May God watch over you," he said as she closed the door.

"Where are you going?" Dan asked as Amy snatched clothes from the wardrobe and tossed them onto the bed. "And for how long?"

"The continent, just a couple of days," she said, hating lying to him. "A nice safe job. No need for you to worry your wonderful heart." She smiled but there was no warmth there for him to cling onto.

"Get my toothbrush, please my love. I have to be at Northolt in an hour or I'll miss the flight."

"Why not Heathrow, or even Gatwick?" he asked, suspicion growing once again. "Why the RAF?"

"I expect the old man is penny-pinching again," she suggested flippantly.

Dan caught hold of her arm and turned her to face him, looking deep into the amber orbs which had suddenly grown shy in his presence. "Why are you lying to me?"

She smiled and those eyes flitted about on his face. "My darling, Dan, why would I lie to you?"

"You tell me, little one, you tell me. I don't like this one bit. I have a bad feeling in my gut. I'm scared, and that's a hell of an admission for a man like me."

"Don't be." She reached up and kissed his lips. "I can take care of myself. Besides, this is a safe one. I've told you. Stop worrying. I'll be back before you know it." She kissed him again. "Tell you what, you can empty the spare room while I'm away."

"What for?"

Amy stopped what she was doing and looked lovingly at him. "Because it's full of junk, my love, and it's time we turned it back into a guest room. When I come home, I'll organise some wallpaper and paint and we'll do it out properly, together."

No point telling him about her plans to convert the room into a nursery for the daughter she knew they were going to have. Of her plans to paper the walls a delicate shade of pink and white with soft cream paint on the woodwork and lace-trimmed curtains at the windows.

Her heart was aching and heavy as she did what she had to do. This time she would deal with Roushaka once and for all. There would be no peace for her while the woman lived. She was going to kill her old friend.

There was no hope that Pavalovsky had turned her back on her precious Communist Party, nor on the KGB who held a vicelike grip on the entire Soviet Union, while their evil spread itself silently around the world like cancer eating into hearts and souls.

"Okay," he said at last. "I'll sort it out. Leave it to me. And I won't ask any more questions, but I'm warning you, little one, you'd better get your pretty little bottom back here double fast. Do you hear?"

"I hear, and I will. I promise." She zipped the canvas holdall closed. "If I didn't have to go, I wouldn't."

"What did you say?" he asked. She'd been talking into the wardrobe.

Standing in front of him now, she repeated herself. "I said, if I didn't have to go, I wouldn't. This is the last time. I've had enough. We'll move into the country and raise a few chickens. Do you fancy that?"

Dan was beaming down on her. "Of course I do. I want nothing more than a few chickens and you."

They made love before she left the house. It wasn't planned, it just happened. One minute she was kissing him goodbye and the next she was peeling off her clothes and kissing him at the same time. Their lovemaking was urgent and clinging to what they had. They seemed to consume each other hungrily. Devouring, savouring and loving.

Amy cried out when she orgasmed, marvelling at the beauty of her joy. She cried and she laughed, carrying Dan along with her as she soared high in ecstasy.

"Aw, Christ!" he said as he looked into her face. "I don't want you to go."

"I know, my love. I know." She smoothed his brow, wiping away the heavy layer of perspiration threatening to drip onto her face and breasts.

"But I will come back to you, and if you really concentrate, as I've taught you to, we can be together all of the time. Use your mind, Dan. Don't ever forget to use your mind."

Chapter Seventeen

Friday 20 September 1985

Amy arrived in Moscow eighteen hours after the RAF Hercules took off from Northolt. She'd been flown to Helsinki and transported at break neck speed to the Soviet border to where a Finnish soldier in civilian clothing took her on into Moscow.

Bone weary and sick in her stomach she retired to the modest room on the top floor of the British embassy. The Ambassador would have to wait for her to sleep before she was prepared to discuss anything with him.

As she closed her eyes on the world, Amy knew that there had been no new developments. Pavalovsky persisted with her request to be granted asylum in the West, conveying urgent messages, by various means to the British authorities in the city, messages in which she revealed alarming details of nightmare attacks upon her person.

For all the urgency of the situation, it took her three days to make contact with Amy via another young peasant girl laden with freshly harvested vegetables for the kitchen staff.

The girl asked for Amy by name and refused to budge until she had seen her face and spoken the words memorised by her during the journey into the city.

"Let her speak to me," Amy called as she entered the kitchen where everyone appeared to be yelling at each other. They'd sent for the Ambassador who in turn had summoned his personal secretary and then the official interpreter arrived. The kitchen staff, cooks, cleaners and servants all succeeded in talking at the same time. The hullabaloo was deafening.

A vision of two men attempting to assassinate her old friend had clutched at Amy's mind as the young girl with the vegetables and the frightened eyes entered the building. Suddenly Amy was not so certain that Roushaka was lying.

Amy could not readily comprehend the rough country dialect and she reached for the girl, taking her arm to lead her deeper into the building, away from the din. "Médlenno!" she said firmly but with compassion. "Slowly!" And then she told her that she did not understand her. "Ya ne ponimáyu."

The girl studied Amy closely, her eyes narrowing with suspicion and then she spat a single word into her face, "Slúshayte!" "Listen!" Repeating herself more slowly now, she gave Amy the message. "Pavalovsky. Danger. Soon too late. She dies soon."

"Well?" Ambassador Ponsford asked, having waited for Amy in his study. "What's going on, Amy?"

Troubled by what she'd sensed more than by the message itself Amy sat heavily. "I don't know, sir. It seems the KGB no longer trusts Pavalovsky. It's likely that her request is genuine."

He frowned. "That's not what you said when you arrived."

"I am aware of that, Ambassador, but two attempts have been made on her life and she has been severely beaten several times. She has no food and little money. Her room was ransacked and then they withdrew official permission for her to remain resident in the city. They took her room off her. She's been hiding in a derelict building until this morning when one of her more loyal old-Russian friends took her in."

Amy paused briefly before adding, "Her mind is closed. Blackness came on her. I think she's dying. I do honestly believe she's in danger of assassination."

"Whose mind closed?" he asked, sounding confused.

"Why, Roushaka Pavalovsky's, Ambassador." Amy couldn't understand why he was being so obtuse. Everything she said was crystal clear - to her it was clear.

"What the hell are you talking about? 'Her mind is closed.' What does that mean?"

But Amy simply looked bewildered.

"Look." he began. "A peasant girl asked for you and you spoke to her and she left. Now you're talking as if you've spoken with Pavalovsky herself. Who was that girl?"

"I really don't know, sir. Someone who knows her, whom she could trust." Amy shook her head slightly. "Sir, I thought the commander had explained about me and..."

"Your psychic capabilities!" he scoffed. "I am well aware of your capabilities, Mrs Jones. You have a degree in psychology and you're very quick on the uptake. An astute young woman I'd say." He sounded so damned patronising Amy wanted to laugh. "All that psychic business is nothing but poppycock," he added.

This was a new, yet seemingly ancient challenge for her. "Is that so, sir?" It took her seconds to glean all the information she needed in which to prove she was genuine. "Forgive me, Ambassador, but after you'd made love to your wife this morning, I do believe you dressed in rather a hurry, and Mrs Ponsford raced after you with your briefcase and tie."

His eyes were wide. Nobody could have known about that, not unless his home was bugged again. But no, he had it swept twice a day, there was no way...not even he had planned the little roll in the hay with Marjorie that morning before work. It had been a long time since...completely spontaneous...the black nightdress was transparent and she looked so inviting he couldn't resist touching her breast, and that was it, they did it on the floor in the bedroom. Nobody could possibly have known.

His face was hot and red and he loosened his tie so that he could breathe again.

"Your wife is a very beautiful lady," Amy added with a knowing grin. "Especially in black." He coughed and spluttered, fidgeting uncomfortably in his seat. She would never tell him the truth that she'd caught a brief glimpse of the couple as she passed through the building that morning.

"Ahem! What...how...look, there's no way..."

"No, sir, as you say, there is no way I could possibly know, unless, of course, your home really is bugged, even though you have it swept twice a day," Amy agreed. "And as you also said, it's nothing but poppycock. And the answer to the question you are about to ask is, in a way, yes, I can. Sorry, sir, but you really are like an open book."

His mouth sagged open, the unspoken question dangling there in mid-air. "You can really read my mind?"

"Yes, and no," she replied. "It's actually more a sensing thing. I seem to absorb emotions and thoughts. I perceive your mood. I can't read a mind, not the way you think of mind reading. Besides, your thoughts are as private as your love life. Had you not been thinking about your...your romantic interlude this morning, I could not have sensed it. It is obviously quite fresh in your mind, Ambassador." She was laughing at him, but gently.

"Cooper said you were different and special." His colour began to settle again as he heaved his tired body back in the chair.

"Very well, Amy, I have to believe you. Nobody could have known, nobody. But tell me, Pavalovsky; is she the same as you? I mean, does she have the same psychic abilities?"

"We are very similar in many ways, Ambassador. We each of us have our weaknesses and our strengths. I can usually overpower Roushaka when I expressly wish to do so. She is rather flippant and loses concentration too easily. Her main topic of thought is the naked male form." Amy chuckled. "She spends a great deal of time concentrating on that subject."

"You obviously know her very well."

"Yes, I do. We were at university together. We shared a life; we were so closely linked we were as one. We communicated frequently with pure mental transmissions. We helped each other with our studies and we even cheated from time to time. I helped her with her English and she sorted out my maths exam for me. We were very close, closer than sisters. I knew her as well as I knew myself."

"Does this...this power thing wear off? Can you outgrow it, or lose it?"

"Oh, yes." She was happy to answer his questions; most people were shy of her once they tasted her power.

"It seems to be something children frequently have from birth. They see and hear things that are lost to others, but they grow out of it, or should I say, they are encouraged to grow out of it by adults who believe them to be living with figments of their overactive imaginations. - the invisible friend syndrome, the constant daydreaming. They are such beautiful times that it's sad that it's driven out by ignorance.

"Roushaka is not nearly as strong nowadays, of that I am fairly certain. She seems to have wasted her youth. Grown mentally lazy. At times I had difficulty keeping up with her when we were young. She thought in her native tongue, in Russian. I thought in English. We were both conversant in each other's language, and at first, we struggled to understand each other. She'd been trained from childhood to speak English, prepared and nurtured for her future with the KGB; she could not quite get the hang of using it in telepathy. If it hadn't been for Roushaka, I don't suppose I would ever have taken up the career I chose for myself." Amy sighed. "Perhaps I should hate her for that."

"You have regrets?" he asked, sounding surprised.

"Yes, sir. I have many regrets. I have a husband whom I adore and I'm stuck here, behind the Iron Curtain, surrounded by the only people whom I can genuinely refer to as my enemy, whilst Dan is at home painting the spare room blue and yellow instead of cream and pink."

Ambassador Ponsford smiled a paternal smile, seeing Amy as if for the first time. He had never really had a proper conversation with her in the past, not like this, and only ever in the line of duty and usually in words of one syllable. She was never really a human being before this day, just another operative sent out from London to do a job and leave again as quickly as possible, someone else to watch over and worry about.

"Does it matter?" he asked. "Him painting it that colour I mean."

She shook her head. "No. All that matters is that I get back there to him." With a tired sigh, she went on. "Now, if you could arrange for that to happen, sir, I will be most grateful. But in the meantime, there's the small matter of Miss Pavalovsky to be resolved. She's dying out there and she wants to come over to us. I have made contact with her but she doesn't make much sense. She's ill and feeble."

"Is there any way she could deceive you?" The dark-eyed man asked her.

"I don't honestly know the answer to that question, Ambassador. I know of no way her mind could project the images I am now experiencing. It is possible for her to withhold information but not to show me the pain and suffering as clearly as she is unless it is genuine. Her fear is great and I believe her to be genuine. I have to stake my life on that judgement. I want to go and collect her and take her back to London."

Ponsford nodded. "Very well. I'll contact London and tell them what's happening. They'll arrange transport for you both. The sooner she's in London the happier I shall be."

"Sir, there will be a written message from her tomorrow, delivered by the same young girl, until we receive that I don't think we should make too many plans."

"Very well, Amy. Just let me know if there's anything I can do to help."

The child with the responsibilities and worries of a grown woman returned at first light as promised. She delivered a handwritten message. It was barely legible and despite the fact that it was written in the English language, it took Amy a considerable time to decipher it. There was what appeared to be blood stains on it.

Amy, I am desperate for your help. I am at Ivanovskoye 2117, Reutov. My health is poor and I am very frightened that my comrades will find me. If they do they will kill me. You are my friend. Please help me. The access routes to your embassy are being watched. Be careful. I am dead if you do not help me. You are my very last hope for life and freedom and my only true friend in this sad world. Roushaka P.

"Have you made any decisions yet?" the Ambassador asked when she entered his office an hour later.

"Yes, sir. I need a fully armed combat-trained soldier in civilian clothing to drive me. He has to know what he's doing. No stuffed shirts, please, Ambassador. Just a good reliable fighting man."

"Amy!" The man pulled himself up in his seat and puffed out his chest in indignation at the suggestion that he would provide her with anyone but the best. Her request for a fully armed fighting man troubled him deeply.

"There is no open conflict here, we do things with diplomacy and discretion. No urban guerrilla warfare tactics out here, I'll have you know. And I'll make it abundantly clear to you once again, we do not need anything that will give the Soviets something to blow up into a full-scale international incident. An incident, which would undoubtedly end up with the expulsion of my entire staff."

He shook his head. "No, Amy, you'll adopt a quieter method of conducting your business or I can't help you. Under the present climate, the only way can be the quiet way."

Silence filled every corner of the room and then Ponsford spoke again. "I'll give you one of my best young men. Basil Raymond is an intelligent young man who speaks the language like a native, what's more, he knows this country like the back of his hand."

He paused for thought and then he went on. "He'll take you to Reutov by a rather roundabout route. It's most fortunate that we have a diplomatic package to be delivered to the British Agricultural Mission further west - much further west. You can drop it off and return via Reutov, it's good cover. Find Pavalovsky and bring her back here as swiftly and discreetly as possible. No heroics."

Amy was smiling at him again, unnerving him, letting him call the shots, and knowing that she would do it her way in the end. She experienced only the briefest moment of shame for playing such a childish game when precious lives were at stake. In her wisdom she knew that her recent immature thoughts were due to nerves, as was her compulsion to drink copious amounts of water all of a sudden. Of course, the more she drank the more she needed to pee, and with the forthcoming trek through the countryside of Moscow it was a very impracticable situation to find herself in.

"Yes, Ambassador. Thank you, sir," she said seriously as she stood to leave but felt obliged to have the last word. "What sort of a name is Basil?"

Ponsford laughed. "He's a good man."

At 10:15 Ambassador Ponsford introduced her to a tall almost delicate young man with a pale face and ash blond hair. His cornflower blue eyes reminded her of a porcelain-faced doll she'd loved so dearly as a small girl. The same doll that the spiteful boy next door chose to poke the eyes into the back of her head with a stick. She never forgot Rosie and wondered briefly if her knight in shining armour would object to being called Rosie.

"I say, Mrs Jones," the knight began in near-perfect Oxford English. "I'm most awfully pleased to meet you at last."

"Likewise, Mr Raymond, likewise."

"I've heard such wonderful things about you," he went on, unable to take his eyes off her. "Do you think you could possibly bring yourself to call me Bas, Mrs Jones?" he asked most earnestly.

"Okay, Bas it is, and I'm Amy. Now, shall we get started?" There was an urgency in her to get this over with so that she could go home to Dan, and it had nothing to do with him stripping the wallpaper off the spare room walls with an eye to a bold deep purple pattern in the sample book. He had a very strange colour sense. His daughter would not appreciate such bold and masculine shades, but on the other hand, she was his child, and she might actually like it.

A terrible foreboding hung over her as she settled into the passenger seat of the old Rover saloon. She shrugged it off, there was no time for such nonsense, work was work and becoming sentimental at this stage would never achieve anything worthwhile.

They found the Agricultural Mission, dropped off the diplomatic package and headed full speed for Reutov in the western sector of Moscow. The black Rover sped along the dusty road towards the post-war concrete metropolis and as he steered the car Basil Raymond confided in Amy that he was a little nervous of what they were about to face. "I'm strictly an intelligence man you know. I've never had the opportunity to get out in the field like this. I'm a tetch nervous. How about you?"

Amy sighed; she didn't need this, and certainly not right now. "I'm nervous too," she told him. "It's good. It heightens the senses, keeps you on your toes. But don't you worry, Bas, I only want you to do exactly as I tell you, nothing more and nothing less. I'll give you clear and specific instructions when the time comes."

So much for her request for a fully armed combat trained soldier in civilian clothing. Amy sighed - one out of four had to be better than nothing. This man was at least dressed in civilian clothing!

During the drive she warmed to the innocence of the young man with the unspoiled mind of a child. "I love this place," he confided in her again. "Poor and plain and everything my home is not, but I love it." He half-smiled; it was a fleeting movement of his eyes and mouth.

"I suppose this sounds strange, but I never wanted for anything as a child and I only signed up for a slice of excitement. You see, money and breeding become terribly tedious after a while. Here, in Moscow I have a cheap room; pretty squalid actually, and mother would have a fit if she knew. She thinks I live in the tsar's palace. I eat what I can get in the local shops, just like a native, and I enjoy being alive. I'm terribly proud to be British, and to be working for my queen and country."

Yes, Amy liked him. She pitied all the men who could never be like this young man, unspoiled and untouched by the pain and cruelties of life that harden a man's heart and prevent him from loving and being loved. Even so, she longed for Dan to be with her now, in the black Rover, speeding towards the city and to…to God alone knew what.

Dan with his muscles and his bloody determination, Dan who would hold up the world for her if she as much as hinted that she needed it lifting. He was a natural survivor. He was her wonderful Dan and exactly the sort of man she needed with her when entering enemy territory. But Dan was still busy stripping wallpaper off the walls, filling the many cracks and stirring the non-drip paint.

Suddenly she heard his voice inside her head. *'Aw Christ! It's bloody non-drip! It'll go everywhere now I've stirred it. Amy would have noticed right away. What an idiot I am.'*

The sound of his laughter mingled with sadness echoed all around her now, filling her senses. *'Better not let on I cocked it up,'* he said to himself. *'I'll never live that one down.'*

'Oh, Dan!' she whispered within her conscious mind. *'I love you, Dan. You are impossible and I love you.'*

At 15:00 they arrived in the suburb of Reutov and found Ivanovskoye without too much difficulty. Grey dilapidated and neglected tenement blocks, row upon row of them stood like grey-clad Soviet soldiers on parade. They were buildings waiting for life, and for the living. Here, in this grey world, poverty and misery were rife. There was nothing to inspire life or joy, nothing outside of the hearts and souls of those who dwelt within the concrete walls. These were not homes, merely places in which people existed.

"Dear God," Amy gasped as they parked the car some distance away so that she could brief the young man by her side. "It's not just those who have been, and who are being tortured in the concentration camps who are the victims." Feeling all the pain from within those concrete walls reach out to touch her tender heart, Amy wanted to cry.

"The KGB has created a living hell for every Soviet citizen, even the Party members suffer one way or another," she went on as Basil Raymond turned and studied her pretty face. "Their victims include everyone who is forced to live in fear and mistrust of each other. They watch and listen, waiting for them to come for them. Never knowing when they will strike. Who guards the guards, Bas?"

"I never thought of it like that, Amy."

"Well, do. Stop using this place as a way of avoiding who and what you are. Stop hiding amongst this misery. Look around you and see the true colour of things. Feel the pain of these precious souls. The KGB is responsible for murdering, maiming and terrorising countless millions. We, in the West, will never know the truth. We can only scrape the surface off and do our level best to assist those who cry out to us for help."

He sighed. "Will it always be like this?"

"No," she said. "I think it will get worse. I believe the walls of totalitarianism will crumble and these people will be unable to deal with life. The culture shock will be too much for them. Generations to come will perhaps benefit from all of this, but I don't know. I can't see how the damage can ever be undone. It's up to us to do our bit, now, while we can."

Basil spoke to her but she failed to hear him. The child inside her and the fear wrapping around her soul were far too great a distraction. She looked at him. "What did you say?"

"I wondered what you want me to do."

"You can drop me close to where Pavalovsky is alleged to be in hiding. I'll go inside. If I fail to reappear in precisely twenty minutes from leaving this vehicle, you are to turn around and report back to the ambassador. If you hear any sounds, such as gunshots, you abort this mission and leave. Should anyone approach this vehicle other than me, you leave. Do you understand?"

He was horrified by her orders, and he told her so. "I don't like that plan. I can't leave you here should you get into bother. I cannot simply drive off and leave you, it isn't done."

"You will drive off and leave me here!" she repeated emphatically. "Because I will either be dead, dying or captive. You must leave. You must not set foot outside of this vehicle. Do you understand me?"

"Yes. I understand, but as I said, I don't like it."

"Like it or not you will obey my instructions to the letter, Bas." She reached for his hand and squeezed it. "Obeying the instructions of a woman will do nothing to diminish you as a man. You have my respect. Just do it, please, Bas."

He watched her slip silently from the car the instant he pulled off the road. He checked his watch as she closed the door silently, turned and disappeared into the gloom of an entrance corridor. Basil Raymond felt a powerful sense of warmth for the enigmatic woman. He had never come across anyone like her before, in all of his twenty-four years. He knew that the tough streak of granite in her personality did nothing to diminish her feminine essence in any way.

Her powerful insight was such that within an hour of meeting him, and with only a handful of words and limited conversation, she succeeded in boosting his morale and building his confidence so much so that she had left a lasting impression upon him. It was an impression, which would remain with him until his dying day. He prayed that he would not have to leave her here, but he knew that he would obey her every word. And now, as he sat alone, he primed his senses. He checked his watch again. He was totally alert and waiting, just like the grey depressing buildings, waiting.

With increasing unease Amy climbed the concrete staircase to the first floor. The building was silent and the only sound to reach her ears was the patter of her own footsteps. Instinct told her that this was a trap - that she was making a monstrous mistake, however, the die was cast and she told herself that it was too late now to turn back.

Feeling an overwhelming compulsion to move on into some predetermined fate, and powerless to resist, she continued making her way to number 2117. There was neither sight nor sound of life as she walked along the stark first-floor corridor, passing doors as drab and grey as the concrete they were set in, and then she was there, outside 2117. She knocked and waited, too frightened to do anything other than to go on.

The door opened and Amy faced Roushaka Pavalovsky for the first time in a long time. She had aged beyond her years. Pale and gaunt with deep-set dull eyes and grey threads streaking her once lustrous black hair. Her left cheek bore the tell-tale signs of having been broken - the bone was deeply indented. Her flesh was black and blue. A heavy scab hung from a split in her swollen lower lip. There was little sign of her previous beauty; she had been so badly marred by beatings.

She reached forward and urged Amy into the single room, closing the door behind her so that she could cling to her old friend and then she wept silently whispering her genuine gratitude. "Thank you, Amy. Thank you for coming for me."

"Get your coat," Amy spoke sharply to her, in no mood for sentimentality. "We have to leave immediately."

Roushaka nodded and attempted to smile, wincing as blood trickled from the split lip that had torn open again. "I understand," she said as she crossed the room to the bed.

Amy moved further into the room to watch her every move. She saw her lift her threadbare coat and then she saw the pistol in her hand.

"Why are you in such a hurry to leave, my dear friend? Do you not wish to visit with me for a while?"

"Rou!" Amy snapped. "Put that damned thing down and let's get out of here now."

Pavalovsky shook her head and smiled as fresh blood flowed freely down her chin from the tear in her lip. "I think not, dear friend. I suggest you sit down before my comrades decide to apply a little pressure upon your delicate body. You can see with your own eyes what they are capable of."

Amy spun on her heels but all too late. Two athletically built females, almost identical in appearance, with round sallow faces, barrel chests like bulldogs and pistols levelled with her heart, prevented her from going anywhere.

A stocky, balding man in a brown leather jacket, baggy trousers and wire-rimmed glasses stepped between them. "Good afternoon, Mrs Jones," he said, speaking to her in his own tongue, knowing exactly what she was capable of understanding. "We have been expecting you. We need you to help us. You will come with us please. We know you are an intelligent woman and you will by now be aware of the foolishness of attempting to escape. If you resist, or you attempt to shout out, we will shoot away your legs." He continued almost without a pause. "You see, we do not need your legs, only your mind."

Amy froze. Her mind began spinning recklessly. Her instincts told her that she had to survive, no matter the cost. Resisting the urge to place her hand protectively on her belly, slowly she moved her eyes around the room until they fell again upon her former friend, but Pavalovsky could not hold her gaze. She turned away and checked her pistol. She'd known exactly what she was doing; this was no act of the oppressed. Roushaka Pavalovsky had submitted herself to the most horrendous of beatings for months. She'd starved herself and lived in poverty. Her mind was tortured, just as her body had been tortured. She knew exactly what she was leading her oldest and most dear friend into.

This woman had betrayed her only true friend to the KGB in the name of Communism and the Soviet State. She felt no compassion for Amy and no remorse for her evil deed. In return she would be given a luxurious apartment in the heart of the city. No more sharing a bathroom with three other tenants and no more poverty. The betrayal had not been difficult. It came naturally. She remained convinced that uniting her mind with Amy was the answer for the Party. They would be linked to a computer and together they would conquer the world.

"Do not look at me that way," Roushaka said at last. "Alone I am not powerful enough to carry out the project, but now, with you, we have everything we need."

Amy felt sick; she was unable to contain her revulsion and contempt. "What project?" she asked coldly, knowing exactly what she was talking about but stalling for precious time.

"The advancement of our science, Mrs Jones," the man with the eyes of a pig proudly informed her.

"I am on an official British diplomatic mission. You will not interfere with me in any way lest you cause an international crisis, which your country cannot afford." Her words were brave and useless, her voice steady and strong.

With that she took a bold step forward in an attempt to walk through the formidable Russian trio, but the man stood his ground and barked out an order to the fur-coated females. They immediately holstered their pistols and reached for Amy, taking hold of her arms to pin her between them. It was not dissimilar to being clamped in the jaws of a massive vice.

She attempted one final verbal gesture. "I warn you, I am accompanied and I am expected at the British Embassy in Moscow."

"My lady," the Russian mocked. "You know that a little woman like you is expendable. We hold the initiative in this 'Cold War' as you decadent Westerners like to call it. Your people will not risk a crisis over someone like you. They will forget you and erase your name from the records as if you never existed. As for your young man outside, he will soon be leaving without you. My men will scare him away the instant he sees them. You see, you belong to us now, to do with as we wish."

Amy recognised only too well the truth of his words. All was now lost for her. She withdrew into herself, thinking only of Dan, of how she had walked away from him again in a desperate effort to keep him alive. Now he would live and she would perish. The child within her would never be British, she would be taken from her body when she came to full term, and used in scientific experiments. In the depths of utter despair, Amy cried within herself.

'Dan! Oh, Dan! Find me. Please find me. I'm so sorry, Dan! I need you' The sharp point of the hypodermic needle broke through the flesh on her left arm and before she could whisper her husband's name once more, she was plunged into a black abyss.

PART FIVE

Chapter Eighteen

Friday 1 November 1985 London, England

Daniel Jones held his breath and counted to ten as he felt the energy drain from his body. It was as if he was being sucked dry by some force outside of the room. His senses began reeling and he dropped the book he was holding and fell to his knees in submission. This was a new sensation and one he could well have done without.

Amy had been gone for six long weeks. During which time he'd received letters from various places in West Germany. Letters allegedly written by his wife. Postcards with brief messages and a single vague scrambled telephone call from her, which left him even more frustrated. Whilst he'd snatched at and held on to everything connected to her, common sense prevailed and a niggling suspicion told him that none of it was genuine. The spurious messages were too stilted. The words on the sheets of paper were too cold and unfeeling, despite the numerous terms of endearment. The things Amy would have written were never there for him to read and take solace from.

Every letter or postcard opened up a deep wound in him and the void in his life was so great now it threatened to swallow him up at any moment. The black hole of his existence would collapse if anything were to happen to the woman he adored beyond reason.

"Amy!" he called into the nothingness that had been their home. His voice echoed in the empty room. It returned to him and he repeated his words. "Amy! Where are you, little love?"

"Dan!" Her voice was but a shadow in his mind. He reached out and clutched at that shadow, mentally taking hold of it, grasping at it and listening ever more carefully to what was being said. "Come for me. Find me. I need you, Dan...we need you..."

He shook his head as the shadow cleared and he was alone again. This had been happening to him for days, ten days in all - visions of Amy. Words from her mind projected over land and sea. Yielding to the terrible fear that was threatening to drown him, he began to cry. There was no longer any room for doubt. Amy had reached out to him for help, she'd drawn from his strength, leaving him weak and helpless.

Huge sobs convulsed his formidable frame as he buried his head in his hands; plunged into the depths of despair by the profound sense of loss he was feeling. He knew without doubt that the KGB had snatched his wife. He had no idea what they would do to her, or how long they would permit her to remain alive if she continued to resist them, as he knew she most surely would. He felt as if the end of his world was imminent.

Suddenly he leapt to his feet. "No, by Christ! As long as there's breath in my bloody body, I'll search for her!" He sprang across the room, raced down the stairs and snatched up the telephone receiver.

"Commander Cooper," he said abruptly to the switchboard operator. "Dan Jones."

"Dan!" the old man said, sounding nervous.

"Where is she? Where's Amy?"

"Amy? Err..."

Silence met his ears and with even more conviction sounding in his voice he repeated himself. "Commander, this is Dan Jones. I'm asking you where my wife is. You've been fobbing me off for six weeks now and I'm not having any more of your lies. Amy told me she'd be gone a couple of days at the most. You as good as said the same thing. I know I've heard from her; at least, I got letters from someone in Germany, but it's not enough."

"I've spoken to her in the past few days, Dan. I know she's..."

"Sir, no more bloody lies. I'm not some snotty-nosed little kid you can fob off with your professional storytelling." After a brief pause Dan picked up where he left off. "If she is there, I want to know where, because nobody in Germany seems to have even heard of her." He knew that for a fact, having contacted every single military base in Western Germany, British and American, asking for his wife by name, giving a full description of her to clear up any possible ambiguity.

"Either you agree to see me today or I'll come down there and break every bone in your bloody body without your permission."

"Dan, don't you think this is a little, err... unprofessional?"

"Mr Cooper," he growled in a low resounding voice that filled the old man with profound fear. "I've got no time to mess about with words. I want you to listen very carefully. I have good reason to believe that the Soviets have taken Amy, and that she's in mortal danger."

"This is preposterous..." Cooper began. "I must warn you..."

"Have the courtesy not to interrupt me, Commander," Dan snarled. "I'm deadly serious. I'm about to leave my home. I must see you in person. When I reach you, I want answers to the following questions. I suggest you make a note of them."

He paused for a couple of seconds and then he made his demands. "Where have you sent her? What was her assignment? What's happened to her and what have you got planned for getting her home?" Another brief pause and then, "May I respectfully suggest that you begin enquiries immediately? I haven't got time to waste." He slammed the receiver down.

The instant the line went dead Cooper pressed a button on the desktop intercom and spoke to his superior upstairs. "John, we have a problem developing. I'm on my way up."

Minutes later he entered the lavishly furnished office of John Baker - Director of Operations - six-feet tall and thirteen stones of austere but worldly naive flesh and blood. The fifty-year-old was prematurely aged and physically faded due to desk-bound inertia.

"Sit down, Bernard," he said smoothly. "What's troubling you?"

"As I said, we have a problem developing. One hell of a problem to be more precise." He sat down slowly, his joints beginning to ache, seeming to have aged in minutes. "I've just had Jones on the blower. He says he believes the Soviets have taken Amy and that she is now in a life-threatening situation. He's on his way in. He wants answers. He's in a dangerously determined frame of mind."

Baker was safe behind his mahogany desk. Nothing could harm him there. "He can't possibly know anything," he said. "Where would he get such information?"

"I don't know," Cooper replied. "But I do know that there's a report on file about Amy, from the Training and Assessment College, which states that they have irrefutable proof that she has strong psychic capabilities. I've never really let on to her, but I have always kept an open mind on it all, in fact, I'm convinced that she's the operative she is purely due to that ability.

"Dan Jones is a different kettle of fish, however. He's neither the biggest nor the strongest of men, nor is he the most agile, that's one of the reasons the SAS turned him down, but with what he does have, combined with his survival and combat skills, he's about the most lethal one-man force I've ever seen. He has a keen sense of smell when it comes to nosing out trouble and avoiding it, and when he decides to move into action, he won't let anything, or anyone, stand in his way. Unarmed he can kill with his fingertips."

Cooper was warning his superior. Warning of the storm blowing his way. He went on. "If you'd ever seen the two of them together, you'd know they have some unshakeable bond between them, the attraction of two opposites, two minds as one. Together they make up two integral parts of a single force. He's bound to be more receptive to her psychic powers, and it's more than likely she has contacted him with something like telepathy."

"What a load of nonsense!" Baker exclaimed, laughing at such an idea, having barely understood a quarter of what he'd just been told. "Telepathy indeed! Phooey! We've obviously got a leak in the department. There's nothing supernatural about that. You're going to have me thinking you're getting senile, Bernard. You've been in this work too long."

"You're probably right," Cooper agreed. "But I am warning you - Jones is on his way here and he'll arrive within the hour demanding answers as to what's happening with his wife. I know for a fact that he's made contact with all our establishments in Germany - searching for her in his own way. There's no way he fell for the counterfeit letters, even though our lot got the handwriting spot on. Amy is unique and Dan knows it. Get on the blower to Moscow and find out how the assignment is moving, because the Dan Jones I know, won't be satisfied with anything less than the truth, not this time."

Baker nodded, agreeing with him for once. "I take your point, Bernard, but I'm sure they'd have contacted us if anything had been amiss." He pressed the red button on the intercom. "Moscow, Ann. Get Ambassador Ponsford on the scrambler."

Two minutes later the telephone rang and a distorted voice asked, "What made you call me, John? I was about to give you a shout."

Baker felt a shiver travel the length of his spine. This was déjà vu. He had definitely had this conversation before. Suddenly his mind whirled him back to six weeks earlier to when he spoke to Ambassador Ponsford with regard to Amy Jones.

Heavy distortion caused by the scrambling devise had made the conversation that ensued strained and awkward, then, just as it was now. "Repeat, please," Baker had said slowly and precisely.

"Amy Jones is missing." This time the message came through more clearly.

"What happened?" Baker probed, rerouting the call through the desktop speaker as Cooper edged forward on his seat, anxious to hear what was being said.

"She went to collect...but it looks very much...our man is...trap...he came back alone...orders...unhappy..."

Baker prevented him from continuing. "Please repeat. Your voice is breaking up. Repeat slowly."

"I understand. Mrs Jones went to collect Pavalovsky...Can you...me?"

"Slowly!" Baker shouted impatiently. "More slowly, for God's sake, man, slow down."

"Will do my best," came his slow and precise response. "Amy Jones went out to bring Pavalovsky in. We are certain she walked into a trap. We've got wind of a rumour that she's on her way to Tobolmennaya. That's all I have. Orders are orders and I was not happy with the plan from the onset. I think you'd better..." The line crackled again and his voice faded.

"Please repeat last part of the message," Baker yelled into the mouthpiece.

"I was saying that I think you had better implement safety measures immediately, John."

"I will be the one to make that decision." His hackles had risen at being advised how to proceed by a diplomat. "I want a full report from you and your lot. I want everything on my desk by morning. Is that clear?"

"Perfectly."

Commander Cooper's worst ever fears became reality that day. His blood ran cold, as he'd listened to the conversation between the two men.

"I bloody well knew it!" he'd said, leaping to his feet, exploding with anger. "I tried to warn you!"

"Sit down, Bernard!"

"Sit down!" he'd spat at him. "I'll bloody well sit down when you decide to listen to me. Are you too damned stupid to know what goes on inside Tobolmennaya? It's an experimental facility, a laboratory. A psychiatric institution where they take people's brains apart and put them back together again to suit their needs. Christ almighty! They'll destroy Amy there! I'll sit down when you tell me you're going to get that woman out of there and not a minute before."

"Insubordination!" Baker exclaimed that day six weeks earlier.

"Too-damned right it's insubordination! I'll tell you what I'll do. I'll see this thing through to the bitter end and then I'll resign and ram my resignation right up your...your stuffed shirt! Until then I'm working to try and sort something out for Jones. Those two are the best in their respective fields. They trusted us. I warned you that this operation was too much of a risk, yet you still pushed on with it. You hoped to gain a prestige coup for yourself and now you've got one of them a death sentence and ruination for the other."

"Losing your nerve, Bernard?" Baker had asked smugly, unruffled by Cooper's outburst.

"What the hell do you know about nerve? By God! You've never suffered a day's hardship in your damned life. You came straight out of university into a desk intelligence job. Bootlicking your way to where you are now and me working for you. I wish to God I'd had the balls to retire from the Navy and gone into an office like a normal officer instead of allowing myself to be coerced into this filthy business with the likes of you. Inducing good men and women to put their lives on the line for cowards like you is not my idea of man management. You're right, I am losing my nerve, in fact, I'm sick to my guts of it all!"

Still attempting to reconcile the situation whilst retaining a modicum of seniority, Baker tried once again. "They all know what they're in for when they sign up."

"Do they?" Cooper asked. "I wonder. Besides that, I find it totally abhorrent to lull them into believing they're going on a routine safe operation when you know damned fine that you're sending them into an obvious trap."

"Don't worry, Bernard. Our people will handle this. He'll never suspect anything. The dust will die down and either Amy Jones will be released back to us or she'll be involved in a fatal road traffic accident."

It had been as cut and dry as that and six weeks ago Baker was quietly confident that he could handle the situation. Cooper had succeeded in keeping Dan Jones calm and at bay until now, and the bomb was about to go up.

"We have confirmation from our reliable sources out here that Amy Jones is definitely being held at the Tobolmennaya Institute," Ponsford told him. "We believe her to be alive, although, to be honest John, I know of no way we can help her from here. I've done my level best to secure her release through all of the regular channels. They deny all knowledge of her every time we make an enquiry. I'm sorry. I know it's been a long time, but until now I have done my level best to help that young woman."

"Yes, we know you have, Ambassador. Thank you for your help. We'll be in touch."

John Baker sighed as he settled back in his chair and informed Cooper, "The official channels are now closed. There's nothing more they can do. I'm afraid we're going to have to implement the RTA. Get things set up, there's no other way."

Cooper wanted to cry. They were going to cut Amy off with no hope of being returned to her husband, or to her homeland. They'd fake a fatal car smash and they'd just leave her there for the KGB to do whatsoever they wished with her mind and body, if indeed she were still alive.

"Not yet," Cooper advised. "It won't help solve the current situation. Dan Jones is on his way in. If you try fobbing him off with anything other than the truth, he'll slaughter all of us."

He could see that Baker was going to argue yet again, despite his numerous warnings. He leaned over the desktop. "Now you listen to me, John Baker, Jones will be here very soon. He'll want answers. If you can't cover this properly, you'd better take a suicide pill right now, because that man will tear your throat out if he has the slightest suspicion of what's happened to his wife and you start lying to him."

"I can handle Jones." Baker said sounding somewhat blasé.

"For God's sake, man!" Cooper exclaimed, completely frustrated by this man. "Let me handle him my way. Don't utter a sound or I won't be responsible for what happens to you. I want you here. I want you to see what you really are up against this time. You might just learn something that will save your stupid, arrogant neck at some time in the future."

Suddenly Baker lost some of his confidence. "Is this man violent?" the coward in him asked.

"Jones is the gentlest of men, and the most reasonable I've ever met. He's lethal in combat conditions only. But what we have here is a terrible combination of circumstances. We've robbed him of his wife and he's half out of his mind with frustration and worry. The only way is to let me handle him. I'll level with him. Nothing but the truth will do with this character."

Baker sighed resignedly. "Inform security. Take every precaution as regulations insist we must. I want to be certain that this is done by the book. Issue him with form C/109."

"Naturally." Cooper was sick and tired of the regulations and the red tape. "I'll brief security on how I want them to handle the situation. Leave everything to me."

Cooper left the office and headed straight for the intelligence bank room on the fourth floor of the building, to where all classified documents were securely stored. He let himself in with his electronic security clearance scanner card and searched the rows of cabinets, stopping only when he arrived at the letter T. Thumbing deftly through the buff files his hand closed on one of the thickest in the cabinet.

It took him only minutes to photocopy five pages of vital information, return the folder to the drawer and leave the room. The security card would have recorded him as having entered the room, together with the time of day and the length of his visit. He would deal with the consequences if and when questioned.

His secretary typed in the relevant details on form C/109, the document that would terminate Dan Jones's involvement with the Department. Cooper took the form out of her hand and sealed it in a large buff envelope together with the photocopies.

By taking this action, he was jeopardising his own freedom. Should Baker get wind of it he could forget retirement, but it was a risk he was prepared to take. He would probably never be able to put right his wrong, but by God, he was going to give it his very best shot.

As the powerful form of Daniel Jones stepped into the foyer of Victoria House, there was an air of concentrated menace about him, which appeared to paralyse everyone, as if a primed atomic device had been timed to explode at any second. Typists stopped typing. Telephonists stared in awe, and visitors looked up from their newspapers and documents while a heavy presence of white-shirted security officers fidgeted nervously where they stood.

All eyes were on him as he walked straight up to the security inspector and held out his ID card for him to study. "Dan Jones. I've come to see Commander Cooper."

"Ah! Yes!" the man said politely. "We've been expecting you. Please follow me." He turned and walked through the double security doors. Dan, together with five of the security team, fell in behind him.

All seven men travelled to the ninth floor with Dan holding his ground in the centre of the lift. His legs spread wide and his arms folded over his fully inflated chest. They travelled in complete silence. There was nothing to be said, he had no business with these men. They were pawns, just like him and Amy.

They stepped from the lift on the ninth floor and moved procession-like along the corridor, coming to a halt in front of an elaborately ornate door. The inspector knocked and a voice from inside commanded them to enter. He opened the door, motioned to Dan to enter and remained outside with his colleagues.

"Do come in and sit down," Cooper invited him sombrely. "This is my director, John Baker."

Dan afforded Baker only the very briefest of scrutinising glances as he sat down on the chair strategically placed in front of the long table, behind which the two intelligence officers were sitting. His eyes fell upon Cooper and remained fixed unerringly on him, waiting for answers.

"I shall get straight to the point, Dan," Cooper began. "I'll give you the facts, the truth."

"You will," Dan growled. It was not a question. It was an order. His eyes narrowed as suspicion and distrust grew within him. He had never for one minute expected an easy ride with this man, but he wanted him to know that he was not being offered options.

"No need for threats. I owe you that much at least." He took a deep breath and began. "As you have already guessed, Amy was sent to Moscow. Pavalovsky, her old university friend, expressed a strong desire to defect. We checked it all out as best we could and it seemed like a genuine enough request. One of the Pavalovsky family members has recently been executed on trumped-up charges, and the rest of them have been incarcerated in some ungodly hell-hole.

"We knew Pavalovsky was on the run and in hiding. She was thrown out of Moscow, denied the right to occupy a room there, beaten and persecuted. We had no clue as to exactly where she was and we asked Amy for her help so that we could get the woman out of there. She...she blackmailed Amy into accepting this assignment by threatening your life. Amy had no choice other than to go. If Pavalovsky had as much as snapped her fingers, both of you would be dead by now."

Dan frowned. There were flaws in this story. "Beaten," he said. "Persecuted and on the run, yet blackmailing my wife and in a position to have us both killed at the snap of a finger."

Cooper sighed and confessed, "It was all wrong from the start, Dan, a complete mess. Our people over there have been running around like headless chickens for the best part of a year. Messages coming in and going out - garbled messages half the time. Until we could put Amy into the position of being able to assess the situation, we had no idea what to think. It was very much a 'can't do right for doing wrong' situation."

"Huh!" Dan huffed and Cooper went on.

"Amy went straight to the embassy in Moscow and located Pavalovsky. She and one of our men went in to bring her out. They walked into a trap." He sighed again and looked to Baker before adding, "We have heard rumours that she's been taken to..."

Baker leapt to his feet. "Silence, man! You have no right to..."

"Shut up!" Cooper breathed the words and Baker fell instantly silent as he sat down again. "Amy could be in the Tobolmennaya Institute. I can tell you no more than that."

But it was much more than Dan could have hoped for, and somewhere to begin the search. He sat in thoughtful silence while Cooper finished what he had to say.

"Being the type of man I know you are, you would want me to lay everything out for you, and so I will. The Soviets deny all knowledge of Amy being held by them. As you are aware, Amy is lost and there is nothing more this department, or the British government, can do about it. The reasons are obvious and politically motivated.

"If any of this information leaks, we will also deny all knowledge of Amy. In fact, while I speak, the process of erasing all reference to her has begun. Amy never existed in this department. Your involvement with the Department will also be terminated forthwith. You will be required to hand in your passport and any other documents that link you to this department. This instruction includes your ID card. You have twenty-four hours in which to comply. We'll set you up with a new identity and the means with which to establish yourself in any country you so wish."

He lifted the buff envelope and handed it to him saying, "I am obliged by the Official Secrets Act of 1970, to serve upon you form C/109 contained within this envelope. You will sign to say that you have received it from me today."

Baker shoved the book across the table, together with a ballpoint pen; taking satisfaction in what he believed was Dan's submission.

Dan signed and then he said, "And for that I have to keep my mouth shut." The words came from him but his lips hardly moved. His face was ashen and lined with tension.

"Dan, believe me, your silence is guaranteed," Cooper assured him. "These people will destroy you if you refuse to conform. They have the law, the dirty tricks brigade and other more severe and questionable means with which to ensure your instant silence. Don't take them on." Cooper strafed Baker with a look of utter contempt.

Cooper was choking as he said, "I want you to know that…I…I had it in my power to prevent Amy from going. I could have used any number of devious means, but no, I went along with it, knowing full well the terrible risk involved. I'm as much to blame as the rest of them. I want you to know that. I'd be a bloody hypocrite if I asked you to forgive me for my actions, but I wanted you to know the truth and how deeply I regret my part in this. I'll see this thing through and then I'm finished. I can say no more."

Commander Bernard Cooper was a visibly broken man. Gone was the astute and authoritative military air from his bearing. His head hung and his hands trembled on the tabletop.

The hard and forceful glare in Dan's eyes began to evaporate, giving way to a look of compassion for the old man opposite him. Still in silence he reached forward across the table to place his hand lightly over both of the commander's hands.

"I speak for Amy and myself, sir, when I say we forgive you and bear you no malice whatsoever. You were always a good officer, and you are a very fine man. You obeyed orders and treated us always as best you could under difficult circumstances. Unlike the rest of these desk-bound idiots, you have a good heart and a conscience. You can be assured always of our respect and affection."

Through misty eyes Cooper thanked him. "I value those words. Thank you."

Dan went on as he withdrew his hand. "What I need from you now is advice and direction. Would you mind if we speak alone?"

"Mr Jones," Baker said loudly and offensively, finding confidence in what he believed was Dan's apparent softening of resolve. "Let me remind you that I am Director of Operations here and you will take whatever orders and advice are necessary in this situation, from myself alone. I'm most awfully sorry about your wife, you have my sympathy, but we will do what we have to do, as there can be no sentiment in our line of work."

"John!" Cooper warned. "Leave it! Leave it to me!" He saw the anger being re-primed in Dan, but it was too late. Ignition had already taken place.

"You bloody hypocrite," Dan hissed through his teeth. "You snivelling cowardly bastard." He was roaring with fury now as Baker began to almost shrivel up with fear. "Sorry! You're not sorry. Amy was nothing to you. She was just a number on a piece of paper. She's my wife. I killed my way out with her years ago, out from under the noses of the bloody Reds. I entrusted her into your care - my own country, my own people, and you put her back into their hands, and for what, for an impossible dream? For prestige, or to boost someone's ego but whose ego? Yours? You who have never seen active service. You who send others to their deaths while you hide in a hole like a sewer rat. Now I'll show you what it's like to fear death."

Dan stood up and reached out towards Baker with both hands. Baker had already lost his nerve and was leaning heavily on the security button strategically positioned close to the edge of the table. Taking hold of him by his jacket lapels, Dan's hands became steel power clamps as his thumbs pressed into either side of Baker's larynx; stopping his breath instantly and preventing him from crying out as he was dragged like a rag doll, across the table top towards his attacker, stopping inches from his face at precisely the same time the six-man security team burst into the room. Baker's eyes were already beginning to roll up into his head.

"How about my ripping your bloody throat out in the next few seconds?" Dan asked with an eerie calm.

"Dan!" Cooper shouted. "Stop! You'll kill him." The inspector and his sergeant were attempting to prise Dan's fingers from around Baker's neck whilst a third man grabbed him from behind, his hands around Dan's forehead in a futile attempt to force his head back.

Baker's body belly-flopped onto the table as Dan released him suddenly so that he could shimmy to either side in an instant, both elbows jabbing under two outstretched arms and into unprotected gut. The men who had been flanking him crumpled and fell winded on the floor. Dan compacted himself and swivelled inside the head grip, turning to shoot a pile-driving punch into the groin of the third man.

With four men writhing and moaning in agony, each gasping for air, one across the table, three on the floor, Dan took up a stance that warned that he was ready for any action they cared to put his way. He was like a compressed coil of steel waiting to spring into instant action, yet the onslaught never came.

While the commander restored Baker to his chair and patted some life back into his face, the other three security men, as yet untouched, stood unnerved, apprehensive and leaderless before him, frozen in awe and making no move towards him.

"No, gentlemen," he said quietly to them. "Don't even think about it. I have nothing to lose. I've lost my wife and my life goes with her. You still have your lives to live. The three behind me will recover, but you make any move and I'll kill you instantly and think no more of it than having a haircut."

The seconds ticked by in silence save for the heavy breathing of the injured men and the commander, talking quietly to reassure Baker that he would live. When Dan decided that further hostilities were unlikely, he relaxed and walked leisurely towards the door. Unable to resist one last final flaunt of dominance. As he passed close to the biggest of the standing security men, he gave his right arm a quick twitch and the hapless fellow jumped back out of his way."

"God! You're jumpy," Dan said over-condescendingly, and then, "Don't worry, I won't hurt you. You're only doing your job."

On reaching the door he turned and addressed Cooper, "I'll be back tomorrow with the documents you requested, Commander, but I'll only deal with you."

Pointing to Baker he added, "Keep that thing out of my sight and these monkeys out of my way for their own safety. Thank you for your honesty, sir." He closed the door quietly behind him.

"You bloody fool," Cooper chastised Baker. "I had him eating out of my hand and you blew it by opening your big mouth. Now you know what you're up against."

"He's an animal," Baker croaked, sitting up rubbing his bruised throat whilst the shattered security team helped each other to their feet.

"Dan Jones is one of the finest and most loyal men I've met," Cooper informed him again. "The animal side of his nature was developed in the service of this country and it's always kept well under control and out of sight until a complete cad like you triggers it."

"We can't let a dangerous man like that stay loose under these circumstances," Baker argued, choosing wisely to ignore the derogatory remarks made by the man senior only in age and wisdom. "I'm going to inform New Scotland Yard Special Branch."

"You're an even bigger fool than I thought you were!" Cooper shouted now that they were alone in the room again. "I'll tell you how that'll end - bloodshed and death. He's not going to give in to the police. He'll probably kill a couple of innocent young family men in self-defence. A siege situation will develop and that poor man will die in a burst of gunfire like a common criminal. He doesn't deserve that.

"As it is now, he's under my control. I trust him like I've never trusted anyone. He'll be back here tomorrow with his documents as promised, and I can take him from there. Besides that, John, I'm afraid you have no option. If I put a confidential report to the Foreign Secretary, who you know is a personal friend, and I describe your appalling blunder in this affair, your career will be finished."

"Very well!" Baker conceded bitterly. "But I warn you, Bernard, if anything goes wrong from here on it will be on your own head. The sooner I have your resignation the better."

"I agree." Cooper turned away from him with a satisfied smile; he'd scored another valuable point. "Now, let's clear up and get on, shall we?"

But Commander Bernard Cooper, after a lifetime of handling real men, had a good insight into the thought process of Daniel Jones and he knew full well that he would go for the impossible and for Amy, even if it killed him in attempting it, as it most certainly would.

He knew that he would prefer to die in trying than sit back and mourn the loss of his lovely wife. All that remained to be done was to keep the authorities off his back for twenty-four hours, allowing Dan breathing space to leave the country. He'd be gone before dawn, free to do whatever he had to do with regard to his wife. Cooper knew he owed him that.

The good commander had been spot on. At 2135 that same day, a Lufthansa DC10 lifted off the tarmac at Heathrow Airport. Daniel Jones was on board. The aircraft was bound for Hamburg.

After leaving Victoria House, Dan returned home long enough only to pick up his combat rucksack, ready packed with survival gear - always there in readiness for any eventuality. He gathered up all of the necessary documents, passport and credit card. A medium-sized holdall was sufficient for a few changes of clothing.

He turned off the gas and electricity, locked up and left the house keys with his next-door neighbour. He also handed over a single sheet of paper containing contact numbers for his family, should he or his wife not return within a month.

After posting a letter to his sister Stephanie he called at the bank, purchased sufficient German currency to last a month and took a cab to the airport where he managed to obtain a ticket on the next Hamburg flight, leaving him enough time to snatch a bite to eat. He needed to keep his strength up, more now than ever before.

Looking back through the aircraft window, he saw the red sunset fading in the west. Ahead of him lay the blackness of the night. With a heavy heart Dan slumped in his seat, closed his eyes and focused his thoughts on his beloved Amy.

"Where are you, little one?" he asked, regretting that he'd waited such a long time to take this action. "I'm on my way. Just hold on."

PART SIX

Chapter Nineteen

Saturday 2 November 1985

With great effort of will, the man lifted his body from the comfort of the armchair and silenced the telephone by lifting the receiver to his ear. "Hello?" he said sounding grumpy.

"Major Philips?" a voice from the past asked.

"Speaking." It had been a long time since anyone addressed him that way - another lifetime ago in fact.

"Dan Jones here, sir. The old regiment – Berlin - sixty-seven. Do you remember me?"

"Dan Jones!" he exclaimed. "Good Lord! Remember you! Hang it all, man, how could I ever forget you? Where are you? What are you doing with yourself these days?"

"I'm in Germany, sir. I'm on a desperate mission - a matter of life and death. I need to see you urgently. I can answer all of your questions later." He spoke positively and deliberately slowly in order to impress the urgency of his mission upon the man on the other end of the telephone line.

"You're serious! Of course, splendid." The very sound of some action returning to relieve the monotony of his life instantly lifted his flagging spirits. He'd almost forgotten what the thrill of adrenalin surging through his veins felt like. "Where are you?"

"Lübeck railway station." He was kilometres away. He'd walk if necessary.

"What! You crafty sod! Don't change do you, Jones? Same old 'stop at nothing' man I remember. Dump yourself on my bloody doorstep then ask if I'll see you. Cheeky young bugger. I suppose if I refuse, you'll break my door down and threaten my life."

Dan remained silent and the major chuckled as he pictured his face as he remembered him. "Sit tight, old chap. I shall be with you in a jiffy...well, thirty minutes or so. I live just out of town."

"Thank you, sir. I'll start walking if you give me directions."

"You'll do no such thing. You'll stay right where you are, do you hear me, Jones?"

"I hear you, sir. I'm outside the railway station."

In just over an hour, Dan was being shown into a compact and rather modestly furnished lounge in a large old Teutonic residence. It appeared to him that Douglas Philips was living in only a handful of the many rooms in the mansion-like place.

"Do sit down, old chap, and as long as you're here you might as well make yourself at home. What would you like to drink?" the major asked as he jack-knifed his colossal seven foot frame to open the drinks cabinet.

"A cup of tea would go down nicely, sir, thanks." Dan was relieved to find him looking much like he'd remembered him. Just as tall and standing just as proud. This was a man the regiment could be proud of, he was greyer, and with a little less leanness to his body, but the same Major Philips with the same shock of red hair.

"Of course," he said as he closed the cabinet. "I remember now, never one for tippling, were you? But if I recall the rare occasion that you did take a drop or two, you always seemed to end up with some form of controversy hanging over you. Oh, I know, you'd never actually start anything, but by God, you'd certainly finish it!"

A fleeting smile crossed Dans ruggedly handsome face, relieving him temporarily of the worry lines, which were now part of him. "Some things in my murky past are best forgotten, sir." He looked about him. There was something, or someone, missing. "Tell me, Major, do you live alone or is there a Mrs Philips?"

"I live alone," he said as old wounds opened up and his pain became intolerable again. "Least I do now. I lost my wife a year ago. The dreaded leukaemia you know. In a way I regard her as still being with me, although it's not the same without her companionship."

Dan let him go on, watching his eyes mist with sadness and a deep longing to return to life as it had been with his wife.

"Anja was a local woman, an absolute angel, but never overly strong. The disease must have been lurking about for years, undetected, of course. We had three wonderful years before she became too ill to enjoy life. Then it was all over within months. Sadly, no children, but I never regard myself as being alone, not completely alone. I find her everywhere. Do you know what I mean, old chap?"

"Yes. I do. I'm sorry, sir," he spoke softly as he fingered his thick moustache. The major seemed to be looking inward at something deep inside him. Dan knew that type of pain and despite everything he'd said about not being alone, he was alone, and he was in pain.

"Thank you, old chap. Now, don't say any more about it, please. I'll never get over losing Anja but I will eventually learn to live with my loss. She would have wanted it that way. But tell me, what about you? Why are you here? What have you got yourself into this time?"

For the next forty minutes or so only Dan spoke while the major sat in deep concentration, puffing occasionally at his pipe.

"So, you see, sir," Dan concluded. "Time is desperate. As it is I don't know what will be left of Amy when I do find her." There was no doubt in his mind that he would find his wife, but there was uncertainty as to whether he would be in time.

"God Almighty!" Doug Philips blasphemed aloud as he jumped up and began a steady pacing of the living room floor. "This is far too much to absorb all at once." And then he lowered himself back into the chair and faced Dan with what was on his mind.

"Right. Listen. Questions. First things first, how did you find me?"

"Last year I met an officer from the old battalion who worked with you - Colonel Cutler. He gave me your address and phone number. I filed it away for future reference."

Doug Philips nodded acceptance of his reply. "Cutler. Hmmm! That's okay. Tell me, how do you know that this laboratory exists? How do you know the location and how are you so damned certain Amy is there at this time?"

"Pavalovsky constantly tried to get Amy to join her in research after their stint at university. The KGB were itching to get hold of her ever since then. Commander Cooper put his career on the line by slipping me everything I need, all the information his department holds. I know exactly where it is. It's 500 kilometres north of Leningrad and 322 kilometres in from the border with Finland."

He then took the five photocopied pages provided by Cooper, some were blueprints of the layout of the place and others were photographs, and he handed them to the major who said, "So that's what it looks like. I remember hearing rumours about it many years ago, but no names were mentioned at the time."

Doug Philips was staring at the image of the drab single-story building, the Tobolmennaya Institute. The place bore all the similarities of a wartime concentration camp, set in a clearing surrounded by pine trees.

"It's five kilometres off the main Leningrad road," Dan commented as the major turned to the second sheet.

"That's all the information on a number of the key personnel in the place. The third page is an internal layout, a blueprint if you like, and the others have all the information for a navigational fix and details of manpower etcetera."

Before the major could take a proper look, Dan was pressing ahead. "Now, how do I know she's there? Logic, Major, pure logic. The KGB is only interested in acquiring Amy for two reasons." He held out his left hand and held up the index finger. "They need her vast knowledge in the field of psychology." And then he held his middle finger alongside the other. "And they need her strong psychic faculties, which have been well documented for them by Pavalovsky. Therefore, as we know of no other psychiatric research establishment with the special apparatus and facilities this one has, Amy has got to be there. I'd stake my life on it." He lowered his hand.

"The other thing is that Amy and I have developed a certain telepathic rapport. I couldn't, or wouldn't, get the hang of it before, not really if I'm perfectly honest, but lately I'm getting better at it. I get impressions, strong ones now that we're separated. I know it's hardly credible, but I only have to close my eyes and I can see the place and feel some of the great distress she's suffering." With steel-like determination he finished off with, "I don't just believe she's there, sir, I know it. But time's running out for her."

"Very well, Dan. I'll accept all of that, my memory of Amy and the way she works is perfectly clear. Now, my last question - why me? How do you think I can help you?"

Dan smiled as he said; "I'm going to get her out of there, sir. I'm going to bring her back and I want you by my side." He spoke with a deep conviction that penetrated the older man's subconscious, rendering him temporarily speechless.

"Why you, sir? That's simple. Trust. There's nobody living and available whom I know and trust like I know and trust you. Who else is there? Nobody! Where've they gone? Dead - either killed or killed themselves in some last-ditch suicide. The ones that are left have run to fat and they're all but useless, some with alcoholism and others just with old age. If there's anyone up to this, I haven't got time to find him. I'll put it bluntly to you, Major - I'm asking you to put your life on the line to help me rescue Amy.

"On the face of it, it's an impossible mission. But if you think about it, you'll know it can be done and why it's possible. It'll certainly involve killing and intense physical and mental anguish. The odds are stacked against us. It could end in death for us both or misery if we get either injured or captured. But I know it can be done." He took a deep breath. "That's about the size of it, sir."

Major Douglas Philips sat very still as his colour and entire aura seeming to alter. While the man himself hadn't diminished in size and bearing, his air of authority, natural to his previous rank and standing, appeared to have been obliterated before the power of Dan's personality and resolve.

"I know there's no time for dithering on this, Dan, but we can't start anything today. It's already very late." He took another second or two for his thoughts and then he added, "I'll give you my decision first thing in the morning. Even if I decide against joining you, I'll give you all the help I can. Now, let's put a bloody-good supper inside us and get some shut eye."

At 07:00 Dan heard footsteps on the stairs. The bedroom door creaked opened and the major spoke to him. "Breakfast is served, old chap." He saw that Dan had shaved his chin, showered and dressed. "Come down when you're ready."

The aroma of fried bacon drew the big Welshman and his grumbling stomach down the carpeted stairs and into the kitchen where Doug Philips placed a huge platter of bacon and eggs on the table. "Do sit down, old chap," he invited and his guest obeyed in hungry silence.

"Put that away and we'll talk over coffee."

The food smelt wonderful and Dan was grateful to him for his hospitality. This meal would set him up for the day. "Thanks," he said without further talk before wolfing the lot down within minutes, leaving the plate shining as if freshly washed.

Doug Philips poured two mugs of coffee and slid one across the scrubbed surface of the kitchen table. "I've decided to join you," he informed him watching him physically relax. He'd been in suspense all night.

"I'm going to put my body and soul into this, Dan. I know the risks, in fact, I think it's damned suicidal, but like you, I've given it much thought and I know it can be done. Besides, I've really got sod all to live for now I've lost my wife, and frankly, I couldn't give a hang if I were to join her wherever she is. But don't go worrying about that, I know survival is what counts. I'll be no good to you, or to Amy, dead. I'll give it my best shot.

"I've always held Amy in the highest possible esteem. I'll even go as far as to say that when she first arrived in Berlin, all those years ago, I was madly in love with her."

Dan grinned broadly. Liking the man all the more for his honesty. "I know, sir."

"You do?" He looked utterly astounded by the news. "Hang it all, man! There was me thinking I'd kept it hidden so bloody well!" He sighed. "Went about it all the wrong bloody way as usual. Cocked it up first day, of course, but when I saw the pair of you together, I gave up even trying. Couldn't wish for a finer man for her, if you'll excuse me for saying so."

In order to cover any embarrassment he might have caused, he hurried on. "Count me in. What do you want me to do?"

"Thanks, sir," was all Dan could manage to say, he was too choked for more. "I want..."

But the major interrupted before he could even begin. "Now listen to me, Dan. You're the boss on this one. I know I far outranked you in the service but I can't hold a candle to you in this type of operation. So, drop the 'sir 'and the 'major', and all that. All right, old chap?"

"No, sir," he told him. "It isn't all right. I don't want to be in any way inhibited by what not to call you when we're under pressure. I'll call you what comes naturally. Okay, Major?"

He nodded and Dan went on. "Besides, it's a mark of respect that's firmly fixed in my mind for all time. It's like asking you to drop saying things like, 'I say, old chap. Backs to the wall' and all that crap."

Doug Philips laughed, as he hadn't done in years. He laughed until he cried and then he said, "Point taken, old chap. Point taken. So, get on with it, man!"

For the following three hours, Dan talked while the major made notes on a large pad. They concluded that they would need military type compo rations, something lightweight but nourishing, firearms, including ammunition and numerous other necessary bits and pieces. They would carry only the most essential items.

"Do you believe in fate, Dan?" he asked when the planning was over.

"Never given it much thought, sir. I suppose I do. Amy kept on coming in and out of my life, especially when I needed her most. Then I thought that fate had given her to me at last and she's...she's been taken away again by those bloody bastards."

He felt all the anger boiling within him again; the anger he'd kept locked up since learning that Amy had been sent to Moscow. "Sorry."

"No need to apologise, old chap. I understand fully how you feel, believe me. But what I meant was more in line with the fact that I just happen to be a shareholder and business adviser to FCP."

Dan was lost. All of his years in the service had taught him that everything in life could be abbreviated into short form. Initials, codes, pass words - acronyms: NAATO. HQ. SGT. CPL. MJR. NAAFI. CQMS. RSM. And of course, there was Amy's special one: PA - Puff Adder, alias Major Douglas Philips, the very man who was about to help save her life, if he had any say in the matter.

"FCP, sir?" Dan repeated. "What the hell is that?"

"Finnish Computer Products," he told him. "Everything to do with computers and computer technology. But the point is this; I really am quite au fait with Finland, what is more, I just so happen to have a very good friend in Helsinki who deals in arms. All legit mind you, nothing underhand at all. Oh, no, I would never be a party to anything illegal."

Dan's mind was racing ahead. It was perfect. It couldn't be better if he'd planned it.

"What I suggest now is this..." the major began and then he paused for a second. "I don't want you to think I'm taking over the show, old chap, but I have a few contacts and I would like to help."

"Help all you like, sir. This is exactly why I came to you in the first place."

Major Philips nodded his thanks. "I suggest we take the car to Hamburg and hop on board a flight to Helsinki. We can have a word with Minivaanen, my arms dealer friend, and take it from there."

"Sounds like a plan, sir. Let's go."

Chapter Twenty

They parked the major's BMW in a long-term car park quite close to the airport at Hamburg and then they boarded the first flight to Helsinki which offered two vacant seats. A smartly uniformed chauffeur from FCP met them outside the arrivals area. One quick call from the major before leaving home and all of the arrangements were made by the company secretaries, who fortunately worked shifts right throughout the weekend.

The limousine was long and sleek and bright red. There was sufficient space in the boot for all of their gear, and enough left over for luggage for a family of four. The interior of the car was soft cream hide that moulded to their forms as they sat back to enjoy the short swift journey to the hotel.

They checked into adjoining single rooms. Clean, modern and ultra-sterile rooms lacking the warmth and charm of an English hotel. The hotel gave them somewhere to lay their heads for the night and somewhere to put together their final plan of action.

They washed and ordered a light meal and drinks from room service before settling down to talk. Douglas Philips planned to pay a visit to Minivaanen the following morning and all they could do was bide their time. Neither of them was in the mood for sightseeing, nor for drinking in a smoky bar. They retired early and lay awake for hours, longing for morning.

Breakfast arrived courtesy of room service once again, and then they left the hotel, stepping outside to chilling fresh air. Dan buttoned his jacket knowing the chill was deep inside him; it had nothing to do with the winter air.

Minivaanen welcomed the major as a long-lost brother. He embraced him and then he held him at arm's length to study him more closely. "Good. You look good, my dear friend, you have survived your loss, but not easily I think."

Doug Philips needed no words, he simply waited until the Finn had completed his inspection and then he introduced him to Dan. "A friend from my army days," he said and Dan felt glad he'd gone to him for help. This man was indeed a true friend and an equal.

"I am pleased to meet you," Minivaanen said as they shook hands. His handshake was firm and reassuring. His eyes were cold but his smile was warm. "Tell me what I can do to help you?"

"Rifles," Dan said, getting right down to business. "And pistols, plus ammo. That'll do for starters."

"Come through." The big Finn led them from the office into the warehouse - with a vast concrete floor, tables and gun cases around all four walls, where hundreds of weapons ranging from the smallest pistol available to heavy machine guns on tripods were laid out for inspection. The tools of death were displayed to the best advantage so any man could feast his eyes upon them and make his choice.

"This is what you want," he said as he reached for a Kalashnikov AK-47 7.62mm Assault Rifle. "This is the best combat rifle I have. It is totally reliable and you will not damage it easily in whatever you do. You need not fear for it becoming wet. It has single shot or automatic fire."

Dan took it out of his hands, felt the weight of it and nodded in agreement. "Okay, that's one for the major." He then proceeded to lay it carefully on the wooden counter so that he could search the racks of guns with a restlessness built on a longing to be reunited with his beloved Amy. And then he spotted exactly what he was looking for - the well worn, good old reliable, SLR.

He looked to Minivaanen for approval and when the big Finn nodded, Dan reached out and lifted the weapon down to examine it. He tossed it in the air, caught it and twirled it around his right hand like a baton before proceeding to strip it down. He noticed with satisfaction that there was no filth pitted on the end of the gas rod. That was a bonus. It was in prime condition if just a touch too dry.

As he reassembled the weapon he said, "I'll take this one. It's what I used all through my military service. I'm comfortable with it. I can make it sing to me." He sighed, feeling slightly more at home with that familiar weapon clutched in his big paw.

"There is a range next door," Minivaanen told him.

"Right. Give me a few rounds and I'll try it out. I need to adjust the sights. Meantime I'd be grateful if you could get me seven magazines ready loaded plus a pull through, cloth, sandpaper and some linseed oil. Oh yes, and a couple of slings."

He tried all three firing positions - standing, kneeling and lying prone on the mat. After each grouping he made a minor adjustment to the sights, until his last set of shots appeared dead centre in the target at a distance of 300 metres and he was satisfied.

They were not alone in the range and Minivaanen spoke to his employees and potential customers with pride. "This man is very good."

"Not just good," the major interjected with even greater pride. "He really is the best."

"Yes," the Finn agreed. "This must be so."

They re-entered Minivaanen's office an hour later with rifles, pistols and the addition of six hand grenades, a last-minute suggestion by Major Philips.

Minivaanen waved aside the usual paper work. "We know the major is our friend. He is not a robber, nor a murderer, and we know that he has no connection with any mercenary organisation or terrorist group."

He smiled at his guest and added, "We also trust him to have good reason for wanting these weapons, and so we ask no questions as we adjust the figures in our books to show we never had them. Is that good?"

Dan nodded just the once. "Good enough for me, sir." They accepted coffee and open sandwiches, which left Dan wanting more, shook hands with everyone in the building and loaded the weapons into the boot of the hire car.

"Sir," Dan said before they moved off. "I want to pay for this trip. I insist."

The major waved his hand and brushed aside the suggestion of reimbursement. "Forget it. I can afford it."

"That's not the point, Major. This is my..."

"Mine too," he interrupted. "Amy was mine before she was yours." He grinned broadly at him and thumped the big Welshman on the upper arm. "Make me happy by forgetting it. Let's just get her out of there and all debts will be cleared. Agreed?"

"Yes, sir. Thanks." Dan would remain indebted to him; despite everything he'd said.

By the time they'd sorted out a supply of dry rations and all of the equipment necessary for a successful mission, it was late when they returned to the hotel. There was nothing they could do about finding a reliable driver and a vehicle suitable to take them as close to the Soviet border as was possible. That would have to wait until morning. One more day and they could begin.

When Dan entered the bedroom occupied by Douglas Philips the next morning, he knew they would not be going anywhere for some time. The man lay soaked in perspiration, shaking hard enough to cause his teeth to rattle. He was clinging feebly to the bedclothes to prevent himself from falling out of bed.

"What the hell is wrong with you, sir?" he asked as he held a hand towel under the cold tap, wrung it out and wrapped it around Doug Philips's burning head.

"Touch of...malaria..." he stammered. "Bugger all, old boy...a few...hours rest...be fine...need quinine."

There were options open to Dan. He could go it alone; he had the weapons he needed and the food and equipment. He could abandon the major. Or he could find a doctor and help him back onto his feet. He contacted reception, arranged for a doctor to visit immediately and he put his plans on hold. He could not abandon him now; a few days were neither here nor there.

It took more than a few days. He'd arrived in Hamburg on the 2nd of November, the weapons were purchased on the 4th and it was the 13th of the month before Douglas Philips was able to walk to the bathroom unaided.

Through Minivaanen they acquired the services of a driver and a Toyota 4x4. The man who came highly recommended was very expensive. His vehicle was guaranteed to carry them over virtually any terrain, it would be money well spent.

By 05:00 on the 15th, they began the journey north-east out of Helsinki. It was their intention to be at the Finno-Russian border before nightfall.

Information pertaining to that area told them that the Soviets felt it unnecessary to lay land mines in the death strip that far north. How reliable that information was, would remain to be seen. The death strip was the cleared stretch of land alongside the border fence. Usually mined and always patrolled by vicious guard dogs. It was known more familiarly as 'No man's land'.

They crossed hundreds of kilometres of seemingly unending and very beautiful countryside, along winding roads, with unchanging landscape of forests on rolling hills and lakes lying still and deep beneath them.

Dan relieved their driver from time to time and the major was fit only to sleep and eat. There was a weakness about him that put the fear of God into Dan. He claimed to be strong again, yet there was little evidence of anything more than mental strength.

Both men were sleeping soundly when the driver spoke to them in broken English - explaining that they were only a matter of kilometres off the border. He'd intentionally parked the vehicle halfway up the side of a steep hill, turning off the engine before waking them, yet neither of them had heard a thing.

"Be careful not to make war," the man with the grizzly face and twisted mouth advised as he helped unload the gear. "Enough for us in thirty-nine."

Dan assured him that there would be no war as an outcome of what they were about to do. In his mind he could hear Amy calling to him. His heart ached for her. All he wanted to do was run to her, to take her in his arms and carry her off to safety. He was so close to her now he could almost reach out and touch her. He felt it in his heart and soul; so near and yet so far.

As the Toyota pulled away from them, they lifted the heavy rucksacks onto their backs and got off the road as quickly as they could, heading directly towards the border, using the trees and vegetation as cover.

They made swift and silent progress and when they eventually reached the border road and the death strip beyond it, Dan stopped walking and spoke to his companion.

"Are you fit for this, sir?"

"I can assure you, old chap, that I wouldn't be standing here if I wasn't capable." Doug Philips placed his hand on Dan's shoulder. "Stop worrying about me. We're going to get Amy out. I won't let you down."

Dan nodded, that was good enough for him. "Okay. You go 600 metres south and I'll head north. Turn and return to this spot. I need to know exactly what there is by way of guard towers and manpower. If there's anything or anyone out there, we've got to know before we begin."

Doug Philips nodded understanding and turned to walk off into the darkness. Without being told he followed along the edge of the grass verge so as not to make a sound. Dan smiled wryly, the man was good, and he'd always been a good soldier. Amy had seen his true worth, despite all the name-calling and mickey taking. She knew that he was trustworthy and completely dependable and in her own way she loved him too.

They met up thirty minutes later; their recce had been thorough and enlightening. "Nothing south," the major informed him.

"Same here," Dan said, sounding relieved. "We'll cross the fence one hundred metres apart. That way if either of us happens to stand on a mine the other one won't cop it too." He was simply repeating their previously discussed plan of action - the plan formulated before the bout of malaria struck his companion.

"You go fifty metres south and I'll take the north again. Once we're across and clear, we'll meet up and take it from there."

Doug Philips readjusted his gear ready to climb the fence as Dan continued confirming their plan. "If there's any trouble and you cop it, I leave you where you drop and carry on. If you're alive, I'll find a way to get you back over the fence and onto the road. The Finnish border patrol will pick you up. If I cop it, you'll have to decide if you go on or abort the mission. If you don't think..."

"I go on," he interrupted resolutely.

"I'm grateful to you, sir." Dan punched him affectionately. "Let's go."

"God speed," the old man called to him as he walked away into the unknown.

Dan paced out the fifty metres and had no difficulty scaling the tall fence, despite the weight of the equipment on his back and his own bulk. His steps were tentative once he landed on the ground on the other side, and with the dexterity of a ballet dancer he moved across the open ground arriving at the tree line safe and sound.

He was about to move off again when a powerful heavy muffled thump shattered the silence of the night, obliterating his thoughts and confusing his senses. Seconds later a shower of small stones rained down on him and he was forced to crouch low to shield his face.

With the restoration of silence came a searing fire of fear and bitterness that cut through his gut. He knew what had happened, exactly what had happened. He'd just lost a loyal and very valuable friend.

He moved towards the large crater at the edge of the death strip, knowing that he had to look for the major despite the obvious risk. There was no way he'd turn his back on him, not now.

The hole in the ground contained nothing more than loose dirt and stones and a handful of twigs and splintered branches. He searched the edges and then the surrounding ground but nothing, not a sign of him and hope began rising within him. The old man was still alive. He was hiding, waiting for the dust to die down. In that case the only thing to do was head for cover and wait for him.

As he moved back into the dense undergrowth, he stumbled and fell over something solid and relatively large. He reached down and touched the flaccid mess that had once been Douglas Philips. His lower limbs had been torn off and as Dan probed around the pulp, the stench of blood and body fluids churned his stomach and he heaved, turning his head to vomit bile into the long grass.

With tear-filled eyes turned to the heavens he cried aloud into the night, "Oh, God! Please forgive me. I brought him into this and now he's gone. Forgive me."

With profound anger and bitterness, he dashed the tears away, sniffed hard and set about removing the only evidence that proved the man was anything but a Russian. He buried the service pistol, holster and back pack deep in the ground, well away from what remained of the major and before he took off into the woods, he returned to the mutilated body to pay his last respects.

"You will never be forgotten, Major." Without any intention he recalled a short passage from the New Testament and he spoke the words aloud into the depth of the night and the now silent forest.

"Greater love hath no man than this, that a man lay down his life for a friend." He swallowed the lump in his throat and added, "Thanks, old buddy...Major. Thanks." He snapped to attention, saluted smartly and crisply before taking off before the Soviet border patrol converged on the scene.

A beam of light from the Red Army troop carrier fell upon the ground and a polished boot kicked out at the gory remains of what was once a human being, and then a Russian voice cut through the silence of the place.

"I've searched it, Commander, there are no papers. Looks like one of our rustics trying to cross the border, but I can't think where he came from. There's no form of habitation around here. He's stolen a Kalashnikov but what is he - a trapper or a hermit?" And then he answered his own question. "He is certainly a nobody now."

"You are correct, Lieutenant," his commander replied. "Just a piece of mutilated meat in rags. Not worth the paper we've got to use to write up the report. But, as you say, why was he attempting to cross the border?"

"For the same reasons we would like to cross, Commander," he reminded him. "Looking for the opportunity to escape to a better life than the drudgery we have all of us got to put up with on this side of the wire."

"Careful, comrade!" the commander warned. "We all think along those lines but it is very unwise to speak the words aloud. I will forget we had this conversation." He sighed and made as if to leave. "Arrange a work party and have them bury that thing. I think we shall leave it at that. No paperwork and no further mention of this day."

The young, fresh-faced lieutenant saluted his superior. "Very well, Commander. Thank you."

Chapter Twenty-one

Saturday 30 November 1985

The fifteen-day journey east had taken its toll on the big Welshman. He'd travelled through driving sleet and the dankness of the forest had gradually ground him down. Dan Jones was feeling the strain that only intense hardship, and the total isolation of wilderness travel, can wreak upon a man.

However, this was no ordinary man. His dexterity in survival had enabled him to keep his sleeping bag completely dry and his legendary skill at being able to kindle a trapper-style fire over a pool of water had enabled him to provide hot meals and dry clothing with each break in the clouds.

No ordinary man would have gone half the distance already covered, but even so he was beginning to feel a strange sense of detachment from reality. A single recurring nightmare haunted his sleep. The corpses of the dead East German border guards, he'd killed to rescue Amy in 1967, sat up in coffins pointing accusing fingers at him. He saw the most terrifying visions of Major Philips being blown apart by the land mine. His legs flew off one way and his mutilated body the other. All of these signs were the initial symptoms of intense fatigue and emotional stress.

He began muttering to himself as he crouched under cover of the Taiga - Russia's seemingly endless tracts of coniferous forest. He was keeping watch on the Tobolmennaya Institute where he believed his wife was being held prisoner. It was difficult for him to comprehend that he really was so close to her yet still so far away. Only the instinct to survive and to win, kept him from rushing headlong into the place, guns blazing like some half-crazed cowboy.

The fact that he no longer picked up any form of telepathic messages from his Amy disturbed him enormously, yet he remained convinced that she was still alive. Instinct and the deep love he held for her told him that she was waiting for him to arrive.

He waited a further six days, watching and waiting until he was ready to put together his plan, talking to himself through it, the trees and birds his only witnesses.

"Two armed guards. Four male civilian staff - they must be the boffins. One tall female who's gone out once in the week I've been keeping watch, and she's back inside now. The information sheet tells me there'll be more, but they're all I've seen. I'll take the guards first and the rest should be no problem. I'll deal with whatever comes my way when it happens."

He scratched the beard on his once clean-shaven chin; the itching was driving him crazy.

"They seem bloody sloppy with security around this place must be the isolation of it I suppose. Godforsaken hell-hole is too. One guard comes out of the main door at 19:00 spot on and gazes around for a few minutes when he's obviously supposed to be patrolling the bloody perimeter fence. He'd patrol it if I was in charge! Idle bastard!

"But the woman...the woman could be Pavalovsky. It looks like her. Tall and smart. Same bearing. "Yes! Everything fits!" He saw Pavalovsky everywhere he looked, he held her solely responsible for the fate of his precious wife. She would answer for her deeds before too long.

Quite suddenly he decided he'd sleep for what remained of the daylight and he crawled stiffly into the bivouac. This way he'd conserve energy. It was the wisest thing he could have done.

He woke automatically at 07:00 on the 6th of November and prepared a hot meal. After warming himself he packed his gear, depositing everything on the edge of the forest and he was ready for his lone assault on the laboratory two hours later.

The stubby figure of a fur-trimmed, parka-clad Russian pulled the door shut behind him and began waddling outside, but before he got two metres into the open, a vice-like grip clamped over his mouth and nose, drawing his head back to expose his unprotected throat. Simultaneously, and with a savage swiftness, the knife in Dan's right hand sliced through flesh to the spinal column.

He left the man exactly where he dropped and went quietly inside, easing the door shut behind him. Inside he saw that the nearest door on the right of the corridor was ajar, and by peering through the crack, he could see a second guard sitting at a table, facing him. His interest lay wholly and solely in the glass of vodka in his hand.

Dan knew that there would be no element of surprise with this one, but once he'd taken care of him, he could get on with setting up a good defensive position against whatever else was thrown at him.

Stepping boldly through the door, he levelled his pistol with the startled face and fired once. The guard was hurled backwards off the chair to smash against the wall, collapsing in an untidy heap. A red mark stained his forehead between his eyes.

Footsteps clattered down the corridor as Dan leapt out to face them, seconds later two white-coated figures crumpled to the floor. Two empty bullet cases lay next to them.

Dan moved on, making his way down the corridor, hugging the wall, watching and listening. The door at the far end of the long corridor was wide open and he entered cautiously, stepping into a high-tech jungle of modern electronics mixed with antiquated Soviet engineering.

Lights flashed and blinked. Machines buzzed and hummed. Reel-to-reel tapes spun noisily as they wound their way endlessly around the room. A high-pitched whine filled his mind and confused his senses.

Shaking his head to clear the sound, he returned his attention to staying alive and to finding Amy. He swept the room most thoroughly with eyes and pistol, and then he caught sight of a small patch of white, beneath the bench at the far end of the room.

In an instant he stepped to one side as a single shot whistled past his left ear, embedding itself in the plastered wall behind him. Instinctively he fired two shots into the white-clad figure, which had now emerged.

The force of the impact at ten metres knocked the man backwards, leaving him spread-eagle astride an electronic switchboard, which began crackling and sparking as he writhed in agony, his hands clutching at the bullet holes in his upper chest and right shoulder.

With several long strides, Dan was on him, finishing what he'd started, knowing he couldn't leave him alive, not if this mission were to succeed.

He finished him with a single bullet through the temple. The dull thud that sickened his stomach also sent a familiar thrill through him.

"God help me," he said to the dead man. "I'm almost beginning to enjoy this bloody carnage." The sound of approaching footsteps from behind a large computer console told Dan that there was another door concealed there.

Having estimated that the oncoming stranger was approximately five metres away, Dan found the door and yanked it open, firing a shot that pulped the fellows left eye before passing through his skull.

Several unarmed white-coated scientists were beginning to spill out of a room further along this second corridor, they were panic-stricken by what they'd heard and terror struck their souls at the sight of Dan standing menacingly before them.

They scrambled back into the room in blind panic, clawing and clutching at everything and everyone standing between them and freedom, but Dan was already making his move. He unhooked a grenade from his belt, pulled out the pin and tossed it into the room after them just seconds before the door closed on him.

Flattened against the wall of the corridor, he waited for the explosion that drowned out the sounds of screams and terror. When silence rang loud around him, he kicked the door open to peer into the smoke-filled interior at the scene of brutal carnage - at the dying and the dead.

The smell of fear danced around inside his head as he used his pistol to extinguish the life of those who began screaming and writhing with agony as they briefly recovered consciousness.

When all eight men had been despatched to their maker, Dan fixed a new clip on his pistol, checked the crumpled plan of the building and continued his search, heading in the direction of the recreation and living accommodation area.

Time was running out for him. He knew that the sounds of the shots and the grenade blast would have been more than enough to alert everyone left alive inside the Institute.

"No time to mess about," he told himself quietly as he powered ahead. "Kill everyone except Pavalovsky." He was assuming that the woman was actually inside the building. "Need her alive to help me."

With laser-like concentration, he moved swiftly and silently along the empty corridors, turning first left and then right around corners, which almost doubled back on themselves. The place was a maze of passageways, with rooms leading off on both sides.

He saw operating theatres that were none too sterile. Laboratories filled with equipment and wire cages housing small animals - guinea pigs, rabbits, mice, rats and small rhesus monkeys. It needed only a caged human to turn the place into a regular chamber of horrors.

His blood ran cold as he imagined Amy strapped down on one of the wooden tables, wired to a machine, frightened and helpless. That image drove him on in his relentless quest.

Suddenly he heard a tumult of voices united in panic and confusion. They were ahead of him, around the next corner.

Dan waited, listening intently to what was being said, assessing the number of bodies he would have to deal with. Then it came to him, it came clear and sharp above the din, it was the voice of Pavalovsky.

There was no obvious way he could know what was being said, nor which way the woman was facing, and he had to make a decision, fast. Her voice was projecting away from him, raised above the others. Shouting out commands. He would have to take a chance on his being correct.

With a grenade clutched in his left hand and the pistol pointing ahead in his right hand, he turned the sharp corner to find that he was directly behind Pavalovsky and a seven-metre gap between her and sudden death.

"Stand still, Roushaka," he shouted with a touch of familiar irony sounding in his voice. "And drop your weapon or I'll blast a hole through you right now!"

The elegant Russian woman froze and then she let the pistol drop to the floor and Dan called to her again. "Listen very carefully to everything I say. Tell them to lie on the floor."

Having relayed the message all five of her comrades threw themselves down on the floor. "Now, turn around and kick that gun over here," he commanded.

Pavalovsky turned slowly to face him and with brazen contempt she said, "Daniel Jones! I should never be surprised by your foolishness. You will not get away with this. You will be hunted down like a dog before you get a few kilometres. Your brave effort is in vain for your precious Amy is now very far from being as you once knew her."

She kicked the weapon towards him across the highly polished floor and watched as he stooped to pick it up, his eyes locked on hers.

With the pistol stuffed into his belt and with barely contained blind fury, he went to her and shoved the muzzle of the pistol cruelly against her mouth, holding the grenade out at the same time.

In a maniacal whisper he hissed, "I'm not fussed if I kill all of you, but I'll guarantee you'll be the first lump of dead meat that hits the floor."

Dead silence prevailed. Nothing stirred as Pavalovsky boldly attempted to hold his psychopathic stare. Her mind probed and pried into his conscious thoughts and she knew without doubt that the look that burned into her brain was merely a reflection of the hatred eating away at his soul. Her nerve began to crack and her base self-preservation instincts started to override her show of bravado and defiance.

"Dan," she whispered sweetly. "I am on your side. I have been forced to do all of this against my will. They have killed my family. I have to put on a show in their presence or they will kill me too. I will do everything you tell me to do. What do you want from me?"

"Just do what I say. One slip and you're dead," his resolve was rock solid as he spat the words into her face. "I want to lock this lot up somewhere. If you don't show me where, I'll just blow them all to hell and be damned."

She nodded understanding and he snarled out a command. "Get them up. I want them lined up behind each other with their hands on the shoulders of the man in front. Then get them moving. You tell them where to go. You follow closely with me behind you. If anyone tries anything at all, you'll be the first to die, then the rest of them follow."

Pavalovsky spoke in her native tongue and all five men complied, scrabbling to their feet and moving off single file along the corridor with Dan following up behind. His curiosity was drawn to the last man in line.

Unlike the others who were white coated, this man was a giant, clad in what looked to be a filthy brown boiler suit. He stood roughly six and a half feet of wide-boned bulk. Not exceptionally tall but huge nonetheless. His lower jaw protruded like that of a gorilla. His actions were slow and much more deliberate than the others, he lumbered along obediently.

"Who's the ape?" Dan asked of Pavalovsky.

"Ivan," she told him. "He's been here since the mid-sixties when this was a metabolic research institution. They built him up with steroids and experimented on him, operating on his growth glands - the thyroid and the pituitary glands. They used new techniques. It was their intention to take all of the gold medals at the Olympic games with him, but the theory went wrong and they created a monster with very little co-ordination, useless for the explosive trigger of energy and skill required for competition.

"However, he has sufficient intelligence remaining to be very useful here. He is what you would call an odd-job man, a janitor. He cleans up the mess. He holds the keys and gives food to the prisoners...err...patients," she hastily corrected herself. "He is generally docile providing he has his daily injection to dampen down his adrenalin."

"You were right first time," Dan snapped. "Prisoners! You cruel swine! You make me sick inside my gut." He pushed her on with the muzzle of the pistol.

"Just get a bloody move on and keep that poor bastard away from me. I don't want to have to kill him, although I'd probably be doing the poor sod a favour."

They moved into an annexe, closed doors on both sides and one ahead. Roushaka Pavalovsky signalled to Ivan to pass her a large bunch of keys.

"These are cells," she told Dan. "You can lock them in here, this one is vacant." She unlocked the door and the men filed silently in with the exception of the big man who stood solidly outside the door. A deep grumbling, growling sound was escaping his lips as he shook his oversized head slowly from side to side.

"He will not go in there," she informed him. "You would have to kill him first. He suffers with claustrophobia."

Dan stepped back and levelled the weapon at the colossal head, knowing that he was too great a force to waste time upon. The big man turned to face him, still shaking his head, and Dan saw a pathetic pleading there in his eyes. Several seconds ticked by before he lowered the pistol.

Something closely resembling a crooked smile altered the shape of the giant's face as he ambled forward holding out a shovel-like hand in a gesture of sincere gratitude. It was clear that he fully understood his present situation.

Dan hardened his heart to him and re-aimed the pistol. "Tell the bastard to keep away from me or I'll kill him as sure as hell."

Pavalovsky obeyed and Ivan moved back again to stand against the wall. "You are a kind man, Daniel Jones," she remarked over-condescendingly.

"Shut up! I've accounted for two guards and eleven others. How many more are there in this place?"

"No more personnel. Only Amy. I swear it. Only Amy."

He grabbed her arm and squeezed firmly. "If you've lied to me and anyone else shows up, I told you, you'll be the first to go. I'll consider what to do with the ape afterwards. Now, take me to my wife."

She smiled, relieved that he believed her. "Follow me, and please, you will have no trouble from Ivan. He neither knows nor cares about such things as politics and patriotism. He lives from day to day, and besides, he and Amy have found some kind of rapport in each other's company."

Dan tightened his grip on her arm and she winced with pain. "What the hell does that mean?" he demanded as his fingers dug cruelly into her flesh.

"I only know that they have an unspoken understanding. He lifts her and carries her when she needs to be moved. He is tender with her."

"Carries her? You bitch! What have you lot done to her?" he was yelling into her face now, his pistol raised to the level of her heart.

"Please, please. I have had nothing to do with it," she said, attempting to convince him yet again of her innocence in the whole affair. "I have been forced to work here."

"Just take me to her, you lying bitch. Take me to my wife!" His patience was wearing thin.

"But you must appreciate that she is not how she was. She is..."

"Take me to her!" he roared as he shoved her forcefully along the corridor. She stumbled and grazed her left arm and cheek on the roughly plastered wall but Dan felt no compassion for her, not a solitary drop.

"Move!" he shouted when Ivan stopped at a T-junction where three identical corridors met. "What the hell is going on?"

"Confusion," she explained. "One moment." With what sounded like tenderness in her voice, she spoke to the big man who repeated Amy's name over and again, slowly and in a deep gravelly voice.

"A-mee. A-mee."

And then he began moving down the right-hand corridor; moving with purpose this time.

The only emotion Dan could feel for the big man was that of an overwhelming sense of pity, and above all he hoped he had already put a bullet through the head of the person or persons responsible for such an atrocity.

They reached a second large annexe within minutes and Ivan stopped dead outside the room with the steel door that was barred and padlocked.

After fumbling clumsily with the keys, he eventually unlocked all three padlocks and began heaving the door open towards them. He then looked to the Russian for further direction and she turned to look at Dan, saying, "Amy is inside."

"After you," he said, nudging her with the pistol, knowing that he dared not turn his back on her.

He followed apprehensively, scared deep in his gut that he wouldn't be able to cope with what was to come. Despite having prepared himself for the worst, he was very nervous. Amy was a free spirit locked within a cell, isolated from everything she knew and loved. People, places and the joy of life had been removed from her for many months now.

What he saw inside that vast room was not a thin and destroyed woman, it was Amy, beautiful and plump, and very obviously pregnant. She appeared to be sleeping.

He stood back from the bed upon which she was strapped, wired and tubed. He stared at her, even more confused and terrified than he had been before seeing her.

"She is alive," Pavalovsky assured him. "She, as you can see, is carrying a child." She witnessed the anger and the rising fear in him and she instantly feared for her life. If he were to think that this was not his child, he would not hesitate in putting a bullet through her head.

"No!" she exclaimed. "They did not implant this child, or the seed of this child. It is your child. Amy was pregnant when she was abducted. She foolishly said nothing in the hope that she would be rescued or released long before the child became evident, but she was very ill - starved and drugged and mentally exhausted and then they found out that she was pregnant."

With something resembling pride, she smiled as she said, "I alone convinced them that it would be in their best interest to nurture the growing child, to save what remained of Amy and build her up again so that they would have a new life with all the psychic capabilities of its mother. A child they could develop without any resistance. A willing subject. I told them, Dan. You have to believe me. She would be dead had it not been for my intervention."

But Dan refused to believe her. Without needing to be told, he knew instinctively that she was an inveterate liar and that she would tell him anything to save her own skin. "Unhook her," he commanded gruffly.

"It is not that simple!" she protested. "There could be dangers. She is approximately six months into her pregnancy and...it is complicated."

Amy was still and beautiful; in a deep drugged stupor. "Explain yourself," he demanded, feeling his patience running short.

"Her brain waves are being monitored by this machine." She identified a vast network of twisted multicoloured cables leading from a grey steel cabinet. There were dials and meters, flickering lights and wavering needles. The four sticky pads on Amy's forehead and neck were providing the electroencephalogram with all the information it required and with each changing peak on the printout scroll, Roushaka Pavalovsky knew that Amy was mentally aware of what was going on around her.

"She is being intravenously fed. She has a catheter into her bladder and she is bagged for body waste. The drugs within her system will not clear for at least twenty-four hours and you cannot just turn her back on again by switching the machine off.

"Look at them, Dan! There are a dozen pieces of equipment here that cost more than the entire space programme for the past five years. This is not a hospital, and Amy is not a patient. She is being carefully studied. The baby is being taken care of. They have not harmed it, but they have harmed your wife."

She reached out to touch him and he shrugged her hand off. "Oh, Dan, she is my dearest friend. We love each other like sisters. I would never hurt her."

Then he felt Amy reach out to him across the room. It was as if she'd touched his mind with her gentle breath. Her voice whispered to him and he felt his pulses race. It had been a long time since her voice echoed in his mind this way.

'Destroy her!' she said. *'Destroy her, Dan!'* Her voice was weak and distant, and suddenly the encephalograph needle began darting about on the scroll.

Hope sprang to life within him like a living flame. His pulses quickened and his body warmed for the first time in weeks. Amy was unconscious and lifeless, but her mind was active and aware of what was going on.

"Do whatever is necessary to get her off that bloody machine," he shouted. "And do it quickly." He knew that within a matter of hours, relief guards would arrive and he intended being well away from the place by then.

"It cannot be done quickly," she argued in an attempt to slow him down. "I could kill her if I make a wrong move. This is not my work. I am a psychologist, not a scientist."

Dan chose to call her bluff. "Don't give me that crap, just get her off the machines and do it quickly or I'll have no option other than to kill you now rather than later. Please yourself. If I have to, I'll unhook her myself."

Ivan drew closer to Amy as Pavalovsky began turning dials and flicking switches. He watched her as if he understood what she was doing. He had no fear of death because he could not comprehend it, what he feared most was life and the pain of further surgery, just as he feared confinement in a small dark cell. Amy's pain was like his own. He had grown to love her, and to understand her. He heard her voice within his head, talking to him, soothing him. Amy spoke to him in the only language he understood - his own.

Roushaka had turned another series of dials, flicked several more switches and was removing the catheter and bag from Amy's body. The acrid stench of stale urine reached Dan and he wondered how long it had been since the bag had last been changed.

His mind was working on the latest batch of problems. He needed warm clothing for his wife and for himself too for that matter. He and the major decided to head north-west when they'd completed the mission. North-west and to the Finnish border and not due west as the Soviets would expect as it was the shortest route to safety. The other way would be colder and more difficult, not to mention a great deal further. The cold would quickly sap them of energy and would take the life of anyone slightly weak or unwell and especially anyone who was not wearing appropriate protection.

The sounds of deep grunting and the sign of obvious agitation in the large Russian, brought Dan back from his thoughts and planning in time to witness the massive paw-like hand reach out and clutch Pavalovsky by the throat, lifting her off her feet and tossing her away from Amy to lie winded and stunned across the room.

Dan levelled the pistol on his vast bulk and came to within a split second of shooting him dead when the simpleton waved his hands about grunting, "Nyet! Nyet!"

He beckoned Dan to move towards him, so that he could look at what he was pointing to on one of the complicated pieces of electronic equipment.

A large index finger stabbed at a dial, and then he pointed to two switches. "Nyet! Nyet!" he repeated, his head shaking clumsily from side to side and his finger wagging. "No! No!" he was saying, over and again. He signalled in an upward direction followed by frenzied shaking of his head, and then the finger indicated a downward motion and he nodded clumsily. "Da! Da!" "Yes! Yes!"

It seemed Pavalovsky had been turning up the power instead of down and off. She had been making a last-ditch attempt to finish Amy, the woman she professed to love like a sister.

Amy's breath, as soft as that of a baby, reached into his mind once again and he went to her, permitting himself the luxury of touching her cheek with his fingertips for the first time in too long.

"Ivan will help you, my love," she whispered without moving her lips.

Dan sighed. The big Russian had proven that he could be trusted. He would watch Pavalovsky for him. Nobody would be permitted to harm Amy while Ivan was around.

"I'm taking you home, little one," Dan whispered to his wife. "Home for good. This is the last time you leave my side. My old heart can't take the strain." He smiled down on her and kissed her lips, and then his hand rested on the flimsy fabric covering the swollen mound, which was his child, and he recalled the things Amy said before she left him in London six months earlier. He knew then that the child was his and there was no element of doubt about it.

Ivan was continuing the growling guttural noise as he reached forward and touched Dan on the shoulder, gesticulating towards Amy. Dan spoke to him. His understanding of the Russian language consisted of approximately twelve words and he knew that there was no way he could converse with this man, and so he spoke to him in his own tongue, easily, softly and with a vast wealth of understanding.

"Look, old chap, I know you can't understand me, but I'm going to tell you anyway. This is my wife." He placed his hand firstly upon Amy's hand and then upon his own chest.

"I love her more than I love life. She's everything to me, and everything I live for. If she dies then I don't want to live without her. I've come to take her home and I'm bloody tired. I need help. I need clothes and food. I believe you understand a lot more than you're able to show. You've dealt with that bitch and stopped her from killing Amy, now help me again, please."

Ivan moved slowly, reaching out to touch Amy now. Holding her hand in his as if she were a small child, he began shaking it in a futile attempt to rouse her from the depths of her drugged stupor. He returned his eyes to Dan, seeking answers.

"A-mee," he said, "Da. A-mee" He pressed his cheek down onto her hand and then he began disconnecting the vast network of equipment. Flicking switches, pulling out wires and turning knobs. Big wheels stopped turning. Tapes hissed and clicked to a halt and then the room was silent save for the sound of Pavalovsky recovering her senses and Ivan shuffling around the table checking his handiwork.

Before Dan could lift a hand to help him, Ivan raised Amy off the table and into his arms. He moved out of the room and Dan snatched at Pavalovsky, dragging her unceremoniously to her feet.

"Stand up, bitch!" he snarled. "Tell me where I'll find clothes and food. We're moving out of here."

"I can help you," she gasped, still desperate to win favours. "I can help."

"Then help!" he said, tossing her towards the open door.

With her interests wholly and solely in saving herself and her personal comforts, Roushaka Pavalovsky led him to a large, well-stocked storeroom where Dan selected dried foods, powdered milks and cereals, bouillon cubes and several other lightweight packets that he'd selected on smell rather than on sight.

There was no logical explanation why he chose to take the woman with them, and why indeed he permitted her to live, he just did it, and within thirty minutes, he was glad he'd made that decision. She opened a room packed full of cold weather gear. There was featherweight silk underwear that was going to be warm next to the skin. Insulated outerwear that was thick and well padded and guaranteed to protect them from even the coldest of temperatures. Dan knew that unless he kept his wife dry, especially at night, she would surely die. To sleep damp meant certain death.

There were sleeping bags; lightweight and of a quality he had never set eyes on before. Without a doubt, the by-product of man's invasion of space. Dan was tired, bone-weary, but even so, he found the energy to offer up a silent prayer to whoever it was who was watching over him.

"Speshite!" Dan called to the big man as he stuffed himself clumsily into the padded trousers. "Hurry!" Ivan carefully laid his unconscious burden on a stack of blankets. So he could find suitable clothing. Amy was silent and Dan had to force his eyes off her and back on the Russian couple.

"Where are we going?" Pavalovsky asked, knowing exactly where they were going without attempting to pick up his thoughts.

"Away from here. You just do as you're told and keep your bloody mouth shut or I'll blow your head off."

"Amy cannot walk," she reminded him needlessly. "You should not be moving her. It is dangerous in her present condition. The cold, she will not stand it."

"I'll take that risk," he informed her brusquely.

"There is a vehicle," she announced, looking rather pleased. "A four-wheel drive. It is at the rear of the institute, in one of the garages. I know where the key is kept. Here!" she said, thrusting a map into his hand. "This will help you to find shelter."

As soon as the four of them were suitably clad in winter gear, Ivan lifted his precious bundle with seeming ease and began following Pavalovsky out of the room and into one of the many long corridors.

The Lada Niva was perfect for easing their journey north-north-west towards the Finnish border and freedom. Dan intended driving as far as he possibly could under the cover of darkness and in the furthest, most difficult route available. It would be easy to head directly west but that way would have meant certain capture and inevitable death.

No, he'd set out the plan with the major and it would definitely work providing he could keep going and keep Amy warm and alive. With the map recently provided by the cunning Russian woman, he would be able to find shelter for them to rest and eat.

Dan intended following the main Leningrad-Murmansk road, taking a turn west onto a track leading to a hunting lodge.

While he owed Ivan an enormous debt, he knew that his loyalties lay with Amy and no-one else. He would do whatever it took to get her home.

They'd been travelling in virtual silence along a rugged single track when a loud bang, followed by a grinding crunching sound reached into the vehicle from the fast-disintegrating gearbox. The little vehicle had never been designed to carry such a load under such duress, and now that the engine had been set free of its torque it revved loudly and the Niva began a rapid backwards roll.

A sudden surge of adrenalin coursed through Dan as he yanked at the handbrake with so much ferocity he tore it from its roots, rendering it instantly useless. Instinctively he slammed his foot on the brake and that alone was holding them on the side of the steep slope.

They sat in silence for several seconds, save for the creaking and complaining of the brakes under strain and then Dan began complaining bitterly about shoddy Russian workmanship.

"Get everyone out quickly!" he ordered Roushaka. "Put Amy safe and get Ivan to push this bloody junk. Go!" he commanded none too gently.

The big man pushed and shoved until his bulging veins looked ready to burst. At the apex of the ridge, Dan signalled for him to stand clear and he freewheeled the Niva down the other side, taking advantage of the fast-building momentum to deposit it in the lake at the bottom, jumping clear at the very last minute.

Between them, they fashioned a stretcher with freshly cut poles and the skins that had been protecting Amy from the elements. Ivan took the rear and Dan the front with Roushaka walking ahead of them as they turned off the track, moving under cover of the thick forest, following the southern shore of the lake and heading north-west.

To say that their journey was difficult would have been a gross understatement - it was a living breathing nightmare with Dan struggling to pick out deer tracks for them to follow, pushing through the undergrowth with the stretcher, doing everything within his power to keep Amy steady and safe. The ground sloping steeply down to the lake and the thin layer of frozen snow under foot made it impossible to stay upright for long.

Roushaka stumbled over and again, calling to him each time, begging him to help her. He ignored her cries and she grew hysterical, berating him for his cruelty and stupidity in attempting the impossible. She reminded him that it was a mission in which they would all die.

Dan lowered his end of the stretcher and Ivan followed suit. He pulled his pistol from his belt and levelled it with her eyes and with a cold faraway stare he flicked the safety switch. Roushaka shrugged her aching shoulders and gathered up her possessions. There was no way she could argue with his cold-blooded ruthlessness.

The already appalling conditions worsened yet Dan was determined to keep them moving no matter what happened. It was dark when Ivan went down like a felled tree, taking his end of the stretcher with him, pulling Dan into the bushes and spilling Amy off onto the frozen ground.

Dan yanked him to his feet, rebuking him for not letting go of the stretcher and went to gather up his sleeping wife who seemed unaffected by the ordeal.

"Check her!" he snapped at Roushaka and he sank down onto the ground, depressed, demoralised and at his lowest ebb ever.

Having done exactly as she was told the woman turned her attention to the big Welshman, sensing his mood and seizing at the opportunity to win back a place in his consideration by using any method available. This time she opted for seduction. Her sense of self-preservation was as acute as ever.

"Do not give up, my friend," she soothed his nerves with her quiet calm. "I was wrong. You are doing a good job. I misjudged you. I see it now. You have to keep going, for Amy if not for yourself. You are a proud man, a true soldier. I am proud to have seen you in action."

Dan looked across at her and sneered as he said, "Save it for your comrades you Soviet slag."

"Please," she whispered helplessly. "Do not be so hard on me. I want only to survive. This is my country and all that I have ever known."

She moved to his side. "Let us find a sheltered place to make camp. It is dark and we are all tired. We need to eat and drink and then rest."

As she spoke the gentle snowflakes turned into a blizzard and Dan knew that she was right and he hated her even more for pointing out the obvious.

He left them there so that he could scour the area for a suitable place to spend the night and then he led them to the camp, which he'd already set up behind a rock face, sheltered from the blizzard - a lean-to shelter constructed from poles and brushwood.

He laid a long trapper's fire and they ate and slept. Amy lay snugly between Dan and Ivan. Roushaka was securely tethered to a tree, unable to reach either Dan or his weapons while he slept, yet she was under cover and protected from the elements.

The day dawned crisp and splendid. Virgin snow blanketed the ground, and formed exquisite sculptures on the branches of the trees. Sunlight sparkled on each unique flake and Dan grew restless to move on. His fortitude all but spent on what had gone before.

He stirred the embers of the fire into life and commanded the now untethered woman to make food and hot drinks for them, warning her not to put additional wood on the fire. He could not take a chance on the enemy spotting smoke.

Two hours after they broke camp, they arrived at the hunting lodge at the far end of the lake. It was in a clearing and there were snowmobile tracks leading away from the place. Having bound and gagged Roushaka and deposited Amy and Ivan in a safe place Dan followed the tracks until he arrived at a large lean-to at the rear of the lodge that was large enough to house two or more snowmobiles. He saw fuel drums and tools. A stack of freshly cleaned skins and an old generator that was warm to the touch, which meant the possibility of the present occupiers being at home.

Fortunately, the lodge was empty. Dan conducted a thorough search of every room and concluded that it was definitely under occupation by fur trappers, disorderly men who never did any tidying or cleaning up after them.

The main room was a long hall with a concrete floor liberally spread with cured skins. A large and commanding stone fireplace was the one tidy spot in the entire building. It had been cleaned out and neatly laid with logs ready to be ignited when the trappers returned.

The two large dirty white kitchen freezers were crammed full of meat. The desk in the study was piled high with old books and sheets of greying paper. There was a toilet, shower room and sauna, a boiler in the annexe and ten beds in the upper rooms.

Dan collected his Amy, Ivan and his prisoner and took them to the upper part of the house where he signalled for Ivan to keep silent. Roushaka had given up protesting about the gag and was attempting to cajole Dan by fluttering her eyelashes pitifully at him.

Then he settled down behind the door of the lean-to and waited for the return of the trappers. There was no time to consider the option of trust, he would have to kill them or be killed. Time was running out for him and he couldn't afford to take any more risks. He was tired and feeble and without even knowing it he fell into a disturbed sleep as the hours of the short winter day ticked away and darkness fell once more.

The trappers returned noisily on their snowmobiles but Dan was treading the fine line between unconsciousness and coma and he heard nothing. Only the rasping sound of the snowmobile engines penetrated his fevered brain, reminding him, not unpleasantly, of the sound of a chain saw and the days of his youth in the forests of Wales. He muttered a curse to his old friend Tom Pugh and attempted to drown himself in the pleasures of fond memories.

A large fur-clad figure poked at the sleeping stranger with the muzzle of a rifle and Dan shook his head vigorously from side to side returning to reality with a start.

It was dark now and he saw the two men silhouetted by the headlights of the snowmobiles. One stood back with a skinning knife in his hand and the other was poking at his ribs with the rifle.

He cursed his own foolishness and attempted to clear his mind of everything including fear and despair. The mistake was his and now he had to put things right again and get Amy out and safe.

The trapper poked at him again and barked something in Russian, motioning him to get to his feet. Dan moved slowly, moaning and clutching at his chest, working his right hand gradually inside his jacket to the shoulder holster and the gun nestling therein. He writhed as if in pain and then in movements too swift for the eye, he grabbed the rifle barrel with his left hand and brought the pistol out from the holster with his right, pumping an instant round of lead into the man's face. His knees buckled and he fell backwards, dead long before he hit the ground.

In a flash the second trapper launched an attack on Dan, the knife aimed at his heart, but he was ready for him and he rolled away, seconds too slow though and the knife struck his upper left arm, slicing through clothes and flesh with considerable ease. As Dan completed the full roll, he pumped a single round into the stranger. The shot went clean through the top of his head.

He became wild with pain and anger as guilt and remorse joined forces with the pain in his arm, turning him into nothing short of a wild beast. He sprang towards the last man to fall and stamped his boot into his neck, hearing the sound of snapping bones that gave him no relief and only added to his insanity. He put the pistol to the base of his skull and pumped another round into all that was left of his brain.

Leaping across to the other man, he kicked the lifeless figure over onto his back so that he could afford the dead man exactly the same treatment.

"Pituitary gland. Central vortex and spinal column taken out," he said aloud. "No chance of recovery." It was as if he was reading from a survival manual.

The sound of each bullet striking home resounded in his gut and he felt the instant 'buzz' of fresh kill.

The realisation that he was actually enjoying the carnage suddenly took hold of him, shaking him to his core. An awesome fear clutched at him. "Oh, dear God!" he wailed as he stomped about wringing his hands in total despair. "What have I become? I'm a bloody monster."

One thought alone brought him back into focus - Amy. Suddenly a voice not his own grew deep inside his head, commanding him to take control of himself, for him to return for her and take her out.

The sound shocked him into instant action. He shut off one of the snowmobile engines, worked out how to start it again and got familiar with the controls, and then he dragged both bodies to one side and feverishly covered them with a pile of skins. He parked a snowmobile inside the garage, topped up the fuel tank of the other and left enough skins for comfort inside the trailer. Shutting the double doors behind him, he went back inside to his wife.

Dan sat with his back to the roaring log fire and with the hum of the generator sounding in the background he took stock of the situation, speaking aloud to Roushaka who was busily fussing over his wounded arm.

"You cannot put it off any longer," she told him, advancing on him with a curved upholstery needle threaded with a length of strong thread that resembled string. "This will hurt very much."

He and Roushaka had eaten and bathed. They had showered Ivan between them and made Amy comfortable. Now he could think about his own wound.

"How do you British soldiers think you can do this to yourselves and get away with it? It is barbaric."

"Just get on with it, woman," he snarled menacingly as he pulled together the two edges of the deep wound. "Stop bloody chattering and sew."

Dan had warmed to Roushaka for the way she was now tenderly caring for him, and for the way she had washed and fed his wife.

There was something about the fresh feminine smell of her and the fact that he knew she was naked beneath the robe, which she had cunningly ensured to be open to her navel, something that comforted him.

She poured antiseptic into the wound and began sewing the flesh together. The skin was as tough as leather and her work was not easy to complete.

One look into his eyes warned her not to mention the unbearable pain he was suffering and as beads of perspiration stood out on his furrowed brow, she continued the unpleasant task.

His teeth were tightly clamped together and he fought against flinching each time the needle dug into his flesh.

"You must hold still, Dan," she admonished tenderly as he rested his arm on the curve of her hip.

It took twelve large stitches to hold the wound tightly together and then Roushaka applied a generous field dressing, binding it well in place.

Both of his big hands were resting on her hips now and after she'd tied the ends of the bandage together, she eased his head down onto her voluptuous breasts.

He was vulnerable and she knew it. Her timing was impeccable.

Dan had made provisions for all of them to sleep in the main room, with him guarding them from a position by the main door. Amy lay still and silent on a big wooden bunk that doubled as a sofa throughout the day, and Ivan slept soundly on a mattress close to her. Roushaka was to have slept on a mattress next to him, tethered securely to one of the legs of the bunk, but things worked out a little differently now that Dan was falling for her seduction.

She led him to the rug in front of the fire where she stood and unfastened the tie belt on the robe, letting it slip to the floor so that she stood naked and lovely before him. She helped him out of his trousers and then she began kissing his chest and stomach.

He grabbed her roughly, lowered her to the rug and almost instantly covered her with his body, entering her without permission, using up all that was left of his reserves of energy in a two-minute burst of the most intense emotion he had ever experienced.

He hated her as he had never hated any living being, and he felt that hatred in its entirety as he pumped life into her body. He hated her and yet he desired her. He even felt pity for her. He was using her, just as she had used him and every other living being, to serve her own purposes.

This was not an act of love. There was no tenderness. In both his mind and body, he raped her and he relished raping her. He was violent in the heaviness of his thrusting body. He gave her what she wanted and satisfied his own angry lust for an instant. It could almost be likened to the act of a dying man - procreate or become extinct – man's last single desperate act of survival - not to be mistaken for any form of passion.

Dan fell off her the instant his convulsing body became still again. Soaked in perspiration and with a quiet mind for the first time in too long he felt himself falling into the most gratifying of sleeps he'd known since before Amy left him alone in London.

Before his body closed down, his senses picked up the tiny chinking sound of metal on metal and he brought his eyes wide open in time to see Roushaka lining up a pistol on his heart.

Instinctively he grabbed her wrist and she fought like a wild cat to free herself from his grip. The pistol flew from her hand crashing against the stone hearth and Dan lifted her and tossed her in the opposite direction. She yelped in pain as she hit the concrete floor but quickly regained her wits and lay back in her nakedness smiling at him, gloating at what she felt was her victory.

"It does not matter that I have failed to kill you, Dan. My people will be dropping in here by helicopter any time now. While you were showering and preparing yourself for me, I sent a radio signal from apparatus in the wall of the office. It has already been acknowledged by our communications base in Leningrad."

Speechless with rage Dan glowered at her long and hard before shaking his head in disbelief.

"Go and look!" she yelled at him. "The key is taped beneath the bureau. Go!"

He pulled on his trousers and grabbing her by the hair he dragged her unceremoniously to her feet and pushed her towards the door.

The key was there, as was the radio transmitter, just as she'd said they were. Roushaka was bathed in euphoria, feeling very pleased with her accomplishments. He shoved her back into the main room and tossed her down onto the hard floor where she continued to gloat.

"So you see, Dan Jones - big British hero, you are doomed."

Throwing her head back, she laughed loudly at him. "You have come this far only to be caught. Your lust for sexual gratification has finished you both. You fell for all of my tricks, even in the presence of your beloved Amy. She may have lost her means of communication, but her senses need not necessarily be impaired."

She glanced towards Amy and Dan followed with his own eyes. "Look and see how you have destroyed her, Dan Jones. I despise you for who and what you are."

He saw a single tear trickle slowly down the pale flesh on Amy's cheek and an overwhelming sense of remorse flooded over him; tearing at his heart as it washed through his very soul.

In an instant, the remorse within him changed and he aimed a piercing knifelike glare at Roushaka, slicing through her armour and striking fear into the very depths of her pitiful soul.

All too late she realised that she had overplayed her hand; having based her own preservation upon the quality of compassion, chivalry and reason she'd seen in him. She knew that he was beyond all of that now, beyond everything and anything, and with one last effort to save her own life she began to bargain yet again.

"I can still save you, Dan. I can get them to put you both over the border to safety. I have status in the government medical office, with the military and the KGB. They will do what I advise. You are both of no use to them now."

By way of a reply, Dan recovered the pistol and advanced upon her, still maintaining a murderous stare, shaking in cold fury all the while.

The now-hysterical Roushaka progressed to threats. "If you kill me, they will rape Amy until she dies. They will torture you and send you to a work camp where you will starve, freeze and rot."

The rapid talk gave way to an animal-like howl as her mind disintegrated in the face of advancing certain death.

She scrambled, crab-like, to one side and curled in a foetal ball covering her face with her hands, whimpering softly.

Dan held the pistol steady until he'd emptied the magazine into her head. Her fingers flew across the room, bone splintered and blood and brains splashed about until the contents of the magazine were spent and all that remained of her noble Slavonic face was a shapeless pulp that had been a head.

He stared down on the mutilation with glazed eyes until the warm fetid stench pervaded his senses and he retched violently. Shaken from his lassitude he threw himself down beside Amy taking her hand in his, sobbing bitterly, begging her to forgive him.

Her eyelids flickered slightly as another tear made a silent journey down her cheek. Ivan touched Dan on the shoulder and smiled dumbly at him. His compassion great for the man he trusted. "Nichego."

Dan looked at him and cried again. The big man had told him that it did not matter. He understood far more than was apparent. This was a true friend indeed, but there was no time now for more sentimentality or regrets. They needed to leave as quickly as possible; the enemy was closing in for the kill.

"Brown Bear to Control. Target located. Cloud cover moving in fast. Await orders. Over."

"Control to Brown Bear. Destroy target immediately. Over."

"Brown Bear to Control. Pavalovsky might still be in there. Request wait for assault squad drop to take target. Over."

"Control to Brown Bear. Do not question orders. British criminal too dangerous. Pavalovsky expendable. Destroy target! Repeat - Destroy target! Acknowledge. Over."

Precious seconds ticked by and then the voice came through once again.

"Brown Bear to Control. Confirm target now destroyed. Over."

"Good work Brown Bear. Return to base. Out."

Dan looked back and saw the brilliant flash of light that lit up the whole area, it was promptly followed by a powerful muffled thump. He stopped the snowmobile as it laboured beneath its load in a valiant attempt to mount the steep incline, and from the vantage point he could see back across the miles of forest they'd travelled through since leaving the lodge.

Far off in the distance a massive ball of flame rose from where he knew the lodge had once been. The sound of a jet banking away to the south reached his ears and he knew without doubt that Roushaka had succeeded in giving away their position.

It had been his hope that the Soviets would believe that they had all been vaporised in the missile attack, but if they spotted the snowmobile and trailer, they would most certainly assume them to be making a dash for the border. With luck on their side, the massive black cloud reaching into the heavens would blot out the stars and bring snow to cover their tracks.

He sighed a deeply tired sigh that was laced with bitter regret, and turned back to the others. All he could do now was to keep on moving, or all would be lost.

As he twisted the throttle, the small but powerful engine struggled to get the heavy load in motion again. The vast bulk that was Ivan straddled the pillion seat, his hands upon Dan's shoulders like the paws of a mighty brown bear. The trailer contained Amy who was lying on a soft bed of furs with all that remained of their meagre possessions, including a can of fuel, Dan's rucksack, a bivouac, ammunition for his rifle and a belt of hand grenades surrounding her.

The horror of what he had done at the lodge and the most primaeval of all emotions - survival, drove Dan towards the border before the might of the Soviet military came down upon them.

At the top of the ridge, he turned off the engine and spent a few precious moments searching the horizon and listening intently for any sign of the enemy. He checked Amy and found that she was breathing more regularly than when in the care of Roushaka Pavalovsky, which led him to believe that the woman had been administering some chemical to his wife unbeknown to him. Ivan too was brighter and more lucid, which was also further evidence that he too had been receiving some form of medication to suppress him.

They had covered little more than ten kilometres since leaving the lodge. The going was slow and there was no fresh snowfall to cover their tracks. Dan glanced east and saw a cluster of lights moving about in the distance.

"Oh, God!" he cried aloud. "They're searching the ruins of the lodge. They'll find our tracks. We've got to move."

There was no time to feel either the pain in his arm or the ache in his gut and he mentally brushed aside the ghosts of those he'd murdered, becoming little more than a killing machine whose sole aim was to survive.

He was devoid of all but the basic human emotions save for the love of his precious wife, a love that still burned hotly in his heart, that and a remote and very gentle compassion for the impaired Ivan.

Dan struggled to steer the snowmobile, dodging trees and rocks in the now sparse forest rising and falling at the most unpredictable and difficult angles. He was correcting a particularly awkward manoeuvre when he caught sight of a light in the sky; it was approaching from the south.

When he looked more closely, he could see that it was not a single light but four individual lights. He turned the key and silenced the vehicle, plunging them into darkness as four Mil Mi-24 Hind helicopters flew by not 200 metres away, searching for them. He froze and waited but the pilots did not deviate from their course and the instant they were out of sight he started the snowmobile again and turned north.

The sound reached out to him - a constant heavy pounding ahead in the distance. It was drawing closer and he knew exactly what it was. The helicopter search party was strafing the area in a systematic manner with cluster bombs. He knew that the Soviet gunships bristled with a variety of armaments. Ahead of them lay certain death for he was still pushing on regardless.

Columns of flames rose high into the night sky just a handful of kilometres away and the explosions were growing louder by the minute. Dan felt unsuppressed panic rising inside him. It was a feeling alien to him and it gave him no pleasure to think that he was beaten after so much bloody slaughter.

He crashed blindly on in a rapid descent to the bottom of the valley feeling the tracks of the vehicle beneath him biting into the ice of a frozen stream. He stopped and balanced the odds, to follow the course of the stream would mean a rough ride for all of them, but more so for Amy who could do nothing to help herself.

To go on into the gunfire was foolhardy and would mean certain death for the three of them. He would take his chances with the frozen mountain stream.

With a great deal of shuddering and protestation, the snowmobile slipped and slid along the meandering course until Dan steered it back under cover of the trees at the very first opportunity.

A track, he'd found a track, and it was wide enough for them to move freely and relatively easily. Things were beginning to look better for them, until a handful of cluster bombs burst in a sheet of flame along the path they'd just followed. Shrapnel and splinters of timber ricocheted around them, hitting the metal tailboard of the trailer protecting Amy.

Ivan yelped like a wounded hound as a sliver of metal cut through the fur coat on his back. A piece of hot metal cut a groove along the side of Dan's head, slicing away the top of his ear lobe.

As Ivan tightened his grip, Dan accelerated away from further injury. Despite his pain he drove on for what seemed to be a safe distance and then he stopped to listen.

There was no evidence of them having been pursued and all that was visible of the search party was a powerful searchlight playing up and down the creek. The helicopter gunships were fading away to the east.

The snow came at midnight, the snow Dan had prayed for hours to fall. It drove in from the east with a terrifying force, covering their tracks and assisting in their flight to freedom.

Chapter Twenty-two

By the time Dan stood high above the border road, he was nearly mad with pain from wounds and frostbitten fingers and toes. He was a kilometre away from freedom, concealed by the forest. He'd seen irregular traffic; single troop carriers, passing both ways on the snow-covered road. They came and went at intervals ranging from five to thirty-five minutes. There was no pattern to their behaviour and Dan decided that they would have to make their move to get over the border late into the coming night.

The pounding of explosives to the south of them suggested to him that the search had taken a new turn – the enemy was now attempting to burn them out. By opening up observation areas between the tree cover and the death strip, they would make escape virtually impossible. They intended incinerating anyone hiding there, waiting for their chance to break cover.

Wearily Dan returned to the bivouac four kilometres from the lookout point on the hill, overlooking the road. Amy lay safe in the arms of Ivan. He would get Ivan up and moving, pack Amy tight with furs and move off when the time was right.

It was afternoon, on the second day since their escape from the gunships. They had travelled somewhere in the region of 192 kilometres, mostly by snowmobile until they ran out of fuel. They left the machine hidden and continued on foot following a parallel path with the border, but now they'd eaten the last of the dry rations and they were growing weaker by the minute.

Dan looked at Ivan and said, "Perhaps the time's right, my friend. If we stay any longer, we won't make it anyway."

He sighed deeply and smiled at the big Russian. "I'm taking you home, lad. Home to Wales."

Ivan grunted acknowledgment of the words that soothed his aching body and mind. Dan was his friend and he trusted him implicitly as he had never trusted before.

"But with respect, Colonel Sergeyev," the Soviet officer argued, "On that principle you might as well burn a line up to the Arctic Sea and that I think would be in vain, because I believe that our infamous former British SAS soldier is back there in the Taiga. He is surviving as he is trained to do, waiting until the search is called off, when he is then going to make his move. All we need to do is let everything go quiet and saturate the border with troops. In fact, wait for him to come to us. Right now, we hold the initiative."

His senior officer puffed out his chest indignantly and took back control. "Incidentally, Major Vlasov, our intelligence reveals that he is not SAS. He is something far more lethal if that is at all possible, but we do not know exactly what. Not even Hitler or our Stalin in the darker years bred such an animal as this one. They were chivalrous compared to the savage who is obsessed with shooting people in the face. We first knew him in East Berlin, years ago, when he did just that to three border guards. He was getting a woman through a check point."

Sergeyev nodded in agreement at last. "However, you are probably right, with this man anything is possible. He might just have got that far. Keep napalm bombing at intervals for 300 kilometres from here. You might even flush him out or let him starve or freeze to death. But whatever happens, specific orders from KGB headquarters are that he must not, and I repeat, he must not get across the border."

"I understand, Colonel. This will be done. I just felt that I should give my views."

"You have given them, Major. It is not a problem; that is why I called this briefing. One final point, I see that the Finns are keeping us well scrutinised across the border. They are wondering what is going on. Have no dialogue whatsoever with them, because although to us, and the British government, this Jones and his woman do not exist, the Finns, if they get to know any of the facts, could just release the story to the press and that would be very embarrassing. Is that understood? You tell them nothing."

"Understood, Colonel. Thank you."

Major Vlasov saluted crisply and left the room. He nimbly negotiated the wooden steps down from the mobile field headquarters, and trudged through deep snow fifty metres to the communications vehicle where his men snapped into instant action.

"Sergeant, get me Wolf Pack leader," he commanded the radio operator. Major Anatoli Vlasov was of typical Slav peasant stock. Short, square and thick set, immensely strong, with a broad flat face and piggy eyes. His hair was light brown and beginning to grey since his fortieth birthday. At forty-two, he was proud of his rise through the ranks, a rise brought about by sheer hard work and dogged determination.

Vlasov, however, lacked the intellectual vision of his colonel. He could not imagine anyone reputedly half-mad, wounded and starved, carrying a shell of a woman, with a Frankenstein-like monster as a prisoner, ever reaching as far north as the colonel anticipated, not through the Taiga Forest in midwinter, and certainly not on an ageing and ailing snowmobile.

Even if they survived the blanket of bombing, the rest was too far-fetched to be possible. He was convinced that troops carrying out the ground search with tracker dogs would eventually find their remains. Until then he would obey orders, go through the motions, and then smugly he would patronise his colonel. It was an attitude he had adopted of late, which would serve only to alienate him in the eyes of the colonel and ensure no further promotion before retirement, but that was Major Vlasov, and he did things his way.

"Wolf Pack leader to control Major. Awaiting instructions - over."

"Control Major to Wolf Pack leader. Wolf Pack to remain tasked. You alone to return to base for up-to-date briefing. Acknowledge - over."

"Wolf Pack leader to Control Major. Message understood. Making my way down. Out."

Holding on tenaciously to the fragments of consciousness and sanity that remained his, Dan trudged wearily through the last kilometre of the Taiga to the border, leading the now pathetic figure of Ivan by the sleeve of his fur coat. Ivan held on firmly to Amy, clutching her to his chest, stumbling along like an automaton. Amy was barely alive. Her breathing was shallow and her heartbeat nothing more than a fluttering deep inside her.

Ivan had become belligerent and refused to move at all. Dan knew that his behaviour was most certainly caused by fatigue, lack of food and having to endure the suffering of frostbite and the pain of the shrapnel embedded in his back.

There was nothing Dan could do for him. He'd examined the wounds and decided that to inflict more pain upon him would have been morally wrong and most definitely cruel. The best plan was to push him to the border and into a Finnish hospital, along with Amy, provided they could make it alive.

Dan had used his last field dressing to pack his wounded ear and the fact that he could not hear clearly had become a terrible handicap. His left arm was stiffening now, swollen and infected. His eyes were also swollen with infection and the right one was completely closed. During moments of rationality, he knew that the severity of his mental stress was not improving his situation. He knew that in another twenty-four hours he would be virtually blind, and as helpless as a new-born infant.

The border fence would have to be crossed that night. There was no question of waiting for a better moment; for that time would never come. Amy was dying. Ivan was becoming violent and a danger to them all, and he was anything but healthy himself. He'd dumped all but the clothes they stood up in and the skins cocooning his wife. There was no way they could survive another night without help.

With daylight fading rapidly, Ivan suddenly stopped dead in his tracks, shaking his head and breathing heavily.

"Come on, you bloody oaf!" Dan cussed as he tugged at his coat, but the big man stood firm. In sheer exasperation Dan took out his pistol and held it close to Ivan's face.

"Now move, you bloody peasant or I'll kill you where you stand."

But Ivan was not in the least intimidated by either the weapon or the threats. He shook his big head from side to side and grunted Amy's name over and over with a tongue so tied the words were barely audible.

In his state of moral derangement, Dan could so easily have pulled the trigger and thought no more about it than blinking his eyes. It was instinct that told him that he needed the help of the big man to get Amy over the border fence, and it was only that fact that made him lower his trembling hand and put away the pistol.

He looked deeply into the eyes, which told no tales and listened to Ivan say, "A-mee...A-mee...A-mee."

"Yes, Amy. We have to save her, Ivan. Help me, man. Please help me. I can't do this without you. Christ! I'm all but finished."

"Da!" Ivan seemed to understand. 'Yes,' he'd said in his own tongue, as clearly as any man might say it, and then he resumed his steady plodding with renewed vigour. There was no need for Dan to tug or pull now; he was going well under his own steam.

Ivan had been constructed in a laboratory - a genetic experiment to build the perfect athlete. His body had once been solid muscle but since the moment he left the Institute with Dan and Amy he'd lost over half of his body weight. His immense compassion and dedication for the woman in his charge was all that was needed to keep him struggling on.

As Colonel Sergeyev's napalm consummation of the border forest moved rapidly northwards and ever closer, two men, tormented beyond human endurance, staggered over the last kilometre to freedom. One carried the body of a woman barely alive, the other mumbled over and again two simple words: "Hold on. Hold on."

The heavily laden Hind was carrying a full load of napalm. It appeared to labour in its ascent from lift off before swinging north, passing high above the smouldering forest adjacent to the border road, until the front line of the burning operation was in sight of the three occupants. Pilot Commander Captain Mironov, Armaments operator Zalozny and Major Vlasov strapped in next to the pilot.

"Take her down to operational level and keep going north as slowly as you can. Put your arch lights on. I want to see what it looks like down there. Drop a burn at intervals when I tell you to, Commander."

"Going down now, Major. What do you have in mind?"

"I have in mind, Commander, to get this operation over with as quickly as possible. With all due respect to the colonel, it is my opinion that we are not going to find our British savage up this far. Ground search is going to find him back south, somewhere in the interior. There has not been a track found or any sign that he is heading this way, but I am obeying orders and going through the motions. We will lengthen the intervals of these burns to cover ground faster and get this over with." He looked about him. "This is far enough. Drop one now."

Mironov pressed a button, pulled a lever and immediately swung the aircraft away to the east to avoid the updraught. A vast ball of fire burst on the ground beneath them, sweeping ahead for several hundred metres, consuming the forest in flame as it travelled with awesome power.

"These are amazing devices, Commander," said the major with eye-sparkling delight at the havoc he was wreaking in the beauty of the Taiga.

"New development. Many times more powerful than anything the Americans have. You would find no trace of human remains down there in its path. They would be vaporised in the explosion and cremated to dust in the run on."

"It concerns me that no warnings have been given to the trappers that work in this area. Watch out for them."

Vlasov was displaying a rare trace of compassion for his fellow humans and it surprised Mironov so much so that he asked, "Another expendable group, Major?"

"Not where I am concerned, Commander," suddenly there was bitterness on his palate. "My people were farmers eking a meagre living from the land. They were forced to spend most of the winter months trapping furs in order to earn enough to survive. I worked with my father many times as a boy. I have a feeling for these people and I do not want them hurt.

"They would normally smell what is going on here and keep clear, but if they have traps in any of these river beds, they will want to check them no matter what. They are like that. Get all of your men to watch for them."

Mironov nodded agreement and continued on course. Leaving the holocaust behind them Mironov swung back around, easily picking out the tree line and the border road in the powerful arch lights. He flew directly over the two hundred-metre strip of cleared land between fence and forest and continued northwards waiting for the next command from the Major.

Dan had picked the perfect high vantage point in which to lay up and watch for approaching vehicles. During a lull in passing military patrol vehicles, he went down to the fence and selected his crossing point, hiding a solid chunk of felled conifer trunk that he intended using to prop against the wire to assist in their break for freedom. Alone he could have heaved his weary body over the fence, but with Amy and Ivan in his charge he knew he needed all the help he could get.

Six hours after darkness descended racked with pain and still fighting the oblivion hovering over him, Dan saw a new menace looming up rapidly from the south. In the pristine freshness of the clear and frosty night, he'd watched the burning operation far to the south. He heard the explosions and saw large columns of flame rising into the star filled heavens. A mushroom-like cloud of smoke and flame filled the southern horizon. Then he spotted the powerful lights of the Hind.

'Danger! Mortal danger!' Amy's voice sounded inside his head. He crashed to his knees alongside her and saw that she was as still and silent as ever. He placed his hand gently on her forehead and felt her fevered state. Her flesh burned and was clammy. Her eyelids flickered and he heard her voice again inside his head.

'Dan! You have to move or we perish!'

A sudden surge of adrenalin shot through his body like an electric shock, blotting out all pain. His mind became sharp, lucid and calculating. He looked south again and knew that the next bomb would be dropped roughly in the area in which they were presently hiding. The arc light was moving rapidly towards him. His thoughts raced - it was too late to make a break for the fence. He had to get the ship down out of the sky or fry in a napalm hell.

He checked his weapons. Felt for his grenade belt. There were three remaining, all primed and ready for use. "Ivan, come!" he said as he pulled at the sleeve of the giant who stood instantly, lifting Amy into his arms, offering no resistance.

Dan led him to the edge of the tree line and took Amy from him, laying her on the ground. He covered her with skins. Stood and removed the field dressing from his head and dangled it on a nearby overhanging branch. It was his marker, so that he could recover his wife when everything was safe.

"Come with me!" he called to Ivan, beckoning him to follow. Dan ran and the big man kept pace in long heavy lumbering strides. On and on they ran straight towards the oncoming Hind. They'd covered three hundred metres of ground when Dan stopped running at the edge of the border road. The helicopter was less than two kilometres away now, approaching at a steady speed with arc lights playing over the ground ahead of them.

"Now then, boyyo," Dan said to Ivan as he waved his arms over his head and Ivan copied him. "Keep it up, lad. You're doing great." Ivan fixed his eyes on the oncoming lights waving his arms in large circles like windmill sails.

Dan sprinted into the cover of the forest, no time to even pray, but time for regrets.

"Sorry, lad, but I have to make you expendable. If you get through this, I swear I'll take care of you for the rest of my life."

In merciful ignorance of the fate that was more than just likely to befall him, the pitiful giant continued to wave his arms about and the Soviet helicopter moved closer for the kill.

"Do you now see how I want you to work it, Commander? Space the stuff out at longer intervals. It will be less complete but it will still serve the same purpose and the colonel will call a halt all the sooner."

"I understand, Major. It is easier for us this way. How many more drops..."

"Sir!" Zalozny interrupted. "What is that down there?"

All three men looked out of the window to their left, straining their eyes to try and make out what it was down there.

"Nothing there," Mironov replied tersely.

"What did you see?" Vlasov asked with something close to patience sounding in his voice.

"Something was moving about down there, by the roadside. The lights have passed it now." Zalozny was positive he had seen something.

"Circle. Come back in front of it," ordered the major, despite his reluctance to waste time.

"Taking her around, Major. Weapons primed, Zalozny?"

"All ready, sir."

The large assault gunship helicopter banked steeply in a wide circle, picking up the border road again in the powerful lights and slowly following along above the treetops.

"There! Straight ahead!" Zalozny called with great satisfaction.

"It is a man, waving his arms about! Who could he be and what is he doing out here?" Mironov observed suspiciously as he brought the aircraft hovering over the stranger.

"Obviously trying to attract our attention," Vlasov remarked sarcastically. "Put us down about forty metres in front of him, Commander and I will go and see what he wants. As I said earlier, probably a trapper trying to keep us off his run."

The Hind touched down lightly with the side hatch open ready and Vlasov jumped down. Instinctively he kept his head tucked low until he was clear of the rotor blades and then he began a leisurely stroll towards Ivan who had stopped his frantic waving and was attempting to shield his eyes from the strong lights and the cloud of dust flying about him.

Dan broke cover at the rear of the aircraft; the sound of his feet crunching in frozen snow was lost in the noise of the powerful motor.

Ivan was confused and frightened as the stranger approached him. He cowered away and began whimpering.

"What is it, man?" the major asked, not without some concern. "Tell me what is wrong with you."

Growling now with pain and fright Ivan began to move towards the man who took a step back towards safety, trying once again to get sense out of the big bear of a fellow. "Can you not speak?" he asked. "I am here to help you."

Advancing, Ivan continued growling and shaking his head. The major took in the fullness of him and becoming aware of his mental impairment it was as if a thunderbolt struck him with the realisation of exactly who he was dealing with.

"Zalozny! Zalozny!" he screamed. "Come here, quickly!" He fumbled with his hip holster and drew his revolver as Zalozny jumped out of the hatch and began running towards him. Two rifle shots rang out in quick succession. The impact of the first knocked Major Vlasov metres beyond Ivan, and the second stopped Zalozny stone dead in his tracks.

Commander Mironov had been granted a grandstand view and was at panic stations as he slammed the controls into instant lift off.

Dan moved towards him, a true force to be reckoned with, his rifle slung on his shoulder and both hands free. Two metres from the aircraft he lobbed a grenade into the open hatch and the machine rose noisily above him.

Mironov knew that he had a live grenade on board. He'd heard it clatter in aft of the cockpit and helpless though he was, with the knowledge that he was most certainly a dead man, irrationally he clutched on to the hope of survival. His last action was to bank the aircraft well over the forest in a futile hope that the thick tree canopy would cushion the impact as it fell from the sky.

It took him seven seconds for that thought process. The eighth second he used to focus his mind on his wife and child at home in their Leningrad apartment. The ninth second shut down his existence.

Mironov had pressed the 'Emergency 'button, which gave his position to those in operational headquarters, and every military aircraft and ground patrol in the border area would be sent speeding to the scene of the crash within minutes.

As the helicopter veered over the forest, Dan knew that he had approximately six seconds left in which to save himself and Ivan. He took the big man down as well as he had ever dropped any man in a game of rugby. The wind left Ivan in a massive 'huff 'that was instantly drowned by the volume of the explosion.

Ramming Ivan's head down into the snow Dan covered him with his own body as the mighty explosion shook the ground beneath them. The Hind was down and a fireball of napalm shot high into the night sky. A searing wave of heat rolled over the bodies of the two men, scorching their clothes and singeing their hair. The beard on Dan's face shrivelled to stubble as the uppermost layer of skin exposed to the heat was instantly burned off.

As swiftly as the heat came it seemed to be sucked back again and both men lifted their heads to breathe, but there was no air, the mushrooming fireball had eaten up the oxygen from all around them.

Dan struggled to his feet and dragged Ivan off the ground, forcing him to run with him to where he knew he would find Amy.

"Amy!" Dan screamed at Ivan. "Faster! Move! Get Amy!"

"A-mee," he repeated as he tried to keep up with Dan without actually exerting any energy.

Dan slowed his pace to search for his wife. Breathing was easier now but he couldn't find the marker. In desperation he cursed aloud as he felt the darkness closing in on his mind. No time to waste in searching, they would be on him at any minute. The might of the Red Army would fall upon them like a disease. He sank to his knees and pummelled the snow-covered ground with his clenched fists.

"Oh, God!" he cried aloud. "If you're out there, help me now."

Ivan took hold of Dan by the shoulders and lifted him, placing him on his feet. Ivan found Amy. He pointed back the way they'd just come. Dan had gone too far in his frantic search. "Show me, man. Show me where Amy is."

Fifty metres back, the field dressing was still dangling from the branch of a tree. Ivan was not as simple as Dan had first believed. He'd remembered everything and at his slower pace he'd spotted the dirty white rag.

Ivan scooped Amy up lovingly and touched his face to hers as Dan began pushing him towards the open ground and the fence. It was all that lay between them and freedom - a piece of ground and a fence - that and the men who were hurrying in their direction.

A sense of unreality overcame Dan for an instant, as the darkness of unconsciousness hovered ever closer, never far away. There was no time for pain now, only for living.

On reaching the fence he took Amy from Ivan and laid her on the ground so that he could prop the great chunk of tree trunk against the wire, indicating to Ivan exactly what he wanted him to do. With the Russian's thick fingers clinging to the wire above his head, Dan shoved at his backside with his shoulders, pushing and heaving until both feet were on top of the wood and he was standing three feet off the ground.

Dan lifted Amy and handed her to Ivan and then he scrambled over the wire, seriously doubting that he would be able to get Ivan over in time. He could hear the sound of vehicles approaching, engines revving and gears grinding as wheels failed to grip the icy ground.

Suddenly the headlights of the lead vehicle broke into the open ground. "Drop her, man!" Dan yelled at Ivan who was holding Amy over the wire.

"In the name of God, drop her! Speshite!" Dan was screaming at him to hurry, motioning with his hands. Ivan shook his head and growled deep in his throat as he tightened his grip on his charge.

"Drop her you stupid bastard!" Dan yelled again as he reached into his jacket again for the pistol. Before he could do as he intended, the sharp rattle of machine-gun fire rang out from the turret of the leading armoured car.

The sudden sound startled Ivan who moved a fraction on the log and lost his footing. As the log rolled away, the big man was left hanging by his arms and upper body on the barbed wire strung across the top of the fence. Amy slipped from his grasp and fell crashing into Dan on the ground below.

Dan clutched her close to his body, turned and ran into the cover of the forest on the Finnish side of the border, knowing that he was abandoning Ivan to violent death. Above the continuous stream of machine-gun fire came the plaintive cries of a desperate and frightened human being.

"A-mee! A-mee!"

A pitiful wailing from the soul abandoned by the world followed the cries. He was a man forsaken even by the friends he had so quickly learned to love.

Dan was nearing the tree line when Ivan's cries stopped abruptly. The termination of the cries was by far worse than the silence of his death. Dan turned and saw that the entire area of their escape was lit up as bright as day. He'd turned in time to witness the final horror of Ivan being torn apart by the bullets from the weapons of the blood-lusting cold and calculating enemy. What had once been a noble and gigantic being was now nothing more than great strands of bloody shredded flesh spread across the fence.

Knowing that the Soviets would not deliberately violate Finnish air space but that a few precisely aimed 'stray' bullets were a definite likelihood, Dan headed for cover, Amy clasped to his chest. He was desperate to get out of range when he crashed through a thicket of trees and became aware of a bright beam of light moving behind him. A machine gun opened fire, splintering timber nearby and he knew that he would be cut down for sure if he attempted to run; besides, he could no longer run, but he could crawl, and crawl he did, dragging his pregnant wife alongside him as the bullets raked the forest all around them in one last desperate effort to take his life.

He found a hollow behind some substantial moss-covered rocks and lay there shielding Amy with his own body as the Soviets lobbed mortars over the fence.

Amy was cold, as cold as ice and Dan feared the worst. He couldn't detect any sign of life within her body. He ripped back the skins and pumped her chest. He shook her and swore at her. He threatened her and cajoled her and, in the end, he laid his head on her swollen body and wept aloud.

"Oh, Jesus! Not now, not after so much! I can't live without this woman. Amy!"

A storm blew up inside his mind as visions of horror came and went. Amy. Ivan. Roushaka. Bloodied bodies. Slaughtered human beings. Shattered skulls and skeletons pointing accusingly at him. Now he was falling with them, heading into a bottomless abyss, gaining velocity as the maelstrom dragged him down.

An explosion inside his head instantly silenced the agony within him. A searing white light rapidly dwindled to a mere pinprick, which remained single-pointed in a universe of blackness, as the tortured mind of Daniel Jones finally collapsed.

PART SEVEN

Chapter Twenty-three

TILKKA SAIRAALA - Finnish Military Hospital on the outskirts of Helsinki.

Two men with grim expressions on their faces walked slowly and quietly into the intensive care unit of the neurology department. Rauno Jukola, Professor of Neurology, led the way, closely followed by Mikko Kauppinen, Chief of SUOPO the Secret Service Branch of the Finnish Federal Police. This man was sober-suited, bullet-headed and very heavily built.

The Professor stopped at the foot of the first of two beds separated only by machines. One bore the body of a female and the other a male. Each was connected to a labyrinth of drip tubes and wires. He motioned to the Chief of Police to walk between the beds.

"I want you to look, that is all," he told him in a low voice, barely above a whisper.

With a photographic memory, developed from twenty-six years of special policing duties, Kauppinen made a mental note of every detail that his finely trained mind could possibly absorb, and then he said, "Both patients obviously comatose. The woman is mature in years, hair flecked with silver. Somewhat emaciated except for a swollen abdomen. A tumour possibly, or perhaps she is pregnant."

He looked long and hard at the face of the male patient and then he studied the rest of his body. "Approximately one-point-eight metres in height. Sturdy in structure but with obvious massive weight loss."

He cast his eyes back to the face. Noted the grey in the sparse hair - the haggard face and sunken eyes, the features he recognised as those of Daniel Jones.

An overwhelming sense of admiration warmed the big Finn's heart knowing that this man had done exactly what he set out to do, he had brought his wife out; but at what cost?

He turned back to the Professor and with a sigh said, "My God, they are in a terrible state. What have they been through?"

Professor Jukola placed his finger to his lips. "Not here. Come to my office and I will tell you what I know."

He pushed two folders across the desk to Kauppinen. "You can study them at your leisure, Rauno. One is from Border Watch and the other is a medical review of both patients from myself. Meanwhile, I will give you an outline."

He settled back in his chair, took a deep breath, let it out slowly and then he began. "For the past three weeks Border Watch had been monitoring massive Soviet activity. At first it appeared to be some large-scale exercise, but when they began burning the forest in a hundred-kilometre radius of the border with napalm, then the whole thing took on a much more sinister appearance, as if they were trying to prevent some escape or other.

"However, the affair came to a head two nights ago with a powerful explosion of napalm further north. It appears that a helicopter gunship carrying napalm crashed into the forest right on the edge of the border. It was hardly an ill-timed accident, more than likely our fugitive patient found some way of bringing it down. It then appears that he got himself and the woman over the wire and into cover on our side, but only just in time. One man, who was probably with them, got shot on top of the wire.

"When Border Watch arrived at the scene some twenty-five minutes later the Soviets were picking bits of the man off the fence and putting them into a canvas bag. As soon as it was light enough, our men began searching for any signs of escapees. There was enough evidence to suggest that the Soviets were raking the area with everything they could lob over.

"They found this man and woman behind some rocks. He was holding on tightly to her. At first, they thought them both to be dead, possibly frozen. When they tried to move him, he seemed to regain consciousness. He attempted to stand, continuing to hold on to her, and he lashed out at everyone who came close to her. He was quite mad, and he had good reason to believe her to be dead, which would explain his mental state. It is understandable after all he had gone through. He tried to pull a pistol but was disarmed by one of our men. Even then it was very difficult to wrench the woman free of his grip.

"When they were brought in, she was taken for dead and laid to one side until the doctor could deal with her and sign any necessary paperwork. He later found the woman to be alive but only after a very thorough examination. Her breathing was so shallow it was undetectable. However, there were no obvious signs of death such as discolouration of the skin. No indentation of the flesh when touched - dehydration, in other words, and despite the stiffness of her muscles they did not have the total rigidity of rigor mortis. Blood had not pooled with gravity on the underside of her body and there was still some obvious circulation.

"Tests then showed very faint heartbeats and the slightest of brain activity. She was in fact very much alive and not even brain-dead as was suggested. It appears she was in some kind of catatonic trauma of the type that has caused premature burial in the past.

"Now, what is the cause of this, you might well ask? Extensive testing showed no sign of organic damage to the brain. What it does show, however, is extremely weak brain waves, or in other words, a low electrical charge. Like an intricate computer, the brain functions on a mass of minute electrical impulses, or charges, which pass from cell to cell by means of connecting nerve fibres known as neurones. In this woman's brain, not only the impulses are weak, but also the activity is the slowest I have ever known. This causes me to suspect that the brain has been overdrawn of its power by artificial means. This, plus the presence of certain marks upon her scalp, indicates that she has been subjected to some kind of experimentation.

"If this woman was known to have some kind of special faculty, such as heightened psychic capabilities, it is possible that they exploited, and over-enhanced this capability, subsequently overdrawing her brain waves. This condition would be loosely termed, 'burn out', and it is not new to us.

"Mengele engaged in this practice at Auschwitz and we have always suspected that the Soviets, who were first to liberate the camp, have engaged in this practice since taking hold of the case notes. Therefore, we can only conclude that she has been experimented on in a Soviet laboratory, and that this man, whoever or whatever he is, has achieved the impossible by getting her out."

The policeman nodded with a knowing smile upon his lips.

"You know this already?" the Professor asked eagerly, sitting forward on his chair.

"I am sorry, Rauno. I can say nothing. I am intent on listening to you. Please continue."

"You are so very tight, my old friend. One day you will be honest with me before I begin such a lengthy explanation. I do not have the time for this, I am growing older by the second." He laughed, settled back and told him more.

"She is pregnant, approximately twenty-six to thirty weeks' gestation. We cannot be accurate, but it is a miracle that she has not aborted the foetus. On first examining the pregnant woman and declaring her lifeless, the doctor searched for life signs in the unborn infant and found none.

"It is a miracle, as I said, that the foetus was not aborted long ago, yet the child is surprisingly healthy, despite the emaciation of its mother. It does appear from the scans that there could be some damage to the spine, but until birth we cannot be certain. Other than some spinal damage the infant, a female, appears normal enough and as far as we can tell she is a little undersized, but that is all."

"What about him?" Kauppinen asked. "The man."

"He is suffering complete mental breakdown and severe physical exhaustion. It was caused by whatever he went through in the process of rescuing this woman. Remember that he would have been convinced that she was dead after all of his efforts. He also travelled for at least a week with half of his right ear torn away and a badly infected knife wound to his upper left arm. Burns and frostbite mean he will lose most of his toes; however, we can save his fingers.

"I have never known anything like this," the professor admitted. "I think he must be British. Only one of that dogged mongrel race would be mad enough to attempt a mission as impossible as this, and to have the indomitable grit to accomplish it." He was silent, and then, "What do you think, Mikko?"

"Prognosis?" was all Kauppinen said.

"They will live, and they will recover in due time, but to what degree they will recover is impossible to assess at this time. She will suffer, at the very least, from permanent brain fatigue and he will suffer the classic symptoms of what today is known as 'combat fatigue', plus massive guilt complex, manic depression, and he is likely to be extremely aggressive.

"His adrenalin will now be out of control and it will be secreted into the bloodstream at the slightest sign of stress. I have already taken steps to dampen it down because his heart is pumping too fiercely and his blood pressure is sky high."

Professor Jukola placed his hands together and pressed them to his lips as if praying and then he asked again, "Will you tell me what you know about this affair?"

"No. I cannot," Kauppinen told him firmly. "I am sorry, but it is all a matter of the most stringent national security. Officially those people must not exist, but as they are in your care, I will tell you only what you need to know and I will hold you to the National Secrecy Laws."

Jukola nodded agreement - that suited him.

"We are leaking to the Soviets that two bodies have been found shot and frozen to death. They were taken for post-mortem examination and will be buried in a common unmarked grave in the municipal cemetery here in Helsinki. Thus, we will make a show of burying two earth-filled coffins tomorrow morning, and will ensure that it is leaked to the press. We have to do this or their agents will cause havoc here and leave no stone unturned. I will be flying these people out of the country as soon as you tell me that they are fit to be moved."

"That will not be for six months at the earliest," Professor Jukola informed him. "There is the birth to consider and although they could regain consciousness to a degree quite soon, we are going to keep them in drug-induced comas for at least three months to permit their brains to rest and recover. We will let them come back to us slowly. I will inform you when that time is close."

Kauppinen stood to leave, taking the folders off the desktop. "Thank you for your help, Rauno, it will not be forgotten." He shook his hand and walked to the door, turning back to add, "Your assessment of the situation was most interesting, but please do not express those views to anyone else."

As he walked away, he knew that his next task was to make contact with a certain Commander Bernard Cooper in London, and he also knew that getting through to him was not going to be easy.

21:00 Monday 18 August 1986

The Finn-Air Ambulance jet touched down at Whitecross Airfield in Southern England. A private ambulance and a team of medical staff were there to meet it. Three patients were transferred into their care - two adults and a twenty-one-week-old infant girl.

As the ambulance sped away to a private nursing home, an elderly distinguished-looking gentleman turned pained and haunted eyes away from the sleeping patients and spoke to the nurse.

"Can I err...hold the baby?" his request was offered tentatively. "She is awake."

"I would prefer it if you didn't, Commander," she replied. "You will have to wait until we arrive."

"Dammit, woman, just for a second or two!" he growled. "I am paying for this damned expensive ride!"

"Oh, very well," she said with a resigned sigh. "But be very careful."

She lifted the baby from the carrycot and placed her in the commander's arms. His heart warmed with eternal gratitude to see the child look so perfect and doll-like with her large blue eyes and sweeping dark lashes. He touched her cheek and she smiled a lopsided smile and gurgled with contentment.

His tired eyes took in her precious beauty and smiled down on her as inside his head a voice cried out to him: *'You are responsible for everything that happened to these people. You and you alone.'* His conscience was, without doubt, the cruellest of all masters.

'This child looks perfect, but she is not. You know she's crippled. You know she will never run and play - that she will never know the joy of being able to walk. You, sir, are wholly responsible for this crime against humanity.' His conscience reminded him relentlessly.

As tears filled his eyes, he handed the baby back to the nurse and turned his face to the mirrored window so that for the first time in his adult life he could break down and weep bitterly for what he should have prevented.

PART EIGHT

Chapter Twenty-four

Tuesday 19 August 1987

Exactly one year after returning to the country of her birth Amy was sitting alone on the floral sofa shrouded in bright sunlight when the smartly suited tall thin man entered the room.

She studied him closely, remembering another tall thin man a very long time ago - a lifetime ago. Major Douglas Philips. Seven feet of arrogance, but that was when she first met him. Whilst he remained 'exceedingly long', as she had so succinctly put it, he turned out to be a very loyal and caring man, a man whose prime concern was the welfare of those in his charge. She had learned to trust that man, and now she had to trust this one too.

Christopher Bates was not unlike Douglas Philips. His hair was not quite as red but it was auburn and he was concerned only with those in his care. "How are you feeling today?" he asked, hitching his trouser legs up and squatting on his heels to look directly at her.

"Fine," she told him. She'd learned a great deal about him in the many months following their return to England. Not one person had given her cause to distrust them. Not one had made any attempt to keep her from her husband or to harm the child they named Katherine.

"Can we talk?" he asked. "Informally I mean. Not work. You being in the same profession, and me not having had time to...to...chat."

Amy half-smiled. "We can talk if you'd like to."

"Has Dan gone for a walk?" he asked looking around the comfortably furnished apartment.

"He gets restless," she explained. "Cooped up."

He stood to his full height, flicking his legs one after the other to straighten his trousers, and went to sit in an armchair where he had a perfect view of her face.

"Um that has something to do with the fact that he's an extremely fit man again, physically that is," he said. "He's made a remarkable recovery and I'm confident that he's strong enough to balance up everything that's going on inside his head."

"Time," Amy said. "It heals, or so they say."

"Precisely." He swept a lock of hair back off his forehead with a well-practised flick of his head, unceremoniously shoved the thick-lensed heavy brown plastic spectacles back up to the bridge of his nose and asked, "Are you happy?"

Her expression remained unchanged, there was no real way of knowing how she felt, she rarely smiled unless she was with her husband and daughter, and conversation amounted to direct replies to direct questions, never a spontaneous thing for her. "Yes."

"Do you have any regrets?"

"No," she said. "It was how it was meant to be."

Christopher Bates was entirely fascinated by this enigmatic woman, this delicate yet strong female who had survived torture and experiments, who had been kept virtually comatose by her adversaries, and who had never been heard to complain. She was a remarkable woman being repaid with denial and exclusion by her own government, her own people.

He knew about her from Commander Cooper and it repulsed him to think that one so brave and intelligent should be locked away and intentionally forgotten. He knew almost all there was to know about Amy. Her history was truly fascinating and made for compelling reading.

"You brought a lot of people out from under the cloak of oppression," he commented quietly, it was the first time he'd felt it appropriate to broach this subject. "Quite an accomplishment. But tell me, do you remember exactly how many you rescued?" This was one piece of information he did not have on file.

"Yes, I remember." How could she possibly forget? "Ninety-two adults, twenty children, and two dogs. We could never risk a cat or a bird, and only quiet, well-behaved dogs."

"So many!" He was genuinely in awe of her. "You must have been in a few tight corners over there, Amy. How many were you forced to kill?"

"None," she replied, looking surprised by the question, sensing that more than an informal chat was taking place. Not only was this man satisfying his curiosity but he was also applying psychology to this informal interrogation.

"None?" he asked. "Not ever?"

"No." It was as simple as that.

"But you carried weapons, you must have."

For the first time, he witnessed a smile creeping mischievously across her lovely face and then she whispered, "Two."

"What were they?" He was sitting forward now and almost drooling over her every word.

"My tongue and my mind." The smile became a cheeky grin and he laughed quietly, enjoying her company and her dry humour, which was in itself, a remarkable thing considering everything. How he envied her husband the constant pleasure of her company.

"Would you do it all again, Amy?"

"Yes, of course, I would. Would you change any part of your life?"

"Well, yes and no," he quickly replied. "I suppose I would..." He stopped speaking and looked at her, shaking his head and tutting. "Don't do that to me, Amy. It's neither professional nor polite."

"Do what?" she asked innocently, looking like a very young 42-year-old, her hair flecked with grey and her face bearing tiny fine lines that added to her loveliness.

"You turned the tables on me and I'm pretty certain you were probing my mind."

"I would never do that," she protested quietly. "It is both unprofessional and impolite. Besides, I can't read minds. I don't do any mental probing, that's science fiction. I only sense emotion. I'm an ordinary woman." She sighed, tired of repeating herself for so many years.

"The rest is a fallacy. A rumour spread by those who know no better. I never pretended to be a mind reader. I don't perform for money in a circus ring. You should know better than that, Doctor Bates, and besides, this is an informal chat, is it not?"

He nodded and smiling said, "Touché! But I find some contradiction here, if you are so very ordinary, as you constantly claim, how come you are alive and mentally intact?"

"Am I?" she asked, clearly amused by his puzzled expression. "Or am I dead, as are you, Dan and the others? Is this not heaven, Chris?"

"Hardly, but I suppose it must seem like it after the USSR."

"Um," she mumbled, that was food for thought. Then she looked up and turned her eyes to the door, there was no sound, yet she knew someone was there. "Dan is coming."

"Will he talk to me today?" he asked.

"Maybe," she said as the door opened. She looked at her husband and loved him with her eyes. He was without doubt, the most special man on earth. "Hello," she said with an incredibly gentle tone of voice.

Dan nodded and smiled as he went and sat next to her, taking her hand in his. He knew that Bates was there and he purposely avoided eye contact with him. His distrust of all human beings ran so deep within him now that he dared not let his emotions become agitated lest he kill again. He couldn't stand the thought of more blood on his hands.

"It's a beautiful day," Chris Bates commented.

Dan nodded and looked at him, waiting for the questions he knew would follow, they always followed a polite comment like that.

"Good walk?" There it was, as anticipated.

"Yes," he grunted, wishing to be left alone with his wife and child. Longing to take them home to Wales, to where Cooper promised they would go one day soon. He felt every one of 47 years and he looked older. The nightmare trek across the USSR had taken its toll on the force that was Daniel Jones. He walked with difficulty on permanently mutilated feet and lay at night with the ghosts of the past.

"How are the saplings coming along, Dan? The ones you planted last month I mean."

"Fine." Dan released Amy's hand and clenched one fist inside the other. "Look, I don't need this psychological hogwash. All I want to do is take my wife and daughter out of this place. I'm perfectly in control and capable of looking after my family on my own."

"Are you?" he asked.

Dan almost jumped up but instead; he forced himself to slow down as he stood, his face growing red with his rising impatience. "Yes, I am. I'm not stupid, I know I might never get over this lot, but I'm damned lucky to be alive and to have my wife with me. I thought we were dead back there. There was no way we could make it, but we did, and we've earned a life of our own."

Chris Bates nodded agreement. "You're right. As a matter of fact, that's why I came to see you both today. You've been here for...let me see...twelve months.

Katherine only knows this place, so how about taking her to your own home?"

Dan looked hard at him; ready to break his neck if he thought for one moment he was behaving in the least bit deceitful, and then he looked to his wife who was sitting open-mouthed and stunned. She hadn't sensed what was coming, and that was most unusual.

"Is this on the level? If it isn't I'll..."

Dr Bates held up his hands as if in surrender and said, "I have no reason to lie to you. I'm here to help you. It's what I get paid for. Commander Cooper is coming to see you both later today. He has all the information you need. All I ask of you is that you undergo some simple tests for the next few days, Amy too, and then I'm prepared to discharge you."

Tears of joy were running down Amy's face. She stood on shaky legs and went to the doctor, taking his hands in hers and then she hugged him. "Thank you for your patience, Chris."

"Hell, it's nothing, all in a day's work really. I'm going to miss you, all of you, but especially Katherine. You'll have to promise to keep in touch." He too was feeling the emotion of the moment and wanted to leave before he broke his own set of rules and blubbered like a baby.

It was Dan who spoke, "Anything you want." He'd have bargained with the devil himself if it meant leaving this place with his wife and daughter. "Just let us go." He was a prisoner, no matter where and when, he was a prisoner. With Amy and Katherine, he would be a prisoner only within his mind.

Commander Bernard Cooper arrived at the nursing home mid-afternoon on that lovely sunny August day. He was a tired and bitterly disappointed man, but the great level of his disappointment was with his colleagues, his government, and the laws, which give mankind the right to hunt down and destroy their own people as easily as they are able to abandon them. Save for his burning desire to see Amy and Dan free and happy, his life was over.

Every penny he'd once owned was gone; spent on bringing the couple home to England, on medical expenses, on the nursing home fees, private doctors, and on his peace of mind. The cottage he'd set up for them in West Wales was on the outskirts of a small coastal village that consisted of 50 homes, 140 people, 50 of whom were children under fifteen, 30 pensioners and 60 adults under 65. There was a church, a school, a shop, a village hall and a health clinic. The cottage had been provided by the British government without them even knowing it existed.

Cooper went there personally and found the place. He knew the village and felt deep in his heart and soul that it was the perfect place for Amy, Dan and Katherine. He paid outright for it with money from a special rehabilitation fund and then he wiped all record of it from the computer memory, just as easily as they had done with Amy and Dan.

When that was sorted out, he accessed classified files and erased all mention of the couple, for despite all the talk of eraser, there were secret documents locked away in deep vaults. Facts were stored, risking disclosure at a later date. Cooper did it properly this time and he gave them the freedom they'd earned.

They were issued with new National Insurance and National Health numbers. New birth certificates and a marriage licence, but they retained their surname. Jones was about the most common name in Wales, and nobody would ever be any wiser.

Cooper left no stone unturned and made certain there was nothing that could ever be used to destroy them. He gave them back what his colleagues had so freely taken away. All that remained was to get them to Llanheddwch and settle them in and then he could leave England for good. He'd bought a farmhouse deep in the heart of France, it was waiting for him and he was ready for it. He would die there, with his memories and his regrets.

"Tea?" Dan asked him.

"Please." He removed his hat and placed it on the dining table and then he sat down on a straight-backed dining chair and watched Dan ignite the gas under the kettle. "How is Amy?"

Dan turned and saw how old the man had become. "Seems okay," he replied. "See for yourself."

He turned just as Amy entered with Katherine in her arms. He went to them and embraced them as one. Katherine squealed in recognition of the love Bernard Cooper felt for them. She knew him and loved him in return. He was her friend and her grandfather.

Cooper kissed both of them and took Katherine out of her mother's arms so that he could hug her in a more personal way. "You've grown so big," he whispered as he settled her on his knee, his nose pressed into the mass of dark hair on her head. "You really are a very beautiful and precious jewel."

"Dog," she said, pointing to her mother. "Mamma, dog." Her words were clear and precise; she was a child who would never struggle to learn.

"We saw a big old sheepdog and she fell in love with it," Amy explained." She kissed Dan and sat down next to him, her hand in his. They were rarely separated any more. "How are you, Commander?"

"I'm fine," he said, meaning the exact opposite. "Especially now I can take you out of here at last. It's been a long year. I think I must have aged twenty in just one, but it's time to move on to better things. I hear Bates let the cat out of the bag."

"Not a cat," Amy told him. "A sly old fox more like." She smiled lovingly at her old friend. "Tell us where we're going, please."

"Llanheddwch," he told them and watched as the word took on meaning for Dan. "Village of Tranquillity, or Peace," he translated for Amy's benefit. "Sounds about right for you, my girl. It's been a long time coming."

"In Wales?" she asked, her eyes brimming with unshed tears.

"Yes, on the coast of West Wales, a beautiful place. You are going to love it there."

"When do we leave?" It was Dan this time.

"On Saturday. The twenty-second. That gives Bates time to complete his tests and you have a few days to sort yourselves out and pack."

"Commander," Dan said quietly but firmly. "It will take me exactly fifteen minutes to pack for the three of us and be standing by the main gates." And then he sighed deeply. "Tell us about this peaceful village."

He told them with immense pleasure. "Your cottage has a commanding but comforting view of the Irish Sea and a pretty little garden. You'll be on the edge of village life there - not too close to feel uncomfortable. The village shop is one of those open all hours places with a post office counter and everything you need within four walls. There's a nursery school and both primary and secondary schools in the village for Katherine to attend. You'll be safe there."

"How safe?" Dan asked.

"Safe. Trust me just this once, Dan. I would die rather than send you back into that sort of life. You will be safe for as long as you live, providing you keep your mouths shut about what has gone on before. The local doctor has been briefed that you were involved in a road traffic accident in Iceland, one in which you almost died. You both suffered frostbite and various other cold-related problems. He won't ask awkward questions. Your medical files will cover everything. This time everything is in order.

"Officially you both died in Finland, as the Finnish government files show. You're buried there. This is a new start. A pension fund is all set up to support you for the remainder of your lives and £500,000 in Barclays Bank in Aberystwyth."

"Commander!" Amy declared. "We can't take any more of your money."

He smiled knowingly and shared his secret; "This one is on the government, Amy. They owed you that much. You enjoy it."

"We'll try," she said looking at him through a hot mist of tears.

"Life insurance and endowment policies are in place for you both, and the records show them as having existed for years." He laughed aloud. "Computers are marvellous things when you know all the right people."

Amy relieved him of her active daughter so that he could drink his tea. Cooper glanced into the biscuit tin, which was now devoid of chocolate biscuits, Dan having cleared the lot in record time.

"We had to tell the doctor that you lost your parents in the car accident, Amy." She looked about ready to protest at that but he hurried on. "We had no choice, we needed a reason for your..." but he was lost for the correct word.

"Slowness?" she suggested.

"Yes, why not, your slowness. You have made a remarkable recovery but let's face it, you went through hell and it scarred you, both of you. It was necessary to paint a grim picture that would excuse you in the eyes of the locals. The doctor will tell the district nurse in confidence, who in turn will tell the milkman, and so on and so forth.

"It's a small place. They watch out for each other. This way they'll assist you without thinking of you as eccentric outsiders. Dan being Welsh will also make your acceptance there easier. I know you'll do okay."

"I'm sure we will," Amy agreed. "But what about you, Commander?"

"Oh, I'll be just fine. I've got a farmhouse in the Bourbonnais area of France, a quiet place. It's private and just right for me to get back to my oil painting. I never did quite perfect the art of painting a nymph-like nude. Perhaps I can get a Friesian cow to pose for me."

"Perhaps," she said, wanting to hold onto him, to keep him in their lives. "How can we ever repay you?"

The words he spoke almost choked him and tears filled his eyes. "By surviving and by being happy, the three of you." He and he alone accepted the responsibility for what had happened to these people. He knew of no other way to make amends.

Commander Cooper promised to see them again before he left England. His last words to them were: "It's your time now. Enjoy it." He kissed Amy and then Katherine. Shook Dan by the hand and walked out of the door and Amy wept silently for the man who had always commanded her deepest respect.

The journey to Wales was long, tedious and very hot. The private car was comfortable and fast. Amy slept fitfully and Katherine was content to lie in her father's arms dozing and waking to watch his face as he stared unseeingly at the countryside.

His mind unkindly showed him the horror of all that had gone before. Pictures of mutilated soldiers - the sound of terror - the screams of the mortally wounded and those in their death throes. Over and again he mentally travelled the route to the USSR and to the Tobolmennaya Institute and on into Finland.

A dozen times in a single hour he witnessed Ivan hanging on the fence, his big gentle body decimated by Soviet bullets. Once again, he planned how he would handle it if he had the opportunity to do it all again. How he would save him and take care of him for the rest of his life, just as he'd promised he would. And then he remembered it was over - gone. Ivan dead. Major Philips dead. Roushaka dead. How many had he killed, or caused the death of? And the answer came silently to him, too many. And how much had he actually enjoyed the power of those acts of brutal murder? He sighed; knowing he'd enjoyed it all too much - far too much.

He prayed to God for forgiveness. He prayed that he could be spared the constant torture of it all.

The journey was long, and it was safe.

Amy and Dan Jones carried their daughter into their new home and knew instantly why Cooper had chosen it. It was comfortable and welcoming. It was home.

They said very little to each other. There no longer seemed to be an urgency to be constantly chattering. Neither let the other move far out of eyesight for long.

Amy wandered into the cosy living room to where boxes were stacked against the far wall. She opened one and almost cried out with delight.

"What's that, little one?" Dan asked following closely behind her.

"Look! Oh, look, Dan! Our treasures from our London home."

Cooper had personally packed their private bits and pieces and despatched them to Wales. Amy couldn't see through a veil of tears. "Look, Dan, our wedding photograph. That vase Stephanie and Chris gave us on our first anniversary. The book I gave to you. Everything is here. He thought of everything."

Dan lowered Katherine to the floor and placed his arms around his wife, kissing her head as she leaned her body back against him. "He's a good man," he said. "Always was. Good men rarely have jobs that aren't dirty at times." Dan was an expert when it came to dirty work.

They made a pot of tea and fed Katherine and went to bed early, too exhausted to think about anything for the remainder of that day. The bed was clean and aired and for the first time in years they slept a deep and contented sleep in each other's arms. There was no time for dreams or nightmares. No ghosts invaded the privacy of their rest. It was a peaceful sleep.

The sound of someone moving about downstairs brought Dan out of bed and on his feet in a flash the next morning. He pulled on a sweater and stuffed his legs into a pair of trousers as he moved towards the stairs. He was ready for action. Alert now that the lethal adrenalin was pumping through his body.

"There you are!" A woman declared seeing him filling the doorway. "I'm Ellis. Mr Bernard told me you'd be here when I arrived this morning."

She was neither Welsh nor English and Dan found it impossible to place her accent, she was aged anywhere between fifty and sixty. A woman who looked as if she permitted her hairdresser to use a rusty shears on her head and who took little care over the way she dressed. She was tall, five-eleven or more and flat-chested. Her complexion was ruddy with no hint of make-up. She was a very plain woman.

"Is it Mrs Ellis?" he asked somewhat suspiciously, watching her working in his new kitchen.

"No, just Ellis," she replied without looking at him again.

"And what exactly is it that Mr Bernard expects you to do here, Madam?"

She smiled the smile of the wise old woman and moved closer to him. "He told me that you are a very sharp man." And then with a wave of a large spoon she explained, "I'm part of this cottage. I come here to help out, to help your wife settle in. I cook and clean and then I go home. I get every Saturday afternoon and the whole of Sunday off and four weeks of holidays every year.

"I expect to be treated with a modicum of respect, and for that I return the same. I am about to cook breakfast, so tell me what you both like to eat and leave me to get on with it. I have boxes to help unpack and this afternoon I'm to take Mrs Jones and your daughter to see Doctor Alun Griffith at the surgery."

"Humph!" Dan grunted rendered temporarily dumb by this fireball of a female, wondering what his wife was going to make of her. "Scrambled eggs on toast," he said at last. "Tea. Three sugars, not too weak." He'd spoken to her in headlines.

"And your wife?" Ellis accepted his curt orders with dignity.

"Err..." He thought carefully before replying. Amy ate very little, especially before noon. Her stomach had never fully recovered from all those months of deprivation. "Fruit juice. Toast and marmalade."

Ellis nodded and began rooting about in the refrigerator. "Orange, pineapple or..." Her head was buried deep inside now as she spoke to him. "I see you found the apple juice, Mr Jones."

"That's Dan, and yes - sorry."

She closed the door, a carton of orange juice in her hand. "No need to be. Orange juice will be healthy. Go and shower and let me work."

"You ought to know about Ellis," Dan said, meeting Amy on the stairs.

"Ellis who?" she asked, holding his arm for support.

"Ellis who is downstairs cooking breakfast - Ellis who is part of this cottage - Ellis whom Mr Bernard told I was sharp. Now, on a process of elimination, I have to deduce that this woman - this Ellis is our housekeeper and that she was taken on by Commander 'Bernard Cooper' our benevolent benefactor."

"We have no need of a housekeeper." Amy was beginning to look vexed. She wanted only to be left in peace with her husband and child.

"That's what I thought you'd say, little one. Do you want to tell her or shall I?"

A barrage of delicious smells bombarded their nostrils as they entered the kitchen together. Ellis was hovering over a sizzling frying pan. Dan's taste buds danced greedily and his stomach began to protest loudly in earnest.

Ellis turned and smiled at Amy as if she had always known her. "Good morning, Mrs Jones. Sit down. Breakfast is almost ready."

They waited until they'd finished eating before addressing the subject of dismissing the stranger. "Sit down, please," Dan said and she obeyed, although with some obvious discomfort.

"Whilst we appreciate the help," Amy began. "We are in agreement that we do not require a housekeeper, Miss...Ellis."

"My goodness!" the woman declared, eyebrows raised and eyes wide and aghast. "I am not a servant. Oh, no."

"Then what exactly are you?" Amy asked, sounding more her old self again.

"As I told your husband, Mrs Jones, I am part of this building. I cook and clean and make things easier for you."

"I don't need your help," Amy informed her, trying not to sound too ungracious and failing dismally.

"It's what I do," Ellis repeated. "Besides, Mr Bernard specifically instructed me to help you."

Dan was both surprised and at a loss as to what he should say when his wife stood and left the room. He nodded a half apology to the stranger called Ellis, and went after her.

"I don't understand," he confessed, going to sit next to her on the bed.

"Just leave it, Dan." She was beginning to tremble.

"Leave what? You got up and left me there. What's going on?" When he received no reply he asked, "Is it that woman? Is she dangerous?" Still no reply, but she was looking at him now. "For God's sake, Amy, talk to me." He wanted to shake her.

"She's not dangerous. She means well."

"Then what's wrong?"

"Nothing." As she spoke tears filled her eyes and her lower lip began to tremble. Dan hugged her to him.

"Shush! No need for this now is there? You'll wake Katherine if you go blubbering."

"I'm sorry," she sobbed quietly. "I...I can't believe we're safe. So much...the things that happened...all that pain..."

"Hey, you're safe now. Your pain has gone."

"Not my pain," she said. "Yours and Ivan's." She raised her left hand and looked at her misshapen fingers, the fingers that would never function properly again.

"They did that to you, didn't they?" It was the first time for him to ask her about her mutilated fingers. There were many things he needed to know, but he would never ask.

"Yes," she whispered. "They severed them to test my reaction to pain. To see how I could control it."

Dan shivered, as the old hatred burned hotly within him once again.

"No," she said, holding on to his hands. "No more hatred. They did what they felt they had to do, just as you did when you came for me."

"What they did to you, little one, that was inhumane. It was wrong. Morally, ethically, wrong."

"And what you did was not?" It was the first time for her to speak out about any of it too, and now she had begun she was the angry one.

"I didn't say that," he started in his own defence.

"No! You're attempting to justify your actions and your hatred by blaming the Soviets for what they did to me."

"They were messing with your mind. They cut halfway through your bloody fingers. They drugged you senseless. They kept you alive because you were pregnant and they could steal away our child for future experiments and mind warfare."

"Not quite senseless," she said more calmly now. "They did all of that, and yes, they drugged me, but I retained my senses. It seems you lost yours out there somewhere, Daniel Jones."

Dan was hurt and it was abundantly obvious. "What happened to the compassionate Amy I met and fell in love with?" he asked as she pulled away from him.

"She grew up," came her curt reply.

"Aw, Amy, don't do this."

"I'm not doing anything, Dan, nothing more than being candid. I've kept quiet for a very long time now. I've been the perfect little woman. I've listened to everyone's problems, been a shoulder to cry on. I have feelings too. I hurt. I care. I get scared. I'm not a freak who performs psychic tricks. I can't keep on proving just how genuine I really am. I can't keep on telling people I don't read minds. I'm sick of it."

Dan sighed. They'd warned him that she might react this way one day. "You never had to prove anything for me, little one. I love you exactly as you are each day that dawns, good or bad, nice or nasty. I love you. I know you've had a hard time with ignorant beings. I know those bastards hurt you, but it's over, Amy. It's finished."

"Is it? Can you promise me that it really is finished, Dan?"

"Yes." he replied positively.

She looked at him with jaded amber eyes and sighed deeply. "You have never lied to me before today, Dan."

"I..." but he gave up, knowing that she was capable of sensing his emotions and any effort on his part to tell another direct lie would only prove futile."

"I love you too," she said quietly, sensing all of his love for her. "Please stop smothering me."

"Am I?" he held her hands at arm's length.

"Yes."

"Then I'll try not to do it." He paused. "But it won't be easy."

"And Ellis?" she asked.

"She stays. The commander knew what he was doing. Agreed?"

"Agreed."

Dan hung around the house, helping to move boxes, stack books and wash dishes. He chopped wood until there was a stack of logs high enough to keep the stove burning for a year and then he took to going for long walks, exploring the area.

One day when he was out on one of his rambles Amy carried Katherine into the kitchen and sat at the table watching Ellis preparing vegetables for dinner. The sixteen-and-a-half-month-old girl was happily occupied scribbling with crayons on a sheet of paper Amy held down for her. The child was contented and rarely cried. They'd been in the cottage in Wales for two weeks and felt that they'd spent a lifetime there. Already Amy was more at ease with herself.

Suddenly Katherine screeched with delight when a squiggle on the paper turned instantly into a shape she recognised and loved. "Dog!" she shouted as if her mother was in another county.

"Darling, don't shout. I'm here. Yes, it looks like a dog. Colour him and you can give it to your daddy when he comes home."

"How long has she been that way?" Ellis asked, her eyes on the carrot in her hand.

"Since before she was born," Amy replied quietly.

"I hope you don't mind me mentioning..."

"No," Amy interrupted. "My daughter cannot walk. She will never have the use of her lower limbs. Her spine was broken when I fell whilst pregnant. We're very fortunate to have her in our lives."

"She is a very special child," Ellis agreed. "But she needs to be with other children of her own age at times. You should get to know some of the young women in the village, they have small…"

"Ellis," Amy silenced her. "When I am ready to mingle with the ladies of the village I will do so. I do not need you to tell me what my daughter needs or does not need. When Katherine is old enough, she will attend school. Before that we have to teach her to use a wheelchair."

"I meant no harm," she said apologetically. "She is a joy to be with and the other children would benefit greatly from her placid nature."

Amy smiled. "I'm sorry. Forgive me." She beckoned for the woman to stop what she was doing and sit down opposite her. Ellis obeyed, wiping her hands on her apron.

"Tell me, Ellis, what was it like in Estonia when you were last there?"

The older woman smiled and the lines on her face joined together to lift ten years off her appearance. "He warned me about you," she said quietly.

"Commander Cooper?" Amy asked, mentioning his name for the first time in her presence.

"Yes."

"Tell me about it."

"It was very beautiful there," she began. "Clean and big. There were magnificent trees and lakes and our living was slower paced but very hard. We were happy in our own way, contented with what we had. We farmed the land and survived the long cold winters by keeping busy." She paused momentarily and then she asked, "How did you know? Did he tell you?"

"No. I just knew. How long have you known him?" The questions came one after the other - so many questions.

"Don't you know that too? You can read my mind."

Amy shook her head. "No. I sense things. I pick up feelings and hopes. I know you miss your homeland and your family and that you remain very sad."

"I am sad," Ellis agreed, "But I am also happy to be alive. Commander Cooper saved my life, many, many years ago. I am deeply indebted to him."

"Is that why you work for him?"

"Oh, Amy, I do not work for him. I help him, as he helps me. I want for nothing. This way I have a roof over my head and food within me. The Commander bought a tiny cottage in the village; he gave it to me twenty-five years ago. When he told me about you, what had happened, how those people almost destroyed you, I knew I would help you too. You can tell me to leave if it is what you wish. It is not my intention to interfere. I want us to be friends."

Amy sighed as a massive wave of sadness washed over her. "I think we are already friends, Ellis."

"You believe me?" she asked, sounding surprised.

"You spoke the truth." Amy lowered Katherine to the kitchen rug and reached out to hold on to Ellis, clutching both of her hands, and then she saw it all as it was. Women were being dragged out of buildings. Their clothes torn open and their bodies raped by shabbily clothed, rough-skinned soldiers. Children were shot through the head. Babies tossed down the well like bundles of rubbish.

Amy shivered violently, chilled through by what she was feeling. "Where were the men?" she asked.

A frown knitted her brow. "The men? I do not understand."

"You were younger then. Your son and daughter taken away and...and shot." Ellis gasped and paled. "Your mother was raped in front of you and your father hanged from the beam in his own home. You were beaten and raped. You almost died. Where were all the young men? Only the old and the children remained."

"Hiding," Ellis said at last, recovering only slightly from the shock of this conversation, and of the memories being evoked. "They went into hiding so that they could stay alive to fight off the soldiers they knew would come."

"Did they fight?"

"No." Her eyes were full of tears. She believed she would never shed a tear again. Her heart was filled with shame. "Most of them ran away when they saw what was happening in the village. Some came down when it was over and buried the dead. My husband...he ran away. I never saw him again."

With a deep sigh, Ellis continued. "I walked for many weeks. I knew which way to go. I stole a ride on a goods train and when I woke, I was in Stockholm. I had travelled through Finland and been unaware of where I was. In Sweden I met an English naval officer who offered to help me in any way he could. He wanted nothing from me in return, not money or sex. He was a good man, with a kind heart."

"Commander Cooper," Amy whispered.

"Yes. He found me when I was almost dead. He broke many rules to get me to England. He spoke to important people. He begged many favours and I was given permission to stay." She smiled as she fought back the tears.

"I am a British citizen and I am very proud to be so. Will you permit me to help you?"

"Only if I can help you in return," Amy bargained.

"How? I do not need help. Not now."

"We all need help," Amy told her. "But it is all a matter of degrees." She sighed. "Now, Dan will be here in a few minutes. I think I'll make us a cup of tea. You finish what you're doing and we'll sit and chat."

Every night Dan cradled Amy in his arms until she fell asleep. He frequently lay awake listening to her whimpering. He couldn't make love to her. He was impotent. Rendered so by the vision that filled his head each time he lay down next to his wife - Roushaka Pavalovsky, naked and beautiful. Dead though she was, she would not stop haunting him. She laughed at him and whispered to him. She mocked and taunted him and he hated her so much that he longed for the satisfaction of killing her again, just to feel her blood hot and thick upon his flesh. To smell the bitter-sweet odour of death once again would be satisfaction for all the damage she'd done to his mind. For the damage he continued to permit her to do to his mind.

Dan wondered if he would ever feel the way that he had before Tobolmennaya, to love life again and to know the joy of a peaceful mind. He marvelled at his wife and the speed with which she had recovered. From the moment she regained consciousness, her thoughts had been lucid if a little slow. Apart from those two misshapen fingers on her left hand, there was no apparent physical damage. Everyone who had seen her said the same thing, 'She's a miracle,' and it was true.

There had been times when he knew without doubt that he would not bring her out alive, and times when he was uncertain as to his own fate. Only sheer determination and his steel-like will power carried him through it all, that and the strength of his love for Amy. He'd driven himself over, and through everything, right to the edge and well beyond it. He'd slipped dangerously along the thin blade of sanity and he'd won through, defying all odds.

Days went by slowly and peacefully until one day, seven months after moving into the lovely cottage in the village of peace, the 19th of March, 1988 and the eve of Katherine's second birthday. Dan was sitting quietly in the armchair by the fire. Katherine was asleep in the room over their heads. Amy was teaching herself to crochet.

"Why did you go?" he asked out of the blue.

Amy looked at him, knowing exactly what he meant. "I had no option. They threatened to kill you."

"You could have called their bluff." His tone was mildly accusing.

"Why now, Dan?" she asked. "Why dredge it up now?"

He looked across at her, curled up on the sofa, her auburn hair soft around her face. He knew she had never looked lovelier. He also knew he needed her.

"We had everything then. We were young and in love. We had everything. I asked because I need to know. You never tell me anything. We used to talk. Now all you do is keep it all inside you and read my damned thoughts to save speaking to me."

"That is not true!" she said, tossing the ball of cotton to one side to stand and face him. He too was on his feet, in one of his pacing moods again.

"I don't need to read your thoughts. I would never...I find the very thought of it offensive. I do sense your moods, but I can't tell you what you need to know unless you speak out. Things still hurt me, Dan. I too have painful memories. I get flashbacks. I don't mean to exclude you. I love you, but it's all so horribly private, like grief."

"Tell me about it!" he sniffed, standing still only long enough to look down on her. "Are you the only one grieving, Amy?"

She moved away without touching him and he asked, "How many men and women do you think I killed over there to save your life? Have you any idea, woman?"

"Yes," she whispered.

"Then it's time we were able to communicate again. Time you let me back into your life. It's time we were a real family. Katherine can't understand this even if you can."

"Katherine understands much more than you realise, Daniel Jones."

"Katherine is just a baby, she's nearly two, that's all for God's sake."

Amy smiled knowingly as she spoke to him, "I advise you never to become lulled into believing that our daughter is 'just a baby'. She has been sensing telepathically since she learned to speak. She is far more capable than I was at her age. I was four before I knew what I could do. At five I went through a cruel phase. I hurt people who hurt me. Stabbing them with shafts of pain. But that phase went quickly and I taught myself what I could do. Katherine has me to help her to learn. Me to chastise her mentally, and you to depend upon just as I do."

"Do you?" he asked, his voice still as cold as ice.

"You know I do, Dan. Without you my very existence would be hell. I know I would be dead by now. Why are you like this? What has happened to trigger this again?"

"Nothing's happened!" he shouted at her. "I'm like it because you don't talk to me, and because I can't understand why the hell you went running to them in the first place, especially since you knew you were carrying my baby." He sat down with a heavy thump. The truth was out at last.

"I'm sorry if you feel I am uncommunicative," she began. "But I never was much of a talker. I went to Moscow because they blackmailed me. You know that. They threatened to kill you. Because I was so wrapped up with maternal excitement, I failed to read the signs. I missed all the vital messages. The images and sense of deprivation and destruction that Roushaka succeeded in sending to me was skilled, clever and something I would never have expected from her. I believed her.

"I loved Roushaka, and knowing that I'd gone there to kill her, well, my senses and judgement were turned around and confused." Suddenly she saw surprise in her husband's expression. "You didn't know the commander ordered me to kill her if I couldn't turn her?"

"No. He never said, but then, I guess it never came up."

"She was the only person who was capable of destroying me, the only one who could ever understand my capabilities and my vulnerabilities. Despite my doubt, I knew she'd never betray her leaders. Her family were less important than them; they were expendable, as was I.

"I went because I was afraid for you and for our future. I went knowing I had to end it, one way or the other. I had no intention of staying long enough to harm our child." She laid heavy emphasis on 'our'.

"Yet you did." He then whispered the cruellest words he could have mustered. "Look at her sometime, if you've got the time between playing mind games, she's a cripple, maimed."

It was as if fate had dealt another hefty cruel blow to Amy. She shook from head to toe as she responded. "Katherine is neither a cripple nor is she maimed. She is a very special little girl. Her back was broken, Dan. How many times did I fall? How many times did I slip off the trailer? How many times did Ivan, or you, fall on the ice and drop me? I had no control over that, nor did Katherine. None!"

Amy walked out of the room and poured a glass of water. She drank deeply from it and returned to find him standing on exactly the same spot where she'd left him, his arms folded across his broad chest and a defiant set to his mouth.

"How could you?" she asked of him.

"Why did you leave me?" he countered.

"How many times do I have to tell you in order to get through your thick skull? I did what I considered to be correct at the time. I went out there confident that I would return. I went when they threatened to kill you."

"You risked my child." His child again.

Amy sighed. This was not easy, and she was not nearly as strong as she once was. "If I had to choose between you, my husband, and my unborn child, I would choose you every time."

He turned and looked at her, there were tears in his eyes. "How can she survive like that?"

"Very well," Amy told him. "She will teach the others about courage and bravery, about coping with life. Dan, if I could make her a whole person, don't you think I would?"

"That's not the point."

"Yes, it is. You are blaming me entirely for our daughter being different. For her being unable to walk. You blame me, but you also blame yourself. You believe you could have rescued me more efficiently. You see the dead men. You taste the blood of your victims. Nights haunted by ghosts and days so wrapped up in guilt you have no room left for living."

"No!" he shouted. "You know nothing about it!"

Amy knew what was in his heart and it was not what was coming out of his mouth. Confusion, anger and remorse were just three of the reasons behind this sudden outburst.

"I've told you why I went to Moscow; now you tell me why you went after me, Dan."

He stared long and hard at her before speaking. "To get you out. What are you getting at now?"

"Humour me, please." He nodded imperceptibly and she went on. "You heard my cries for help. You went to save me. You collected the major who was later killed when he stepped on a land mine, and you journeyed on alone in unfamiliar territory. When you found the Tobolmennaya Institute where I was incarcerated, you were forced to kill - to remove dangerous obstacles. You found me, and you got me out of there. Roushaka provided certain equipment that aided in our escape. Ivan, bless his heart, was your packhorse. Many died. We did not die.

"At the hunting lodge you...you were forced to kill Roushaka. We moved on. You fought and you won. At the border fence, you watched an innocent man perish; a man who knew nothing of what happened. Who had no concept of fear, as we know it. Who lived only for each moment and who had no preconceived ideas of death, and so had not given it any thought.

"We returned to England barely alive. Our child was ill. Her spine had been broken and she was paralysed from the waist down. She had been bumped and bruised and was suffering whist inside me from the drugs they forced into my body long before they learned of my pregnancy. We grew stronger, the three of us. We learned to live again. We came to this wonderful place and we have friends again in just seven months. We have each other.

"If this is not enough for you, Dan, and you cannot find it in your heart to forgive yourself, then I will take Katherine and go away."

"No!" His eyes were wide with the shock of her words. "Never again! Never! I won't let you leave me!"

"Then you must forgive and learn to lay all the ghosts to rest. What is done is gone. You cannot bring Ivan back, or Doug Philips. Nor can you go back and undo what you did with Roushaka."

"Aw, Christ!" he clutched his gut and cried out as if in pain. "You saw! You know! Aw, Christ!"

"Dan, what I saw has no bearing upon anything. I know the circumstances in which it happened. I know how powerful Roushaka was. Her mind was bright and alive. It was also slightly evil. She had a nasty sadistic streak in her. It suited her leaders and her cause. She used her mind to manipulate you at every opportunity. You had no idea what she was doing to you, there was very little that happened that was not her doing.

"Roushaka knew exactly when she could destroy you, and exactly how to do it. You did not rape her; you only believe you did. In fact, it was she who did the raping, she took everything from me by manipulating you into intercourse and the moment you gave in to base instinct, she felt she'd won." Amy sighed. "I took everything they did to me because of Katherine. Had she not been inside me I could have fought them with my mind. I could have turned the tables on them, just as Roushaka did with you. It really is time to stop blaming yourself."

"It's easy for you to say that," he argued. "It was me who did all the killing."

"I have never killed anyone or anything, nor have I wanted to, yet it doesn't mean that I don't understand." She reached out and held his arm. "I adore you, Dan. I love and need you, just as Katherine needs you. We can, and we will survive this. Come back to me; please come back to me. Open your heart and your mind and let me in again."

As he began sobbing, Amy took him into her arms. This had been a long time coming. He'd borne guilt, remorse and self-pity and the weight of his load finally became too much to bear. "I'm sorry," he sobbed. "So sorry. Can you ever forgive me?"

"There's nothing to forgive. Just let me help you from now on and let's start living again. We have a child who will need us until she grows older and becomes independent. We can't let her down."

He wiped his eyes and blew his nose, quickly hiding the handkerchief, still conscious of his breakdown being a sign of weakness. And then he nodded once and admitted, "I'm a very lucky man."

The next day Dan returned from one of his long walks with a large shaggy-haired puppy in his arms. He swept passed his wife and Ellis who were preparing their midday meal, and stomped through to the living room to where Katherine half lay, half sat on the carpet, surrounded by the toys and books she'd received that morning for her second birthday.

He knelt by his beautiful daughter and lowered the bundle of grey and black fluffy hair to the floor and watched her face light up when the young dog moved boldly towards her to greet her with a gentle lick. She opened her arms to him and said, "Ivan." She hugged him, and then she looked back at her daddy and smiled her thanks.

Dan was crying when the women went into the room. He was crying unashamedly and there was nothing Amy could say or do to console him. When at last he was able to speak he asked, "How is it possible?"

"How is what possible, my love?" she asked lovingly of him.

"She called him Ivan. He walked up to her, slowly and carefully and she said 'Ivan' and put her arms around him to hug him like an old friend. Did you tell her about him?"

Amy shook her head, feeling the same choking emotion overcoming her sensibilities. "No...I...I was going to, one day, when she's old enough to understand."

"Not a word?" he asked.

"No, I swear." Amy smiled at him, here was the proof he needed that Katherine was no ordinary child, and evidence she would cope very well with whatever came her way.

The puppy grew into a large friendly hound whose capacity for loving far outweighed his common sense as he careered and bounded around their home knocking objects flying off tabletops. Katherine filled his entire thoughts, and she became his life. He lived for the little girl, watching over her at all times, playing, loving and learning with her. It seemed then to Dan that he had indeed saved Ivan and fulfilled his promise to the big Russian.

Dan and Amy loved again with a passion that never once caused the earth to move beneath them, but which gave them the confidence to overcome all of the ghosts and horrors filling their memories and starving their souls of love.

EPILOGUE

On the fourth day of November the following year, 1989, one million East Berliners marched for change, they gathered in Alexanderplatz, East Berlin, half a kilometre from the hated wall. Two days later half a million marched through Leipzig. On 9 November 1989, the Berlin Wall was breached and on the 10th day of the same month, one million East Germans poured into the West - free at last to leave their country without special permission. Holes were bulldozed in the wall and the people partied day and night.

Amy wept with a joy mingled with sadness for all the wasted years. She wept for those who died unnecessarily, for the families who had been torn in two by the acts of a handful of politicians. She knew then the 'Cold War' was at an end but it would live on within the hearts of the oppressed until they too were dead and scars could begin to heal. The 'New Germans' would in time make good the damage done by communism and the world would eventually learn to forgive.

In the autumn of 1990, Dan took Amy to Berlin. He returned her to the place where they first met and they walked together through the city of fear and pain to places they'd walked before. In awe they strolled beneath the towering Brandenburg Gate into what had been the eastern half of the magnificent city. Amy thanked her maker for giving her back her life with each precious step she took.

The nightmares hadn't ended, nor would they ever end. She and Dan would never forget and they were determined their daughter would never know.

'With food comes warmth
With warmth comes hope
With hope all things are possible.' Russian Proverb

Printed in Great Britain
by Amazon